Bloodied Conscience

I hope you enjoy it

RAYMOND HUGH

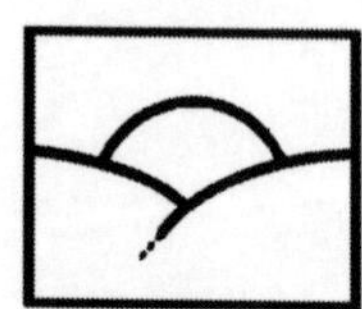

Poole
Dorset
BH16 6FH
Email. info@morningmist.co.uk

A CIP catalogue record for this book is available from the British Library

ISBN 9781838409265

Printed in Great Britain by
Biddles Books Limited, King's Lynn, Norfolk

My thanks to all who helped me in my research for this book and understandably wish to remain anonymous. You know who you are.

Dedicated to all those, who through no fault of their own were born in the wrong place at the wrong time.

Continued from *Bloodied Waters*

To fully understand the story you will have had to have read Bloodied Waters first.

Chapter 1

Tinworth Street, London, England

It was the strangest silence he'd ever experienced.

First there had been an almost blinding flash and then a deep, deep silence. A silence that penetrated every nerve left in his body. The silence appeared to go on forever, though in reality it lasted under a second. What followed can only be described as hell on earth. The ground shook followed instantly by an ear blasting roar which subsided to a dark and deathly sounding rumble.

The air filled with projectiles, a mix of organic and inanimate objects. The inanimate consisting mainly of masonry, the organic mostly human flesh.

Ian had been thrown to the ground with the flash. His head hurt, not just from connecting heavily with the pavement, but with the burns from his singed hair. A blend of masonry dust and acrid smoke dried his mouth descending to his lungs with every rasping breath. He could just about feel the battering his body was taking from the projectiles that seconds before had been thrown into the sky, returning to earth. With each hit he knew he should be screaming in pain but his body was already numb. As the rumble subsided, other sounds filled the air. High pitched screams that once heard would live with the receiver for the rest of their lives. Throat rattling moans and heavy uncontrolled sobbing. These sounds were quickly followed by shouts, shouts shrill with urgency. And finally the rhythmic sound of sirens, sirens from all three of the emergency services.

Ian's face lay flat on the pavement, facing the chaos that was unfolding. His fuzzled brain strained to take in what was happening, what had happened to him. He had simply been walking home and now he was laying helpless on the ground with insanity all around him. He tried to get up but he couldn't feel, find his arms. He couldn't feel his right leg either but the odd twitch, he could feel, coming from his left leg. He put all his concentration into moving his left leg but all that happened was the twitches became spasms and more frequent. A dampness that felt warm began to seep through his clothes, cooling quickly in the stiff autumn breeze. The dampness began to spread and Ian began to sense that he was slowly sinking into an ink black sea. The liquid that had soaked his body now appeared about his head. Through the mist that shrouded his vision he could just make out it was red. Involuntarily his mouth drew up some of the liquid and onto his tongue. He vaguely recognised the taste. The inky water was now drawing him deeper and deeper below the surface. His last conscious memory was of hearing sirens all around him, but there was always the sounds of sirens in London. There was nothing out of the ordinary in that, it was part of the city's make up.

A light appeared before him, a warm welcoming light. In his mind he started to swim towards it. As he approached he found himself starting to drift through a garden. A beautiful flower filled garden, sweet smelling and full of bird song. How strange, what on earth was he doing in a garden?

Chapter 2

The Hilton, Park Lane, London.

Roger Denton of the NCA was sitting in an unmarked car, parked roadside in Hamilton Place, approximately 30 metres from the main entrance of the iconic Hilton hotel on Park Lane. He'd wanted to be in on the action but the subject of their attention, an international debt collector, John Mitchell, knew him well and he couldn't risk even a flicker of recognition from the man they were tailing. His colleagues were trained to recognise the slightest of facial expressions and they would spot any sign of recognition, no matter how minute, immediately. No, although this was his sting operation, he had to be content with being a bystander, in command, from a distance.

It was very frustrating, even more so because his view of the hotel entrance was hindered by passing traffic, both people and cars. Doubly so because he could not let their subject, his ex- colleague and friend come out of this sting operation alive. Somehow he'd have to engineer an accidental shooting. And he still hadn't worked out how he was going to do this. And now to make matters worse, his sting operation appeared to be going terribly wrong. Somehow they had managed to lose both their subject and the operative who was tailing him, also a plant. That is despite having two unmarked cars outside, more operatives discreetly positioned in the hotel reception and five in the Windows, Sky Bar on the 28th floor, where their subject was last in view. What a bloody fuck up.

Roger couldn't help himself any longer. He had to get in on the action, after a two second mental risk assessment, he was out of his car and walking briskly towards the hotel entrance. He wanted to run but he daren't bring any unwanted attention upon himself. One, if he ran and John their subject, were close by, he would spot him, and two, they hadn't informed the hotel of their operation. Something he was beginning to regret.

His operatives couldn't hide their expressions of surprise as he entered the spacious hotel reception. The slightest of hand signals ordered them to stay in position. Glancing only briefly to his left and right, Roger strode purposefully towards the lifts. John wasn't in reception, of that he was sure, he would have spotted him. The first slice of luck that day he mused sourly. A lift was free, waiting for him. He immediately hit the button for Windows and waited. The ride up felt like hours, he had to keep his calm. He couldn't at all costs let his team see that he was panicked. They were trained to read signs of stress. This was going to be his biggest test, and he knew his operatives in reception will have radioed to warn those in the Windows, Sky Bar that he was on his way up. They would be waiting for him. Discreetly watching his every move. Shit, what a bloody mess. John where the hell have you gone?

As he stepped out of the lift two women were waiting to take it back down. Both were wearing a hijab, one, slim and sporting colourful, flowing Arabic robes, the other wearing much more sedate colours and a Western style suit that failed to hide an impressive burlesque figure. Roger found himself strangely drawn to the second woman which was probably a godsend, for, for a split second, perhaps longer, his mind was elsewhere and the tension so evident in his face faded away. After stepping aside to let the women take the lift, he strode, as casually as he was able to the Windows, Sky Bar.

Roger immediately, spotted all five operatives. To anyone else they appeared to be just another Joe public, enjoying the unique experience of the Sky Bar. But Roger felt their attention, no matter how discreet. After briefly glancing around the room, just as anyone would, he made his way to the bar, ordering a bottled IPA. Seconds later one of his operatives, a grey man in a grey suit and carrying a laptop he'd been pretending to work on joined him, ordering a lime and soda. They at first, for show, joined in casual conversation before Roger asked.

"So where the bloody hell is John Mitchell?"

His colleague, with exaggerated nonchalance, leaned on the bar scanning the room.

"I was hoping you knew."

Roger smiled.

"No we fucking don't," he took a long sip of his beer. "We've lost his tail, our plant too." Another smile.

There came a dull thud and the windows shook. Roger knew immediately that it was a bomb blast, or at the very least, a significant explosion. Nervous but excited conversation started to fill the bar and its occupants, including the operatives, made their way to the windows on both sides of the bar. In the distance, to the south a plume of smoke could be seen rising above the London skyline.

"Shit," Roger whispered. "What now? "I'm going back down," he nudged his colleague. "You stay here, and make sure with whatever the fuck is going on out there, that Mr Mitchell doesn't slip past us."

The man in grey nodded briefly, smiling goodbye. Seconds later a message came over the radio. It was too late, his boss had gone. Outside the sound of sirens from all three services filled the air.

A House Somewhere in Mayfair, London

Ariana, alias Fatima found herself sitting in a luxurious oak panelled room. After her meeting with the apparent head of the 'organisation,' she had been swiftly led into the hotel corridor, taking the lift to reception. As they'd walked through reception three women of similar build and attire to themselves, walked ahead of them, got into a taxi and sped off. Fatima never saw their faces. Instead of taking a taxi, Fatima found herself being led on foot, turning right and doubling back along Pitt's Head Mews into the labyrinth of plush streets that make up Mayfair. After little more than ten minutes they arrived at a five storey town house, fronted with highly polished brass topped black railings and carefully manicured window boxes. A set of spotless steps, led up to the front door lit by single black lantern hanging by a chain from a stone cover supported by two round stone pillars. There was, from what Fatima could see, no name, not even a number identifying the house and everything about the house shouted money. A great deal of money.

The door opened without anybody knocking and Fatima was ushered into a long tiled hallway with a wide curving staircase at the far end.

"Welcome to my home, Ariana." The woman Fatima now knew as Orme motioned to the hall in which the three of them were standing. Orme and the woman with her remained fully covered, despite being indoors. Abiding with habit, Fatima removed her hijab and let her long hair tumble loosely down her back. Neither of her two companions looked bothered by this.

"It's very nice." Fatima knew she sounded pathetic and her response was, she considered, pathetic too. She could have been much more resourceful, for example commenting on the glistening and elaborate chandelier which dazzled above their heads.

"I think so," Fatima sensed a smile in Orme's polite response. "Come, you must have many questions, but first we must sort you out."

Fatima wasn't sure what was meant by this, 'sort her out?' Orme didn't wait for a response, indeed Orme had that sort of presence that you stay silent until spoken to. Instead she walked to the bottom of the stairwell where her colourfully dressed assistant took over.

"Please follow me." The woman who'd first introduced herself to Fatima in the Sky Bar as Nefret, gestured for her to follow her up the curvaceous stairway. On the second floor Nefret showed Fatima into a wood panelled room with two floor to ceiling windows affording views over what Fatima considered to be a beautifully intimate park.

"Please take a seat," Nefret offered. "He won't be long."

He? Who was he? But Nefret didn't wait to answer a question. Silently she glided out of the room, to be replaced by another, much younger woman carrying a Turkish style tray on which sat a small clear glass, and a typically Arabic teapot. Egyptian, Fatima recognised the subtle difference, and two small bowls, one full of cubes of sugar and one with fresh mint. The woman placed the tray on the edge of a low table by one of the windows. Without saying a word and not even throwing a glance at Fatima, she placed the glass on the table and started to pour, raising the teapot as she did so. Without asking, with ornate tongs, she gently dropped two cubes of sugar into the glass and stirred. Finally she placed two mint leaves to float on top of the sweet smelling liquid and without once acknowledging Fatima, left the room, taking the tray with her.

At first Fatima had been wary of even sipping the offering left for her, what if it was drugged? However the smell soon got the better of her and throwing caution to the wind, she took a long hard sip. It was good, very good and reminded her of Marseille, even more so Persia when she was a child. Her mother used to make her tea, exactly like this. Standing in front of the window, she gazed down on the people enjoying the park below. How carefree they looked. She began to feel emotional, it was the realisation that she hadn't really experienced carefree, since she'd been a child. How she longed for that feeling again and now after recent events, she wondered if she'd ever experience the feeling again. Just a few hours ago she'd been determined that this would be her last ever job, and now look at her. Her thoughts wandered to Orme. Who was she? She had a presence that commanded you without having to utter a word. And on reflection, Orme had uttered very few words and yet she still held within her this strange and very strong desire to please her. To lay down her life for her if necessary. It just didn't make sense, she'd never felt this way before. Even for Pierre who had done so much for her.

Fatima finished her tea and quickly poured another repeating the actions of the young woman who had delivered it. She gazed around the room. The ceiling as well as the walls were covered with wooden panels. In each corner of the ceiling were carvings of grapes. Voluptuous bunches, ready for an orgy of eating. Portrait paintings from another age hung in strict regulation on the three walls without windows. Fatima wondered who they were. She suspected they may have been here from the time the house was built. All the furniture was of a dark wood, ornately carved. Candlesticks were everywhere and a huge gilded ornate clock took up almost the entire top of a dresser. Unusually there was no ceiling light but this was more than made up for by no less than seven free standing lamps. All the lamps were on and presented a very calming, quite charming atmosphere. Fatima wondered if this really was Orme's home. She doubted it, a base maybe but not her home. Everything was too structured, too formal. This room, the room she was in was almost like a museum, untouched for centuries. There was nothing homely about it, and certainly no glitz from Arabia.

A good ten minutes had passed since Fatima had drunk every last drop of tea in the teapot and she was beginning to get bored. Sitting watching the people in the park below no longer helped pass the time. And there was little else to do, there were no books or magazines she could flick through and she didn't feel like thinking. She was worried where it might take her. A further twenty minutes passed, and she was just starting to wonder whether she should go in search for someone when there was a knock at the door. And not waiting for an answer a middle aged man, late forties to early fifties Fatima guessed, opened the door and entered. Fatima immediately recognised he was wearing a foreign cut suit, with a crisp white shirt. Open collar, no tie and highly polished slip on shoes. As he closed the door, Fatima caught sight on his left wrist an expensive looking watch held with a brown leather strap. He's French, Fatima surmised. With everything combined it was a give- away.

"Axsti." The man smiled.

"Axsti," Fatima could hardly get the word out, she hadn't expected this.

"Axsti, ham.vainti," the man countered.

Every nerve in Fatima's body tingled. This was a language lost to time and yet she understood every word, how did she know? She had no idea. It was scary.

The man switched to French.

"Sorry to keep you Ariana, my name is Abadun, though officially my name is Alain. I work for the French Embassy." He chuckled.

So that explained his attire, she'd recognised the look immediately. His attire was almost a statement. I'm French and I'm important.

"Here I have something for you." Alain, as she now knew him motioned to a large table in the centre of the room. Ariana, alias Fatima, drew back a chair and sat with her right leg over her left. It was unintentional but her position she noticed had caught Alain's attention. Quickly she dropped her right leg and drew both legs under her chair. Abadun, alias Alain drew up a chair beside her. Reaching into his jacket Alain pulled out what looked like an official looking set of documents. With deliberate neatness he lay them flat on the table in front of her. They were actually four pages stapled together. The first two were smaller.

The first gave the address of the French Consulate at Cromwell Place, SW7 2JN. Above the address Fatima, almost dare not look. In capitals – PASSEPORT/CARTE NATIONAL D'IDENTITE. Fatima took a deep breath and quickly flicked to the second page. It was a page containing general information about staying in the UK. With undisguised haste, Fatima flicked to the third page. This was A4 and headed – Ministere De L'Europe Et Des Affaires Etrangeres. Directly underneath and in bold, 'DEMANDE DE PASSPORT'. In the top right hand corner there was a photo of her and somewhere below her real name and the names of her parents. Without warning Fatima started to cry, her shoulders heaving and tears streaming down her face. Abadun, Alain, the man from the French Embassy made no move except to smile broadly. Still, hardly daring to look Fatima skipped to the final page. This was identical to the last except in bold the title -DEMANDE De CARTE NATIONALE D'IDENTITE. She turned to look at Abadun, Alain, whoever, she didn't care. There was no need for her to speak, Fatima's facial expression said it all.

"Yes, Ariana. From this day on you're officially a French citizen, no more false identities," the man paused. "Except if the organisation needs it, you understand." Fatima, Ariana, didn't care. She was official, nearly all of her life she had lived a lie and now she existed, really existed. It was official. For the majority, who have never had to live a lie. To have to on a daily basis hide from the authorities, they will not understand Ariana's state of mind. For her this is like winning the biggest lottery in the world.

"Asha Vasishta, merci, thank you," the expressions of gratitude tumbled one after the other from Fatima's, now Ariana's mouth.

"It's nothing really, the man from the embassy looked a little embarrassed. "Now listen Ariana, you must collect your passport and identity card from the consulate tomorrow. This is very important. And don't please, wear a hijab or cover your face. The Consulate is French territory. it's also important that we get your face on facial recognition cameras, this way we can normalise you, if you will pardon the expression. For tonight and tomorrow night you have been booked into the Royal Lancaster Hotel. Your room affords quite beautiful views over Hyde and Kensington Park. And please forgive Orme, for she has arranged for your personal belongings in your room at the Hilton to be collected and dropped there. In fact I believe you'll find they're already in your room. I'm sorry if you feel we have invaded your privacy but all of us felt it too risky for you to collect your belongings yourself."

All of us? Just who are all of us? Ariana, or Fatima whichever you prefer made it clear she had a question, more than one but the man from the embassy held up his hands.

"I'm sorry Ariana, I know you have many questions, but not now. Not at this time. There's a car waiting downstairs to take you to your hotel. It's an embassy car so it's perfectly safe. Come I'll escort you downstairs, and don't forget your documents, you'll need them tomorrow."

Ariana, alias Fatima returned the documents to the envelope and placed it in her small shoulder bag. Abadun or Alain, had already opened the door. There was no one to be seen as they descended and entered the hallway. Fatima wasn't sure what she had expected. Not a farewell party, but at least someone to bid her goodbye and good luck. Certainly not this, nobody!

Alain, opened the door and gently holding the fingertips of Ariana's right hand escorted her down the steps to where a gleaming black Peugeot 3008 stood waiting for her. A chauffeur in plain clothes sat at the wheel. Ariana looked at the car, it was lovely but for an embassy car she'd expected something a little grander. As if reading her thoughts, as he opened one of the rear doors Alain remarked.

"We don't want to draw attention to ourselves do we?" He smiled, it was Alain's best feature his smile. "After you've collected your documents, somebody will be in touch, don't worry."

Why worry? Fatima thought to herself, she had long been used to this sort of cloak and dagger contact. It didn't bother her.

"We may never meet again Ariana, at least not in the near future, and for the record, you have never met me. Is that clear?" Alain was still smiling.

"Yes of course," Fatima returned his smile as she slid into the car.

"It's been a pleasure, Ariana, a real pleasure." And he meant it.

As the car moved off Fatima paid attention for the first time to the sounds of London, that evening. The air was split with the sound of sirens from all three emergency services. Nothing new in that, but this was different. This sounded like bedlam. What an earth was going on?

Tinworth Street, London, England

Two men stood over the crumpled body of a man lying on the pavement. The rhythmical shine of blue light from emergency vehicles every few seconds diffused the orange glow from the fire in the building behind them. Before them a recent development Spring Mews had most of its windows blown out or shattered, and uniformed police were hurriedly ushering people out of the building. One of the two men, dressed in the green uniform provided by the London ambulance service knelt on one knee to examine the body. Whoever the man was he had lost both his arms in the blast and his right leg. His left leg was still attached with only a sliver of muscle tissue. The man's blood had created a rough shadow of it's owner on the paving stones on which the man lay.

"He's well gone," the paramedic looked up at the policeman, who was still standing.

"Poor sod, I expect somewhere there'll be a wife or girlfriend, perhaps even kids waiting for him to come home. And someone's going to have to tell them."

To the paramedic, the policeman sounded more concerned about the latter than for the poor guy who had lost his life in such a brutal fashion. Simply for being in the wrong place at the wrong time.

"Well, I'm sorry, but that's your concern, not ours." The paramedic stood up, unfolded the shroud he was carrying under his arm and laid it with as much dignity as he could over what was left of the body. He looked around him. What a bloody mess. There was debris from the blast scattered everywhere and the supposedly sturdy railings behind them, their purpose, to protect the building now in flames were either missing or grotesquely bent. Around twenty metres away the paramedic spotted what was left of the dead man's right leg. His arms were nowhere to be seen.

The policeman tapped him on his right shoulder.

"We've been told to get out of here, they're worried about further explosions, deliberate or as a consequence of what has already gone on. They want the site secured before we do any more. No point in adding to the dead."

The paramedic, was reluctant. From where he stood he could see two more bodies. However it didn't need a trained eye to see it was obvious they were dead. It just didn't seem right to just leave them. A short distance away he saw two more colleagues of his being ushered to safety by uniformed police officers, as well as officers sporting NCA on their backs. Other men, men in plain clothes, mostly casual were becoming more numerous. They appeared to be oblivious to the danger and strangely they were ignored by the uniformed officers. This is big the paramedic thought to himself, very big.

Just over a mile away in a modest three bedroom apartment, a pleasant looking woman who still sported signs of youth waited impatiently with her three young children. Her husband had phoned to say he was picking up a Chinese and would be home in just over half an hour. Over an hour had now passed and she and her children were growing impatient with hunger. She kept trying to phone him but his phone kept going direct to answerphone, Where the bloody hell is he? She cursed silently to herself. I'll bloody kill him when he turns up. Unbeknown to her there wouldn't be any need. Her husband was already dead.

La Manche, (The English Channel), half a mile from the French coast. Close to Cap Blanc Nez

Whilst events were unfolding in London, Didier and his son Mason were just starting their night's fishing. Fishing was in their blood. Didier's father had been a fisherman, so had his grandfather and so on, as far back as anyone living could remember. Didier was one of the few fishermen along the coast who still used a traditional flobart. A flobart is a rounded boat made of wood which hasn't really changed in design since Jesus walked the earth. And Didier was proud that his great grandfather was known to have turned his old flobart upside down and turned it into a house. A tradition once commonplace along that part of the coast. There were just four flobart fishermen left in Wissant and they shared an old tractor to drag the boats down to the water's edge. In the past it had been the job of horses. The launch each evening of the flobarts, had recently become something of a tourist attraction. And nowadays each launch was normally accompanied by a gaggle of tourists with cameras or camera phones at the ready.

The last couple of weeks had been hell, what with those heads and body being found in La Manche and then the girls body found on the beach. His lovely little seaside town had become swamped by the world's media, law enforcement of varying genres and ghoulish tourists. He, if truth be told had no time for any of them. Slowly that had all, thankfully died away. There were still more patrols by the local police than was normal, and the occasional journalist would appear asking questions, but thankfully the wrong sort of tourist had, it seemed at least on the surface, to have at last disappeared.

Part of the reason for the latter may well be the weather. Winter was fast chasing Autumn away, ignoring what the calendar demanded. And this evening was a good example. There was a stiff running breeze which had a cold bite to it. Unusual for this time of year. The sea in response was starting to protest. Both Didier and his son relished in it. Didier took a deep breath letting the cold air explore the deepest reaches of his lungs. He relished the cold freshness and the taste of salt on the tip of his tongue. He never tired of the exhilaration delivered to him by the sea air. And he never grew tired of the power of the sea. If you respected it, it would respect you.

They were now rounding the imposing white chalk cliff head that was Cap Blanc Nez, (White Nose Point). In view to the west were the bright lights of Calais, to the east, a string of faint lights marking the English coastline and in-between more lights moved slowly across the blackness that was La Manche. Didier faced the growing rush of bitingly cold air. If the breeze got much stronger they would have to head closer to the cliff. Where, because of the direction of the wind, they'd be sheltered. Didier wasn't overly worried, the flobart he knew was almost unsinkable and because of its centuries old design could navigate even the shallowest of waters. Perfect for catching bar,(sea bass).

A shout from his son shook Didier from his thoughts.

"Papa, regardes."

His son was standing, pointing at something floating in the water, not more than twenty metres away. Didier swung the light in the direction of his son's pointing finger. If he was honest with himself, there was no real need. He knew already what the object was. He'd been a seaman long enough to recognise a human body, simply by the outline. And in this case a man's body. The way the sea played with a human corpse was sickening, it created the illusion that it was working a puppet. He never got used to it.

"Merde," Didier muttered under his breath. They were only just beginning to get over the storm that had decimated parts of the coast, and the subsequent horrors and now this. And they, he and his son were going to be central to it. He half thought about pretending to have never seen the corpse, but he was a good man and this would be someone's son and probably somebody's father. They had a right to know, and quickly. Secondly his son would never agree to it.

Slowly he manoeuvred the flobart alongside the body. Taking care not to allow the boat to capsize. Between them they managed to drag the body on board and lay it with as much decency as they could onto the nets. Didier gently moved the dead man's head with the back of his hand and let out a cry. This was not just another corpse. He recognised the face immediately, this man laying dead in his boat, had only recently been all over the news. The corpse they had in their boat was Capitaine Maubert, head of the gendarmerie at Calais. Didier had even spoken to him, maybe just over a week ago. Shit really would hit the fan when they reported their find.

"Merde, merde, merde, merde," Didier fisted the side of his precious flobart and turned the boat around, heading back towards Wissant. They had no radio on-board, their find would have to wait until they were ashore. "Merde," he shouted the word this time and this time aimed a kick at the side of the flobart. His son watched on in shocked silence. Unlike his father he couldn't wait to get back to Wissant.

Chapter 2

The Hilton, Park Lane, London

Roger walked as fast as he dare as he left the Hilton. Setting foot in the open air, the blare from the sirens of all three emergency services was almost deafening. Groups of bystanders were all staring in the same direction, where in the distance an orange glow was delaying the fading light. Even worse the expressions on the faces of his operatives sitting in their unmarked cars told a story. They all looked as if they'd just heard the world was coming to its end. Not for the first time that day, Roger Denton thought to himself, what the fuck was going on? Not soon enough he flipped the lock on his car and slid into the driver's seat, knocking over a half finished coffee in his haste. 'Shit, shit, shit.' Roger half-heartedly wiped some of the offending liquid from his shirt. His radio was virtually on fire with chatter. He flicked a switch.

"Will someone please tell me what the fuck is going on?"

"Bomb blast sir, where the hell have you been, we've been trying to reach you. Your team said you couldn't be contacted."

Roger took a deep breath.

"Never mind that, I couldn't risk my cover being blown, where? How big? Casualties?"

"Our office sir," the man's voice went up an octave as he relayed the news.

Roger stopped him in full flow.

"WHAT?"

"Our office, and it's a bloody mess. The Director General wants you to contact her immediately."

"Our office?" Roger couldn't believe what he was hearing

"Yes sir, our office, the bloody NCA in Vauxhall."

"But that's simply not possible," Roger wasn't really directing this at his colleague on the radio, he was more speaking his numbed thoughts out loud.

"Sir you really need to speak to the Director General, she wants you to contact her as soon as you get this."

"Yes, yes of course." Roger terminated the call and then a second later re connected. "Thanks."

From his car Roger stared up at the now blue lit Hilton tower. The NCA, it simply wasn't possible. The NCA building was one the best secured in the country. It simply wasn't possible, and yet somehow it had happened. He radioed his operative, Nick who w sitting in a silver Range Rover Sport positioned in one of the few parking spaces directly in front of the entrance to the Hilton.

"Sir?"

"Nick you've heard?"

"The NCA? Yes of course, it's not possible. How the hell?"

"Yes, I know, but it's happened. Jane wants me to contact her immediately, you're almost certainly going to have to take over here. She'll almost certainly want me somewhere else after what's happened."

"No problem sir. Sir? Any news on casualties?"

"No, I'll let you know as soon as I hear, I promise."

"Yes sir."

"Any news on Mr Mitchell and our man?" Roger already knew the answer.

"No sir, they appeared to have disappeared into thin air." There was a pause. "But don't worry sir, there's no way either of then can leave the hotel without us knowing it."

"I hope you're right." Roger was doubtful. Something was terribly wrong and he was beginning to suspect that somehow John had got wind of their sting operation and had organised some sort of elaborate set up. He just prayed it wouldn't come back to bite him. "Anyway, keep me informed will you, and any news on casualties I'll let you know."

"Yes sir, I will, and thanks."

The radio clicked off. Every one of his team at the Hilton had colleagues, many of whom were also friends that may have been in the NCA building when it went up. It was a gut wrenching feeling not knowing. With a deep breath he made a direct call to the Director General's secure mobile, or at least he hoped it was secure. Nothing after this could be certain anymore.

Jane answered on the first ring. "Roger. How's your investigation going?"

"Not well," Roger admitted. On any other occasion Jane would have launched into a succession of questions. But not on this occasion. Roger was almost thankful. Almost.

Jane continued as though she hadn't heard him, and she probably hadn't.

"Roger you obviously know about the NCA, our offices."

"Yes of course, but only just. You can't very well not know, the explosion has lit up half the London sky."

"Several explosions Roger, not one, but several!" Roger heard his boss take a deep breath. The pause gave him a few seconds to think.

"We're sure the explosions were caused by a bomb are we? I mean, is there a possibility it could simply be a gas leak?" Roger regretted immediately, using the word 'simply,' there was nothing simple about the disaster unfolding south of the river.

"Nothing can be ruled out until the relevant experts have taken a look, but word is, and I mean word from the people who are meant to know these things, that it has all the hallmarks of a bomb blast or rather several bombs."

"How is that even possible? I mean how….,"

"That's the million dollar question Roger. HOW? And it's a question everybody is going to be looking for an answer to, not just here but intelligence agencies, law enforcements and friendly governments all around the world. Who the hell will want to share their intelligence with us after this? We're going to have to find answers Roger, and bloody quick."

Roger stared out of his windscreen at the brightly lit Hilton. He could hear from the background chatter on his radio that his ex-friend and colleague, John Mitchell, and the operative tailing him, due to meet him, and under his direct command were still missing. There was simply no sign of either of them. What a fucking day this was turning out to be.

"Roger, the investigation you're on now. It's pretty big. It's even taken an international turn and involves two of the nastiest gangsters that's ever walked our green and pleasant land. Whoever found and had those two assassinated, had access to some serious resources, and the suspicion is, they could well be involved in the murder and mutilation of those poor children as well. Something as you know, that has now involved government ministers. Well I don't need to tell you, do I. And now this. Do you think it's a possibility that there could be a connection? With the explosions at the NCA offices I mean. If it turns out the explosions are the work of bombers of course, which everyone in the know seems to already accepted that is the case.

Roger thought. Within seconds of knowing about the fate of the NCA, he'd asked himself the same question. There was not even a hint of a connection, but his gut feeling told him there was. And gut feelings were sometimes a better source than solid evidence. However, he had no wish to inform his boss that their one solid lead in their investigation. A Mr John Mitchell, ex-special forces had somehow, and under his watch, disappeared into thin air along with their man acting as a contact. No he would leave her, for now anyway, in blessed ignorance. In any case Mr Mitchell could be found at any minute though the heavy feeling in his stomach was a reflection of his true feelings, that somehow, Mr Mitchell had slipped out of the hotel, taking their man with him.

"I can't see any connection at the moment Jane, not to say that doesn't mean there isn't one of course. But to bomb the NCA, that would need a whole team of people and huge resources. Not to mention intelligence. No, I think it has to be, either an unfriendly country. The usual suspects, who maybe simply want to embarrass us, or to stop the intelligence flow. Quite possibly even, state sponsored terrorism. The worrying thing is, if these explosions were the result of bombs, somewhere along the line there has to have been an informer. There would have had to have been at least one, almost certainly several people, on the inside. Which Jane, doesn't begin to even bear thinking about."

"My thoughts exactly, MI5's too. Yes they've already been in touch. They were sympathetic, but the conversation still wasn't pleasant. They virtually accused me of being asleep on my watch."

They would, thought Roger. The game of pass the buck had already started.

"Have they got any idea who could be behind this? Or why?"

"No, none. Total shock."

Roger wondered if this were true. They may well have a suspicion and possibly had a suspicion something was amiss before the attack. If that's what it was. And if so should have made known their suspicions before the attack took place and now they could be busy covering their backs.

"Do you believe them, Jane?"

"Yes Roger, I do." There was a pause. "Roger, where are you now?"

"Outside the Hilton hotel on Park Lane. We're following up on a lead. Do you want me to head over to HQ?" He heard Jane take another deep breath.

"Listen MI5 have placed me in a safe house. MI5 feel that if the NCA is a target then so could I. I can still operate, direct from here but it won't be easy. You could be a target too Roger, so could any of us. If you want to be placed in a safe house it's there for you. Just let me know.

As for HQ, I'm not sure you're be able to do much. It's crawling with the emergency services and already with specialist teams from MI5. The fire service has cleared the whole area, apparently the resulting fire is pretty intense. They're concentrating on finding if there's anyone left alive in the building and getting them out. So I'm told, the north wings haven't been that badly affected, it's the southern wings which took the brunt of the blasts." Where my office is, Roger bit his lip. "Where your office is," his boss confirmed, as though reading his thoughts.

"Jane, I'm going to go over there. There may not be much that I can do, but I can ask questions and I feel it's important that I be seen there."

"What about your operation, where you are now?"

"It's all under control." If only it was.

"Ok, it's your call, but be careful. Whoever did this has access to some pretty nasty and sophisticated material. The odd gun would be play dough to them. And in all probability they will have their own operatives surveying the scene. Maybe with further intent."

"MI5 will have done a clearing operation."

"They won't have had time. Not a thorough one. Just watch your back Roger."

"Scouts honour," and Roger flicked off. Immediately after he messaged Nick in the Range Rover Sports to say where he was going and that he was leaving him in charge of this fuck up. Though he didn't use those exact words. That sorted, he slowly, so as not to arouse suspicion, pulled his car out of Hamilton Place, onto the busy Park Lane. Not till he reached Grosvenor Place, behind Buckingham Palace did he put his foot down, at the same time triggering the car's siren and blue lights.

Chapter 2

The Royal Lancaster hotel, Lancaster Terrace, London

Fatima loved the room. The design was clean cut, with everything just where you needed it. Designed by a woman, definitely. And just as the man from the embassy had promised, all her belongings from the Hilton had been delivered. Not just delivered but neatly laid out. She'd almost been caught out when booking in, as the booking was under her false name, and she'd needed her false ID provided by Pierre, in France. Without thinking she'd almost handed over her documents enabling her to collect her legitimate ID card and passport from the consulate. A moment of madness, but she'd recovered quickly and checking in had gone without a hitch.

Her room was on the 8th floor with breathtaking views over Hyde Park. Immediately below, the streets buzzed with activity. Just as all London's streets seemed to. She'd thought the streets of Marseille were busy enough but they were nothing compared to London. In the distance, somewhere the other side of Hyde Park, the skyline glowed orange. Together with the bright lights of London, they spotlighted a continuous plume of smoke that on reaching a certain height became part of the blackness that was the night sky. Somewhere there was obviously a fire and a big fire at that. Curious Fatima turned on her TV. After navigating the hotel welcome she quickly found the news. The fire in London was the headline and virtually the only subject covered. There were numerous ground shots, with suitably shocked looking reporters, interspersed by sky shots, almost certainly from a hovering helicopter. The fire it was being reported, may well be the result of a bomb, which was shocking in itself but even more shocking the building affected was the London office of the NCA. The agency that investigated serious crime and supposedly one of the most secure buildings in the country. Fatima watched for ten minutes but the reports went round and round, repeating what had already been covered. Casualties were of course the main concern but so far the authorities were keeping schtum with just about everything. The one sliver of information that had been released, was that all the regional NCA offices were being temporarily closed. Not just for security but to allow them to be checked. This, it was emphasised was routine in such circumstances and there was no need for alarm. If nothing was found, and it wasn't expected that they would find anything, they would reopen in a day or so. Normal service would be resumed and organised crime would not be let off because of this event. The million dollar question, it kept being reported was if this was a bomb, who was responsible and how had they managed it to plant and detonate it within the NCA? Who indeed, mused Fatima. Thankfully it wasn't her country and therefore not her concern.

Her immediate concern was to have a shower and change into something more comfortable. Throwing her jacket on the bed she went into the bathroom and turned on the shower. Disrobing she stood naked in her room gazing out at the orange glow in the distance. It was slowly subsiding, the earlier bright orange was now more of a burnt orange and the smoke more of a whisper than a plume. The fire fighters appeared to be winning.

Standing under the powerful and deliciously warm jets of warm water, Fatima started to wonder. For the first time since she'd arrived in London, she began to question why Pierre had really brought her here. Her given target in the Hilton Sky bar had disappeared with a complete stranger. It was obvious to her now, that it had all been an elaborate set up and that the real reason for her being there, had been to introduce her to Orme. What a strange name. And why such a theatrical route to a meeting? Why not simply knock on the door to her room? And only minutes later, why such a hasty exit? For what purpose? Her thoughts wandered back to Orme. Who was she? Where did she come from? Orme had given nothing away, except to confirm that she was head of the 'organisation.' Apart from that she had hardly spoken a word.

Fatima remembered, around her neck had hung a quite beautiful Croix d'Agadez. The cross meant they both had something in common. But did it go beyond the Croix? It had to. Fatima threw back her head, enjoying the water beating her face, it helped free up her mind. Her train of thought, wandered to Orme's house, if it was her house of course. Fatima still doubted it. The man from the French Embassy, or so he had claimed. His early introductions had been in a language she didn't know, but apparently did know. She understood what he had said immediately and she had replied in the same language. How was that possible? She searched for the language, delving deep into her own mind, but couldn't find or remember a single word. The whole thing unnerved her. She shook her head, and after squeezing her hair , turned off the water and stepped out of the shower. Before doing anything else she fingered her Croix d'Agadez. And now she was about to have a genuine identity card and passport. In all of her life she'd never had that. Whoever, must have gone to a lot of trouble to enable her to have these, to have a real identity. Why? Why? Why? What was the real reason the 'organisation' wanted her here? Who was her real target? Finally she decided there was no point in worrying. She'd find out in good time.

After towelling herself down, Fatima slipped into a long pale lilac Arabic style robe, covering her head in a crisp white hijab which crossed just below her neck with one end draped over her shoulder. On her feet, she decided on a statement making pair of high heels. Last but not least, she slipped the chain holding her Croix d'Agadez over her hijab. Admiring it in the mirror, she had second thoughts and slipped the cross behind the folds of her robe. No need in taking the risk of attracting unwanted attention. She was in unfamiliar territory and who knows, who may be watching. Apart from feeling a little uneasy Fatima felt refreshed, she felt good, and tomorrow she'd be official. She couldn't wait. For now though, dinner. The hotel she understood had a renowned Thai restaurant and she'd never tried Thai. She was really looking forward to it.

Albert Embankment, London, England

When Roger arrived, the Met were busy clearing all traffic off Vauxhall bridge. The bridge itself had been closed to all traffic and, from the look of it, all the streets anywhere near the fire. An exasperated uniform approached his car. Roger wound down the window and flashed his card.

"How close can I get?"

"Not close, the best bet is for you to take the Albert Embankment and park somewhere there, but they won't let you near, it's bloody chaos."

"Thanks. " The uniform waved him through. Just who are 'they,' Roger wondered. More uniform stopped him on the far side of the bridge, beside the polished MI6 building. Again Roger flashed his card. The uniformed officer didn't look impressed.

"Where are you wanting to go?"

"Just close, I need to check on a few things, follow up. I need to speak to some of my officers who are there."

"Well, good luck. You'll have to take the Albert Embankment. The Pleasure Gardens are being used by the fire bods and fuck knows who, as a command post. No one can get near. It's bloody chaos." The officer confirmed his colleague's opinion the other side of the bridge.

"Thanks." Roger swung his car, lights flashing, siren wailing onto the pavement and cut across to the Albert Embankment. Unlike the other approach roads the A3036 that ran along the Albert Embankment had been cleared of traffic. Only emergency vehicles remained, mainly from the fire service, though there were three ambulances, one of them private Roger noted. Nice of them to help out.

Not wanting to block the road, he pulled up on the small riverside green opposite The Rose pub. For a split second he thanked God the pub didn't appear to be damaged. It was where he liked to unwind and think over some of his most difficult cases. There were two other unmarked cars on the green. One he recognised as NCA, the other, no doubt from one of the other security services. Stepping out of the car he felt the heat from the fire immediately, Christ it was intense, and this was with him being some distance away and with the blaze subsiding. What would it have been like when the building first went up? He glanced across the river. Clearly visible on the far bank were the House of Lords and the House of Commons, along with the MI5 building, And only metres away the iconic MI6 building. This had happened under everyone's noses. When everything had settled down there would be bloody hell to pay. In the air two helicopters hovered, almost certainly commissioned by one or more tv channels. Roger cursed, 'ghoulish bloody bastards, go on you broadcast our bloody misery to the world.' He spat, more in disgust than needing to relieve phlegm.

Despite the heat from the fire, the Thames was drawing in the stiff evening breeze and Roger put on his blue Barbour jacket, before venturing across the A3036 to The Rose pub. Police tape was stretched across the entrance to Tinworth Street, Roger guessed it had been put there before they'd decided to close the whole embankment. Several uniformed officers were guarding it and he counted at least ten fire officers pulling on thick heavy hoses. Roger lifted the tape flashing his NCA card.

"Sorry sir, nobody's going down there". Two uniformed officers stood in his way. "It's the railway bridge, the second officer explained, the blast may have damaged it. We've been told it could collapse at any moment. Not even Jesus , if he turned up, would be allowed down." If there was a God, shit like this wouldn't happen, Roger thought to himself.

"Then where's the best viewpoint? I need to make an assessment, and where are the occupants of these cars?" Roger waved to the other cars on the green. The two uniformed officers, indulged in quick discussion, before one asked.

"Can I see your card again sir?" Roger showed it to him. "One minute." The officer turned his back, speaking to someone on his radio. Under a minute l later, he was back. "Your best bet sir is to go down Glasshouse…." Roger cut him off.

"I know it, thanks."

"No problem, sir." But Roger didn't hear him. He was already walking briskly along the A3036, towards the petrol station, after which lay Glasshouse Walk. Arriving beside the Black Dog pub more police tape sealed the entrance to Vauxhall Walk, the approach to the NCA. It would appear, that all access to his place of employment was sealed. Here though he at least, had a view of the NCA building. Or what was left of it. Though prepared, what he saw still shocked him. Where his office had been was now nothing but rubble. The sturdy iron railings that had been placed to protect the building were either no longer there or bent, in some cases even snapped like wood. Windows in all the surrounding buildings he could see, were blown out. Fire crews were working amongst the rubble as were a number of paramedics. Among them were a few men in civilian clothes although with protective jackets. Either MI5 or bomb squad. Roger couldn't be sure. Behind him on the large expanse of grass that was Vauxhall Pleasure Gardens, were all sorts of emergency vehicles. Impressively, several mini marquees had been put up to accommodate both emergency operations and investigations. There was a tap on Roger's arm. Turning he found three of his colleagues gathered together. Each looking shocked as well as helpless.

"What a bloody mess sir, and we all feel so bloody useless standing here like spare parts."

"There's nothing we can do," Roger tried his best to sound reassuring and knew he'd failed miserably. "We've got to let the boys do their jobs, has anybody any news for me? What about casualties?" Seb, short for Sebastian, shook his head.

"Nothing really, we've been politely told to keep out of the way. As for casualties, what we do know is the security office was decimated. There's normally at least three bods in there. There's no way they could have survived. Luckily the streets here are usually pretty quiet. For London anyway. From what we've been told three passers by were caught in the blast, all dead. But I can't confirm that."

"Has anybody hinted at what may have caused this?" All three officers shook their heads.

"Nobody's actually saying it sir, but it looks to all of us as if it were a bomb." This came from Lee who specialised in stopping the drug gangs hitting on young people.

"If it turns out to be a bomb, we will, after the initial sympathy, be the laughing stock of the world's intelligence services." Roger cursed as he thought of the consequences. Without warning there was a sharp blast and flames followed by plumes of black smoke filled the air. Instinctively everyone ducked.

"Right that's it" a fire officer shouted, his face lined with frustration. Can we get everybody back at least another fifty metres." He directed his request to the uniforms strung along the tape. "It's just a car going up, but there could be worse." This was meant for the uniformed officers, but everybody heard him.

"Just a car," Seb complained loudly, That's all, just a bloody car. Nothing to worry about."

"Sir?" For the first time the third officer spoke. He was the youngest of the three, and his face still fresh from having only just joined. He hadn't yet witnessed the sights that scarred the faces of his older colleagues. Roger raised his eyebrows in response. "What are we going to do tomorrow? I mean we can't exactly come to work can we?"

Roger had asked himself the very same question on the way here. What were they going to do? Tomorrow, and the day after, and the day after that.

"I'm sure we'll all be told. My advice to everyone for now, is that you carry on in the field as best you can, until told otherwise. I'm sure the Director General is liaising with the Home Secretary as to a plan of action for the next few days. Just keep your radio on twenty four seven."

"Roger Denton?" Two men, one wearing only an open necked pale blue shirt and mushroom coloured chinos, the other in black fatigues, but with no explanatory insignia on his back, were approaching. Both men looked as though they knew how to handle themselves. Roger nodded, rather than speak a confirmation. "Have you got a minute? We're set up in the 'Tea House', over there." There was no explanation from either, as to who they were or for whom they worked. Roger started to follow, then hesitated. Turning he directed his question to Seb.

"Those two helicopters, are they ours?"

"No, media I expect, it's all over TV. India 98 is on its way." India 98 was the call sign for one of the Mets helicopters.

"Then get somebody to tell the civvy copters to get the hell out of the way will you."

"Yes sir." Seb immediately reached for his radio, glad to have something to do at last.

"Sorry gentlemen." The two men smiled their understanding. Roger followed them to the Tea House. Normally a tea room offering quality tea with lots of moreish cake, all homemade, and a theatre to boot. The Tea House had justifiably won several awards. Today however it had been taken over by just about every emergency service. Roger immediately recognised the Met's assistant commissioner, a couple of the chief fire officers, members of the bomb squad and one member from MI5. A guy called John Johnson, nicknamed JJ, obviously, and who he got along with and secretly liked. There were quite a few in the café he didn't recognise, and the café was a hive of activity, it was packed. Admirably the owner had risen to the occasion and called his staff in to help out. Everybody was being catered for with tea, cake and even sandwiches. Under the circumstances it was very impressive and everything Roger liked about this country. When there's an emergency he thought. People who live here stand up, ready to be counted.

"Roger." It was the assistant commissioner. He waved to a table in a corner and the people who were there, without protest moved off. "Sit down, Roger, please." Roger sat. Two men who Roger recognised from the bomb squad, one of the fire officers and JJ along with the two who'd invited him over, also sat. JJ cast Roger a nod. "Well this is a bloody mess," started the assistant commissioner, I just need a quick briefing and I need to brief you. The commissioner." He looked at his watch, "is briefing the world media in twenty minutes, and it's imperative that we're all working off the same hymn sheet. This is no time for inter-agency point scoring. Agreed?" There was a murmur of agreement from everyone present. He turned to the two members of the bomb squad. "Do we know yet if, this is a bomb?" One of the two from the bomb squad, his face set grim, shook his head.

"Too early to say, though it has all the hallmarks of one. We can't be sure until we, along with the fire service can get access to the scene. And the fire service have informed us that, that won't be till tomorrow morning, at the earliest."

"But your instincts are.....?"

"That's it's a bomb, yes, maybe more than one." Everyone listened in silence. The assistant commissioner still had the floor.

"Just to make it clear, the commissioner is going to use the classic stalling tactic. We will not be making any comment on the cause until all the facts are known. This will give us time to know how to best present this to the world's media. Is that clear? Any comments?" Unusually for those gathered, there weren't. The assistant commissioner turned to Roger. "Roger, have you any idea how many people there may have been in the building when the explosion happened?"

Roger stared at the floor.

"It's really hard to say, there wouldn't have been many administration workers unless they were doing overtime. Specialists and field officers tend to work using their own time sheets. At a very rough guess, maybe thirty."

"The fire people have managed to evacuate sixteen from the north wings, they were hardly affected. Anyone in the south wings." He paused, spreading his hands. "Well there's no hope. The lower floors, no idea yet. Sorry Roger." Roger acknowledged the man from MI5 with a weak smile.

"I'm sorry too Roger," the assistant commissioner did his best to smile. If this is a bomb, have you any idea who it could be? Is there a case your agency is working on that could have upset somebody so much so that they would go to these lengths?"

Roger shook his head.

"Jane and I have already discussed this. Yes we're constantly pissing people off, it's our job. But I can think of no one, or any organisation big enough or organised enough not to mention the resources and expertise needed, to pull something like this off." He paused not wanting to comment further, but he had to. Everybody else would be thinking it. "Jane and I concur. If this does turn out to be a bomb, or bombs, they would have had to have had help from a person or persons inside. We, and it pains me greatly to say it, must have been infiltrated."

"Agreed." It was the man in the open necked shirt and mushroom chinos.

The assistant commissioner turned to face him.

"And has your agency got any idea who could have done this? Who could have infiltrated the NCA? How sure are you that your offices haven't been infiltrated?

"I'm not," the man admitted. "We're doing a complete security overhaul as we speak." Roger closed his eyes, how many times had he heard that. The man turned to Roger.

"What about the case you're currently investigating? That seems to be pretty big. After all I hear even the Home Secretary's involved." Roger thought hard before answering. He wished he knew who this man was. He still hadn't been introduced. He could see no possible connection and as yet no connection had been found between the twelve mutilated children, currently in a morgue in France and his investigation into the beheadings on the south coast and in Spain. Yet for some reason his gut was telling him otherwise. His gut was normally right, but on this occasion he simply could not see how.

"To be honest it's too early to say. The investigation is in it's early stages, and I'm not sure how big it's going to get. For the moment, at the stage we're at, I can't see how there's any connection with my current investigation and with what's happened here, if there is one. Well, we haven't found it yet. Again it pains me to say it, but I'm being honest when I say, I haven't a clue."

"And it pains us too, if knowing that helps you to feel any better. And this may make you feel even better. To be honest we haven't a clue either. And after we've finished here, I have to call the Home Secretary and tell him so, maybe even the Prime Minister. Think of me won't you." He actually smiled at Roger and Roger politely smiled back. Who the hell was he?

The assistant commissioner gestured.

"If that's all you've got Roger I suggest you go back to whatever you were investigating, with the additional brief that you search for a connection. If there is one of course. There's not much you can achieve by hanging around here. You'll be the first to know if there are any new developments. I promise." Roger believed him.

"Thank you sir."

"Anybody else have a question for Roger?" The assistant commissioner looked around the table. Everyone shook their head or mumbled in the negative. "Then good luck Roger and God knows we're all going to need some of that."

With that Roger stood up and left, taking a slice of cake, generously offered to him by a smiling waitress. The man in the open necked shirt followed him out and reached for his shoulder.

"Roger, my card." The man held out a simple business card. Roger took it and briefly examined it. All that was printed on it was the man's name, Jason Mortimer and his mobile number, nothing else. No indication of which agency he was with. "If I hear anything, I'll let you know, promise. I already have your number. Now you have mine. I'd be grateful if you keep me informed. And er." The man hesitated, it was obvious to Roger he was searching for a way to phrase something. "Look Roger, I'm not trying to tell you how to run your investigation. But, if you want my personal opinion don't ignore the French connection. I feel it's worth more than a cursory glance. Roger raised his eyebrows.

"Thank you, I won't."

" Good luck then." Conversation finished, the man turned and re-entered the Tea House. Roger slipped the card into his wallet. Who was that man? Where was he from? What did he know? He would have had good reason for mentioning France. Why then didn't he explain that reason? He must have a reason! Roger tucked his thoughts away. Time to get going.

The way he had arrived through Glasshouse Walk, he discovered immediately was now cordoned off and the only way now was to take the long way around passing through the 'Pleasure Gardens' to the gyratory in front of the MI6 building and back along the A3036. As he walked he radioed Nick, who he hoped was still sitting outside The Hilton. Nick answered immediately.

"Sir."

""'Any news Nick?"

"Sorry sir, nothing. Nothing's changed since you've left." Secretly Roger was pleased. He hadn't wanted John to have been interrogated by his team and possibly say something which could incriminate him. At the same time he was worried that their plant, the man tailing him hadn't been in contact. It didn't bode well.

"They can't just have disappeared Nick, they must both be somewhere in the hotel."

"I know sir, if the worst comes to the worst we're going to have to ask the hotel to look at their CCTV." This is the last thing Roger wanted. He wished now he'd informed the hotel management that they were conducting a sting operation on their premises. At the time it simply hadn't seemed necessary. Hindsight was a great thing. He knew the hotel management would not be best pleased at having not been told. He paused to think.

"Nick we can't have our team sitting up there for hours and hours, it'll start to look suspicious even to the most pissed idiot in the bar. Get them, in stages, to leave and replace them with a couple either who are in reception or in a car outside. They can stay till the bar closes. After that if there's still no sign of them, maintain a skeleton crew, as many as you think you need. If you think it's necessary book a couple of rooms, and rooms not suites. That will allow you guys to get some shuteye without having to leave."

"What if we don't find them sir?" Roger pursed his lips at the thought.

"Then we'll have to examine every inch of their CCTV footage."

"They won't be happy."

"I bloody know that."

"Sorry, I've always been good at stating the bloody obvious. How is everything back at base?"

"There is no base Nick, I'll brief you all in the morning. No one must attempt to go back there, it'll be a complete waste of time."

"Yes sir." Nick had a million and one questions but knew this wasn't the time.

"Any developments Nick, let me know as soon as."

"Yes sir."

"Good luck, Nick."

"You too." Both radios flicked off.

By the time their conversation had finished, Roger was back at his car on the Albert Embankment. Sliding into the driver's seat he briefly leaned back and sucked in a long draught of cold air, enjoying the sensation. What a bloody mess. His officers were good. He knew, without him asking, pretty soon somebody could possibly be detailed to examine John's flat in Covent Garden. They would almost certainly clear it with himself first, but that wasn't a dead cert by any means. He had some very capable and very proactive officers on his team. More than happy to take the initiative without checking with him first. He simply couldn't take that risk, he had to get to John's flat before anybody else did. Remove anything that might incriminate him. Not to mention to also do some detective work of his own. With his history with John he may just spot something that could help their investigation, something that others might miss. It was risky but the risk was worth it. That was wrong, risk had nothing to do with it. He had no bloody choice. Where the hell are you John, where the bloody hell are you? Why are you doing this to me? Your bloody friend.

Chapter 2

Wissant, France

It had taken just over an hour before Didier and his son, beached their flobart at Wissant. For both of them the single hour had seemed more like an eternity. No longer was Didier luxuriating in the stiff sea breeze, instead, it had become an annoyance that wouldn't leave him alone. He felt cold and crouched double, not once on their return to shore had he taken his eyes off the lifeless body of the capitaine, lying motionless on his nets.

Thankfully when they beached, probably because of the weather there was only the odd dog walker on the sand, and none showed the slightest interest in their landing.

"Go home son. Call Benoit, we'll let him deal with the Police." Without saying anything, his son dutifully turned and walked up the beach. Heading for the inviting row of lights that ran along the promenade protecting their small town. A town that for centuries had hidden many a tragedy through its beauty. Now it would have to hide another.

Benoit was a family friend. As a sideline to his taxi business, he also ran a private ambulance service. It took only minutes before Benoit had his blue and white painted estate car parked on the nearest access to the beach. Seconds later he was stood alongside Didier and his fishing boat. Didier's son remained sitting in the taxi/ambulance.

"I told him to stay there," Benoit explained. "This is no matter for a boy his age."

"He's been a man ever since he joined me in my flobart. The sea maketh a man." Didier, fondly tapped the side of his trusted boat but didn't argue further. Secretly he was pleased his son had remained in the car. Benoit was right.

"Right let's have a look."

Didier leaned the flobart to make it easier for Benoit to climb in. Didier then followed making climbing into the boat look like child's play, which of course, it wasn't. The movement from the two men caused the boat to rock resulting in the corpse rolling onto its side. Both men started, repulsed by the movement. Recovering quickly, Benoit knelt. It took little more than a second to confirm the man was dead. Just as Didier had done, out at sea, Benoit with the back of his hand, moved the corpse's head. He needed confirmation and Didier had been right. He was kneeling beside the corpse of Capitaine Maubert, head of the gendarmerie at Calais. Without thinking Benoit made the sign of the cross. The capitaine was, correction, had been very well respected. This would come as an awful shock to the local population, perhaps an even bigger one than recent events. And one the area certainly didn't need.

"Have you contacted the gendarmerie or police?"

Didier shook his head.

"No, I thought I'd leave that to you."

"Thanks." Benoit looked both ways along the length of the beach. The nearest person was around sixty metres away, maybe a little more, definitely not less. "Right let's get him into my car. We'll put the capitaine's arms over each of our shoulders and walk in upright up the beach. That way he won't look like a corpse. The last thing this town needs is the discovery of more dead bodies."

The two men found it surprisingly easy to drag the capitaine upright to Benoit's taxi ambulance. In the car, Benoit didn't even lay him down but strapped him sitting upright in the back seat.

"You know I shouldn't really be doing this Didier. You should have called Samu."

"And they would probably have called you Benoit. I was just cutting out the middle man."

Benoit lit a cigarette.

"Hmmm, maybe, maybe not. But this is no ordinary corpse, this is Capitaine Maubert. There's going to be one hell of a lot of questions."

"I know." Didier looked across at his son who was now standing with them, leaning on the car roof. If only he could keep him out of this.

"Anyway," Benoit opened the driver's door. "I suggest you call the local police, they'll be easier to deal with than the gendarme. Tell them simply that you've found a body, that you've contacted me, and I'm driving it to the morgue at Boulogne. I'll send in a report as well, we'll let the morgue sort out any identification. It will have to be done formally anyway." With that Benoit got into the driving seat, closed the door and after winding down the window and blowing out a waft of smoke, waved his arm. "Au revoir."

"Au revoir," both Didier and his son replied, both with a single wave." Bonne chance," Didier added. And with that Benoit's taxi ambulance disappeared from view. Father and son remained motionless for around a minute staring out to sea. Neither said a word. Didier's gaze turned to the looming chalk cliffs of Cap Blanc Nez at the northern tip of the bay. Why are you playing games with us? Didier questioned silently. What have we done to you? After a brief look in the other direction, he put one arm around his son's shoulders. "Come on, let's go home. I'll get Richard to pull the old girl, (the flobart), in later.

Not ten minutes had passed when an old red tractor started to pull the equally old flobart up the beach. Three people with their dogs stopped to watch the local tradition. None realising at that moment that the little boat they were photographing with their phones, would soon become international news.

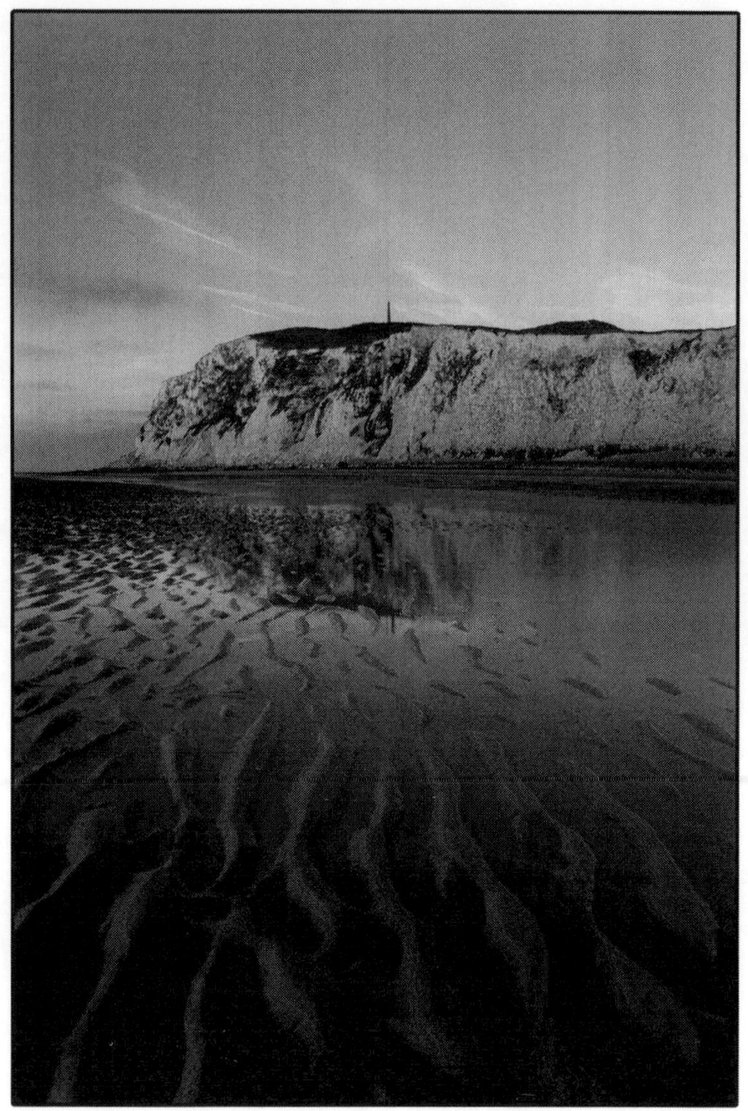

Cap Blanc Nez, France

Chapter 2

Drury Lane, Covent Garden, England

Roger pulled into a side road off Drury Lane and parked with two wheels resting on the pavement. He had to be cautious. Roger's flat may already be under surveillance, either by officers from his NCA, the Met, persons unknown or even John himself! He was pretty certain the flat wouldn't have been searched, not without his say so. If some promotion chasing individual had decided on this as a plan of action, they would need a warrant and that would take hours, probably a lot longer. If a warrant was being sought he was certain one of his officers would have let him know. But that didn't rule out the Met or other agencies with their own agenda. Especially after what had happened at The Hilton. As casually as he could muster Roger exited the car, locked it and walked the few steps to Drury Lane. Although the northern stretch of Drury Lane, was off the main tourist track, the narrow road was still surprisingly busy. John's flat was on a corner and easily visible from where he stood. Holding his phone, he pretended to punch numbers and put it to his ear. To any onlooker he was simply a man having a conversation on his phone. The flat he observed was in darkness. There was no sign that anybody was inside. He gave it a good ten minutes then walked past the front door. There was still no sign of life and no sign, from what he could see of anybody watching the entrance. Playing safe he walked as far as Long Acre and after purchasing a take away coffee, walked back down Drury Lane, retuning to John's door. Once again he pretended to make a call, all the time studying his surroundings. Again there was no sign of anybody watching. Reaching into his wallet he pulled out a small plain plastic card and his set of keys. Turning to face the door he pretended to put a key into the keyhole at the same time trying to slip the lock. If this failed he'd have to pick the lock but this would take longer and may attract unwanted attention. There was no need, the door was already open! Roger pushed again to be sure and the door opened an inch without any complaint. The hairs on the back of his neck stood up and a cold sweat made his hands clammy. Roger hated the feeling. His first thought was that he was unarmed. John had confirmed he carried a weapon and any unsavoury characters in John's world were sure to do the same. If anyone was in the flat he was a sitting duck.

Roger considered his options. What was certain, there was no way he could walk away from this. He would have to investigate. The questions were, should he do this now, on his own, or call it in, get an armed response team here. Just in case. Pulling the door to he thought hard, once again using his phone as a prop. There was no way he could call this in, not yet anyway. It was too much of a risk to himself. He may find himself up in front of a disciplinary hearing, even worse, a spell in prison. A fate worse than death for someone from the NCA. That answered his question. He had no choice but to investigate, despite the risk to himself. Still with his phone to his ear he crossed the road to get a better look at the flat's windows. It was hard to conceal movement, even in the dark, he'd surely spot someone if they were there. Three black cabs passed as he focused. Two with starry eyed tourists, probably theatre goers and one with a smartly dressed man reading a newspaper. Was this man, like himself, surveying the flat? It would be a simple, but clever cover. Anyone standing outside on the pavement for more than a few minutes would soon be identified by those trained to pick up on such things. Or was he being over reactive? No. No, Roger quickly dismissed the thought. One could never be 'over reactive', not in a situation such as this. He continued to focus on the windows. The building being Georgian, the windows were typically large and knowing John's flat as he did, it would be hard to hide any movement inside. Especially with the street lighting, their light was strong enough to identify any moving shadows within. What WAS worrying him was, if there were anybody inside they may be hiding in wait. Roger thought again, but then if that was the case, why leave the front door on the catch? It immediately shouted to anyone who wanted to gain entry, watch out! Things aren't as they should be. No, the more he thought about it, the more Roger thought it unlikely. There had to be another reason. He waited a few more minutes to see if the black cab carrying the man with the newspaper, came past again. If whoever was inside was conducting some sort of surveillance, they would make more than one pass to be sure the coast was clear. Two more cabs passed, both with their orange lights on, looking for a fare. No sign of the man with the newspaper. Conscious that he'd been standing outside for too long, Roger crossed the road and pulling out his keys, pretended to unlock the door. Quickly he pushed it open and stepped inside closing the door behind him. After putting on a pair of disposable gloves he stood at the bottom of the narrow staircase and listened. Nothing, only the sound outside of passing traffic and the odd chatter from passing pedestrians. Roger remained motionless until a point when he considered any sound was more likely to be his mind working overtime.

Taking a deep breath he started to mount the stairs. The stairs being old, made a sound with virtually every step. He might just as well shout, 'helloooo, anybody there?' All the time he was listening for some sort of movement but there was nothing. The flat remained deathly silent. The door at the top of the stairs was open. John never left this door open, so as to keep the heat in. Something was definitely wrong. Slowly Roger entered the lounge, poised to react to whatever surprises the flat may hold for him. The light from the nearest street lamp outside provided quite a good light. He could see fairly clearly. Everything appeared unnaturally still, it was spooky. Even for a trained and experienced detective like himself. Standing in John's lounge, Roger felt a surge of guilt. Yes he wanted, no needed him dead, but standing here in his lounge reminded him that he still counted John as a friend.

Cautiously he started to move around the room, there was no one hiding. Quickly he checked the other rooms and no, to his relief the flat was empty. There was nobody hiding. He was sure. Harder would be the task ensuring the flat contained no evidence linking him to the owner and their recent communications. Meticulously Roger searched every room, every pocket in John's clothing, every drawer, every nook and cranny. Loose floorboards, hems in curtains. Nothing, there was not a trace, and that, in itself, was suspicious. He'd expected to find something, even if it was innocent. Something wasn't right, what was he missing?

In a drawer in the bedroom he found around twenty pre-paid, disposable, or burner as the Americans liked to call them, phones. He would have to check each one, just in case. There was no time now. Finding a supermarket bag in the kitchen he bundled them inside. There was nothing else to do, it was time to leave. Something however kept nagging at him. He was missing something, and worse. Why did he feel strongly that whatever it was, was staring him in the face! Looking around one last time, he shook his head. No, he had already been here too long, it was time to leave. Mouthing, 'sorry John, old buddy,' he descended the stairs and let himself out into the street, pulling the door firmly shut behind him. Happy on hearing the catch click into place as he did so. Pulling off his gloves Roger walked quickly back to his car, all the time looking to see if somebody was either staking out the flat, or worse, tailing him. From what he could see there was no one. He felt an immense sense of relief when he shut his car door. The feeling of security in the car's metal shell he knew was a false one. The reason for so many accidents, but he couldn't help enjoying the sensation anyway. He was running on empty, he knew it, and his body, not to mention his mind was starting to let him know. They were starting to complain, loudly. What a day. Roger closed his eyes, then shook himself. What was he doing? This was dangerous. He slapped his face hard. Think he had to think, be proactive, not reactive. Flicking on his radio he called Nick at the Hilton.

"Still nothing sir, sorry." Nick answered, assuming the question his boss was about to ask.

"No, I'm sure Nick, I have the feeling we've been stitched up. This is going to take a lot of bloody explaining. That's not the reason I'm contacting you though. Look, on the way home I stopped by Mr Mitchell's flat. Just to take a look. All the lights were off but the curtains weren't drawn. We need to take a look. Can you get somebody to get a magistrate to issue a warrant? If they start asking too many questions just tell them it could be a case of national security."

"Yes sir."

"And when we've got it, can you let me know, I want to go in with whoever."

"Yes sir." His boss's radio clicked off. Shit, obtaining a warrant at this time of night wasn't going to be easy.

A Street in Bushey, North London, England

It was another hour before Roger pulled up outside his house in Bushey. There was no light shining inside welcoming him home. That had long gone along with his third marriage. He didn't know anyone in the agency who hadn't been divorced. It came with the territory. Next door was, a pub, his local. Housed in a fine Edwardian building it was one of the main reasons he'd purchased the house. He thought about going in but decided on a large glass of red, a merlot, in the comfort of his lounge instead. Something that was becoming too much of a habit and too often a single glass would turn into a whole bottle. He was aware of it but didn't really care. It helped him get through each day. Instead of sitting down he took the glass, but not the bottle up to bed. A shower would have to wait till the morning. Letting his clothes drop to the floor he climbed into bed, arranging the pillows so he could sit up and finish his wine. With the remote control, since his third wife had left a permanent feature of his bed. He turned on the tv and tuned to channel 40, Quest Red. Bizarrely he enjoyed watching true crime, and often with each case debated how he would have tackled it. As he sipped his wine his mind wandered back to John's flat and the unlocked door. It wasn't easy slipping or picking a lock, it took someone who knew what they were doing. Why then risk leaving the door open? It just didn't make sense. Unless. Unless, whoever picked the lock, had done so and left the door unlocked to allow somebody else, an accomplice to enter later. Someone with a different set of skills.

He may be wrong but then he could have hit the nail on the head. Once more he radioed Nick at the Hilton.

"Yes sir." Roger recognised on this occasion the tiredness in Nick's voice. In return Nick wished his boss would get some shut eye and leave them all in peace.

"Nick, is everybody still there, have you sent anybody home?"

"Not yet sir, I was just about to."

"Well listen, I want two officers to stake out Mr Mitchell's flat tonight. If he has given us the slip he might try and pass by. We can't take the risk. Ask for volunteers first. If no one does you'll have to detail a couple."

"Ok, I wont be popular, everyone's knackered."

"I know, but you'll get volunteers."

"I know."

"Oh and Nick, whoever it is, tell them to do their best to keep out of sight. Drury Lane is not an easy street to stay hidden and remember Mr Mitchell is ex special forces. He's trained in this sort of thing."

"Yes sir, have you got his address?"

Roger gave it to him.

"Tell whoever volunteers, good luck."

"And you get some bloody shuteye sir."

Roger laughed and flicked off. He leaned back against the pillow and took a long sip from his glass. His body immediately started to relax as the mellow liquid trickled down his throat and the alcohol into his veins. The story covered on Quest Red, he'd seen before. Nevertheless he left the channel unchanged, letting his mind wander back to John's flat. Using his imagination he started to create a virtual image of the lounge. Seconds later he realised what he'd missed. He'd missed the bleeding obvious!

Chapter 3

Gendarmerie Nationale – Calais, France

It wasn't even seven in the morning yet and her phone was already ringing. After the events of yesterday, Colette had decided to come in early, to try and get things sorted before it got busy. Whoever was ringing, they'd have to wait, she ignored it. She was still in shock, and the way she was feeling at that moment, wondered if she'd ever recover. She kept running the events of yesterday over and over again in her mind. Her, boss, her ex-boss, she corrected herself, hadn't even bothered say goodbye. Not even after working together all these years. She'd known something bad had happened, when yesterday her boss, her ex-boss, as she now knew, Capitaine Maubert, had exited via the foyer. His face had been ashen, and his expression as though the world had come to an end. Shortly after the commissioner had called her into the capitaine's office. The conversation that followed, explained the expression on her ex-boss's face. It wasn't the world that had come to an end, it was his world.

It was highly doubtful, the commissioner had told her, that Capitaine Maubert would ever work for the gendarmerie again, and if he did. Certainly not as capitaine. Sadly it was more likely that her ex-boss could face criminal charges, maybe even prison. Though, he had promised her he would do his best to see that prison never happened. Your capitaine, he had told her, had been stupid, not intentionally criminal. And even after the capitaine's 'mistakes', he'd try to assure her. He still considered the capitaine to have been a bloody good officer, and almost a friend.

Colette had left the office in floods of tears. On the stairs, she'd passed the station's lieutenant, almost certainly on his way to be debriefed by the commissioner too. He'd looked visibly shocked seeing her in tears, and at the time she'd been in no mood to warn him of what she'd just been told. Now, on reflection, she felt she'd behaved cruelly. She must remember to apologise when she saw him next. As it turned out, she didn't have to wait long, for seconds later the lieutenant appeared. Like Colette, after what had taken place yesterday, he wanted an early start. An early start so he could get things in order before yesterday's dismissal of their capitaine became common knowledge.

Lieutenant Beaufort, on seeing Colette through her window, knocked once, and without waiting for a reply, entered her office. Colette immediately started to apologise for her behaviour yesterday but the lieutenant quickly stopped her.

"Ce n'est rien, rein," he assured her. He was about to continue when Colette's phone rang again. She held up both her hands.

"I ought to get this, it may be urgent, it's the second time it's rung already." The lieutenant made an open gesture, telling her to go ahead.

"Colette?" Colette recognised the voice instantly as belonging to Monsieur Hubert, the chief pathologist at the morgue in Boulogne.

"Oui, Monsieur Hubert?"

Jean-Paul Hubert, confirmed that it was, though there really was no need. Colette had known him for as long as he could remember. Now she had had answered, he really wasn't sure how to approach what he had to tell her. He was still in shock himself. In his morgue lay the body of Capitaine Maubert of the gendarme. His staff had woken him as soon as they realised who had just been delivered. "Colette, it's about your Capitaine."

"So you've heard?" Colette was astonished, the pathologist already knew! "It's the pathologist," she mouthed to the lieutenant. Jean-Paul hadn't been prepared for this response. Did Colette know already then? But how? Who had told her? The lieutenant waved, succeeding in getting Colette's attention.

"I'll take it Colette," he whispered, just loud enough for her to hear. "Can you put the call through to Monsieur Maubert's office." He was sensitive to remember that Colette had never called the capitaine by his title. It had always been Monsieur Maubert. Colette, nodded and informed the pathologist that Lieutenant Beaufort was going to take his call.

In under a minute Lieutenant Beaufort was sitting in the chair that up until yesterday, belonged to his boss. It felt strange, very strange. Uncomfortable even. Taking a deep breath he picked up the receiver.

"Put him through please Colette." There was a click and the pathologist was on the other end. "Lieutenant Beaufort, the lieutenant introduced himself.

There came a stifled cough.

"Morning lieutenant, may I ask, how does your gendarmerie know already?"

"What about? The capitaine?"

"Yes."

"Well the commissioner told me yesterday. Just after Capitaine Maubert had been made to hand in his carte professionel, (warrant card). He briefed me on the circumstances and to expect a replacement though it might take a while." The lieutenant couldn't understand what this had to do with the pathologist. How on earth had he found out so quickly? Surely there wasn't a leak already.

"You mean Thierry, sorry I mean Capitaine Maubert, lost his job?"

"Yes." None of this was making sense. "Yes isn't that why you phoned?"

"No," the pathologist's voice sounded shaky. This news threw a very different reflection on the body that had been brought in overnight. It may even offer up an initial explanation. "No it's not. Have you spoken to Capitaine Maubert since this happened?"

"No." The lieutenant found himself feeling a little guilty at his admission. Perhaps he should have tried. The capitaine had after all, always been good to him. Had his back when it had mattered. "No, I haven't." There came a pause on the other end of the phone.

"Are you with anyone, lieutenant?"

"No, I'm alone in the capitaine's office, why?" What an odd question, the lieutenant was beginning to have a sense of foreboding about the nature of the pathologists call. He wondered where it was leading.

"I'm sorry, very sorry," the pathologist paused. The lieutenant was almost sure he could hear him crying. Another dry cough. "I'm really sorry to have to be the one to tell you this lieutenant, but your capitaine's body was picked up by a fishing boat last night. Just off Cap Blanc Nez."

"Picked up? Body? You mean he's dead?"

"Yes, lieutenant, I'm sorry ."

"Are you sure?"

"Whether he's dead, or is he the capitaine? Yes to both. His body's lying in a fridge in my morgue. I recognised him of course, but he needs to be formally identified. And that really needs to be done by a member of his family." The lieutenant searched for a reply. He was in total shock, this couldn't be happening. Their capitaine.

"Do you know how he died?"

"Not without a postmortem, but my initial observation, and especially after what you've just told me. I suspect suicide from jumping off a cliff. From where he was found, almost certainly Cap Blanc Nez. Can I leave it with you lieutenant?"

"Yes, yes of course, thank you."

"If you need me lieutenant, I'm only a phone call away."

"Oui, oui, merci." With that the phone clicked dead. The lieutenant placed his elbows on the desk and rested his head in his hands. He was beginning to really hate Cap Blanc Nez. When shit happened it always, somehow seemed to be involved. The last couple of weeks had been a nightmare. They had only, in the last few days got rid of the international media. The news of their capitaine's untimely, and they would print dramatic death, will bring them all back to Calais again. His first day in temporary charge, and this landed on his lap. The capitaine's wife had, only yesterday through social media, suffered the indignity of finding out about her husband's affair, along with most of Calais. Now this. And he was going to have to be the one to break the news to her. And quickly before her husband's apparent suicide became public knowledge. He crunched his fists in exasperation. He'd also have to today announce the unfortunate news to his colleagues. How were they going to take what he would have to tell them. They'd all been under so much pressure recently and now this. There came a knock at the door. The lieutenant knew it was Colette. The lieutenant's head dropped. They had been really close, Colette and the capitaine. She wouldn't take this news well. Not at all.

The knock came again and the door opened. In the door frame stood Colette holding a tray with a small jug of milk, a large English style mug and a steaming pot of coffee.

"I always brought the capitaine up his coffee as soon as he arrived. I thought I'd do the same for you" Colette stopped in her tracks, she saw the look on the lieutenant's face. "Is everything ok lieutenant?" Lieutenant Beaufort stood up and gently lifted the tray she was carrying from Colette's grasp.

"Please, sit down Colette. I'm afraid I've got some bad news." He watched Colette take a seat, she was visibly shaking. What a crap start to the day, and why did he have the strongest feeling that the day and almost certainly the week, was going to get worse, much, much worse.

A street in Bushey, London, England

It was five am and Roger was busy making his first cup of coffee of the day. He had already showered and dressed. On the radio sounded Radio 5 live.' Wake up to money', a program mostly dedicated to business. That morning however the program was almost entirely dedicated to yesterday's blast at the NCA building just south of the river and the resulting travel chaos. Some of the reporting, made the events sound like doomsday. Roger shrugged his shoulders, perhaps they were. What every reporter was asking of course, was what was the cause for the explosion. Was it a bomb or bombs? An answer to which, they'd been told would be announced today.

Good luck with that, Roger thought. What idiot had promised them that. Definitely not somebody from the NCA. Probably some idiot, attention grabbing politician. Dropping several thick slices of cheese onto toast he slid his masterpiece under the grill. Waiting for the cheese to melt, he took a long sip of coffee. Better perhaps, described as a slurp. Coffee always helped to move his brain into gear. Jane had already called him. They had a meeting at Whitehall at 10am, sharp. The prime minister would be attending. He was looking forward to that. His team at the Hilton had called him too. Nothing, a big fat nothing. No sign of his ex-colleague John and no sign of their plant, Rory, who at the time had been tailing him. All they knew was his tracker had placed him on the nineteenth floor and after that he'd simply disappeared. With no trace of him since. Roger, reluctantly concurred with his team that their next step would be to look at the hotel's CCTV, which they knew to be very good and covered every floor. Nick, who had managed to grab a few hours sleep, had bravely volunteered to make the request to the hotel management. He would have to deliver some sort of explanation for their request, whilst revealing as little as possible to the hotel about their covert operation. Not an easy, not to mention enviable task.

Good luck with that, Roger thought for the second time, and a faint smile briefly lit his face. Nick had also been successful with the warrant to search John's flat in Drury Lane. Two of his officers had spent the night keeping an eye out for anyone attempting to enter or leave. No one had. Roger, knowing the flat was secure was in no hurry to search it. He would, he had told Nick, go straight there after his meeting at Whitehall. He thought about the 'bleeding obvious.' John owned a laptop. He'd seen it when he'd last visited, on a table by the only window in the lounge. It definitely hadn't been there when he'd made his search yesterday. And John hadn't had it with him at The Hilton. Roger also knew John had no car in London, parking was too much of a pain he had told him. So he could rule that out, the laptop wouldn't be in a car. Other possibilities. Could it be at John's bakery in London? They were going to have to check the place out anyway, as well as interview all the staff. John moved it up the list of things to do. Then there was John's latest love interest, Maureen who liked to call herself Bree. He'd found nothing suspicious on the police computer. He would have to have a more thorough look, And where was she now? And the least palatable possibility, whoever had left the door open had absconded with the laptop. Could the laptop be the reason for the illegal entry. Roger felt pretty confident that any entry had been without John's permission. The latter would be the worst case scenario. He had no idea who it could be and what they were dealing with, not to mention why, why was John's laptop so important. Roger pursed his lips, he felt he was starting to lose this investigation. That it was spiralling out of control. Who or whatever he was dealing with appeared to always be one step ahead. Correct that, several steps ahead. And now the explosion at the NCA, a scenario, if a bomb was responsible, until yesterday, considered impossible. Was there a connection with his current investigation? He could think of none, but his gut continued to nag at him. There was also the French connection and with the delivery of the severed head in north London, it couldn't be ignored. And why severed heads? And why present them in such a disgusting manner? What statement was the perpetrator trying to make? The first two heads had belonged to characters from the gangster world, but not the third. There was no evidence that this poor man had any criminal past. Not that that meant he didn't. He was from a part of the world that was hard to investigate. Roger's thought process turned to the poor murdered Albanian children, supposedly under Her Majesty's care and protection. They now appeared to play some part in this as well. The mystery man, Jason had suggested as much. The possibility couldn't be ignored. The French connection had raised the ugly head of the so called 'red market.' Until recently he'd known little of it's existence. Apparently it was big business. This was another avenue that needed investigating. But just where does one start? Roger remembered that he'd left a message for someone at the gendarmerie in Calais to contact him. To his knowledge, nobody had, not yet. He scribbled a note to follow it up. He underlined his note, not once but twice. That reminded him, he hadn't heard from the policia in Spain for several days either, the same applied to Detective Inspector Johnson at Havant down in Hampshire. Where were they in their investigations. He made another note to contact both.

Shit, something was burning. His breakfast. Roger opened his grill, smoke billowed out revealing a black mass on blackened bread.

"Shit." The second exclamation was spoken out loud. He tossed the blackness into the bin, unashamedly sucking his burning fingers. How was it women never appeared to be affected by anything hot to the touch? His ex wife could handle anything, hot from the microwave or oven, without flinching. Whereas, when he remembered that is, he always needed oven gloves or a tea towel. Refusing to give up, he placed another toast laden with cheese under the grill and prepared a second coffee. He wouldn't leave his house until he'd had three. Over the years three coffees before he left the house had become something of a tradition. It was now superstition. Less than three was bad luck.

Roger had successfully finished his second attempt at cheese on toast, when his phone rang. He looked at the caller ID and froze, it was John! John, bloody John! He took the call,

"John, John, John where the bloody hell are you? The line remained open, but there wasn't a sound the other end. Was John trying to wind him up? If he was, he was doing a bloody good job. "John, John will you, bloody answer." Still silence. Using his land line, Roger dialled Scotland Yard. He had no choice, his office was temporarily out of action. All the time the line to John's phone remained live but no one was responding. There was something very wrong. After jumping through a number of frustrating hoops, Roger got put through to the specialist department, that he needed. It took just over a minute to explain he needed a triangulation track to a cell phone that was live, and that he needed it now, right now.

"Number sir." Roger gave it to the woman on the other end of the line. All the time John's phone remained live. Something was seriously wrong.

"One moment sir." In under a minute the woman kept her promise. "The position is Drury Lane, WC2B 5PD. The phone is stationary. If you wish sir I can operate the phone's camera. I can send you a link, and you can view for yourself."

"Please." Roger could hardly contain himself. There was still no sound from John's mobile and the line remained open. The link arrived within seconds, Roger clicked on it and instantly the image from John's mobile camera was on his screen. He almost dropped his phone in surprise. He recognised the image instantly, it was the ceiling light just inside John's front door, at his flat in Drury Lane.

The image was grainy as it was still dark but it was definitely John's flat. And the image was stationary, frozen. The only explanation Roger could think of was his ex-colleague was lying there injured, maybe fatally injured. He checked his mobile again, the image from John's mobile remained as before, always unmoving. Almost forgetting, he thanked the operator from Scotland Yard. Picking up his radio he called the leading officer on surveillance duty outside the Drury Lane apartment.

"Sir?"

"Our target is in his flat, I have a live camera image from his phone, he's inside."

"But that's not possi……." Roger cut him off, "Not now, we've got a warrant. Gain entry to the premises, use whatever means you have to. Break the bloody door down if necessary."

"Yes sir."

"I'm on my way. Stay in radio contact."

"Yes sir." The second the radio flicked off the officer turned to his colleague, sat in the car beside him. They were both drinking, he thought, a well-earned takeaway coffee. "Shit Mark, we're really in the shit. Our target is in his bloody flat!"

"No way! How did that happen?" Mark despite his fatigue, sat bolt upright. "We'd have seen him."

"I don't know, but he's there, the boss has got a live camera feed from the guy's bloody mobile."

"Shit."

"The boss wants us to gain entry." Both officers jumped out of their car, their coffees forgotten.

Back at his house in Bushey, Roger grabbed his coat. Ready to leave he couldn't help taking a second's glance at his coffee mug. Even under such strained circumstances, superstition held him in its grasp. Only two coffees that morning. That didn't bode well. Would a take away count as three? He knew it was nonsense, but the question still troubled him. He'd pick one up on his way, at the next petrol station. That should do the trick. The thought no matter how ludicrous, gave him a crumb of comfort. He really didn't need another bad day.

Formby, Lancashire, England

James Wade was nervous. Something was wrong, he didn't know quite what, but he didn't like the feel of it. He now regretted ever having getting involved with John Mitchell. Obtaining false death certificates for him, through his position at the GRO, had been easy and easy money, or so he thought. Up until now. Now he was beginning to realise the gravity of what he'd done. If found out he was in for a hefty time in prison. And he was suddenly feeling very exposed.

It was after his last conversation with Mr Mitchell. He had asked for a ridiculous number of death certificates. To have granted his request would have been professional suicide. His bosses would have suspected something immediately. Mr Mitchell had told him his life may even be in danger if he didn't come through, but he hadn't seen that as his problem. In the end he had agreed to provide one last death certificate for the princely sum of £5,000. They had, so to speak, shaken on this. James hadn't heard from Mr Mitchell since, but he had heard from somebody else. A man, a stranger with a foreign accent who somehow knew his mobile number. The man, on phoning him, had been polite but quietly threatening. He wanted death certificates, lots of genuine death certificates and he'd pay four times whatever Mr Mitchell had been paying him. James had told him that what he was asking him to do was simply impossible. The stranger on the other end of the line hadn't threatened him when hearing this. Instead simply a promise that they'd speak again. What, thought James had he got himself into?

After kissing his wife and baby son goodbye, James left in his car for his job with the GRO,(General Records Office), at Southport. When the records office had moved from London, James had moved with it. He could afford a much nicer house up here, and he was quite proud of the fact that he owned a house in the same town where several Premier League footballers had also chosen to live. As he drove he started to relax, maybe he was simply over reacting. On instinct he checked his rear mirror and what he saw almost made him swerve off the road. A man was sitting in his back seat. He wore a grin, a grin that read satisfaction. It was in no way friendly. He had black, neatly cropped hair though in contrast his beard was unkempt. His eyes were dark brown and held no light. What really caught Jame's attention was the man's right hand. Held in its grasp was a pistol. The man's grin widened. Slowly he levelled the pistol at Jame's neck.

"I told you we'd talk again," and the man laughed.

Bodinnick, Cornwall, England

Claire stood, looking out of her picture window, across the water to Fowey. It was a view that was impossible to get tired of, and the very reason she'd purchased the property. As she gazed out now, the morning light, although grey was slowly unveiling the narrow streets of the Cornish harbour town. Directly below the Bodinnick ferry was ferrying its first passengers of the day and further out, nearer the open sea a couple of trawlers were returning from their night's fishing.

It was a view that helped calm her, steady her, and by God, that morning did she need that view. Claire had always had anger issues. In her teens, in Liverpool, she'd almost killed a school friend, over nothing more than sharing a burger. On the plus side, as a young adult being brought up in one of the more deprived areas of the city, her anger had got her through many a tough time. Everyone knew she was not to be messed with, and the usual troublemakers who'd specialised in making many, weaker people's lives a misery left her well alone. This scenario had carried on in her adult life, and it was the reason why she had eventually been so successful in a profession that was almost entirely male dominated. Uncompromising, ruthless men who had no respect for life except their own. To the average man on the street, her job title would be classed as, 'gangster.' And true she did run a hugely successful criminal organisation, the police often described it as an empire. An empire that stretched from, and to every corner of the British Isles. And to some extent continental Europe. But she hated the title gangster being bestowed on her. Claire saw herself more as a modern day Robin Hood. She was the main benefactor for many charities and adored wildlife. She also enjoyed walking, not a pastime normally associated with gangsters, and would regularly spend hours outdoors with her one faithful friend. A Golden Retriever called Tammy.

She was proud that she didn't need to rely on a man in her life. Many worked for her and they were often called upon to do her dirty work, but nothing more. On more than one occasion men had tried to get close to her, for she was not unattractive, but Claire had always rejected their advances. Sometimes brutally so. Like most women in their early fifties she enjoyed a man for sex and she was happy to pay for this service. Rather that, than have a man try and worm his way into her life. With an escort the relationship finished when you closed the door. Perfect. She simply didn't trust men, possibly because of her father, who had deserted her mother when she had been only four. Things simply had got on top of him he had told her when she, in her twenties, after years of searching had found him. He deserved to die the way he did and buried where nobody would look. Claire considered all men to be just like her father. In her view, they were weak, disorganised and tended to make rash decisions. And most important, you could never trust a man. If you needed examples other than her father, simply take a look at the world. It was a bloody mess. A mess created by men.

Now, to her great disappointment, yet another man had let her down. He'd been one of the few men she almost respected. Up until now he'd always carried out his work for her with ruthless efficiency. He'd never questioned her and had always brought her results. Most importantly he'd never tried to climb above his station. He was her employee, an expensive one, yes, but he always made it clear that she was the boss. And respected her for being that. UNTIL NOW.

Reading the papers it would appear her previously model employee had come off the rails in spectacular fashion. In all the national papers the headlines, until the incident at the NCA, Claire couldn't resist a smile, were of a severed head delivered to a woman in North London. A head that had his genitals stuffed in his mouth and his eyes gouged out. The papers hadn't held back on the gory details and all had picked up on a recent murder in Langstone, on the Hampshire coast. In that case, the severed head of a well-known gangster had been found in almost identical fashion. Was there a connection? There must be all the papers surmised. Not as far as Claire was concerned. She had ordered the killing in Langstone and the one in Spain. She was disappointed the one in Spain hadn't yet reached the attention of the media. Both these men had double crossed her, worse still they had both absconded with a great deal of her money. Their murders and the way their corpses were found had been designed deliberately by her for the media to unintentionally carry the story, as a warning to others who may hold similar ambitions. Not to make the same mistake. But this killing in north London, she had not ordered. What the hell was her, up until now, loyal and obedient employee thinking of? Had he gone quite mad?

Taking deep breaths Claire concentrated on the view rather than her anger. She needed to be calm when he rang. If he rang. The phone rang. Claire, after counting to three, answered. Almost touching the glass, another aid to keeping her cool, she spoke. "Hello." A man's voice responded, one she recognised, one she'd been expecting.

"Hello, Claire. How are you?" HOW WAS SHE, Claire almost threw the phone across the room. How was she? She was just about managing to keep her cool. She was doing her best to keep calm. On the surface at any rate. Inside she was boiling.

"Morning, Ryan, well to be honest I'm not best pleased."

"I can guess what this is about Ma'am." Ryan had seen the headlines and had been waiting for the order to call his boss. He never phoned her unless instructed to.

"Can you Ryan?" Claire put the flat of her hand against the window. It felt cool to the touch. She needed to stay cool.

"Yes Ma'am, no doubt you've read the papers."

"Yes, Ryan. Would you care to give me an explanation. Did I give you instructions to target this man?"

"No Ma'am, and I did not target him. That killing has nothing to do with me. It's a copycat killing."

Claire held her breath. She continued to stare out of her window. The Bodinnick Ferry, after unloading was steadily making its way back to the far shore. Its steady motion, had the effect of steadying her emotions. She hadn't considered this, a copycat killing. Was Ryan telling the truth? She prided herself on seeing through a lie and her initial instinct on this occasion told her that Ryan was telling her the truth. If he was, she had some thinking to do. Why go to so much trouble, take such a huge risk in carrying out such a public murder? For what reason? Unless somebody was trying to set her up. But who? Who would be capable of doing such a thing? WHO WOULD DARE? Claire had plenty of enemies, but one key to her success is what she liked to think of as her own private secret service. Her own intelligence network. She normally knew what her enemies were planning before they did. But on this occasion she'd heard nothing, and this could be big. Someone may be plotting her downfall, and if so, she hadn't a clue who it may be.

"Ma'am, Ma'am, are you still there?" Hearing Ryan's voice brought Claire back to the here and now.

"Yes Ryan. Ryan, you are telling me the truth? You know I'll find out if you're not. And if I find out that you're lying to me, you know I'll have someone cut your head off and stuff your manhood down your throat. You understand that don't you, Ryan?"

"Yes Ma'am." Ryan's voice was solid, there was no wavering that Claire could detect. He was telling the truth, of that, she was now sure.

"Any idea who could have done this Ryan?"

"None Ma'am, I'm sorry. Do you want me to ask around?"

"No Ryan, I have my contacts who are better at doing that. But thanks for the offer. Thank you for phoning me Ryan, and for now keep out of sight. No drinking. Tea and coffee at home only. Is that understood?"

"Totally Ma'am."

"Good, I'll be in touch." Claire rang off, she had total faith in Ryan. She should never have doubted him. Now the situation had changed, she needed to make another call. Picking up a second, quite different phone, she searched its address book before placing another call. After six rings the call diverted to an answerphone. Claire listened, though she already knew the message off by heart.

"Hello, this is Detective Constable Havers. I'm afraid I'm unavailable at the moment. Please leave a message and I promise, as soon as I am able, I'll get right back to you." Claire rang off, she'd call back.

Tammy brushed against her leg. It was light now. She wanted her walk. Unhooking the dog's lead from a wall, Claire almost skipped to the front door. "Come on then Tammy, walkies." Both dog and mistress were really looking forward to the next hour together.

Chapter 3

North London, England

Roger took a sip of his third coffee of the morning. It was in a disposable cup, but hey-ho, he was already feeling better. And that, even with the heavier than usual traffic on the Finchley Road. His mobile lay, facing upwards on the passenger seat beside him. There was always the same image but in the background he could hear his officers trying to force the door.

As he'd left, Roger had radioed Jane to inform her of recent events. He'd told her that he feared John may be lying fatally injured inside his flat. If this was the case it changed everything. It would suggest a third party was involved, a third party they knew nothing about. Both had agreed on this and that this added to their original concern. Their concern, following the explosion or explosions, that their agency had somehow been infiltrated by a person or persons unknown. 'These are very worrying times,' Jane had commented more than once. He had come clean on yesterday's events at The Hilton. Jane hadn't been angry, just concerned. She would at some point, if there was no more news, have to phone Rory's wife and explain that her husband was currently missing whilst on duty. Not an enviable task. Jane also emphasised that she wanted this Mr Mitchell thoroughly investigated. Roger had promised to take care of it personally. For his own sake he didn't want anybody else doing it. He was already worried about John's phone. Forensics would go through it with a fine toothcomb. What would they find? Anything on him? It was John's personal phone, so he doubted it but there would be evidence of calls made between them. That may take some explaining. Their conversation had ended with Jane reminding him not to be late for their meeting in Whitehall.

Roger took another sip of his coffee, he preferred his own brew. This coffee tasted as though it had been made by a machine, which it had of course. Following on from his conversation with Jane, he thought hard over John. What had his ex-friend and colleague got himself involved in? And there was that woman, Maureen, or was it Bree? John had sounded besotted with her, even so he was old and wise enough to suspect something wasn't right. What had made him so suspicious and why the false name? He would have to check her out, thoroughly check her out. But again this wouldn't be easy, he'd have to do it on tiptoe or people may start asking questions. Shit he was a bloody fool. A bloody, bloody fool. Frustration ended his patience with the morning's traffic. Activating his lights and siren he swerved into the centre of Finchley Road and put his foot down. As the car responded his mobile almost left the seat. He just managed to grab it before it flew onto the floor. Returning the phone to the seat he took a second's glance at the screen. What he saw almost caused him to crash, and he swore loudly as an SUV coming in the opposite direction came within a fraction of colliding with hm. Steady Roger, steaaaady, he scolded himself. Once more he glanced at his mobile. The lampshade had been replaced by a face. He recognised it instantly as one of his officers charged with staking out John's flat.

"We're in sir," his voice came over the radio. "The phone was simply lying on the floor, there's no sign of our target. Somebody must have put the phone through the letter box." Roger quickly processed this information. What to do?

"Ok, you guys start searching the flat will you, does it look as if anything's been disturbed?"

"First impressions sir, no. All looks in order, but as I said, first impressions only." Roger pursed his lips, swearing at a driver in front, who appeared to be oblivious to his presence behind him.

"I'll be with you in roughly ten minutes. Can you start taking a look around, but make sure you don't contaminate anything. I'm going to book a SOCO team."

"Yes sir. Mark will have to stand guard outside, as we had to break in. We really need a uniform, if the Met can spare one."

"Leave it with me." Roger glared at the driver as he managed to pass the car that had been holding him up. What a bloody dick head. "Can you leave the phone where you found it, I want to get my own impression of the scene."

"Yes sir, will do."

"Ok, see you in five." Roger flicked off. What was going on? Why on earth would someone want to take the risk being seen posting John's phone through his letter box? It didn't make sense. Whoever it was must have had good reason. What was it?

Ardres, France

She wanted to cry, but no matter how hard she tried, the tears simply wouldn't come. A few days back her life had been perfect. Many of her friends had been jealous of her. She'd had a successful husband who'd doted on her and it wasn't long before he was due for retirement. They'd both been looking forward to that day. Or so she'd thought. Apparently her husband had been having an affair with a much younger girl called Marie. It was all over social media. Photos of her husband kissing this girl in his car. Not only had she had to deal with her own personal shock, but the indignity, not to mention shame, knowing most of Calais knew too. For her husband was news. He was, or so she'd just been informed, 'had been,' capitaine of the gendarmerie in Calais. A very powerful position. Many people, she suspected, would be delighting in his downfall, even his death.

'Had been.' Her husband's second in command, Lieutenant Beaufort, who'd only left a few minutes ago, had travelled out to inform her, that her husband was facing disciplinary proceedings. Even worse, her husband's body had been picked up last night, by a fisherman in La Manche, just off Cap Blanc Nez. And was now lying in the morgue at Boulogne. If she was feeling strong enough, they needed her for a formal identification. He could do it of course, he had told her, but the law preferred a family member for a formal identification. She'd surprised herself by saying yes, not only saying yes but agreeing to do it that very afternoon.

The lieutenant had been very kind and genuinely concerned for her wellbeing. He'd come out early he'd told he as he hadn't wanted her to learn of her husband's fate via the media. He'd offered a female officer to keep her company if she so wanted, but she had declined. She wanted to deal with this on her own.

Her eyes moved to the bureau where most of their family photos were on display. Smiling faces, happy faces were the focus of each photograph. All except one. It was of her husband in full uniform standing outside his first gendarmerie at Hazebrouck. He looked so proud. They had been so happy. So she'd thought. Evidently he hadn't, he'd wanted more. She looked in the mirror above the bureau. Without thinking, with one hand she touched her hair. She wasn't that unattractive, was she? Not for her age. Should she have made more an effort for her husband? Was this all her fault?

She picked up the photo with him at Hazebrouck. She'd never really taken an interest in Thierry's work. Perhaps she should have done. Theirry, she allowed herself a faint smile. Thierry, to most people he was Capitaine Maubert, even to some of his friends. That's how he'd liked it. Walking through the hallway, she entered what had been his office, his personal gendarme cave. This was hallowed ground. She never normally entered, not even to clean. This had always been her husband's private space. Still holding the framed photo, she lowered herself into her husband's favourite chair. On the right arm hung a set of expensive looking headphones. Gingerly she put them on. After turning on the equally expensive looking hifi on one side of his desk, she opened the cd tray. There was a cd already there, ready to play. She picked it up. 'Yungblud.' 'Yungblud?' She'd never heard of the artist. She closed the tray, pressed the play button and settled down to listen. As 'The Funeral' began to play, tears at last started to roll down her face. The artist being English she couldn't understand a word he was singing, but somehow she knew the song was apt. Forces the world didn't understand had wanted her to listen to this song. The tears kept rolling and rolling.

The GMC Building, Euston Road, London, England

Arif sat drinking an expresso. He'd quickly discovered he didn't like the coffee served in England. It was too weak, even an expresso. He also didn't like the damp, grey cold that London suffered at this time of year. In Arif's mind it was like living under a funeral shroud. He found the weather depressing and the damp cold seeped through his skin and into his bones. He hoped he hadn't made a mistake. If he passed this exam, the money promised him was eye watering. Never in his wildest dreams had he thought he could earn so much. He pinched himself. He still couldn't believe this was happening to him.

Little over a year ago he was in war torn Syria. Trapped in the greatest hell on earth. He'd been half way through his medical training when the madness started. What had been, up until then a comfortable life descended into simply learning to survive for the next hour, often even the next minute. All of his immediate family were now dead. His mother, his father, his three brothers and his only sister. All killed in a bomb attack his townsmen said were the work of the Russians. What had he ever done to that country for them to inflict on him such pain and despair?

He'd been counting the days when he'd meet his God when out of nowhere a stranger, who spoke a strange form of Arabic, asked if he still wanted a career in medicine. And if he did, he could help him. Of course he had agreed. He'd be a fool not to. That night, along with several others, he had been bundled into the back of a lorry. They'd all been warned to keep quiet, not to make a sound. After the pickup they had been driven for hours. Along the way the lorry had been stopped at several checkpoints. On each occasion they could hear voices, and all in the back held their breath expecting the lorry to be searched, but it never was. Whoever it was driving must have had a close connection with God. The next day, during daylight hours they stayed, along with four others in a simple sand brick room with no windows. A toilet in the corner of the room was of the old style with a smell you could never get used to. It was perhaps a godsend that they were never offered food, just water. For surely if they had, it wouldn't have stayed in their stomachs for long. Whilst held in the room they were again warned not to speak a word, not to make a sound. If anyone did they'd be left there. It wasn't a warning, it was a promise. Nobody did. The following night the group heard two planes land. From the noise, Arif knew they were powered by propeller. He'd been escorted onto one of the planes along with two from the new group, and the four remaining onto the other. The two planes quickly took off with each heading in a different direction. Several hours later the plane landed in open desert. Arif had no idea where they were, even which country they were in.

The year that followed can only be explained as pure fantasy. He trained in an underground medical facility that had the very latest in high tech medical equipment. The professionals who'd trained him were second to none and he achieved in a year what would normally have taken him three, perhaps even four years in a standard facility. Just about everything he was taught went in and stayed there. He was still incredulous as to how this was achieved. In Syria, when training there, he was always making notes, and burning the oil at midnight, to try and retain and make sense of what he'd been taught. In the desert facility, he hadn't needed to make a single note, everything went in and stayed there.

There had been twelve others on his course, including the two who were on the plane with him. There had been other groups of trainees but they had never been allowed to mix. As for the two on the plane, both were medical students and both, like him, had sought to escape having been in fear for their lives. At the training facility, every other trainee told of similar experiences. And they'd been a real mixed bag, from several different countries. Just over half were from the middle east, two were from Eritrea and there was even one from China. None knew who the training facility belonged to and all had been promised a huge salary once they'd qualified. They'd also been offered a choice of four different countries in which they could work. He had chosen England, along with two others. Mainly because he already had a good grasp of the language. The other countries offered, had been France, Greece and Italy. As it turned out he needn't have worried about language as they were all given an intensive course on the language of the country of their choice. Just like with his medical training, he'd remembered everything he was taught and his English was now perfect.

From the desert location, he never found out where it was or which country they'd trained in. There were no roads servicing the facility, just a simple airstrip. It could have been anywhere. He'd been taken to Cairo, where he'd been given a fresh set of papers and passport. The 'organisation,' that's what everyone referred to it as, had obtained authorisation from the GMC in England for him to sit the PLAB. 1 exam at their centre in Cairo. He'd passed with almost perfect results and now here he was, sitting in a London café, The Black Sheep, opposite the GMC building waiting to take his PLAB 2 exam. If he passed, it would allow him to practise in the UK. And if he passed, he already had a job lined up. An incredible job with an incredible salary. Arif finished his coffee, he still couldn't believe what had happened to him. One other student who had trained with him was also enjoying a coffee in the Black Sheep. She was from Eritrea. He wanted to smile at her, to wish her good luck, but they'd been strictly told, under no circumstances, not to publicly show any signs of recognition. He couldn't understand why not. The 'organisation' must have their reasons. The student from Eritrea was playing her role well, not once had she looked at him. Arif looked away, his glance to anyone watching would simply have been interpreted as admiration of an attractive woman. At least he hoped so, for he couldn't get rid of the feeling that somebody was watching him.

Drury Lane, London, England

Roger pulled up right outside the door to John's flat. Standing outside, guarding the entrance and looking thoroughly cold and miserable, not to mention tired stood one of his officers.

"You look like shit," Roger smiled his welcome,

"I feel like shit, we've got no idea how the phone got there sir. We didn't see a thing." Roger listened holding his smile.

"Whoever called me using John's phone, did so at five forty am. There's no CCTV pointing directly at Mr Mitchell's flat, but Camden has plenty of cameras in the surrounding streets, not to mention private. We should be able to pick up something. Scotland Yard are already on to it. Oh and that reminds me. They're also sending a couple of uniforms to take over from you. Feeling better? Roger's smile grew to a grin.

"A little. Poor buggers, I hate this cold. Why two?" Normally in this kind of situation only one would be required.

"Safer with numbers, we're not quite sure who or what we're dealing with. Better to be safe than sorry. Now show me the phone."

The officer pushed open the door, and there lying face up on the floor, Roger recognised John's mobile. "The letter box is low to the ground, so whoever dropped the phone off, literally had to only slide it across the carpet. I simply can't understand how we didn't see him."

"Or she," Roger pointed out.

"Or she, yes." More to the point, Roger thought again. Why? Why go to so much trouble, why take such a risk? Why? Why? Why? Whoever delivered the phone must have been aware that the flat was being watched. Why? It just didn't make sense.

"Where's Mark, upstairs? The officer nodded.

"Yes he's having a scout around, like you asked. I don't think he's found anything out of place though.

"I'll take a look." Roger slipped on a couple of covers for his shoes, along with disposable gloves. Grabbing an evidence bag from his car he dropped the phone inside after first turning off the video. "Somebody else may be watching."

"I did wonder."

"Watch my car as well, will you." Drury Lane was narrow and a delivery lorry passing had almost scratched the side. Throwing the officer his keys Roger mounted the steps two by two. He found the other officer, Mark, kneeling, examining drawers in the only bedroom. "Found anything?"

"Morning sir, no, nothing. It's just as though the flat is waiting for its owner to return. Completely normal. No sign of anybody having been here who shouldn't have been."

Just as he had found it last night. Roger didn't let on, that he'd found the front door unlocked and minutely ajar, that somebody had recently been inside. Somebody almost certainly who hadn't been invited. Just as he hadn't. And unless John had removed it first, there was something missing. A laptop. Roger had one more quick scout around. The flat was just as he had left it last night. Perhaps the door had been left open for whoever it was who had dropped off the phone. Having found the door locked would have been an extreme annoyance for whoever. Had they then left the phone to try and make some sort of statement? It still didn't make any sense. He drew an exaggerated breath.

"Right, Mark. You carry on. A SOCO team are booked to go over the place in detail. Let's hope they come up with something. In the meantime keep looking. Just be sure not to contaminate anything."

"I won't, you know me better than that." Roger did, Mark had been with him for over ten years. "No sign of our target then I understand, nor Rory?"

Rory who had been John's tail, and a plant to entrap him, Roger knew was a very close friend of Mark's. Over the years they'd worked many cases together and as a consequence had built and developed a bond that few people came close to. Even in marriage. Roger shook his head.

"No, I'm sorry. Nothing."

Mark stood up.

"How can they have just disappeared from under our noses? I mean where the hell are they?"

Roger stared beyond where Mark was standing.

"I wish I could answer that. Nick's going to go through the hotel's CCTV's footage this morning. Hopefully we might find some answers there. It's almost impossible to move around that hotel without being caught on camera."

"But not impossible." It was a statement not a question from Mark.

"Pretty much." Roger attempted a grin and failed. "We'll have to wait and see."

"Do you think they're still in the hotel?"

"Honest answer?" Roger stared straight at his officer.

Mark shrugged his shoulders.

"Yes."

"To be honest Mark, I haven't a clue, not a bloody clue. I wish I had."

"Fair enough."

Roger turned to leave.

"Sir, a quick question."

Roger hesitated.

"Yes?"

"Where do we report to?" Mark looked uncomfortable. "I mean I haven't an office anymore. Neither have you. Where's base?"

Roger knew exactly why and how his officer felt and appeared so uncomfortable in asking the question. He felt the same way. He felt naked, as though he had forcibly been made to remove his clothes. And the feeling of nakedness made him also feel vulnerable. He hated the feeling.

"Apparently there's an emergency procedure for such an eventuality, though I've never heard of it. After all I'm just the director, why the hell do I need to know? I'm meeting the Director General shortly. I'm sure she'll have the answers. I'll let you know as soon as I know myself."

"Fair enough," Mark replied for the second time.

"Right, let me know if you come up with anything." With that Roger turned and left, leaving Mark to carry on with his cursory search.

Ten minutes later he was pulling into the Q car park at Leicester Square. He didn't want to park in Whitehall, he preferred to walk the rest of the route. He had his reasons. Turning his engine off, Roger put on another pair of disposable gloves and reached into the evidence bag for John's phone. Systematically , he began working his way through the phone's features. After only a few minutes it became obvious the phone had been wiped. There was no evidence of text messages or any type of message for that matter. The phone registered only two recent calls. A number Roger didn't recognise and his own. And the phone contained no pictures. Only the one video, commenced when the mobile had been posted at John's flat. Somebody had, for some reason, a reason Roger couldn't understand, wiped the phone clean. Again, why? With this case there were so many whys. Nothing seemed to make any sense. He'd been worried that whoever had taken John's phone had wanted to discredit him, to expose his true and murky relationship, with his ex-friend and colleague. To expose how he'd used the NCA's resources to help John answer questions. What he'd done was illegal, he could even go to prison. John's phone could have exposed this, so why wipe it clean? It just didn't make sense. There was that phrase again. Roger made a note of the only recent call registered other than the one to himself. He would call it later, after the Whitehall meeting. With that Roger popped the phone back into the evidence bag, this time sealing it. Digital forensics would take the phone apart. Joe Public, in the main, were unaware that deleted material on a mobile, never really is deleted. It's still there, it's just hidden, not easy to find. He was worried, very worried what forensics might turn up, but he had no choice. Questions would immediately be asked if the phone, as vital evidence wasn't examined by digital forensics. He looked at his watch. Just gone nine. He waited another five minutes. Roger wanted to be sure that no one had been following him. He was pretty confident that nobody had. Following him into a car park wouldn't have been easy. After tucking the evidence bag under his seat Roger started on the short walk to Whitehall.

The Hilton Hotel, Park Lane, London

Nick along with two other officers from the NCA were with the Hilton's security team, going through footage from the previous evening. The NCA officers were all pleasantly surprised by the quality of the footage, not to mention the facilities in the security room. As private security centres go this was amongst the best they'd seen. Getting past the hotel management had been easier than expected. Probably because, as their boss had instructed, they hadn't revealed the NCA had been staging a sting operation in the hotel. If they had, their willingness to help may have been very different.

Nick decided to start with their tail and plant. The hotel's outside cameras clearly showed Rory entering the hotel, and the lobby cameras, him walking past reception to the lifts. Their tracking devices had told them that Rory had for some inexplicable reason exited on the 19th floor. His orders had been to continue to the Sky Bar on the 28th floor. What had made him get out at the 19th? Hopefully the CCTV footage would provide an explanation. Frustratingly the CCTV from the lifts on that day were being upgraded. They hadn't been recording. The hotel operator switched to the camera directly outside the lift on the 19th floor. He started to play back the video from the time Rory entered the lift in the hotel lobby. The video showed people coming and going but thirty minutes of video later there was still no sign of their man.

"Not possible." Nick turned to the two officers with him.

"Why are you so sure this man got off on the 19th floor?" This question was from the hotel's head of security. A tall stocky man of Indian heritage. The NCA had already checked the man's history. He was an ex-officer, with the Met, with an impeccable record. He had taken the job at The Hilton. A, for the money and B, because he'd married and started a family, and no longer wanted the dangers his job as a policeman entailed. Nick wanted to, but because of orders, couldn't reveal the truth.

"Our intelligence is that this man had an appointment on the 19th floor."

"Which room?"

"Our intelligence is the 19th floor, that's it." The Hilton's main security officer, rightly Nick thought, looked on incredulous.

"What! You only have the floor not the room? That's nuts. What was the guy meant to be doing on the 19th floor? Who was he meant to be meeting?" Nick was starting to squirm. The head of security wasn't stupid and his story was beginning to look a little suspicious, weak at best.

"Meeting someone, we simply don't know who. We have our suspicions of course, but I'm afraid we can't reveal them. You as an ex-policeman can understand that. Our informant, simply told us the 19th floor." The head of security, stared at the array of screens, flashing from view to view before them. He sensed the three men in his control room weren't telling him the whole story. He'd been in a similar situation himself. Many times. It was very frustrating, he wanted to help and with clearer information he almost certainly could. He looked at the officer who appeared to be in charge. Nick Harris, his ID had stated.

"Well your informant may have been wrong. He could have got off at any floor. Why don't we start at the bottom and work our way up, we're bound to find him, he must have got off somewhere.." Nick could feel the other two officers pleading with him. Their tracking device had showed him to be on the 19th floor. 'Please no.' It would simply be a waste of time. But Nick could see no other option. Perhaps their device used for tracking hadn't been as accurate as the manufacturers had them believe. It wouldn't be the first time. He reluctantly agreed. The video controller complied.

"I'll start with the first floor, from the time the subject entered the lift on the ground floor and run the film for forty minutes from the lift on each floor. Just in case the suspect travelled up and down, to throw you off his scent. He may have suspected he was being followed."

The head of security nodded in agreement.

"The practice is more common than you'd believe." He grinned, "sometimes it's almost comical."

Nick found himself grinning, he could just picture it. A suspicious husband and all that.

"Good point. Yes do that. But rather than start from the first floor can we start from the 18th and work down, and if nothing, carry on from the 20th till we reach the top." Nick couldn't remember what number the last floor was.

"The 28th, Windows and the Sky Bar," the operator helped out.

Nick agreed, why not? They had to cover all bases. Maybe their man had slipped out on the 28th without their agents placed there noticing him. It didn't explain the information relayed by his tracker, but Nick was beginning to think that there was a strong possibility the tracker had been telling them porkies. He settled himself for the tedious task ahead. Unless they spotted their man quickly, staring at hours of footage of hotel corridors would be very tedious work. That's why you always had more than one officer, doing the job. Just in case one nodded off for a few seconds, and those few seconds invariably would have been the vital few seconds. Nick glanced across at the faces of the two men with him. He saw from their expressions, they both needed fuelling.

"Any chance of some coffee before we start?"

Cromwell Place, London, England

Fatima, or Ariana, the name given to her at birth, hadn't really known what to expect. Certainly not this. In her head she had imagined the French Consulate, from where she had to collect her passport to be a grand affair. Lots of flags and shiny brass plaques, when in fact, as she now saw, the opposite was true. Instead of brass plaques there were a couple of simple white backed signs. One wired onto iron railings and an arrow fixed to the top of a stone post on which somebody had unceremoniously left a banana skin. Removing the banana skin revealed in English, 'QUEUE STARTS FROM THIS POINT.' There was no need to queue as she was the only person there. Fatima wearing a smart dark blue, trouser suit by Lanvin, over which, and keeping the cold out, a tan trench coat by Balmain, felt distinctly overdressed. They were both classic French designers and definitely not average high street wear. She was nervous enough as it was, and now seeing the simplicity of the French passport office, her choice of wardrobe made her feel more than a little uncomfortable. However she'd been instructed by the man from the embassy to dress as if she had money. And that's one thing, with her choice of career Fatima knew how to do. The passport office was situated in the basement but there was a locked gate preventing her from taking the steps down. Eventually after some searching she found a button on the other side of the gate and pressed. Pressing the button several times no-one appeared. Just as she was beginning to fear the button might be faulty a young man came running up the steps and led her down to a simple but functional office. By that time, another woman, presumably also collecting a passport had joined her. There were a number of guichets, (windows), each numbered and Fatima was instructed to go to guichet three. Behind the glass sat a girl, Fatima judged to be in her late twenties. On approaching the girl was chatting and laughing with a female colleague. She looked at Fatima, and without even acknowledging her went back to her conversation. Fatima wanted to slap her but managed to hold a polite smile. If it had been any other place or situation Fatima would have made her feelings known, but not here. After waiting perhaps for a couple of minutes the girl finally turned to Fatima and without even a bonjour, asked.

"What is it you want?" Fatima forced a smile, wasn't it obvious? This was where people came to collect passports and ID cards. Without saying a word Fatima slid the documents she'd been given under the glass. The girl picked them up, examined them and asked her to wait. Fatima stood with her heart in her mouth. After years of living a lie she couldn't help feeling nervous. Any minute she half expected men in uniforms to arrest her, to take her away. As had happened so many times in her past. She needn't have worried, none did. Instead the girl returned and this time she was actually wearing a smile.

Outside Fatima wanted to jump for joy, in her hands she held an official French identity card and a real, a REAL, passport. She simply could not believe it. Not since she'd been a baby, in Persia, many, many years ago had she been officially recognised. Ever since then she'd been forced to live a lie. With a spring in her step, Fatima/Ariana, crossed the busy Cromwell Road in front of the National History Museum, turned right and then left up Exhibition Road. She felt so good she wanted to walk back to her hotel, take in London as normal people did. Yes like normal people, like people who lived daily, normal lives. She knew she wasn't quite there yet but this morning she felt she'd taken one giant step in that direction.

After following West Carriage Drive through Hyde Park, on reaching the Serpentine she took a left along a path that ran alongside the lake. Fatima was falling in love with London. It was cosmopolitan, which helped her feel at home, vibrant, beautiful and had an edge to it which suggested there were secrets. World changing secrets in some cases waiting to be discovered behind closed doors. She paused a moment to take in the statue of Peter Pan. Tourists doing the tourist thing were having their photos taken with the statue. A young girl was playing a guitar and singing at the same time. Another young girl, presumably a friend was busy filming her. A tap on Fatima's arm made her jump. Turning she found an elderly couple smiling at her.

"Do you mind taking our photo?" It was the man who spoke, and he was holding a smart phone. American, Fatima recognised the twang.

"Of course not," she took the phone and focused whilst the couple, arranged themselves in a rather too formal pose. "Relax," Fatima told them. They did and the couple appeared delighted with the results.

"Would you like us to take one of you?" This time it was the woman who spoke. Fatima thought about it.

"Why not? Yes, thank you." Fatima handed the woman her phone. In just a few seconds she had the phone back in her hand. "Thank you."

"No problem," the couple spoke together.

"I love your accent," the man drawled,. "Are you French?" Fatima laughed.

"No Persian, but I've lived in France for a long time. Are you two American?"

"No Canadian, well have a good day." With that the couple wandered off in the direction from where Fatima had just come. Fatima watched them go, what nice people. She looked at her photos, she was smiling. She looked relaxed, happy. Almost with a skip instead of a step she continued with her walk to her hotel. She was close now and the Royal Lancaster was clearly visible ahead. Fatima could even pick out her room.

"Ariana." Fatima, wasn't listening, she was too busy taking photos of the 'Italian Gardens.' She had never done the tourist thing before and she was enjoying doing so.

"Ariana," this time it was a whisper in her ear, and she jumped. "Would you prefer me to call you Fatima?"

Whitehall

Roger looked around him. The room couldn't have been plainer. It was square, had a lino covered floor, duck egg green painted walls, and a painted white ceiling from which hung a head hammering fluorescent light. The only furniture was a plain square wooden table, almost certainly pre war and eight chairs. The kind you tend to find in old village halls. The room basked in anonymity, it was uncared for and nobody cared that it was.

Opposite him, across the table, sat Jane, the director general of the NCA and to his right, his immediate boss, the NCA's director of operations. His name was Charles Reade, he was very much old school, and sported a beard as though it were a badge of honour. For the past few days, he had been off work, receiving treatment for an enlarged prostate. Today was his first day back and from the expression on his face, it looked to Roger as though his battle with his prostate wasn't over. All three from the NCA were wearing, smart casual civilian clothes, whereas the two other occupants of the room, the commissioner of the London Met, one Stephen Cross, and the assistant commissioner, who Roger had spoken to only the day before at the Tea House, were in full uniform.

All five had just come from a meeting held in an underground room in Whitehall. Those present apart from the five in the room, had included the Prime Minister, The Home Secretary, representatives from both MI5 and MI6. The national security advisor, a representative from the joint intelligence organisation, the London Fire Brigade, bomb specialists and a few in plain clothes who were never introduced and whom Roger didn't recognise. Except one, the man who had been at the brief meeting, in the Tea House at Vauxhall. The man who had given him his card. A card which contained only his name, Jason Mortimer and number. Nothing else. On seeing Roger he had thrown a slight smile of recognition but said nothing.

Many who had been at the meeting would be attending the COBRA meeting in the cabinet office later in the day. Following the explosions, it had now been accepted there'd been more than one explosion, at the NCA building. The PM had put out a press release, informing the public that he'd be chairing a COBRA meeting that afternoon. The commissioner, was due to hold a press briefing shortly, in which he was going to announce that first indicators pointed to the initial explosion being caused by gas. That the original explosion had triggered subsequent explosions due to materials, (not specified), being stored on site by the NCA. The commissioner was deeply unhappy about this as all the indications were and confirmed by the bomb specialists present. That there had been three explosions. Each one due to the detonation of an explosive material. i.e. a bomb. He, rightly in Roger's view, believed the truth would come out sooner than later. The evidence would be too hard to hide, and he would be made to look an idiot, even worse incompetent and as a result, probably be forced to resign. No one, if this scenario played out, from the government would step in to help him. Of that he was certain. That was the way of politics. After much fighting, it had been agreed that as a proviso he could follow this statement, by adding, there would be no further comment until all the facts were known. He also had the unenviable task of reassuring the public, whilst at the same time asking everyone to be vigilant. For all the money in the world, thought Roger, I wouldn't want to be in his shoes. A view that he would later tell the commissioner to his face.

What had also been agreed at the meeting was the NCA's new centre of operations. A dormant underground bunker, fully equipped in case nuclear war broke out. The bunker was hidden under Gladstone Park in Cricklewood and accessed via a couple of unoccupied units in a nearby industrial estate. Surprisingly the bunker had been regularly kept up to date with all the latest tech. A few modernisations and adjustments would be needed, that was all. After what had happened, it was felt that the temporary use of the bunker had to be kept secret and a false company would be set up to occupy the vacant units in the industrial estate. To anybody on the outside, it would simply look as though a new company had started trading there. What had also been revealed at the meeting, and something that Roger was vaguely aware of, but never fully involved in, a proposed move of the NCA to another premises had now been rubber stamped by government. The NCA, will never move back to their current address in Vauxhall.

"Well," the commissioner spoke first, slamming a pile of papers on the table. "That was fun."

Everyone present managed a laugh. The commissioner spoke directly to Jane. "

"Have you any objection if I chair, temporarily?" Jane shook her head.

"I'd prefer it."

The Commissioner gave her a rueful smile.

"Thanks." Jane's smile broadened. "I think, despite the public message, we are all agreed that what took place at your offices, was an act of terrorism, i.e. the explosions were no accident. They were the result of manufactured explosive devices." The commissioner of the Met gazed around the table, searching for opposing views. None were expressed. "Which of course, raises all sorts of questions, the main one being, of course. Whodunnit? And to a lesser extent why, and of course how? The commissioner turned to face his assistant. "I believe you may have something to say on this." The assistant commissioner's expression betrayed that he was feeling more than a little uncomfortable, that he felt to some extent that he was stepping on other people's toes. People who were present in the room. However, his role in the Met also included heading up, SO15, the command which covered anti-terrorism and special operations. He was therefore well placed to give an opinion.

"Only that, and we can't be sure, but we believe, if the explosions were the result of explosive devices, that they would have been planted a long time ago. Possibly weeks, maybe even months. You only have to look at the IRA bombing of the Grand Hotel in Brighton, 1984, to see that there is form on this. On that occasion the bomb had been planted weeks before. What I'm trying to say is, any investigation needs to go back weeks, months, maybe even years. Not just here and now."

"And this couldn't be achieved without help from the inside? Is that everyone's view? "

Roger knew just how hard it was for Jane to admit this. What had happened had happened under her watch, and she will eventually be held accountable. Everyone present knew this. The assistant commissioner nodded.

"I think we have to assume that to be the case. I'm sorry Jane."

"Don't be. If we're going to investigate this properly, not to mention thoroughly. We have to accept right from the beginning, that one of our own, maybe several, are somehow responsible. To what degree? Well does that really matter?"

Roger looked around the table, he agreed with everything that had been said so far. Then why was it, his gut was telling him something different? He wished the feeling in his gut would go away. But it wouldn't, it was bloody stubborn.

The meeting had continued for just over an hour longer. The commissioner during that time had promised his full cooperation, and where he was able, would lay the Met's resources at the NCA's disposal. It was also agreed that cross communication was essential if any investigation and prevention of future incidents were to be successful. To this end, it had been agreed that a small group of officers from both the Met and the NCA, they hoped also from the intelligence services would be chosen to work exclusively on cross communication, cross referencing information received, and to pass on leads exclusive to this case. They recognised there may be opposition to this from the joint intelligence organisation. Their role was to collate and share information from all the intelligence agencies, but their track record was hardly one they could be proud of. No all in the room felt new eyes and ears were needed. Despite the circumstances Roger felt the meeting had been a very positive one. The one caveat that nobody liked to admit to let alone talk about. Nobody, none of the agencies or intelligence services had the slightest idea who had carried this out, why and how. Usually there'd be a scrap of intelligence, but in this instance there was nothing. A big fat zero and this sent shivers up the spines of everybody responsible for the country's security.

The Morgue – Le Centre Hospitalier, Boulogne-Sur-Mer, France

They had taken the coast road to Boulogne. This had been at the request of Capitaine Maubert's widow, though the unwelcome title, 'widow,' had yet to be officially confirmed. She'd wanted to see the sea, the coast where her husband had been found. A coastline which had recently witnessed so much tragedy. How could such beauty be home to so much misery? The very same thought had crossed the mind of her recently bereaved husband. She remembered him asking her so.

Lieutenant Beaufort had wanted to take the A16. The autoroute between Calais and Boulogne. His workload after the discovery of the body of his ex-boss, was growing rapidly. He didn't really have time for the scenic route, but he felt he owed, the gendarmerie owed her, this simple request. Her daughter had agreed to meet them at the morgue, and she would drive her mother home. That was her promise. As they drove the Lieutenant quietly hoped the daughter would indeed keep her promise. If she did it would give him a chance to stop by Wissant and interview the fishermen who had found the body. Their boat had already been commandeered by the gendarme, as it was considered evidence and needed to be inspected by the IRGCN. (The gendarmerie's forensics team). He knew the owners would not be happy about this as their boat was their livelihood, and every day it was kept ashore was a loss of income. He was prepared for a belligerent reception.

The daughter was in the carpark waiting for them when they arrived. There followed an uncomfortable few seconds whilst mother and daughter embraced each other, before the lieutenant led them into the morgue's reception. Waiting for them was, Jean-Paul Hubert, the morgue's chief pathologist. Unusually he was dressed in plain clothes, his coveralls being discarded, temporarily anyway. He held out both hands.

"Madame Maubert, I'm so, so sorry."

"Don't be, Papa was a bastard." The daughter despite the circumstances, obviously hadn't forgiven her father's recent mistakes. Her mother squeezed her hand.

"Shhhhh, not now. For me please." A pact was agreed between mother and daughter, and silently they were led into the theatre of operations. The lieutenant had visited the morgue on more occasions than he'd care to remember, but never could he recall seeing it like this. Normally there'd be several tables with corpses being worked on. But today there was only one, and it was in the centre of the room, covered with a light green linen sheet. The folds couldn't hide the shape of a body lying underneath. The pathologist whispered in the lieutenant's ear.

"Under the circumstances, I thought it best I gave everybody a rest. At least until after this visit. Everybody here knew the capitaine. We all liked him."

"Very sensitive of you." The lieutenant whispered back, though he wasn't so sure the pathologist had made the right decision. The unintentional result was a scenario pitched with high drama. He half expected to hear a drum roll.

As it turned out the identification process went rather well. Smoothly even. There'd been no tears, no drama. Both mother and daughter confirmed the corpse's identity and signed the appropriate paper work in Monsieur's Hubert's office. After that the mother had left with the daughter. They'd both even managed to smile whilst saying their goodbyes.

As their car pulled out of the car park the pathologist turned, grabbing the lieutenant's arm.

"Have you got a moment, lieutenant?"

"Of course." Lieutenant Beaufort had wanted a word anyway.

Minutes later the two men were sat in the pathologist's office, sipping freshly brewed coffee accompanied by a mix of goodies from a local patisserie. The lieutenant felt it all to be a little strange.

"I expect you'd like to know my initial thoughts on the death of our capitaine." Our? But the lieutenant said nothing, except.

"Yes if you have some."

"I can't sign anything before I've done the full autopsy you understand."

"Of course." The lieutenant did his best to confirm his understanding whilst managing a mouthful of pastry.

"Good. Well I don't think the cause of death is from drowning. He has a rather nasty gash across his skull, deep enough to have killed him instantly."

"The cause, any idea?" The lieutenant sat up, the pathologist had his attention.

"Well there's a lot of chalk residue in the gash, and of course Cap Blanc Nez, is all chalk. I don't like to guess you understand, but my guess is that our capitaine hit his head whilst falling from a great height. And it was this that killed him, not the sea."

"Suicide?" After recent events it made sense. Had Cap Blanc Nez, claimed yet another victim?

"I know what I said on the phone but that's for you to deduce, not me. I'll have my official report ready for you by tomorrow. But I expect my theory to be confirmed, not changed."

The lieutenant nodded his thanks. The pathologist had answered the question he was going to ask. He was about to rise, to leave, when the pathologist stopped him.

"There's something else. I have stored in my morgue the bodies of twelve unfortunate children and two adults. They were found on a boat. Well you know."

"Yes I do, what about them?" The case was an open investigation, top priority. His boss, ex-boss had been dealing with it.

"Well." The pathologist leaned his hands on his desk. "Well to be honest I simply do not have the room for them. However I've had a request from the British, they want them returned for an ongoing investigation currently taking place on their island. Did you know?"

This was news to the lieutenant, and he said so.

"I thought as much, the request has come via the Ministere de l'interieur, most unusual. I've been told not to hinder, indeed, quite the reverse. I've been told to offer every cooperation to our friends across the water. Most unlike our government."

"Have they given a reason?"

The pathologist shook his head.

"No, none. I mean I'll be glad to get some space back, but something doesn't smell right. I thought you should know."

"Thank you, Monsieur Hubert. I'll make some enquiries, discreetly of course."

"Merci lieutenant."

With that the lieutenant took his leave. He was just about to put his car into gear when he saw the pathologist, running waving at him. He let down his window. "Lieutenant," the lieutenant waited whilst the pathologist caught his breath. "Lieutenant, I thought you should know. We've just received a call from a local paper. The media know about Capitaine Maubert."

"Merde." The lieutenant slammed his steering wheel with both hands. Which scum had squealed to the press. He hated humanity sometimes. No, most of the bloody time. "Ok, thanks for letting me know. This is going to make my job harder."

"And mine," concurred the pathologist.

"Bastards," the lieutenant put his foot down hard, causing his wheels to spin before gaining grip. "Merde, merde, merde bloody merde."

The pathologist watched him go. Walking back to his office he could hear his phone ringing. MERDE. His day, was going to be hell.

Half an hour later Lieutenant Beaufort was pulling into the small public car park at Wissant. The streets he found strangely silent. Wissant was a 'station balneaire,' and it was out of season, but even so, he could never remember seeing the town so quiet. Taking his time the lieutenant walked from the main square, down Rue du Professeur Lelor, to a more recently built square and the promenade. The few people about, gave him more than a cursory glance. He was in full uniform and after all that had taken place over the past few weeks. A gendarme in their town, attracted more than a touch of suspicion.

The lieutenant took advantage of a nearby bench. A bench just beneath a balcony to an apartment belonging to an English resident called Maureen Fowlis. Though he had no reason to know this, and even if he did, at that time it held no importance. Leaning his elbows on his knees, he cupped his chin in his hands and stared out to sea. The weather was clear and the tide out. The eight kilometre wide sweep of sand between the two caps, Griz Nez and Blanc Nez, never failed to impress. In the distance, even in the gloom the famous white cliffs, that identified the English coastline, stood out. In-between the usual myriad of ships ploughed their course East and West. It was an almost perfect scene, much photographed and much painted over the years. He thought about his ex-boss, Capitaine Maubert. How had his body ended up in the now tranquil waters before him? He turned to look at the towering white cliffs that were Cap Blanc Nez. Had the capitaine really deliberately ended his life by jumping off there? Studying their height, at that moment he couldn't think of a worse way to die. It would take several seconds, maybe more before your body reached the water. Horrible torturous, unimaginable seconds. The capitaine hadn't been relieved of his gun. Why not simply use that? To him it just did not make sense. As did none of what had taken place in recent weeks. Every investigation, every lead had simply led to more and more questions being asked. They had yet to find a single answer. The lieutenant got to his feet. Shaking his head, he took one more look about him. Thank God the beauty that was everywhere, did such a good job of masking tragedy. With that thought he started to walk east along the promenade. Somewhere at the far end, was the house of the fisherman who had found the body of the capitaine. He really wasn't looking forward to interviewing him.

The Italian Gardens, Kensington Gardens, London, England

"Would you prefer me to call you Fatima?" Ariana, alias Fatima along with several other aliases, was caught off guard. She spun round. Behind her, smiling broadly stood a man. He was tall, smartly dressed, with French tailoring. On his left wrist he sported a classic style Patek Philippe watch, and on his feet highly polished tan brogues which shouted, English. The only wild thing about Pierre's appearance, was his hair. On his head his hair was a mass of tousled curls. For all the time Fatima had known him, Pierre had never made any attempt to train them. They were to some extent his signature. "Axsti."

"Pierre," Fatima leant across, kissing him on both cheeks. "Axsti." She was genuinely pleased to see him and she knew it showed. I thought you'd gone back to France"

Pierre gestured for her to walk alongside him.

"I'm going back this afternoon, I wanted to see you, have a chat first. Before I left."

Fatima's gaze, returned to the elaborate beauty of the Italian water garden, though she wasn't really looking at all. Her head was filled with questions, questions she knew Pierre couldn't or wouldn't answer.

"Beautiful isn't it? A gift to a queen, I wonder if she ever minded sharing it with the world?" Pierre shook his head, still smiling. "We shall never know."

Fatima could tell, even though he was smiling and looking relaxed, he was in fact, exactly the opposite. Pierre was tense, he couldn't hide it from her. Even though for most of the time he was facing her, his mind was elsewhere. His eyes were a giveaway. He was assessing his surroundings. He didn't want to be there, she could tell. Not with her, but out in the open. As if to confirm her suspicion, Pierre gestured to the gate leading out to the Bayswater Road.

"Isn't that your hotel just across the road?"

"You know it is Pierre."

"You got me there," Pierre grinned. "Shall we have a drink?"

Pierre had phrased it as a question but Fatima knew she had no choice. It was more of an order and allowed him to escort her across the busy Bayswater Road, to her hotel. Every now and again he would lightly touch her elbow. Fatima recognised it as a gesture of reassurance, of protection and wondered, not for the first time if Pierre in his past had attended some sort of finishing school for men. He was always so politely attentive and there was never a hint of the sexual in his touch. Just care. And Fatima loved it.

Pierre had obviously visited the hotel before, for he guided her straight, without hesitating, to what was called the Park Lounge Bar. The bar having only just opened, was empty and they had freedom of choice on where to sit. Pierre chose a lounge sofa beside the wall to ceiling window. The view was spectacular and included the Italian Gardens. Fatima was beginning to believe that it was a requisite of every good hotel in London to have an eye watering view. As soon as they had settled, a waiter appeared. Pierre ordered a spring water and with a little encouragement, Fatima an Espresso Martini.

"Right," Pierre took a sip of his water. He then with exaggeration looked at his watch. "You have me for twenty minutes, no longer. I have a date with someone in Wissant."

"And what am I meant to ask you, Pierre?" A man entered the bar and blushed when Fatima caught him admiring her. Rather than shrink from his attention, she crossed her legs. She knew the man would look again and unashamedly enjoyed the attention. Sitting as she was now, even wearing trousers, she knew the man wouldn't be able to resist taking longer, bolder views. He'd probably even harbour ridiculous thoughts that he could seduce her. Well that was where he was wrong. Fatima was the car he'd never be able to afford. Pierre appeared or pretended not to notice. He was staring out of the window.

"Your identity, you're now a real person. And you haven't even thanked me."

"Am I meant to? How do I know it's you I have to thank. And is my identity a gift, or does it come at a price?

Pierre laughed.

"Nothing in this world is free Fatima, or would you prefer I call you Ariana?"

Fatima held his eyes with hers.

" Whatever you feel more comfortable with Pierre."

Pierre put on a false and exaggerated expression, designed to show that he was thinking.

"For now. Fatima. When you've successfully completed your assignment. Ariana."

"Why do you say that Pierre?"

Pierre in response surprised her. He reached across taking both her hands in his. For the first time since he'd caught her in the Italian Gardens he looked serious.

"If you pull this assignment off Fatima, I believe the organisation, Orme. You've met Orme?

Fatima gave a single nod.

"If you pull this assignment off, Orme has promised me, she'll let you retire."

Fatima drew breath, she was conscious that Pierre was holding her hands ever tighter.

"And if I don't?"

"You will," Pierre assured her.

"And if I don't?"

Pierre let go of her hands and leant back in the sofa.

"If you don't, you'll probably never retire." He took a swig of his water. Fatima remained still, musing over his words.

"For such a prize, this must be a huge assignment."

"I prefer to call it, extraordinary, daring, exciting, a challenge. But I wouldn't call it huge. And you won't be working alone."

"But why is it so important that I have to use my real identity?"

Pierre hesitated. Fatima felt he was debating how much to tell her.

"Because your identity, with your next assignment, is almost certainly going to be checked by the great unseen. False identities, no matter how carefully planned will in time be found out. Now we have embellished parts of your life, but that's all. You are, who your documents say you are."

"Embellished?"

"Somebody else will explain, some friends of mine will be in touch. Now have you had a look at your passport?

"Of course."

"Did you notice your new address?" It was on the documents you handed to the consulate this morning."

Fatima shook her head, she couldn't believe she hadn't noticed. Pierre gestured towards her handbag.

"Have a look now."

Fatima gently lifted the passport out of her bag, handling it as though she were holding the crown jewels.

"Open it." Fatima did as she was told. "There, look." Pierre tapped a place on the page with her photo. Under, in faint blue, the word Domicile was an English address. Pembridge Gardens, W2, Notting Hill, London, ROYAUME-UNI. "You'll be spending a couple more nights in this hotel, then you'll be moving into your new home. It's only up the road from here. You'll like it, I promise. Now," Pierre looked at his watch again. "One more question Fatima, after which I must be off. Just one."

"The Hilton Pierre. What was that charade in The Hilton? That man was never my target was he?"

"He was, but young Bree eventually came good. She got out of him, all we needed to know."

"Where are they both now, my original target and Bree? Is Bree still here in London?" Pierre forced a smile. Fatima knew this time, that his smile was faked. She'd known him too long for him to fool her.

"Your target is in the capable hands of the organisation. Bree, well Bree I'm going to pay her my respects after I've left here." Pierre stood up.

"My new target, who is it?" Pierre lent down and kissed her on the cheek.

"You're out of questions Fatima, you'll be told in good time." And with that Pierre made his leave. Fatima ordered another espresso martini. She looked around the bar. It was beginning to fill up. Three couples had entered, probably married. All the men however were risking a spurious glance in her direction. In response Fatima lifted her crossed leg a little higher and returned to the view outside.

Chapter 3

The GMC Building, Euston Road, London, England

Arif felt as though he were floating on air. He'd found the exams to be much easier than he'd imagined. If anything he thought them to have been too simple. Child's play almost. Buttoning up his coat, he started to walk towards Warren Street station.

"Pitgam," a voice in his ear. Arif turned and without questioning why, started to follow the man who had spoken the word. Two minutes later he was in a car and, fifteen minutes later he found himself booking into a hotel in Bayswater. The New Dawn Hotel, on Inverness Terrace. His room he found was compact but clean and to his surprise, his luggage was already there. On top of his case lay a sealed brown envelope with his name, ARIF, in capitals.

His mind wandered back to the moment he'd left the GMC building. It was strange, he couldn't remember at all, the minutes between leaving the building to getting in the taxi. If it had been a taxi, for the driver hadn't asked for any payment. What Arif did know, he had to stay in the hotel until he was contacted. He couldn't remember who had told him that. Somehow he just knew. It was all very strange.

He picked up the envelope and walked to the window looking out on Inverness Terrace The street lined by trees was typical of photographs he'd been shown of London back home. The pavement was always busy with people going about their daily lives. Everyone looked so relaxed. So very different to where he'd last lived in Syria. There you never knew if your next step would be your last. He tore open the envelope. He'd been expecting some sort of official document. Instead, to his surprise the envelope was stuffed full of notes, British pounds. After getting over his astonishment, Arif started to count. Five hundred British pounds! There was a note too. There were just a few typewritten words. 'We'll be in touch, in the meantime, enjoy London. Stay safe.'

'Stay safe'? After his recent experiences, London was the safest city in the world. What harm could come to a young Muslim man, in a city such as London. London would be fun. He couldn't wait to enjoy it, and now he had the money to do it. Grey skies and the damp cold forgotten, Arif undressed for a shower. He couldn't wait to experience the delights of his new home.

Bodinnick, Cornwall, England

It was late afternoon when Detective Constable Havers, returned Claire's Call. By that time she was almost climbing the walls. She needed to know what the police knew about the severed head delivered to an address in Tottenham, north London. The papers were full of it, but it was all headlines, guesswork and assumptions. Not one report went into the sort of detail that was any use to her. She, really, really needed to know, what was going on, and at that moment her only hope were the police. She'd tried everybody else, and nobody could tell her a thing This worried Claire. Was there a new player in town? A player who wasn't scared to play rough?

"Hello Claire, it's been a long time."

"Hasn't it Havers." The policeman on the other end let out a sigh. She never called him by his first name. She was so bloody rude. If it wasn't for her money, he'd tell her to go fuck herself. The truth was, he'd got himself in too deep. Claire had too much on him. If she insisted he'd have no choice but to provide her with information even if she refused to pay him. Thankfully Claire, where payment was concerned, remained honourable. She always paid him handsomely, and always in cash. If he could help her today, he knew an envelope would drop through his door in a few days' time.

"I haven't heard anything from you, or about you recently. Have you retired or are you just keeping your head down?"

"These days Havers, I spend most of my time walking my dog and enjoying the view."

"So why do you need me now? I hope you don't expect me to walk your dog!" Credit to her, Claire managed to laugh.

"I'm quite capable of doing that Havers. Anyway, I wouldn't trust you with my dog."

"Thanks."

"You're welcome. Tell me what do you know about this murder in north London?"

"Which one?" Over the past week there had been three stabbings, resulting in death in the north of the city.

"The one in all the papers, the severed head with his cock and balls stuffed in his mouth."

A number of seconds passed before Detective Constable Havers responded.

"You mean the one almost identical to the recent horror in Hampshire?" Claire instantly realised her mistake. She should have enquired after both, not just the one in North London. As if to confirm her error, the detective asked. "Aren't you interested in both Claire? Or do you already have the answers to the first killing?" Claire thought on her feet, yes she had this guy in her pocket but at the end of the day he was still a cop.

"Hampshire's not really my patch, north London is. Why do you think the same person or people were responsible?" She hoped the way she'd framed her answer would deal with his suspicious mind. There came another pause.

"To be honest Claire, I'm not involved in investigating either killing. What I CAN tell you, is only what I've heard. Policemen like to talk. You know that." He heard Claire cough. "From what I've heard the killings are similar but not identical. The head in Langstone, for example, still had it's eyes. The one in Tottenham had had his eyes gouged out. And there was no body with the one in Tottenham whereas with the one in Hampshire the body was there too. It was in bits, parts displayed all over the room, but the body was there. All of it. That's all I can tell you for the mo. Do you want me to make some enquiries?"

"Please do but be discreet Havers."

"As always." Seconds after his reply came the dialling tone. Claire never said goodbye, he'd gotten used to it. He pondered over their conversation. Claire knew something about the killing in Langstone, of that, after their brief conversation he was pretty certain. The north London one though he sensed was worrying her. Why? What was going on? He'd try and find out, perhaps there was an opportunity here to benefit him from both sides.

Claire lent against the glass of her picture window, the scene outside was tranquillity personified. How she wished at that moment to become part of it. Havers had mentioned retirement. She wanted to retire, but in her game the big cheeses never retired. They were bumped off, to make way for a new kid on the block. Why did she feel her time was near.

"Get a grip Claire," Claire scolded herself out loud. Her thoughts went back to what Havers had told her. He'd said that the head in north London, had had its eyes gauged out. Why hadn't she ordered that? Next time she would.

The Hilton Hotel, Park Lane, London, England

After hours of trawling through video footage and numerous cups of coffee the team still hadn't found out what had happened to their target nor Rory, their man.. There was just no sign of either of them.

For the first five floors, they'd allowed the video footage to run for forty minutes. This had been quickly reduced to twenty minutes and then ten. Their boss, Roger Denton had rung them whilst they'd been studying the 22nd floor. They'd covered all the lower floors by then, the 19th to the first. No sign. 'Grab a break,' he had told them.' I'll come and look at the footage for the last few floors with you.'

Everyone eagerly accepted. Five grown men in a small airless room for hours, filled with tv static, was beginning to cause the atmosphere to become a little strained. They all needed a break. Obligingly the head of security organised sandwiches and cake for all. To everyone's relief, these weren't ordered from room service but partaken in the bright and airy, Park Corner Brasserie. After the past few hours it was rather like escaping from prison. This is where Roger found them on his arrival at the hotel. The three from the NCA started to rise, but their boss signalled for them all to stay seated. After introducing himself to the hotel's head of security and the CCTV controller, Roger pulled up a chair.

"May I?" Roger let his right hand hover above the platter of sandwiches. The head of security, who had, now they'd worked together for almost the entire day, revealed his name to be Ishaan, nodded.

"Of course, help yourself." Roger did so and took a bite.

"Bloody hell, that's delicious." Roger who throughout his life had lived on a diet of sandwiches, bought when filling up his car or from a work canteen, never thought a sandwich could taste so good. His palate was in shock.

Nick with his mouth full held up his thumb.

"That's smoked salmon, capers, with tarragon cream cheese." He passed Roger a card that had been delivered with the platter.

The next few minutes were spent discussing food and how they all needed to get out more. No one disagreed with that assessment. It was Ishaan, the head of security who suggested they ought to reconvene. He was conscious their little ensemble were taking up valuable space, and the Brasserie was beginning to fill up.

Back in the security control room, the CCTV controller brought up once again, yesterday's footage from the 22nd floor. Roger had been offered a chair, but he'd declined. 'His arse was sore from sitting all day,' was his reason. Nick briefed his boss on how they'd gone about reviewing the CCTV footage from yesterday, and disappointingly, so far with no results. There was still no sign of their man after he'd entered the lift in the hotel foyer. It was a real shame that the lift CCTV hadn't been working.

"And no sign of Mr Mitchell either? I mean he must have alighted on one of the floors. We know he never showed up on the ground floor. On the evidence so far we can only assume, hope, that they're still both somewhere in the hotel." Roger addressed this to everybody in the room. Ishaan immediately picked up on this.

"Mr Mitchell? Nobody's mentioned a Mr Mitchell. You are looking for a second man? Why wasn't I told? Who is this Mr Mitchell?" Roger wanted to kick himself, how could he have been so bloody careless. It was no good trying to fool the head of security, an ex-detective with the Met. He decided to come clean, but not here, not in front of everybody.

"Ishaan, can I have a quick word, not here. In private?"

"I think we'd better, we can talk in my office." Ishaan stood up. Holding open the door, he gestured. Please follow me, we can talk in my office." The remaining three officers from the NCA remained sitting, all looking rather sheepish. The CCTV operator, shrugged his shoulders but said nothing. He looked at the three men who'd kept him company since the morning. It was obvious that nobody wanted to say a word. He went back to his controls and started zooming in and out on floor twenty two.

"You were operating a sting operation in my hotel, weren't you? Ishaan didn't wait for a response. "Why the hell didn't you tell me, I could have bloody helped. You bloody people always think you're above everybody else. You should have bloody told me. The management when they find out, will be furious."

"If they find out, Ishaan, if they find out." Roger held up both hands. "Ishaan can I talk to you as though we are two detectives? Forget your role as head of security, for a moment. Please."

"Sit down." Ishaan, who was still struggling to contain his anger gestured to one of two chairs on the other side of his desk. Roger did as Ishaan requested, at all costs he wanted to avoid a confrontation. Trying to look as relaxed as he could, Roger casually looked around Ishaan's office. It was beautifully informal. There were numerous plants and photos of his family. The office without the desk could have easily been mistaken for a room in Ishaan's house. A real home from home. It said a lot about who the head of security was as a man, and Roger liked what he saw. This was a man who knew what values were.

Roger looked at the man sitting across the desk from him. Apart from, 'sit down,' Ishaan had remained silent. A clever tactic, this man was no idiot. He was leaving him to the talking. Roger decided his only hope for this man's future cooperation was to come clean. He leant back in the chair crossing his legs as he did so.

"Ishaan, if we can talk as though we're simply two defenders of the law discussing a case, I can be open with you. But you have to promise me, whatever I tell you, must not leave this room. Is there a camera in here?" Roger scanned the office.

"No camera," Ishaan assured him. But I'm sorry. If what you tell me affects the hotel, I will have to report it."

Roger let out a breath. He looked quizzically at the man opposite. Sizing him up. Ishaan gave nothing away. This man was a pro, no wonder the hotel had employed him as their head of security. Their hotel was in safe hands, with Ishaan. Roger decided he had no choice. If he didn't confide in him, he knew from here on in, there'd be no or at best limited cooperation. He could push it through official channels but then the shit would hit the fan, with the added risk that covert might become public. The latter would also take time and time was one thing they didn't have.

"Ok, ok. Look Ishaan, yes. You're not stupid, we were active with a sting operation. And yes with hindsight you, the hotel should have been informed." Roger wanted Ishaan to respond, but he didn't. He remained sitting dead still, silent, not giving anything away. He wanted the man from the NCA to do the talking.

Half an hour later both men were back in the security control room. It had been hard going, but Roger had in the end managed to convince the head of security to keep their sting operation between themselves. For now anyway. He'd managed to withhold some of the operational details but had been forced to reveal more than he was happy to. He just hoped Ishaan could be trusted. They'd run a security check, and their records read that there was no reason not to, but people change.

There was a look of resignation on all of those waiting in the control room. There'd been a sliver of hope that their viewing of the CCTV might be delayed for a while, and all could enjoy a longer break. But as soon as they saw their two bosses enter the room, all saw at once that it wouldn't be the case. Both wore an expression of grim determination.

"We continue from where we left off, the 22nd floor." Ishaan, sat on the one vacant chair. "Are you sure you don't want a seat Roger?" Roger shook his head.

"No thanks, I'll fall asleep if I sit down. I'll concentrate better standing up." The three who had been patiently waiting in the control room could relate to that. All were finding it hard to keep their eyes open. Staring at one hotel corridor after another wasn't exactly edge of your seat stuff. "Before we start on the 22nd floor, can we just jump to the 28th? I want to see if our man may have got out there without us seeing.

And at what time Mr Mitchell entered the lift and who he was with, if it wasn't our man Rory. Everyone present thought this to be a good idea.

The footage on the 28th floor was a little more interesting than watching corridor after corridor. Apart from the footage immediately outside the lifts, there was also footage to be viewed inside the Sky Bar and the Windows restaurant where there was a lot more activity. On the head of security's instructions. they started with the footage outside the lifts. To ensure there was no mistake, the footage was played from the time their man, Rory, had entered the lift on the ground floor. Four minutes later, Rory still hadn't exited the lift but John Mitchell was captured entering the lift with another man. Both were smiling. Roger asked for the operator to freeze the image and zoom in on the face of the stranger.

"Anyone recognise him?" Roger had meant the question for his officers but everyone in the room answered negative. "You've no idea if this guy's staying or was staying at your hotel?"

Ishaan shook his head.

"I can ask the staff on reception duty if they recognise him. I certainly don't. Alternatively we can trawl through the footage on reception. See if the cameras there have picked him up."

"Thanks, but no need. Not at the moment at least. If you can ping a few still and clear images of his face over to me," Roger handed Ishaan his card. "To that email address I'll see if we can get an identity through 'face recognition' software." Ishaan took the card and placed it carefully in his wallet.

"I'll do it personally, as soon as we're finished here."

"If we're ever going to be finished here." Nick's comment resulted in him receiving a slap over his head from his boss.

"Wakey wakey Nicky boy. No rest for the wicked. Right let's roll the footage back a little to see what time Mr Mitchell's friend arrived.

It didn't take long. Under four minutes had passed when the man was picked up exiting the middle lift.

"That's roughly the time you'd expect your man, given the time we know he'd entered the lift on the ground floor. If, of course, he was always planning for the 28th floor. At a guess, I think you've been set up, gentlemen." Ishaan grinned ruefully at the men from the NCA. Roger hated to admit it, but he secretly believed Ishaan may be right.

"Right, let's roll the footage for another ten minutes shall we. See if Rory shows up. After that let's have a look in the bar." Roger didn't believe for a moment that Rory would make an appearance, but he had to be sure. The secret to good detective work was to cover all bases. No matter how remote, obscure or seemingly hopeless. Ishaan nodded.

"Sure let's take a look." He signalled to the operator to continue playing the video.

The hours passed, coffee ordered all the more frequently. Floor after floor was played back on video but there was no sign of Mr Mitchell or the stranger with him exiting any of the lifts. At one in the morning Roger had had enough.

"It's just not possible for three men to disappear. Is there anyway out of the lifts other than the doors? The ceiling for example? He directed his question at Ishaan. Ishaan pushed back on his chair.

"No, impossible."

Roger had heard the word impossible during his career at the NCA, more times than he cared to remember. How many times had impossible turned into possible? A lot.

"I'd like to take a look anyway, to make up my own mind. If that's ok with you?"

"What? Now?" Ishaan didn't look impressed at Roger's suggestion.

"No, when we leave."

"When will that be sir? We've been at this nigh on eighteen hours." Nick spoke for everyone there. Roger looked at their faces. Nick had a point, everyone looked exhausted, it was easy to make mistakes when a group were this tired. It wouldn't be the first time a group of officers collectively missed something, because they were all equally exhausted. In a sense it was a group led optical illusion, rather like a hypnotist hypnotising a whole audience.

"Ok, let's call it a day, but we're going to have to reconvene tomorrow." There came the immediate sound of men stretching complaining limbs.

"I can't stand up," Nick complained. Somebody else laughed.

"Neither can I."

"Wait." Everyone turned and looked at Roger. "Look, I know everybody needs to go home to their beds, but can we just see the video footage of me coming out of the lift on the 28th? The response was a collective sound of protests. "After that we can go, I promise. It's just if there's no video of me coming out of the lift then we know somehow the footage has been got at, doctored."

"Impossible," Ishaan was quick to respond for the second time. And on this occasion his operator, backed him up.

"No way."

"Can we just take a look anyway." Roger was close to pleading.

"We might as well," Nick spoke up for his boss. "Seeing as we're all here. It will only take a few more minutes."

"Ok, ok." Ishaan relented. "It won't hurt to, and it won't take long." Nick had recorded the time his boss had entered the lift on the ground floor and the video controller recommenced the recording a few minutes before. Just in case. Everyone there waited with bated breath, and a spontaneous cheer went up, tinged with a touch of sarcasm, as Roger Denton, Director at the NCA could be seen, clear as day exiting the middle lift on the 28th floor. Even Roger couldn't help but grin as he watched himself. The operator switched to a camera covering the Sky

Bar, and there a few seconds later, the camera picked up Roger walking, a little too casually perhaps, to the bar itself.

"You lot are crap actors," Ishaan smiled at Roger. "Now let me guess." Ishaan pointed to each of the NCA's operatives, supposedly working undercover. "Am I right? Tell me I'm wrong." Roger just smiled, but he couldn't hide his embarrassment. Ishaan had correctly picked out from the general public every one of his operatives.

After that, and to the delight of everybody else in the room, Roger called a halt to the proceedings. They would reconvene tomorrow, at 10 am sharp. If anybody wanted a room at the hotel, he promised the agency would pay, but none did. Everyone who had been covering the bar had already gone home. There were just four operatives left and they were sitting in two cars covering the hotel entrance. They'd take it in turns to sleep in rooms already reserved and keep watch. Before Roger left, he asked Ishaan if they could take one trip in a lift to the 28th floor and down again. Ishaan agreed. By the time they'd arrived back on the ground floor, Roger had to agree with Ishaan's immediate opinion, earlier that evening. It would have been impossible for someone to exit through the ceiling. Then where the hell had they gone?

On his way home, Roger once more contacted Jane to give her an update as well as being updated himself.

'It was definitely explosives. The bomb boys have confirmed it,' were Jane's first words. Tell me something new, Roger thought to himself. Everybody knew the explosions had been caused by a bomb or bombs. The 'bomb boys,' as Jane liked to call them had only just been given permission to enter the site by the fire service. Their investigation was in its infancy. The cause was the easy answer. Now they had to find answers to the more important, the more difficult questions. Who? How? And why?

Jane also told him that his immediate boss, the director of operations had returned to hospital and for the time being he was to continue to report to her. Great. Roger liked Jane, she was easy to deal with. As long as you didn't get on the wrong side of her. But then that was the same with most women. The tech guys, were working overtime and she had it on good authority that the more essential personnel would be able to start working from their temporary quarters the day after tomorrow. 'That includes you Roger.' Just in case he hadn't thought himself as 'essential personnel.' Bloody miracle, thought Roger. It just shows what's achievable when the departments get moving. When the chips are down.

MI5, were reviewing their, the NCA's case load. Trying to identify which cases being investigated would most likely result in somebody making such an audacious attack. Their theory so far is that it's almost certainly drug related. There were a number of countries whose governments topped up their coffers through the illegal drug trade. None of them particularly friendly with the UK. If an investigation was threatening their source of income, or threatened to uncover their participation, then that would give good cause to directly attack the offices heading the investigation. It would also explain the resources needed. MI5 hadn't so far, and to Roger's relief, felt the investigation he was leading warranted an internal investigation. As a result of MI5's suspicions, several operatives working undercover had been moved into safe houses. Just in case.

Roger reflected on his afternoon. How it had resulted in nothing but frustration. Forensics have already started examining Mr Mitchell's phone Jane told him. Hopefully that will tell us something. Roger agreed, he just hoped whatever they found wouldn't reveal his closer than known connection to Mr John Mitchell.

"Get some sleep Roger," had been Jane's parting words. Roger hoped he would.

Talk of John's phone reminded him of the number he'd written down. The number other than his he'd found on John's mobile. Fishing it out from his pocket, he punched in the number and pressed the call arrow. It was the early hours and by phoning now he'd probably piss whoever it was on the other end. But tough, he didn't care. He waited in anticipation for the number to ring but it didn't. Instead an immediate message.

"The number you are dialling has not been recognised, please check..."

Roger knew the message. Swearing he dialled the number again, just in case he'd punched a wrong digit. He hadn't, the same message played again. Ringing off he swore again. Another dead end. Let's hope the number could be traced, that it wasn't a pay as you go.

Arriving in the early hours, Roger had to park three streets away. When he'd first bought the house, nearly twenty years ago there were always spaces in his road, always. What will it be like in twenty years' time? He hoped by then he will have retired to somewhere warm and sunny with easy parking. Though now Brexit, it appeared had put paid to that dream. How he hated politics and politicians. Sometimes it felt to him that they were only there to make your life as difficult as possible.

The clock in the kitchen read two thirty eight. What a bloody time to finish work. How he wished on occasion that he had a regular nine to five job. He quickly dismissed the thought. No he didn't. That was rubbish. He flicked the kettle on then changed his mind. Instead he walked into his lounge and picking up a decanter poured himself a large glass of cream sherry. Hardly the stuff of hardened law enforcers, Roger grinned to himself, he didn't care, he loved the stuff. Leaving only the light from the moon to illuminate his lounge, he looked around at what his life's work had given him. It wasn't a great deal. On the walls, the only personal photos he had were of his dog, a cocker spaniel called James. James was long gone but Roger still missed him. More so than his ex-wives. His dog had been the one great personal attachment he'd had all through his life. His last wife had taken him with her when she'd left. He remembered being heart broken. Years later it was only by accident that he had found out James had passed away. He'd never spoken to his ex-wife since. Suddenly the lounge felt sad and lonely. It wasn't the first time, but at that moment it played on him. Refilling his glass, Roger made his way up to bed.

He always did his most productive thinking when he was sitting up in bed, usually just before he was starting to fall asleep. Last time it had been John's laptop, now it was the CCTV. He knew something hadn't been right. Now he remembered what it was. He went to ring Ishaan and remembered the time. Instead he sent a message. 'Ishaan, please bring forward our reviewing of the CCTV to seven,' no that was only three and a half hours away. 'To eight thirty am, important.' He then sent the same or similar message to Nick and two of the operatives who'd been undercover in the Sky Bar. Satisfied, he finished his sherry and settled down to sleep. Except he couldn't. Over and over again his mind replayed the footage of him exiting the lift. Was he remembering correctly or was his mind playing tricks?

Gendarmerie Nationale, Calais, France

Lieutenant Beaufort couldn't remember Colette looking so pleased to see him. She didn't just look pleased, she looked relieved. Very relieved.

"Lieutenant, lieutenant, c'est un cauchemar, cauchemar."

Colette look flustered, Colette never looked flustered. The lieutenant was about to find out why. The death of Capitaine Maubert had reached the eyes and ears of the media and they had descended on the gendarmerie like a swarm of locusts. To keep them off the street and to avoid further unwanted attention, Colette had herded them into the 'salle de reunion,' where they were being monitored by a couple of gendarmes. Gendarmes who were beginning to lose patience or to put in more graphic terms, becoming seriously pissed off.

The lieutenant, swore. How he wished his old boss was here. He never lost his cool. Well up to now it would seem. If suicide was the correct interpretation for his death, his ex-boss had seriously lost his cool. He still couldn't come to terms with the word suicide. Even after everything that had happened to him, he just could not believe that the capitaine would take the coward's way out. It just wasn't in his DNA. Nuclear war could break out, and even if everything was destroyed his ex-boss, if he remained alive, would still be standing, waving the tricolore and telling everybody to keep calm. The lieutenant turned to Colette.

"What do you think Monsieur Maubert would have done Colette?" Colette didn't hesitate.

"He'd call a press conference."

The Lieutenant hesitated, he hadn't enough facts for that. His interview with the fisherman had told him nothing new. And forensics had come up with nothing suspect in his boat. Though their investigation was still ongoing. The fisherman and his son though still had to be considered suspects. Lieutenant Beaufort didn't for a moment believe they had anything to do with the capitaine's death but it would be unprofessional of him to rule them out. A background check on Didier and his son was needed, he'd already requested it and would have the results in the morning. Maybe it was a rush of blood to the head, but the lieutenant decided to deal with the 'populace,' as one of the officers monitoring the press corps described them, now. If he didn't it would be a 'cauchemar' for the night shift. First though he needed to phone the capitaine's wife. She needed to know that the media were onto the death of her husband. He asked Colette to put him through. 'I'll use your office,' he told her.

It took several minutes before Madame Maubert answered the phone. When she did, she sounded relieved to hear Colette's voice.

The press don't stop ringing she told her, and worse still several are camped outside. Have they no bloody respect? After a few soothing words, Colette passed the phone to the lieutenant. For several minutes he listened to the capitaine's widow sob out her despair. They're animals she kept saying, animals. He told her to unplug her landline and only answer calls on her mobile if she recognised the number. He gave her his. After promising to do something about the press outside her house, the lieutenant rang off.

"Bloody animals." The lieutenant turned to Colette. "I'm going to have a word with them now." Colette grabbed his arm.

"After you have, and before you go, Monsieur Beaufort. Can I have a word. It's important."

"It can't wait till tomorrow Colette?"

"No not really, no I don't think it can." Lieutenant Beaufort, hid his frustration. He had enough on his plate. What was so important it couldn't wait until tomorrow. Colette referring to him as Monsieur instead of his rank, had also thrown him. He'd been about to reprimand her, then he'd remembered how she'd never called the capitaine by his rank. It had always been monsieur. For Colette it was a term of respect, more importantly trust. And he knew deep down if Colette thought it important, it was important.

"Ok, Colette. But not here, not in your office. It's too visible. Wait for me in Capt… Monsieur Maubert's office. Oh and Colette, any chance of a coffee?" Colette smiled.

"Of course Monsieur Beaufort, oh and," Colette hesitated.

"Yes Colette?" Colette looked a little embarrassed.

"If you don't mind me giving you some advice." Colette paused. "Be nice to the press, we sometimes need them." The lieutenant laughed. It was good advice. He was all set to give them a bollocking, but Colette was right. Sometimes you had to hold hands with the devil.

In the foyer he bumped into two of his officers returning from their control. Stopping them he quickly explained the situation at their capitaine's house.

"Sort it guys can you, get the bastards well back from the front door." Both officers, even though their shift had finished willingly accepted the lieutenant's request. As they turned to leave the lieutenant thought again. "Guys, guys." The two officers turned. "Try and be nice." The two officers grinned.

"Of course, sir."

Formby , Lancashire, England

What a day. What a bloody day and James wondered how he'd gotten through it. That morning, for a few minutes, he'd even wondered if he'd even get through it alive. To have a gun pointed at his head, was an experience he'd never thought could happen to him. Not in a million years, but it had. That morning. And he never wanted to experience it again.

Now. Sat in his car on his drive back home, what had taken place that morning almost felt like a dream. Except that is, it hadn't been, and if he needed a reminder, there was the same car parked opposite his house. In it sat two men. Men who had, 'don't you dare mess with us,' written all over their faces. And one of the men James recognised, how could he ever forget him. He was the man who had held the gun to his head, and from his voice, the man who had telephoned him before. How the hell was he going to get out of this? He was desperately ruing the day he'd agreed, for money, to obtain legitimate death certificates for John Mitchell. For what, he now was beginning to realise, had been pocket money. He could have demanded a lot, lot more. How could he have been so bloody, bloody stupid. He leant back in his car seat and started to cry. He wanted to but knew he couldn't dare call the police. And if he did, what he'd been doing would all come out. Resulting almost certainly in a prison sentence. And he wasn't stupid, these people, the people who had threatened him would find a way to get to him in prison. Prison would be a death sentence. What was being asked of him by persons unknown was madness. If he tried it would be only a matter of days before he was caught. These idiots had no bloody idea what was involved. And if he refused? He had no doubt something awful would happen. If not to him, to his family. The man who'd held his gun to his head had made that quite clear. He hadn't heard a word from Mr Mitchell since he'd made the call, expressing, if he didn't help him, that his life was in danger. James, after what had taken place that morning realised that Mr Mitchell had been sincere in his message, and that there was a strong possibility he was no longer of this earth. The thought made him want to vomit. No he needed to vomit, he was going to be sick. James opened the car door and heaved. Wiping his eyes he saw his wife running towards him carrying their baby son.

"James, James are you ok?"

Sitting up James tried to steady himself. A quick glance in the rear view mirror caught the man who had put his gun to his head smiling. With his finger imitating a gun he pretended to shoot then blow away the imaginary smoke. This time James didn't have time to lean out of his car. He was immediately sick, this time in his lap.

Gendarmerie Nationale, Calais, France

Lieutenant Beaufort, helped admittedly by the area's PR team, or rather man, a fresh faced smiler called Monsieur Hivin, who happened to turn up at the most opportune moment, dealt with the press rather well. Or so he thought. There'd been the usual barrage of questions, but all the two from the gendarmerie would admit, was there'd been a body, an adult, male picked up in La Manche. That was all they were prepared to say at that moment. A press conference would be held tomorrow at 2pm, here at the gendarmerie. Then and only then were they prepared to answer further questions, and it was hoped by then, they'd have more information. The meeting finished with a friendly but firm warning, to respect the privacy of those involved, or suspected of being involved. And to leave the relevant people, the professionals, alone to get on with their jobs. A special mention was made with reference to Capitaine Maubert's wife. The scenes outside her house, the lieutenant described as a 'disgrace and an embarrassment to La France.' To their credit, some of the reporters actually looked embarrassed.

After the meeting, most of the press left to seek accommodation in town. A hardy few remained outside the main gate. They were not permitted to wait anywhere on the Gendarmerie's land, and it was made quite clear, not to hinder the free movement of traffic along the road outside. The latter would be rigorously enforced they were warned. The lieutenant also warned the PR officer, Monsieur Hivin, not to provide members of the press with refreshments during the night. A practice that had, apparently, been the custom in the past. After that the PR officer hurriedly made his way to his dedicated office, to prepare the outline of tomorrow's press release. Also to start contacting the editors, with whom he had a reasonable relationship, to ask for restraint in some of their reporting. Satisfied there was little more he could do, the lieutenant started to mount the stairs to what he still considered to be, Capitaine Maubert's office. On the way he heard chatter over the radio asking for more support to help with the press corps camped outside the capitaine's house near Ardres. So much for promises. The lieutenant cut in, ordering anybody who was free to ensure that their ex capitaine's widow and anybody else in the house got a good night's sleep.

"I don't want you taking prisoners." He finished. His officers were free to enjoy themselves. And the lieutenant hoped they'd make the most of it.

Now to see Colette. To some extent he was fearing this more than having to face the press. To his surprise, when he entered the office he found Colette sitting in the capitaine's chair. Obviously embarrassed she quickly got up and took her place on one of the chairs to the side. On the desk sat a steaming pot of freshly made coffee. There was just one cup.

"Get yourself one Colette." The lieutenant motioned to the lone cup. He wanted this meeting to be as informal as possible. Thanking him, Colette took a cup and saucer sitting on top of a nearby filing cabinet. She went to pour but the lieutenant stopped her. "Let me do the honours Colette, I want you to relax and get off your chest whatever it is you feel is so important."

Colette thanked him and holding the cup in both hands sipped greedily. The lieutenant observed that Colette drank her coffee black, pas sucre, pas lait. She drank her coffee untainted, black just as it should be. A good 'Calaisien' girl, the lieutenant mused.

"Now Colette. What's so important after all that's happened today, that you can't let me go home." Colette's cheeks reddened.

"Sorry lieutenant. The first, well I've been ordered to tell you. They tried to contact you, but you were unavailable."

"They?"

"Well the commandant. He wanted to tell you personally but as you were busy," Colette paused her head bowed. "Well with you know what, he asked me to pass on his message to you. He said it wasn't normal procedure, but that he could think of no one better to trust," Colette's cheeks reddened again. "He also told me to pass on his condolences." The lieutenant let out a dry laugh. "I think he meant it Monsieur Beaufort," Colette's voice sounded a little more passionate. "He said to tell you that the capitaine had been one of his finest officers and that he'd almost counted Thierry, sorry Monsieur Maubert as a friend. He said all he'd done was to make a stupid mistake, a mistake the finest man could have made. That history," he told me, "was littered with men, fine men who could measure their downfall because of a woman." Colette's cheeks were virtually scarlet when she recounted these last words. "I don't particularly agree with him on that by the way. Anyway, when he spoke with me lieutenant, he hadn't heard the latest. When I told him he sounded genuinely shocked, almost angry. He told me to tell you that he'd call you tomorrow. Around eight in the morning and to be sure to be ready to take his call."

"Merde," the lieutenant sighed. "That's all I bloody need."

I'm sorry Monsieur Beaufort. I'm just passing on a message." The lieutenant held up both hands.

"Sorry Colette I wasn't aiming that at you."

"I know." Colette looked fit to burst. The lieutenant poured some more coffee. Colette accepted it, almost as though it were her last day on earth.

"Is that it Colette?" Colette shook her head.

"No not at all, I haven't really started. Sorry." She saw the look on the lieutenant's face. The main reason the commandant rang was to tell us Monsieur Maurbert's replacement will be with us tomorrow afternoon. A Capitaine," Colette reached for her notebook." A Capitaine Vendroux, Capitaine Olivier Vendroux."

"WHAT?" The lieutenant almost stood up with his surprise. "But the capitaine's chair is still warm. Normally it takes weeks to appoint someone. TOMORROW?" Colette had her head down.

"The commandant said the same thing. The appointment isn't his. The appointment has come direct from Paris. Apparently the powers that be feel, with everything that's happening here and under the glare of the world's media, that it's important to have someone take over immediately. As the commandant put it. Paris do not want the media concentrating on Monsieur Maubert's demise."

"Bit bloody late for that."

"I know, I thought the same as you. This came today, couriered from Paris." Colette handed the lieutenant a spotless A4 envelope. It's the new capitaine's file." The lieutenant held it aloft.

"It's really thin, there can only be a single page inside."

"I don't think you're meant to know much, just the basic details. Everything else will be deemed confidential."

"Ok, thanks Colette, is that it?"

"No." Colette shook her head. The lieutenant thought she looked nervous. What the hell was coming next? With her feet Colette pushed a black filing box from under the late capitaines desk.

"When I heard that we were getting a new capitaine, I took it upon myself to clear Monsieur Maubert's office." Colette looked down at the floor. "After everything that's happened, I didn't want anything else to be found that would further blacken Monsieur Maubert's name. I was going to take everything home with me, but I thought if I did so, I might be guilty of a criminal offence. And I am not a criminal Monsieur Beaufort. However I can't bear the thought of complete strangers pawing over Monsieur Maubert's personal effects." Colette paused. "So, so I put everything in that box. I thought you could deal with everything. It's up to you what you do with it." Colette looked straight at the lieutenant, a single tear trickled down her left cheek. Angry at herself she quickly wiped it a way with the back of her hand. The lieutenant, reached down and touched the lid. Changing his mind, he leant back in his seat.

"Can you give me an idea of what's in there Colette?" Colette, placed both her hands on her knees.

"Personal stuff, all his family photos. Of his daughter when she was just born, his wedding day. You know that sort of stuff, oh and his framed certificates, awards. That sort of thing." The lieutenant had thought the office looked bare. So that was why. "Monsieur Maubert also kept a personal file, hand written on every case he was investigating. Official reports are listed on the computer of course, the written ones were personal to him. Once a case was closed or gone cold he'd take his personal notes home. The notes in the filing box," Colette touched the box with her foot, "are recent. They, I think cover the latest investigation. The investigation that has caused so much trouble." Lieutenant Beaufort raised an eyebrow. This was news to him, the capitaine had kept that quiet.

"Anything else? Is that it Colette?" Colette shook her head.

"No. No, no, Monsieur Maubert kept a diary, an appointments diary, not a personal diary. Purely appointments. Of course part of my job was to organise Monsieur Maurbert's diary, but he liked also to keep his own. I've had a quick flick through and.." Colette reddened and further tears, rolled not trickled this time down both cheeks. The lieutenant didn't interrupt, he'd allow Colette to get off her chest what was troubling her, upsetting her so much. After wiping her face with a hanky Colette went on. "I feel disgusted with myself, but I just couldn't help it. I had a quick look inside. Well, well there's appointments in there I knew nothing about. Monsieur Maubert, I thought told me everything, but it looks as though he kept secrets. Secrets from me, his PA for years. And they don't look good Monsieur Beaufort. They don't look good."

The lieutenant felt embarrassed. The gendarmerie training manual, didn't explain how to deal with a situation like this.

"Do you want some more coffee Colette? I'll make it." It's the best he could come up with. He needed time to think. Colette's next words and action saved him.

"No thank you Monsieur Beaufort. It's very kind of you to offer, but no. I need to get home to my family."

"Of course," the lieutenant stood up.

"I'm sorry to burden you with all this Monsieur Beaufort, I'm so sorry."

"It's nothing, and you did the right thing Colette, don't worry I'll protect the capitaine's good name."

"Merci, merci." And with that Colette left the office, waving as she went down the stairs. The lieutenant resisted looking in the box. Instead he strolled to the window and waited until he saw Colette's car, a burgundy Citroen C3, leave the car park. He then buzzed the duty officer and told him he was working late in the capitaine's office, and that he didn't want to be disturbed.

"I'm not here." He told him.

Sitting back at the desk, Lieutenant Beaufort pulled the filing box nearer to him and lifted off the lid. Inside packed neatly, that was Colette all over, lay a snapshot of the capitaine's life. The lieutenant felt deeply uncomfortable, about touching even the photos. He'd always respected the capitaine and he didn't want that respect to be tainted any further. Finding something in the box that may change his view, would be very unpleasant. Both a feeling of duty spurred on by curiosity eventually overcame his reluctance. One by one he carefully lifted the framed items out of the box, sliding them neatly under the desk. Underneath, sitting on a neat pile of document wallets was a small black book. On the cover embossed in gold, the words, 'MON AGENDA, and underneath in numerals, the year they were in. The lieutenant hesitated, not until he had taken several deep breaths could he bring himself to reach in and lift it out. For several minutes more the diary lay on the desk, unopened. The lieutenant simply couldn't bring himself to look inside. To open it felt like breaking into somebody's life. He remembered the capitaine used to keep a bottle of two for special occasions and guests. Surely Colette hadn't taken those. He went to a bureau where he knew they were kept. With a sigh of relief he found several bottles along with glasses. One of the bottles, had a hand written label, 'calvados.' The lieutenant uncorked the bottle and poured. The calvados poured like silk, some of the liquid sticking to the glass. An excellent sign. Lifting the glass to his lips he savoured the smell for a few seconds before taking a sip. It hit the spot, Mon Dieu, did it hit the spot. Before the immediate affect of the alcohol wore off, the lieutenant returned to the desk. After sitting down, he placed the glass on a mat in front of him and took hold of the diary. Right then capitaine, let's see what secrets you have in here.

Wissant, France

Around the time Lieutenant Beaufort was about to delve into Capitaine Maubert's diary, a tall well dressed man was entering a woman's apartment on the Digue de Mer, Wissant. Hidden under his jacket he carried a single red rose. He had no business being in the apartment, for the owner was away and he'd entered uninvited. Walking slowly, from room to room he touched various items of furniture, as though he were stroking a lover's cheek. The atmosphere, and he sensed it, hung heavy. It was as though everything around him, inanimate objects, were in mourning.

After pausing to look at the view of La Manche from the apartment's sea facing window the man walked softly into the bedroom. Taking the rose from beneath his jacket he kissed the flower gently before laying it on the bed. After wiping a single tear before it reached his cheek, he left as silently as he had entered.

CHAPTER
–4–

A Street In Bushey, North London, England

Roger Denton had hardly managed to have any meaningful sleep. His mind had simply been too active. And yet, for some inexplicable reason he almost felt as though he'd just had the best sleep of his life. The body sometimes works in mysterious ways. By four thirty he'd showered and now at five thirty he was dressed and on his third coffee. That meant luck was with him. He felt it hadn't been yesterday and it was all the coffee's fault. Mad yes, but that's how he felt. Rather than listen to the radio, Roger had switched on the tv in the lounge. He had a thing for Sally Bundock, and that morning she was presenting the BBC's early morning business and news programme. If he switched on the programme and she wasn't presenting it, he'd turn on the radio instead and listen to Radio five live. Once more, most of the news was taken up with the explosion at the NCA's headquarters in Vauxhall. For the last two days the news had been shocking, today it was tragic, as nineteen people had been confirmed dead and that figure was expected to rise. Jane he knew, would be preparing to visit personally, the nearest relatives of all of those who had lost their lives. He made a note to ask her for their names and job function. 'The authorities,' the announcer continued, 'still believe the explosion was caused by a gas leak.'

"Crap," Roger's spoken aloud opinion was expressed whilst eating a mouthful of toast. He wiped his face with a tea towel and took another swig of coffee. He looked at his watch. Five more minutes and I'll get going. The next article, considering the tragedy in Vauxhall, was somewhat appropriate. Another private hospital, built by the emerging private health care company, New Dawn was to be officially opened today. Cutting the ribbon and unveiling a plaque would be done by the Secretary of State for Health and Social Care, one Victoria Adams. In a pre-recorded interview, Victoria proclaimed that again, this was an excellent example of how private enterprise and government can successfully work together to benefit the hard pressed NHS, not to mention the British public. It was the second private hospital to be opened in the UK by New Dawn in a week. Something of a miracle. Next came a live feed from outside the hospital, close to East Midlands Airport. It was an interview with the company's head of European operations. A Frenchman by the name of Francois Debreu. Mr Debreu, enthusiastically praised the British government for their generosity in helping build what he proudly proclaimed to be a state of art complex incorporating the latest technical achievements in healthcare. Not only that. The hospital had a whole wing dedicated to research, and it was hoped by New Dawn that the hospital would become a world leader in medical science.

To repay the government, the hospital would take on many of the operations on the NHS's rapidly growing waiting list, and at a heavily discounted price. For its private healthcare, the hospital , as well as UK patients would be treating well off patients from abroad. The government had helpfully promised to ease entry restrictions if an operation had been pre-booked, and the patient had a return ticket. This is the right sort of health tourism the UK needs, Francois Debreu enthused. A line the Secretary of State, picked up on in later interviews. Finally he promised the hospital would be manned by some of the best trained medical professionals in the world. Their expertise to be richly rewarded. New Dawn would he declared, have no problem in keeping its staff. Was that something of a dig at the NHS? Roger thought so and found himself smiling. Carefully planned no doubt, as Mr Debreu was being interviewed, a brand new shining ambulance sporting the company's logo passed slowly by in the background. Roger Denton drained the last of his coffee from the mug, turned off the tv with the remote, returning to the kitchen where he rinsed his mug under the tap. As he pulled out of his road, on his way to the Hilton, Park Lane, his mind wandered back to the last report. Something, something silly no doubt was nagging at his subconscious. Of course, the ambulance. He'd seen an ambulance, just the same, not all that long ago. Where was it? It was one of those stupid considerations that always clouded, hindered even serious thought. Roger pushed it from his mind. He needed to concentrate on the task ahead. Had his mind been playing tricks? He was about to find out.

Royal Lancaster Hotel, Lancaster Gate, London, England

There came a knock at the door.

"Room service."

Fatima, after quickly wrapping herself in a robe, pulled open the door.

"Thank you," a young Asian waitress wheeled in a trolley. After asking Fatima to sign, she quickly left. Fatima sat down to eat. The best thing about hotel living she considered, were hotel breakfasts. France excluded, she laughed to herself. How could a country so famous for its food deliver such a poor breakfast. Pouring herself a coffee, she turned on the tv and sat down to eat. For a few minutes she flicked between the news channels from the country she was in. Fatima quickly tired, they were so inward looking, you could tell Britain was an island. After a few seconds search she found Al Jazeera and settled back to enjoy her breakfast. So much of the news she found depressing, the world was falling apart. The British reports were almost entirely concentrated on the explosion at the NCA. Fatima had no idea what the NCA was but she noted the news was causing waves all over the world.

"Now some good news," The news anchor smiled. The good news turned out to be a new hospital being opened today, near East Midlands Airport by the Secretary of State for Health and Social Care. The report quickly turned to an interview with Francois Debreu. The head of European operations for New Dawn Health Care. Fatima almost choked on her Shakshouka for she recognised him instantly. He was an associate of Pierre's, she'd met him several times in the past. And if she was right, his name wasn't Francois Debreu and he certainly wasn't French, he was Lebanese!

Hilton Hotel, Park Lane, London, England

Everyone present was delighted to find when they arrived that, Ishaan the head of security for the hotel, had organised bacon butties and fresh coffee for everyone along with cheese rolls in case there were those who couldn't eat pork. Roger quickly apologised to everyone for asking them to be there at such an early hour and hoped it wouldn't turn out to be a waste of their time. The tray of rolls almost exhausted and with all holding a takeaway cup of coffee the gathering settled down to look at the tv monitor replaying the footage from the day of the 'big fuck up,' as the director, Roger Denton, from the NCA referred to it. Roger turned to Ishaan, asking silently if he could start giving the hotel CCTV operator directions. Ishaan shrugged his shoulders, meaning why ask, 'of course, go ahead.' Turning to the controller, Roger asked.

"Can we go back to the same time yesterday, the moment when I exited the lift on the 28th floor." Roger turned to Nick. "What time would that be again Nick?" After referring to his notes, Nick gave the time his boss had entered the lift on the ground floor.

"So it'll be just seconds after that," Ishaan chipped in.

"Yes, almost where we left it yesterday."

Just to be safe the operator started the footage a good minute before the officer from the NCA had recorded his boss entering the lift on the ground floor. Just over a minute later, just as yesterday there came a shout, though this morning it was a little more playful. Roger could be seen clearly, exiting the lift.

"Freeze it, hold it there." Roger almost shouted. Everyone stared at the screen, nobody could see anything unusual. "There's nobody there." To everybody else Roger was making no sense.

"You're there sir." Nick risked stating the bleeding obvious. He felt stupid pointing it out.

"No, no," Roger exclaimed. "When I came out of the lift, there were two women waiting for it. Two Arab women, I'm sure of it. They should be there, but they're not." Roger waved one arm at the screen. "But they're not," he repeated. "It's just me. Me on my own." By the looks on their faces, Roger could see that nearly all were disbelieving, a couple perhaps thought he may even have lost it. Ishaan stepped in.

"The camera doesn't lie Roger, if there's no one there, there's no one there. It can only be your imagination, perhaps it was somewhere else you saw them. It must be your mind playing tricks."

"You haven't had a lot of sleep sir," Nick added. Roger recognised that Nick in the kindest way he could was telling him he may be wrong. Was he right? Could it be his mind, his memory playing tricks? This was the question that had kept him awake most of the night. He hadn't been looking for two Arab women, so they hadn't really registered. He'd been looking for Mr Mitchell and their man Rory . He only really remembered the two women because he'd found one of them to be incredibly striking. Even in the most trying of circumstances, when he'd been extremely stressed she'd somehow, without really looking at him, aroused his basic male instincts. You don't really forget a woman who manages to do that. Roger stared at the still screen. There he was, stepping out of the lift. There were people in the background, by the look of it waiting to enter the restaurant but nobody waiting for a lift.

"Play it slowly," Roger instructed. "Frame by frame until I enter the Sky Bar." The controller did as he was told but apart from a young woman dressed in office clothes, and definitely not in any way Arab looking, making for the ladies there was nobody.

"Do you remember her?" the controller asked pointing to the young smartly dressed woman. Roger shook his head. He had to be honest.

"No I don't," he admitted.

"You see, with the greatest of respect," Ishaan looked embarrassed. "It could just be your mind playing tricks. Well you know what sometimes happens when we ask witnesses to pick out someone from an album. Their mind starts to play tricks and they pick out who they feel they should be looking for rather than who they've seen." Roger knew he was right, it happened all the time but he still felt strongly that he wasn't wrong.

"That's why I asked you two," Roger turned his attention to the two operatives who hadn't been in the control room looking at the CCTV yesterday. One male, one female, both in their late thirties, they had been in the Sky Bar on the day in question, working undercover. " Now I want the operator to work around the Sky Bar, minutes before I arrive. I need you to study the footage carefully, see if you spot anything wrong. By wrong, I mean anything different from what you remember on the day." The two tensed with concentration. "Ready?" The woman nodded and the male operator signalled yes, with an upturned thumb. Roger nodded to the operator. "Let's start the footage around ten minutes before our target is escorted out of the bar, by the man still unknown to us. After that continue playing until I enter."

The operator nodded. Thirty seconds later all were watching footage from the bar. The operator skilfully switched from camera to camera. The bar was fairly busy, their target, John Mitchell was enjoying a drink, minutes later the female operative who had been undercover, now watching the CCTV came and sat beside him. Just over five minutes later the stranger introduced himself to their target. He was carrying a program for the Tina Turner musical, just as Rory, their plant had been instructed to. Minutes later they both left. Nothing out of the ordinary appeared to happen before Roger Denton entered. The girl who had passed him as he entered the bar could be seen prior with what looked like a bunch of workmates. She was seen laughing as she stood up. A few minutes later, just after Roger had stood at the bar with a colleague she returned and sat down with the same group.

"Ok stop." Roger turned to the two who had been undercover. See anything unusual? Anything different? Specifically were there two Arab females in the bar?" The female operative shook her head.

"I don't think so."

"You?" Roger turned to her male colleague. He shook his head.

"I'm, I'm not sure, I seem to remember a woman sitting in the window seat in the corner, but I can't be sure."

" And there's nobody on the video footage." Ishaan cut in.

"Peter," (the CCTV operator), "can you go back to when Mr Mitchell" Ishaan looked at Roger, checking he'd got the name right. Roger nodded. "When Mr Mitchell was sitting on his own."

Peter, immediately played the footage back to when their target was sitting on his own.

"Look at his face, his eyes," Ishaan directed. "What do you think he's looking at?"

"The view." Nick immediately responded, there came noises of agreement from the others.

"Wrong." Ishaan pointed, "look. He's not, he's staring at the table, more accurately the chair and if you play the footage slowly, they're rather furtive glances. Why would he do that with a chair. I'd say he's trying to be discreet, the sort of behaviour when a man's secretly admiring a woman."

"Except there's no woman there," murmured Roger thinking hard. Can either of you remember someone, or more than one person sitting there?"

"It's a prime window seat, Ishaan cut in, they're normally the first to be taken. It's very unusual for it to be free, even when the bar is quiet." The female operative shook her head.

"No, I'm sorry, I was concentrating on our target, not the window."

"There might have been, an Arab woman possibly, but I too was concentrating on our target. I'm worried with the direction of our conversation that I might be tempted into imagining things." Her male colleague shook his head, more in frustration than anything else. Roger turned to Ishaan.

"Can I talk to you outside a minute?"

"Of course," Ishaan went to open the door.

"Before we go, can my guys study the footage from when the bar opened till a good hour after I arrived? Ishaan shrugged his shoulders.

"Of course."

"Sorry guys, I know it's as boring as hell." Roger really did feel guilty.

"Any chance of some more coffee? Nick looked desperate.

"I'll organise it." Ishaan promised

"Can we talk outside?" Roger asked, immediately after leaving the control room.

"It's bloody cold," Ishaan reminded him

"Do us both good then." Roger countered

Minutes later the two men were leaning against a wall, drinking more coffee from takeaway cups.

"You know what I'm going to ask you?" Roger looked at his shoes.

"Can images from our CCTV, have been doctored, altered in any way?" Roger nodded. "I don't see how, and there's no software I'm aware of that could have altered our CCTV images without us knowing about it. Our security is really tight and I'm pretty sure we would have spotted any attempt to hack into our system. We really do pride ourselves on our online security."

"But it's the only explanation." Roger was adamant. "I'm more than sure now that there were two Arab women waiting for the lift as I got out. And how can three men, counting the guy who met and walked off with our target. How can they just disappear. Not just from us but from your bloody video footage?"

Ishaan finished his coffee shaking the dregs out of cup onto the pavement. He looked up at the steadily lightening sky.

"I don't know what you guys are investigating. You've only really half told me. And I'm no longer in the force, but if there's a Middle Eastern involvement in this, that puts a whole new complexion on things. That's not just NCA."

Roger hated to admit it, but Ishaan was right. If there was Middle Eastern involvement investigating it would be way above his pay grade.

"Look Ishaan, let's allow my guys to examine your CCTV footage. See if digital forensics can find if it's been got at in any way. If it has then the next step will be to find out who did it. I'm going to get my guys to do a face recognition check on everyone in the bar, starting with the stranger who abducted our target. He was carrying a programme for Tina Turner. You know the musical. That was a prop our plant was using. So either the guy in the Sky Bar with our target, abducted him somewhere between the ground floor and the bar. Or somebody already knew about our operation..

"Sting." Ishaan cut in, "and I'm still very unhappy about that."

Roger smiled weakly.

"I've already apologised for that. Anyhow the rather distasteful alternative is, that somehow somebody already knew about our operation, and set us up."

"You mean you have a mole inside your agency, working for the other side."

Or moles, Roger thought. Though he didn't say so. He was thinking of the explosions at his office. Planting explosives could only have been achieved with inside help. Almost certainly using more than one individual. That was the generally accepted view coming from the professionals. More and more he considered it looked as though his gut feeling may actually be turning out to prove correct, albeit there was still a long way to go before it would, or rather could be proven to be the case. Ishaan spoke again.

"If the latter is proven to be correct, your Mr Mitchell must be something of a VIP. Someone's gone to an awful lot of trouble to abduct your Mr Mitchell. Again, I'm no longer in the force, and it's nothing to do with me, but are you sure your intel is correct on this guy? Are you sure you know everything there is to know about him?"

Roger pursed his lips. He was beginning to wonder. And what the hell had John got himself into? Was he a victim or was he somehow involved? Was he even the mastermind? His ex-colleague over the years had mixed with, sometimes held hands with some pretty unsavoury characters. He thought he knew John, maybe the unpalatable truth was, he didn't?

"We were pretty sure of our intel on Mr Mitchell, but you can never be sure. Well you being an ex- cop will know that." Ishaan laughed.

"Only too well."

The two men chatted for another ten minutes before Ishaan returned to the hotel's control room. Roger promised he'd join them in a few minutes. He needed to make a couple of calls first. That morning his team were raiding both John's house in Goring. His 'country estate,' as he liked to call it, tongue in cheek and his bakery in Putney. The bakery in Putney was considered a high risk raid as many of the men who worked there were known to the intelligence services. Nearly all were ex special forces and all knew how to handle themselves, with or without a gun. Roger wanted to be with the team when it went down, but under the circumstances the importance of the raid had moved up the list to top priority. The raid would start at eight thirty sharp, which was in ten minutes. There wouldn't be time for him to get there. And his presence it was felt, especially by Jane, was needed at the hotel until all leads had been exhausted. The call to his team in Putney was brief. Everyone, it was confirmed was in position. Nearly all the delivery vans for the morning had left. This was a pain, it would have been better to have organised the raid in the early hours, with everybody still in the building. But there hadn't been time to get everybody and everything together quickly enough and now it was felt, the bakery was too important to leave it until the next morning.

"Keep me updated," Roger requested, and rang off.

His second call was to Jane. Most of her day, today was to be spent with Scotland Yard and MI5. Mainly structural stuff so the NCA could use their specialist services with the minimum delay. She re-confirmed that key staff could move into their temporary offices under Gladstone Park, tomorrow morning and that he could set up anytime after eight am. 'Its only down the road from where you live,' Jane had sounded jealous. Forensics would probably be finished with Mr Mitchell's phone by tomorrow morning, and they'd give him a call when they had. Roger had felt his stomach churn at this. What would they find? In return Roger updated Jane on what they had found at the Hilton so far. He needed a specialised team to check the CCTV, to see if it had been doctored in anyway, plus a face recognition check on everyone in the bar at the time. Priority being the gentleman who had escorted their target out of the bar. He'd organise the footage to be sent over to whoever in an hour or so. He just had to clear it with the hotel's head of security. But he couldn't see a problem. 'The guy's an ex-cop from the Met.' Jane hesitated on hearing this.

"Roger, have you considered the possibility that he may be involved? Head of security for the hotel, may not be his only job? He's in the perfect position to play you if he's working for who knows who."

Roger could have kicked himself, it was bloody obvious, he should have considered the possibility from the very beginning. Why the bloody hell hadn't he. He was too worried about himself, that's why.

"Roger, Roger, give me his name, I'll run a security check on him, ask a few discreet questions with the right people."

"Ishaan, hang on Jane, I've got his card." Roger fumbled for his wallet. "Ishaan Thakor, he comes across as genuine."

"All the clever ones do Roger, you should know that. Right I'll get him checked out. Keep me updated on the raids. Have you discovered any connection with what happened to us at Vauxhall, even the slightest?"

"No Jane, sorry." He couldn't bring himself to tell his boss that his gut feeling was telling him otherwise. Not yet anyway. "Are we any nearer to knowing?"

He heard a long sigh on the end of the phone.

"Nothing, not a squeak. Not even a hint. Everyone's mystified, not to mention nervous. The question that no-one wants to ask but everyone's asking silently, is where else has been infiltrated. The Americans as you can imagine are very skittish, and I understand have drawn up the drawbridge where sharing intelligence is concerned. As have several of our European counterparts. It's a bloody mess, sorry wrong word to use. I wasn't thinking."

"That reminds me Jane, can you get me someone to keep me updated on the fatalities. Where necessary, I need to pay my personal respects."

"Already done Roger and remember. Trust no one. In our game it's always the first rule." Roger was about to reply but the line went dead. His boss had rung off.

Calais Plage, Calais, France

Pierre stood with his hands in his trouser pockets looking at the view from his penthouse apartment, across La Manche to the white cliffs of Dover. Everything was coming together nicely. They were ahead of plan on many of their projects and starting to play with the people who didn't want to be played with. The more they panicked the easier it would be to have them in the palm of their hands. As for the UK, they'd considered it to be one of the harder nuts to crack but it was turning out, at least so far, to be one of the easiest. So far ahead were they, that they were almost ready to start making their final preparations. If everything went to plan, the UK would be theirs without anybody realising it. He smiled to himself. Both Hitler and Napoleon were reputed to have stood on Cap Blanc Nez, enviously eyeing the coastline of Britain. They had both famously failed in their attempts to conquer the island, whereas, he was confident, very confident they would succeed.

He looked at his watch, a Patek Philippe held by a leather strap. It was gone nine, eight in the UK. Fatima would have been up a long time ago. She always got up at the crack of dawn. He still thought of her as Fatima, not Ariana, her real name. It was going to be hard to adjust. He wondered if the organisation would contact her today, it wasn't his call but he couldn't help wondering. He cared about Fatima. Every other man found her irresistibly sexual. She hardly had to make an effort, it came naturally to her. Whereas he, he looked upon her almost as a sister, and as a result he cared for her wellbeing. Very unprofessional but he couldn't help it. He desperately didn't want her to go the way of Maureen, alias Bree. She hadn't deserved that, but they'd had no other choice. She'd become a liability.

He needlessly looked at his watch a second time. They had a new shipment arriving today from Turkey. He wanted to be there when it arrived. He had a couple of hours. That was plenty of time but he liked to be organised. Time was so unpredictable. Whistling softly to himself, Pierre made his way to the bathroom for his morning shower.

Gendarmerie Nationale, Calais, France

Ten minutes' walk away from Pierre's penthouse apartment, around the time Pierre was studying the English coast line, Lieutenant Beaufort was in the capitaine's office looking at the pile of papers on his desk. Capitaine Maubert's death was on the front page of every rag, even the national papers such as La Monde and Le Figaro. Several had photos of Didier, the fisherman who had found the capitaine's body floating in the sea. Nearly every photo had him standing proudly by his flobart. The lieutenant stared at them. If the law would allow him, he could happily strangle that man. He'd even given a couple of television interviews. The connard was basking in his five minutes of fame, with no apparent consideration to the dead man's family or colleagues. A press conference had been called for two that afternoon. He would have to stand and smile at the animals who had written all this stuff. Worse still, answer questions from them.

If that wasn't enough he also had their replacement capitaine arriving to take up his new post, that afternoon. He'd looked at his file last night. What had surprised him, their new capitaine, an Olivier Vendroux, had worked for a while for the BRB. He had only been a capitaine with the gendarme for a couple of years and that was in Paris. He'd find Calais very different. Why on earth did he want a post here? Unless he'd had no choice. It was possible he may have been forced to take the post.

Last night he'd also examined his ex-boss's papers that Colette had given him. The files were mainly his notes and thoughts about the latest case they'd been working on. The one that had caused so much trouble. There wasn't much he didn't already know, and most of what he had read was already officially noted on the gendarmerie's computer files. What had come across however was the capitaine's apparent obsession with Cap Blanc Nez. He simply couldn't see why. They'd already checked and found nothing suspicious there. The headland was simply geographically in the centre of everything. Nothing more, nothing less. His personal opinion was that all their troubles had come from La Manche, maybe even from British waters. It was simply the way the tides and currents ran that had dumped the bloody mess on their doorstep. As for the theory that migrants were going missing. So what? Migrants had been going missing for decades. The theory that they were being kidnapped for God knows what reason was some stupid little girl's fantasy. The girl. Marie, as far as he was concerned had always been an enemy of the gendarme. And now look at the trouble she'd caused. He made a mental note to warn the new capitaine about her.

He'd left it late to look at the late capitaine's diary. He'd felt uncomfortable with the idea of looking through it. As though he were intruding on something deeply personal. Something that was meant for the contributor's eyes only. Even after death. It had taken a good hour of contemplation before he'd managed to overcome his discomfort, and start reading. As it turned out, it was altogether rather boring, that is until he altered the way in which he approached his examination. Rather than start from the beginning of the year, he'd decided to start from the final entry and work backwards. When he started doing this a name kept slapping him in the face. A name he'd never heard of but with whom the capitaine had had a flurry of meetings. The name, Fatima. Who the bloody hell was Fatima?

A Street In Calais, France

In a small Flemish brick terraced house, a young lady by the name of Marie sat sobbing her heart out. Somebody had just shoved a local paper through her letterbox. I say somebody because Marie never had papers delivered. Unfolding it, she read to her horror the apparent suicide of Capitaine Maubert. The theory, and the paper stressed it was, at the moment only a theory, that the good capitaine had committed suicide by throwing himself off the top of Cap Blanc Nez. This after pictures of him kissing Marie Lefevre, appeared all over social media. It is believed that Marie, a local resident, well known for her support for the migrant population, and the capitaine, may have been having an affair. Handwritten in red ink across the top of the paper were the words. 'Thanks Marie, you've done us all a favour.'

Marie threw the paper across the room. How could people be so cruel. Ever since the pictures had appeared on social media, she'd been spat at, called names, even on a couple of occasions punched. All because of an innocent goodbye kiss that someone for some reason had photographed and posted on the internet. Of course people being people had put two and two together and come up three. An affair had been created in the eyes of the masses that had never existed, never started.

Marie made up her mind there and then, that she had to get to Thierry's wife. To tell her the truth. That the photo wasn't what it appeared to show. It was the least she could do. Capitaine Maubert, Thierry had single handedly smashed all her pre conceived ideas of the gendarmerie. The capitaine she had come to discover was genuine, sincere and most importantly he'd had a heart. She would have to get to his wife, she couldn't bring herself to call her a widow. Tell her the truth, if she would listen. The gendarmerie too, they had to know. The least she could do was preserve Capitaine Maubert's reputation. Her mind was made up.

Le Week-End café/Bar, Sangatte, France

Le Week-End café sits on the main thoroughfare through town, the D940 coast road from Calais, through Wissant to Boulogne. Just a few kilometres from Calais, Sangatte is famous for its sand dunes and long sandy beach and is the last coastal town if driving from Calais, before the climb to Mont Hubert and Cap Blanc Nez. As a consequence in summer the café tends to become busy with both holiday makers and day trippers. Now as winter approached, trade was scarce and almost entirely local based. That morning however had been much busier than usual. In addition to the usual locals, there had been quite a few strangers, mostly English speaking. Now it was nearing ten, the café was beginning to empty. Jean, the only waiter that morning had worked as a waiter in the café since he'd left school some five years ago. He liked his job and had no ambition to do anything else. From his few years' experience, he knew that from eleven thirty the cafe would start to fill up again with the lunch time trade. Knowing this he busied himself clearing and wiping tables, taking the used china to the bar to be washed. When there were only two tables still occupied his boss brought him a fresh coffee and told him to take a break. Grabbing a used newspaper left by one of the clients Jean took his coffee outside. He liked to smoke and the cold weather didn't bother him. Settling at a table furthest from the café entrance, Jean lit his cigarette, almost at the same time taking a sip of his strong black coffee. It was something he did around this time every morning, and a habit he always looked forward. And one that never failed to disappoint. Sitting back he took another, longer drag of his cigarette, enjoying at the same time the taste of the salt air blowing in from the sea.

Comfortable, he unrolled the newspaper and set it on the table. After a single glance he froze. His cigarette and coffee forgotten. Picking up the paper he read hurriedly. Before he'd finished reading the front page, he placed the paper back on the table and reached inside his apron pocket for his mobile. It took just one touch to place a call to his girlfriend, Camille. She answered on the third ring. Jean didn't wait for her to speak, he was far too animated.

"Camille."

"Oui. You know it is." Jean heard her laugh. He loved her laugh.

"No, Camille have you heard the news this morning? Have you seen the papers?

"Non, pourquoi?" He should have known. Camille had no interest in the news, only music. He related the story on the front page, about Capitaine Maubert's body being found by a fisherman in La Manche. And how it was thought to have been a suicide, that the capitaine almost certainly threw himself off of the cliff at Cap Blanc Nez.

"We know that's not true Camille, we saw what happened. He didn't jump he was pushed." There was silence on the other end of the phone. "Camille? Camille, are you still there?

"Oui."

"Camille, we need to tell the police."

"We can't be sure Jean. We thought we saw something. We were busy with each other. It might have been something completely different. Do you really want to get us involved? What if you're wrong? The police might even consider us suspects."

"I know, I know. We weren't certain what we saw, but now after reading this, I'm sure what we saw was not a suicide, but a murder."

"Jean, calm down. You can't even be sure it was the gendarme, the capitaine something that we saw."

"He was in uniform Camille, it must have been him." Camille conceded this, whoever they'd seen from their car that night had been wearing a uniform.

"Don't do anything rash Jean, let's think about it first. Let's talk about it when you've finished work." There came a faint, unconvincing, 'ok.' "Jean?"

"Yes, yes, ok."

Reassured Camille, as she always did, told Jean that she couldn't wait to see him and rang off.

Jean finished his coffee with a couple of gulps and after stubbing out a half finished cigarette returned to the warmth of the café. Background music was playing. Jean recognised the song instantly, Tahitialamaison by Keen'V. It was their song, his girlfriend's and his song. It was also the song that they'd been playing on a loop when making love in his car on Cap Blanc Nez. The night, he was now convinced they'd witnessed Capitaine Maubert murdered, by somebody pushing him off the edge of the cliff. Tahitialamaison, continued to play. Fate works in mysterious ways.

Formby, England

The morning's weather echoed James' mood. It was grey, cold and very depressing. The only good thing that morning, was the car with the two strangers, one of whom had threatened him yesterday was no longer outside his house. Throughout his drive to work, the government's General Register Office in Southport, he kept checking his rear mirror. No they weren't behind him, he was positive he wasn't being followed. By the time he'd arrived for work his mood had lightened a little.

Perhaps the people who'd threatened him yesterday had come to their senses. They'd realised what they were asking him to do was impossible. He bloody hoped so.

The Hilton, Park Lane, London, England

Roger took the call just after ten in the morning. It came as a relief, he was sick of poring over hours of monotonous video. Video that should, but failed to, reveal what had gone wrong with their sting. The caller was his man in charge of their raid on John's bakery in Putney. It had gone without a hitch. All the employees found on site had been very cooperative. No one had given his team any trouble. The only mystery was that nobody seemed very surprised to see a team of armed NCA officers raiding the place. Of course not, Roger thought. For he had tipped John off that his bakery was coming under surveillance. John would have told everybody to behave impeccably. To keep their noses clean. And probably to expect a raid at any time. The team he was told had done an initial search but they'd found nothing suspicious. Of course they wouldn't. A team of SOCOs were about to take over, they might find something. They wouldn't, Roger was confident of that, not unless John's laptop was there.

"Ok, job well done. Let me know if the SOCOs find anything. But I want nothing moved until I've taken a look myself, is that understood?"

The voice on the other end of the phone confirmed it was. He went on to say, that everybody they'd found working at the bakery had been taken to the police station at Jubilee House for questioning. Something that the Met weren't best pleased about. There were still five delivery vans out, but going by what they'd experienced so far, he expected all to return and with complete cooperation from the drivers. With that the officer rang off, promising to keep Roger informed.

After a few minutes reflection, Roger called the team raiding, if that was the right term, John's house in Goring. Roger knew John hadn't visited the house for some time and that for his ex-colleague, it was something of a bolt hole. If he knew John as he did, the man wouldn't have risked contaminating the place in any way. It was where he escaped from the pressures of everyday life, and perhaps criminality. The officer in charge confirmed Roger's opinion. From where they'd searched so far, the house was completely clean. Nothing suspicious, not even remotely. Again a specialist forensics team would have to be deployed before they could write the place off. Because of resources that may not happen for another couple of days. Before then the house would be sealed off and guarded by uniformed officers from Thames Valley Police. Satisfied that everything that needed doing was being done, Roger rang off. He was just about to re-enter the control room when his phone rang again, it was Jane. He'd not long spoken to her, what could this be about?

"Roger we've got a face recognition match on the gentleman with your target. The face recognition process also confirmed your target as being John Mitchell. I thought it necessary to check." This was great news. At last they were getting somewhere. At long bloody last. Whoever it was who had vanished with their target had made his first mistake. He hadn't considered the possibility of being traced by face recognition.

"Who is he?" Roger could hardly wait for Jane's answer. There was a pause, he could hear Jane tapping on a keyboard.

"A Peter Fitch. According to our searches he teaches history at a local comprehensive in Wellingborough, Northamptonshire. I've organised a couple of uniformed officers to go and pick him up. There's been a slight delay because I feel, considering the possible severity of what we're dealing with, that an armed response team accompany them. They will not however, for obvious reasons accompany the officers inside the school. And there will be no arrest inside a classroom whilst he's teaching. They have instructions to only act during the break, and even then with the utmost discretion. We don't want another international incident."

What a brilliant cover, Roger considered. Who'd suspect a school teacher. But what the hell was he doing, who was he acting for? Is this something much bigger, an organisation that was placing 'sleepers' inside publicly respected positions? It was a terrifying thought.

"Does the system have anything on him?" He heard Jane tap the keyboard again, though he knew she didn't need to. She'd have committed everything to memory.

"No. According to what it says here he's perfect citizen. Born and brought up in Wellingborough by perfectly respectable parents. Still lives in the same house in which he was born. It's in Burns Road after the poet. Attended local schools. Went to teaching college and has taught at the current school for the last fifteen years. He hasn't even got, or ever held a passport. From the looks of it, he's never travelled abroad, not even on a school trip. His credit rating is excellent, there's no police record, so he's kept his nose clean. And from what the system shows me he's never even received a parking fine. No, from what the records are telling us, Mr Fitch is a model citizen."

"The perfect cover."

"Yes." Roger's boss agreed.

"Who's going to interview him?

"The uniformed officers have instructions to take him to the local nick. At this stage I want to keep it low key. It's important if he's working for some sort of clandestine criminal or terrorist group that our actions don't attract too much attention. At the same time it's important that we do not give him the opportunity to make any sort of contact with the outside world, not whilst he's in custody. Peter Goodson and Raymond Ballinger are attending from the NCA, they're both very experienced interviewers. Do you want to attend Roger?"

Roger knew both men, he had no reason to complain. They 'd both cracked some pretty hard nuts in the past. He'd like to attend but he wanted to visit the bakery first. He was still worried about John's laptop and what might be on it.

"See how they get on first, Jane. If I'm needed, Wellingborough is only a couple of hours drive. I'm going to be another couple of hours here yet, then I want to visit Mr Mitchell's bakery. I might spot something the team didn't." Jane accepted this.

"Ok. Still nothing? I've instigated a security search on Mr Thakor, the head of security there. So far nothing. He has an exemplary record with the Met, but that doesn't mean we wont find something amiss. It might be an idea to run a check on all those working for security there."

Roger whistled.

"That won't be easy, Jane, not without revealing to their HR department or management that we were operating a sting operation inside their hotel."

"We may not need to. Let's see what Peter and Ray get from Mr Pindar. And then there's the staff you have in custody from Mr Mitchell's bakery. They may tell you something. When are they being interviewed? You can't hold them for long."

Roger knew this and his team he knew were already drawing flak from the Putney nick. Interviewing should be starting at any moment, if it hadn't already, and he told Jane this. She appeared not to hear, her attention was suddenly elsewhere. She had to go. There was a click and the phone went dead.

The Gendarmerie Nationale, Calais, France

There were so many journalists in the gendarmerie staff parking that many of those working inside the building had to move their private cars to the nearest available parking, almost one hundred metres up the road. As you can imagine this did little to improve the mood amongst many of the serving officers present, many of whom already had utter contempt for anyone who represented the media. Immediately in front of the gendarmerie reception a makeshift stage had been put together, made from wooden blocks. On the stage stood a visually very nervous Lieutenant Beaufort, ready to hold his first press conference. To make matters worse, Monsieur Hivin the gendarmerie's PR representative was having difficulty with the PA system. He couldn't get it to work. Holding the press conference without its aid was a nonstarter as the wind was coming in from the sea and would carry anything the lieutenant said away in the wrong direction. Colette was inside, watching proceedings from her window. Her heart went out to the lieutenant. The press conference was turning out to be a PR disaster and that's before it had even started. Following the proceedings closely, from across the road, in an obviously brand new silver Alpine A110 with Parisian plates, sat a man in full gendarmerie uniform. Rather than just a shirt he wore a dark blue jacket and on the lower arm of each sleeve were sewn three gold stripes.

After a further fifteen minutes, the PA system suddenly sprang to life with a loud squeal, that represented feedback. A few more adjustments and a tap of the microphone and Lieutenant Beaufort's voice sounded across the gendarmerie car park. A spontaneous round of clapping sounded from the gathered media along with a few sarcastic cheers. Ignoring them the lieutenant bravely launched into his pre-prepared speech, confirming the media reports that the body found in La Manche, off Cap Blanc Nez, was indeed their dearly loved capitaine of the gendarmerie. Capitaine Maubert. He continued, aided by a sign language interpreter recruited by Monsieur Hivin, outlining the circumstances in which the capitaine's body had been found and recovered. Risking the media's impatience, the lieutenant brought to their attention, the capitaine's glorious career and his commitment not only to his gendarmerie but to the citizens of Calais. He'd always done his best to protect. Predicting the questions that were bound to follow, he tackled the circumstances of the capitaine's tragic death, even touching on the possibility of suicide. Lastly, as he had the night before, the lieutenant asked all present to respect the privacy of the capitaine's immediate family. This was not a time either, he stressed for media speculation. Please he urged. Report the facts, not journalistic supposition presented as fact. Colette clapped furiously from her window. She thought the lieutenant had rescued a very difficult situation and turned it into a success. There followed a barrage of questions. All were predictable except the last. This was from an American journalist who spoke perfect French. His question had nothing to do with the salacious theories posted on social media.

"Sir," he started. "Have you and your team considered the possibility that your capitaine's tragic death might have something to do with the recent case you've been investigating. The one that has made headlines all over the world?"

The question caught the lieutenant completely off guard.

Sat in the Alpine A110, Capitaine Olivier Vendroux, the newly appointed capitaine of the Calais gendarmerie, felt the hairs stand up on the back of his neck.

In a café in the village of Sangatte, a young waiter watching the proceedings live on tv, froze as he heard the question, translated. Did the journalist's question, explain what he was sure he and his girlfriend had witnessed from his car on Cap Blanc Nez?

Mont d'Hubert/Cap Blanc Nez, France

Pierre watched the live broadcast on a television screen in the Tunisian restaurant, cleverly built in a converted German bunker from the last war, on the summit of Mont d'Hubert. The press conference had been going well, very well, until the unexpected question from the American. They would have to be careful. The last thing they needed at this time was the gendarmerie snooping around Cap Blanc Nez and Mont d'Hubert again. Their one saving grace, was now at last, they had someone working on the inside. It was hoped, expected by the organisation, that that person would nip any new enquiries involving Mont d'Hubert in the bud.

The organisation and he personally had invested a hell of a lot of time and money in the operation hidden under Mont d'Hubert. And after the successful delivery today from Turkey their next planned stage, could start to become a reality. He'd enjoyed his chat with Antanois. His management of their operation here was superb. Despite, much higher demand than anticipated, his team had been able to cope. So successful were they, it was thought that it may soon be possible to invest in and operate a second van, picking up desperate migrants without attracting unwanted attention. With this operation too, they now had someone working on the inside. She was very anti establishment and a bit of a loose cannon, but as long as they were careful, her hatred for the establishment that was Calais played into their hands. Of course the organisation wasn't paying her. She was in effect a blind asset, she had no idea that she was working for the 'organisation.' But her obsession with bypassing the official channels, even if they were unofficial played right into their hands. Not only was she leading migrants, 'cargo,' was the word the organisation used, right to them, she had also, by publishing photographs of her once colleague, with the late Capitaine Maubert on social media, eliminated someone who may have been considered a risk to their operation, here on the French coast.

Pierre's thoughts wandered back to Antanois. He really was doing an excellent job, accepting his punishment without question. He had always considered his punishment to be overly excessive. The storm was never Antanois's fault, he had been a victim as much as the organisation. He would have words with the powers that be. He could see no reason why Antanois couldn't go back to living in the old farmhouse on the outside. After all the organisation, to date had failed to find a suitable replacement, and they needed 'anchors' in the surrounding villages. Agents who could mingle and act on local gossip. Antanois had built up a good circle of friends, one day soon they might be needed.

Ardres, France

The wife of the late Capitaine Maubert and her daughter sat comforting each other on the sofa, as they watched the live broadcast of the press conference from the gendarmerie in Calais. The daughter, no matter how hard she found it, was determined not to cry. She needed and wanted to support her mother. Even if her father had turned out to be a complete bastard. She still couldn't believe it.

Her mother, watching the press conference, surprisingly hadn't shed a tear until the lieutenant had started to sing her father's praises. Finishing with how, her father, her mother's husband, Capitaine Maubert had, 'loved and always sought to protect the citizens of Calais.' On hearing this the tears started to roll down her mother's cheeks. This was the man she had fallen in love with, the man she knew, or thought she'd known.

Outside on the doorstep, oblivious to the press conference, stood a young woman called Marie. After reading the newspaper, she was determined to put things right. On making up her mind she'd caught a train from la Gare at Calais to La Gare de Pont d'Ardres. From Pont d'Ardres it had been over an hour's walk before she reached the house she was looking for. The home that had been Capitaine Maubert's and now solely the home of his wife. For ten minutes she had been standing on the doorstep, questioning whether she was doing the right thing, and what reception she may receive. Twice she had walked back down the garden path, losing the courage of her conviction, only to find it again and return to the front door. Only when a suspicious neighbour asked if she could help, did Marie find the courage to knock.

Putney, London, England

Roger Denton, wearing shoe covers and disposable gloves, looked around what had obviously been or was, for they hadn't to date found a body, John's office. There was a stand alone computer on the desk, surprisingly old, but no sign of a laptop. The other office held three desk top computers, but again no sign of a laptop. A team of SOCOs, all dressed in white coveralls were carrying out a forensics check. Considering the number of people employed in the bakery and that both delivery drivers and Joe Public were welcomed, Roger didn't really expect them to find anything that would help in their investigation. Their one hope was that a fingerprint may throw up somebody with a serious criminal record, or who was under suspicion.

The team had hoped they might find something other than that uncovered by forensics. A stash of guns, a stash of money or files proving some sort of criminality had been taking place on the premises. But there was nothing. Everything they'd uncovered so far suggested that Mr Mitchell was simply running a legitimate bakery business. One of his team responsible for raiding the bakery pointed this out. Roger responded curtly.

"Bollocks, who's ever heard of an ex special serviceman, retiring to run a bloody bakery. You're more likely to find the Queen on a till in a supermarket."

"I get your point," the officer conceded.

"How's the interviewing going at the local nick?"

"Again, nothing sir, I'm sorry."

"Don't be," Roger's attitude softened. "This Mr Mitchell is one bloody clever individual." Not to mention the fact that I tipped him off. But Roger kept that to himself.

"There is something maybe that background checks are throwing up."

"I'm all ears," Roger already knew what was coming but he faked interest.

"Well, the one seemingly in charge and all the drivers, plus a couple of maintenance type guys are all ex special forces. As you point out hardly a chosen occupation for men of their experience. Normally you'd expect them to be involved in private security, most likely in the middle east where they can earn shedloads with their experience. Not carting bread and cakes around in the back of a van. Mr Mitchell must be offering them something pretty special to keep them here."

"Maybe he was just offering them a chance to have a quiet, stress free life." Roger pointed out.

"Men like that? No, from my experience once they've got the taste, they always want more of the same." Roger knew he was right but had no wish to continue or encourage this train of thought.

"What about the others, the employees who weren't ex special service. What about them?"

"From what we can see, they're all genuine bakers, and pretty good ones at that. We've also checked out the company and from all accounts, pardon the pun, they appear to be pretty successful. We've even discreetly chatted to a couple of their customers. Cafes in fact, and they're both full of praise." Roger was impressed, his team had been pro-active in their investigation. Outside their original remit.

"Have we checked the home addresses, everyone's given us? Do they check out?"

Again the officer's response was to impress him.

"Yes sir. All have been checked, and they all appear to be genuine. We've even checked them with the personnel files, held here at the bakery. Everything corresponds." At that moment a call came through on the officer's phone. After what appeared to be an intense two minute conversation, the officer offered his phone to Roger. "It's Kevin, (the officer in charge of the raid), at Putney nick. He wants to speak with you." Roger took the phone.

"Hello Kevin. How's the interviewing going?"

"To be honest boss it's not. All anyone talks about is the bloody bakery and how, by our actions, we could be ruining the business. And if I'm honest they've got a point. I don't see how we can hold them much longer, and the Met want their station back."

"Have we any reason to believe, that if we let them go they will disappear?"

"We can never be sure, but no, I don't think so."

"Ok, organise their return here will you. I'm going to hang around. See if I recognise anybody, and if I do, something about them that official records won't show up."

"Fair enough sir, traffic depending it shouldn't take us more than half an hour. Their transports still here."

"See you shortly." Roger rang off and handed back to the officer, his phone. He then filled the officer in, warning him to expect a bunch of disgruntled ex-interviewees. "I'll wait in Mr Mitchell's office," Roger added. "I've got some calls to make."

Settling himself in what he assumed must be John's chair, Roger made a call to Nick and Ishaan at the hotel. They both confirmed what he'd expected that the CCTV footage gave up nothing new. They'd drawn a blank, everyone of interest had simply vanished into thin air. Not quite, Roger thought. The two men weren't aware they'd got a face recognition hit on the man who had replaced their plant, who had enticed John Mitchell out of the Sky Bar. And that two officers should be picking up their suspect anytime soon. Roger checked his watch. Actually around now.

Nick and Ishaan, both sounded exhausted and Roger gave instructions to Nick to stand everyone down, but to continue outdoor surveillance from cars parked outside the front entrance. He knew he needn't tell Nick this, but to be sure, as whoever they were dealing with were obviously professional. And therefore, not to arouse suspicion, he reminded Nick that the surveillance cars and personnel needed to be changed at irregular intervals. 'Already done sir,' Nick had replied.

After that, Roger spoke briefly with Ishaan. Thanking him and promising to keep him informed if they found anything suspicious with the CCTV footage. Even if they didn't, in return Ishaan promised to keep a special eye out on all activity in the hotel. Roger believed he would, too. He considered himself a good judge of character. It was the key to successful law enforcement, and his gut feeling was telling him that Ishaan was one of the good guys.

To pass the time, Roger idly cast his eye around the office. Everything in it was simple, basic and showed the scars of having been well used. The filing cabinets looked as though they'd been around long before the war, perhaps even the Great War and the desk, John's desk, was covered in penned graffiti. The walls were painted white and where the paint had peeled and cracked, shades of sky blue and yellow were revealed. The office shouted, 'neglect'. No one cares for me. Everything in it and about it was the exact opposite of the John he knew. After years of living and working in the world's worst hellholes, he had developed a taste for the luxurious. His house in Goring he guessed would be the epitome of comfortable country living, and his flat in Drury Lane, although small and simply furnished, smelt of money. All the furnishings were toned with one another. Nothing had been purchased as part of a set. Every piece was uniquely individual and yet, together they combined to create that family feeling. Roger was also pretty sure every piece had been hand crafted, nothing in John's flat looked as though it had been mass produced. The carpet was so cushioned, you could easily sleep on it and the drapes so heavy they wouldn't have been out of place in a theatre. So why the exact opposite here? Sold at an auction Roger doubted if everything together, all the contents, would fetch as much as a fiver. Perhaps his ex-colleague simply didn't care. That the bakery was simply a means to an end. A necessity he didn't particularly enjoy.

His mind turned to John himself. He knew John carried a gun. He'd admitted it to him. And half of his employees were ex special service. Everyone one of them could kill using just one hand, and all would be extremely useful with a firearm. He didn't doubt each and everyone would have access to a weapon, probably owned one. Maybe even legally licensed, though initial checks hadn't shown this. No guns had been found here, none at the Drury Lane flat and to his knowledge none at Goring. John he was pretty sure, would have had a stash of weapons. So where were they? From his seat he could see the men in white coveralls going about their business. If there'd been guns and ammunition stored here they should find evidence of that. Should, Roger reflected, but I bet they don't.

There came the sound of vehicles entering the yard, followed by heated exchanges. The bakery's employees had arrived back from being interviewed. Roger went out to meet them. Although he wasn't wearing a uniform it was very apparent to everyone there that he was in charge. Using a loud confident voice, he apologised to everyone present for the inconvenience their investigation had caused. But they'd acted on information received and if they hadn't it would have been negligent, perhaps even a dereliction of duty. He hoped everyone would understand. Everyone was now free to go home or return to work. Though if they wouldn't mind he'd like to ask a few more questions of, Roger read out a list of names. They were the employees who'd been ex-military.

"If you guys could just give me a few minutes of your time in your bosses' office that would be great. No obligation, but if you could I'd be really grateful." Roger smiled and turning strolled back to John's office. In under a minute seven men were gathered in front of him. They all looked relaxed but their stance gave away their military background. Once a soldier always a soldier. Who had originally coined that phrase? They were so right. Roger leant back in the chair, his hands placed behind his head. He wanted to appear as unthreatening as possible. He needed to gain the confidence of these guys. He needed to gain their trust.

"Can one of you shut the door please." The nearest to the door, closed it softly. "I'm going to be candid with you guys," Roger started. "I know all of you are ex-military, ex-special forces and I know some of you even served with John, as did I." He paused, letting this snippet of information sink in. No one gave any hint of an expression. They were good. Roger, undaunted continued. "Now I know it was no accident that you guys ended up here. What I don't understand is why. It would be really helpful for me to know." Nobody moved a muscle. "Ok." Once more, undaunted Roger ploughed on. "I know because of your training you're all loyal to John." Using John Mitchell's first name only was a deliberate tactic. "However, we, I feel that because of certain activities John is in danger, maybe in mortal danger. Now I find it very hard to believe, I may be wrong. But I find it very hard to believe that all that was going on here, was the baking of bread and cakes." Roger had expected to perhaps get a laugh from this, but he didn't. Nobody even twitched. "Ok," Roger sighed. He leaned forward. "Well ok, if any of you have second thoughts, I'm leaving my number, here on the desk." With a blue biro, Roger worked into the wood his name and mobile number. "Looks good doesn't it?" He smiled broadly and to their credit two or three of the men gathered had the grace to smile back. "Ok, thank you for your time gentlemen." Roger stood up and one by one the men filed out. All except one, who remained standing, motionless, until all his workmates had left. After the last one had left the office he closed the door. Roger tensed sensing the man might mean business, the wrong kind of business. One of his officers had evidently seen what was happening for the door was pulled open quickly.

"I just want a quiet word, that's all." The lone man's voice was soft but full of metal. Roger recognised it came from his training. He turned to the NCA officer framed in the doorway. "You might want to hold on there whilst I check something." He turned and spoke directly to Roger. "I'm sorry Mr Denton, but I need to check you're not wired." The officer in the doorway with his gun in his hand looked quizzically at his boss. Roger nodded and raised his arms.

"Ok, go ahead." The man stepped forward and expertly ran his hands over Roger's body, even checking the cuffs and collar of his shirt.

"You're fine, sorry about that. Now may I have a quiet word with you Mr Denton. Alone."

Roger motioned to the officer in the doorway, to leave. It was ok. Or at least he hoped it would be.

"Why don't you sit down," Roger motioned for him to do so.

The man pulled up a chair, but rather than sitting on it, leaned on its back. "I feel more comfortable like this. If that's ok with you?"

"Sure," Roger shrugged his shoulders. "You wanted to speak to me?"

"Yes, I'm Mr Mitchell's 'second in command.' The manager of his bakery. Mr Mitchell's spoken about you. All favourable or I wouldn't be speaking to you now. The men, I mean everybody you had in here are happy to let me speak to you. They trust me."

"Go on."

"Well, I thought you might have some questions. Something's happened to Mr Mitchell hasn't it? That's why you raided the place."

"Happened? I don't know. We don't know where he is." There were a few seconds silence whilst the two men eyed each other up, both trying to work out what the other was thinking.

"Neither do we." It was John's 'second in command' who broke the silence. "I've heard nothing from him for over two days. I've tried ringing his mobile, but nothing. I've left messages and received no reply. That is not like Mr Mitchell at all."

"What are you really running here....I mean it's not just a bakery is it?"

"You already know it's not. And we're not stupid. If you ever try and use what I'm about to tell you against any of us, we will all deny everything, and you'll never find a scrap of evidence. I can promise you that. You may though have to spend the rest of your life looking over your shoulder." Roger smiled. He knew the man standing in front of him wasn't making idle threats. If needs be, they'd be carried through with ruthless efficiency. He also knew the man to be right regarding any evidence. They wouldn't find a thing, not a bloody thing.

"I know, and you have my word. Don't forget I'm SF, same as you. You have my word."

"That's good enough for me," the man visibly relaxed. Over the next twenty minutes or so, he explained how his boss using his ex-military staff, ran a high end debt collecting service through the bakery. 'If somebody was reluctant to pay, our special skills could be very persuasive.' He'd actually smiled when he'd said this.

"And you know how it is Mr Denton, you never lose that yearning for action, trained aggression. Mr Denton not only gave us work and a decent salary. Now and again the men could work out their pent-up aggression, all the time whilst being a respectable member of society. You know how it is."

Roger did, only too well. Over the years as a law enforcement officer, he'd given the odd offender a punishment the courts could never hand out. He wasn't proud of the fact, but he'd be lying, if he told himself he hadn't enjoyed it at the time.

"How big were these debts?"

"Big, sometimes in the millions. The really big ones Mr Mitchell dealt with on his own. We didn't always know about them. I know he used to cut them some sort of deal. But that's all I know. The last one, I think could potentially have been his biggest."

"How much?"

"Quarter of a billion. Quarter of a billion pounds, sterling."

Roger whistled, feigning surprise. For he now knew the man was talking about their plant. Their sting operation. He even found himself feeling guilty in front of John's fiercely loyal employee. For appearances sake, Roger asked questions about their last job. Already knowing the answers. Finally he had two genuine questions.

"You know we are going to trace all the calls made to and from this phone." Roger tapped the phone on the desk.

"You can try. It's an internet phone, you'll be traveling all over the world trying to trace calls made from that. Anyway, the system's been programmed to auto delete after an hour."

"Maybe here."

The man simply smiled at Roger's short answer. Roger ignored him.

"Guns, I knew John had a gun, he told me. There must be others, are you prepared to tell me where they're hidden?"

"I don't know what you're talking about."

For the first time the man in front him was lying. Roger knew it and the man in front of him knew he knew it. Roger smiled, a way of accepting the man's lie. The man grinned back.

"One last thing. You said that you've been trying to contact John. How?"

"On his mobile."

"This number?" Roger read out John's number from his phone.

"That's the one."

"And which number are you ringing him from?"

"My mobile."

"Can you give me the number?" The man read it out. After that they shook hands, each demonstrating mutual respect. "I promise you…?"

"Ed." Edward Quainton, Roger already knew.

"I promise you Ed, if we hear anything, you'll be the first to know." The man thanked him.

"Likewise, Mr Denton, I promise." With that the man left.

Wellingborough, Northamptonshire, England

The two officers, both CID, looked at the man, across the desk. Outside the door sat two armed officers. They were there, as the NCA had warned that the man sitting in front of them, one Peter Fitch, a local schoolteacher, may be highly dangerous. Possibly, probably, carrying a loaded weapon.

Well, they couldn't see it. The man, when they had picked him up, had looked genuinely shocked and was still looking shocked. In fact, he looked petrified. He hadn't even accepted the offer of a legal representative, claiming there was no need. At the time the officers had suggested he was in London at a posh hotel on Park Lane, he'd explained he'd been teaching at the local comprehensive. And thirty two teenagers, plus the head, he promised could act as witnesses. A quick call to the head at the school had confirmed this. At the time they'd suggested he was in London, Mr Fitch had been teaching a class of thirty two in year four. In fact, on the day in question, Mr Fitch being a very conscientious teacher had been at the school since seven thirty that morning and hadn't left until seven in the evening. Mr Fitch, the head had repeated, being a dedicated and conscientious employee of the school had, the same day, after school hours, taken a number of private tutorials. The NCA, the two CID officers agreed, had made an almighty cock up with this one.

Two agents from the NCA arrived just ten minutes later. The two officers, whilst all were looking through the one-way glass of the interview room, explained their interview process, You've got the wrong guy, they told the two from the NCA. We know what the photograph says, but it's wrong. There's no way the man in there, is the guy you're looking for.

"Let us be the judge of that." Agent Ballinger spoke for both of them. "Join us if you like."

For the next two hours, Peter Fitch, on and off was interviewed, by all four officers. Not once did he flinch or stumble. At the time presented to him by the officers he was teaching at his school. In the evening, he'd filled up with petrol. There would be CCTV somewhere, and he'd purchased a takeaway from his local Chinese. They would vouch for him as he's a regular customer. Yes the man in the photo looked incredibly, yes exactly like him. It was bizarre. But IT WASN'T HIM. Towards the end, the incredibly calm and so far, patient Mr Fitch had started to become a little animated.

Understandably so, the four officers concurred, when they'd finished. Raymond Ballinger took responsibility for giving Jane the bad news.

"There's no way this guy is our man, ma'am. I know what the face recognition is telling us but this guy's got more alibis than I've had hot dinners. Either the face recognition system has made an error, it has been known, or someone has got to the hotel's CCTV. Somehow doctored it." Jane was aware they were already checking for the latter but decided not to pass this on. The fewer people who knew the better.

"Ok, thanks guys. Sorry you've had a wasted journey."

"That's alright ma'am. Oh, by the way. The chief up here wants to know who's paying for all of this? Firearms officers aren't cheap apparently." He heard the line go dead. Turning to all who were gathered. "Well, she took that well. Let's say goodbye to Mr Pindar shall we. This will be embarrassing."

Ardres, France

Marie took a deep breath and knocked. There was no going back now.

Inside, the late Capitaine Maubert's wife and her daughter were glued to the tv, watching live coverage of the press conference at the gendarmerie in Calais. The knocking was an annoyance, the timing couldn't be worse.

"If that's another bloody journalist, I won't be responsible for my actions." The daughter got to her feet. "You can record it, mama." Her mother's facial expression was one of complete confusion. "Like this." The daughter grabbed the remote from her mother's hand and pressed. A red box with the letters 'rec' appeared on the screen. She gave her mother back the remote. "There, now we won't miss anything. Now who the bloody hell can it be." The daughter marched, rather than walked, into the hallway.

Marie was just about to knock again when the door was thrown open. For several seconds both women eyed each other, neither said a word. Neither of them had expected to see the other and both were silenced through shock. The daughter, recovered first, she had inherited the Gallic in her from her ancestors. Blood rushed to her cheeks and she screamed.

"Hooooowwwww could you. You dirty little slut. Connasse, poufiasse,petasse, salope."

Marie had never heard so much foul language in one sentence, and especially not from a woman. She began to shake. This was a mistake. She had made a massive, massive mistake.

"I'm sorry." In comparison to the daughter's, outburst it was nothing more than a whimper.

"Degage, DEGAGE!" The daughter advanced on Marie.

"Marie?" The name was softly spoken. "Why have you come here? To gloat?" The voice remained soft, there was no threat, no menace. It was obvious that Madame Maubert had been crying but her composure was holding and, if anything, she looked remarkably calm. She looked at Marie, not with hate, not with disgust but with complete neutrality. Almost as if, she wasn't there.

"Don't talk to her mama, don't talk to her. SALOPE." The last word was directed at Marie."

"Shhhhh, cheri. Let her talk, it can't have been easy for her to come here. It must have taken a lot of courage. Why have you come Marie?"

Her daughter had never seen her mother like this. Her mother had always been the quiet one. The steady woman, doing good deeds. The perfect, loyal little housewife. Watching on, her daughter was caught between disgust and surprise.

"Why have you come Marie?" Her mother said again.

Marie was struggling to speak. She was finding it hard to express herself, to find the right words. Before she'd knocked she'd prepared a speech in her head but that was now shredded into a million little pieces.

"Marie?"

Marie took a deep breath. She was wary of the daughter and thanked God she wasn't carrying a knife. Finally she managed to work the muscles in her mouth to say just one word. 'Sorry.'

"Huh." The expression was uttered in contempt.

"Shhh Cheri, let the girl speak." The mother's voice remained soft but now it also carried notes of strength. A strength that grew with every word spoken.

"To say the photos aren't what they look like. Your husband and I never had an affair. He was one of the few gendarmes who listened to me. He was the best, your husband, Madame Maubert." Everyone stood for a moment, even the daughter, without a word being uttered.

"You'd better come in, Marie." Madame Maubert stood back to allow Marie access. Her daughter's eye's blazed in anger. "Not a word cheri." Madame Maubert smiled gently at her daughter. "I want to hear what the young woman has to say, can you make us all coffee. How do you like your coffee Marie?"

"I'm not making that…."

"S'il te plait cheri. For me." The daughter relented.

"Ok for you, mama. But that bitch will have it as it comes."

"How you wish, cheri but try and be courteous in front of your mama. This is MY house you're in, after all." The daughter actually blushed and stormed into the kitchen to make coffee as asked, ordered more like. She still couldn't believe that that salope was in her mother's house.

The next hour passed with surprising cordiality. The first ten minutes were tense but as Marie grew in confidence, she started to relax and was able to get her side of the story across. And her story started with her first approaching Capitaine Maubert regarding the missing migrants. I never thought he'd listen to me, she had said. But he did, he took me seriously. A gendarme. Your husband and later she also used the word dad was a good man. She kept repeating this. Marie, hoped she'd managed to convince both the woman that the kiss had been nothing, and she stressed that she had no idea who had taken the photo. Obviously it was someone who either didn't like her or didn't like the capitaine. Perhaps both. Finally she spoke about Ismail, how she had introduced Capitaine Maubert to him. How Ismail had stayed with some friends of hers and now her friends had disappeared, and Ismail's decapitated head had ended up being delivered to his wife in London.

"I'm scared, really really scared," she kept repeating. "I've got no friends. All of Calais now hates me, and I've been desperate to tell you the truth." Marie started to cry. Mother and daughter looked at each other. No longer was there hatred in the daughter's eyes. Suspicion yes but not hatred.

"You're not alone Marie, if you're telling the truth, you have us. We will find strength together in this. You're welcome to come and see me." Madame Maubert looked across at her daughter. "Us, as often as you want. Whenever you feel scared, you can come here. And I'm sure the gendarmerie will do all they can to protect you."

"The gendarmerie hates me. They hated me before. They hate me even more now. Many there would be pleased to find me lying dead in the street." Marie stared straight at mother and daughter, they both looked to be visually shocked by her outburst. Marie immediately felt a pang of guilt. She hadn't come here to shock, but for forgiveness. "I'm sorry, I'm a bit emotional. And thank you for your offer, it means a lot."

"It's a genuine one Marie." The mother rose, walking to the bureau. She opened a small notepad and started scribbling. Returning she handed a page to Marie. "That's my number, and that's my daughter's. If you ever feel the need, or if you're scared. Please feel free to call either of us." Marie looked across at the daughter. And to her surprise the daughter nodded.

"Yes Marie, please do." Tears started to roll down Marie's cheeks. "Thank you, I'll text you both my number now."

Ten minutes later, the daughter was driving Marie back to her terraced house in Calais. The mother watched them go. Poor girl, she thought. She's lonelier than me. I have my family and Thierry's soul is still here. She hadn't asked after Marie's family. Thierry had spoken often about Marie, she'd never been a secret. And in the past hour Marie had corroborated much of what her husband had told her. She also remembered him saying that Marie often referred to the migrants as 'her family.' More than once he'd told her that he suspected Marie either didn't have or was estranged from her family. After what she'd just witnessed she believed her husband had been right. She needed to speak to Lieutenant Beaufort. She dialled his number. Answerphone. She dialled again. Again answerphone. In frustration she called Colette. Colette answered. Of course she would. Colette always did. She was to be disappointed though. The lieutenant was in a meeting with the replacement capitaine.

"What's he like?" She couldn't help wondering.

"First impressions? He's rude. Typical bloody Parisian."

The late capitaine's wife smiled at this. That was so unlike Colette. He must really be rude, arrogant too if she knew anything about Parisians. After finishing the call, she found she needed Thierry. She needed to feel his presence. Where better than hallowed ground, his office. Not for the first time she found herself wallowing in the high-backed chair that had helped her husband's escape from the pressures of being a capitaine in the gendarme. Turning on the stereo, she picked up a CD that she'd found lying by itself on the desk. Flipping open the cover she extracted the last CD, Yungblud, and replaced it with the new one. After closing the tray she pressed play. Slow exotic music began to sound, and a lady's voice, soulful, wailing, desperate began to sing a story. She loved it. She'd never heard anything like it. Picking up the CD case she looked at the cover. It was paper and on it handwritten biro the words, 'A gift, Ya Sidi, Orange Blossom. She leant back, closing her eyes. The music stirred her. It reached deep inside her soul. Extracting feelings that for a long time had been buried deeper than deep. A pleasurable moan parted her lips. Never had she felt so turned on by a simple tune. She really shouldn't be feeling like this but she couldn't help herself.

Gendarmerie Nationale, Calais, France

Capitaine Olivier Vendroux watched from his car as the press conference finished and the journalists started to disband. The replacement for Capitaine Maubert after his tragic death was not impressed. In his opinion the press conference had been a complete shambles, an embarrassment in front of the world's media. And that last question from the American, he would never have allowed it. In his view the whole proceedings had been nothing but a performance wallowing in self-pity. At times like these the gendarmerie had to demonstrate it had a spine. Not that they were a bunch of blubbering wimps.

As the last of the media squeezed out of the car park, the capitaine roared his car in, coming to an abrupt halt in front of the stage. Stepping out, he grabbed a case from the passenger seat, and on seeing a gendarme, threw him his keys.

"Park that for me." The gendarme hesitated. "I'm your new capitaine," he flashed his card. Now park my car. And why haven't you saluted? I'm in full uniform." The gendarme after a quick salute rushed to park the Alpine A110. Colette saw what was happening from her window, and after smartening herself in front of a mirror, waited in the foyer, ready to greet her new boss.

Lieutenant Beaufort also saw, who he assumed was their new capitaine pull up in front of the stage. Flash git, he murmured under his breath and walked across holding his right hand out in welcome.

"Lieutenant Beaufort sir. I assume you're our new capitaine, Capitaine Vendroux. Bienvenue a Calais."

Instead of taking the lieutenant's hand, their new capitaine saluted.

"Were you responsible for that excuse for a press conference? I assume you were. It was a bloody mess." The lieutenant was stunned.

"Yes sir but I don't…."

"Think." The capitaine finished the sentence for him. "No you didn't think, why didn't you use the Hotel de Ville like my predecessor?" The capitaine didn't wait for an answer, instead he made for the doors accessing the gendarmerie's reception. Lieutenant Beaufort, shocked as well as feeling angry, followed. On seeing the two enter Colette stepped out in greeting.

"Bonjour Monsieu…."

"Capitaine, you will address me as capitaine, what sort of place is this?" The capitaine turned to the lieutenant, "a bloody holiday camp? I thought it was meant to be a gendarmerie. Am I in the wrong place?"

"No sir."

"Well prove it, lieutenant." The capitaine turned to Colette. "I assume you must be Colette?"

"Yes Capitaine Vendroux." The capitaine's tone softened.

"I've heard very good reports about you Colette, I hope we will work well together. Now would you mind bringing myself and the lieutenant some fresh coffee. Lieutenant will you show me to my office."

"Up the stairs sir." The capitaine started to mount. Before he followed the lieutenant turned to Colette and mouthed, 'connard.' Colette tried not to laugh.

Five minutes later, Capitaine Vendroux, (the lieutenant knew from reading the file that the capitaine's first name was Olivier, though he doubted from what he'd witnessed so far that he'd ever use it), and Lieutenant Beaufort were sitting in what had been, until a few days ago, Capitaine's Maubert's office. The lieutenant was finding it hard to accept that a new man was now sitting behind the desk. The capitaine's first question surprised him.

"Tell me about yourself, Lieutenant Beaufort. I've read your file, of course but tell me about you, the man. Your family, your likes and dislikes. Where you'd like to be a year on from now."

The lieutenant told him and the capitaine listened. For the next hour the conversation continued in the same vein. The capitaine asked about the men and women who worked under him. Their characters, who the lieutenant trusted the most and who was best in a tight or dangerous situation. After a bad start, their conversation flowed surprisingly easily. The lieutenant even found himself beginning to relax. Lastly, the capitaine asked about his predecessor. What sort of man he was, or rather had been. How had he run the gendarmerie. At the end, the capitaine praised his predecessor. 'They're big boots to fill but fill them I will,' were his exact words.

For the following hour, the capitaine asked to be taken over the case that most of the gendarmerie had been working on. The case that had made world headlines. The lieutenant went over everything, in detail but felt it wise not to mention that he had in his possession Capitaine Maubert's personal files and diary.

The last conversation came as a complete surprise.

"Lieutenant, your first assignment, or order under me. Tomorrow morning there's specialist transport coming from our friends across the water. Le Royaume-Uni. They will be picking up from La Morgue, Centre Hospitalier Boulogne. They will require an escort back to the ferry port and there are to be no custom checks. The douanes already know as do the UK's border force. On our side you must ensure that no overzealous douanier, (customs officer), interferes with the cargo. The pick up and delivery have been authorised and agreed at the highest level in both governments."

"Can I ask what the cargo is?" The order came as a complete shock to the lieutenant. Not since he'd joined the gendarmerie had he ever heard of or been involved in anything like this. Not only was it a shock, but he felt it to be highly suspicious.

"Yes I'm authorised to tell you." The capitaine leaned forward, resting his elbows on the desk. "But what I'm about to tell you, does not leave this room. You understand?"

"Of course not, sir."

"A few days ago, a boat was brought into harbour, and on it you discovered the bodies of twelve unfortunate children along with two adults. The British via Interpol requested the DNA of the victims. From all accounts, they know who the bodies belong to and are part of an ongoing investigation on their soil. Their government has bypassed us and requested our government for their immediate return. Our government has sanctioned their request. Not just sanctioned it but ordered it, and that their passage is not to be hindered in any way. That's where we come in."

The lieutenant couldn't believe what he was hearing.

"But those bodies are vital evidence in an investigation that is very much live."

"I appreciate your concern, lieutenant, I really do, but this I'm afraid is out of our hands. There's nothing you or I can do."

Lieutenant Beaufort stared at the floor, this wasn't right. The whole thing stank. He had a question.

"If the British authorities know who these people are can we at least have that information. We may be able to connect them with what's been going on here?"

"I've already put in that request, lieutenant. Now can you see to it that there's no hiccups tomorrow. I don't want anything embarrassing to happen, not on my first day."

"I'll take personal charge, sir."

"Good and after that, I'd like you to report back here. I want to go over this case with you. After that I'd like to start being introduced to the men. Not by group, one by one."

"Yes sir, what time is the transport due tomorrow?"

"I need you to meet it at the morgue at five am. And I want four cars acting as an escort."

"Four!"

"Yes lieutenant. Our government regard the cargo as high risk, as do the British. We must assume that somebody else, a third party might want to get their hands on this cargo. And it's our duty to ensure that doesn't happen."

"Why aren't the military involved if it's that important? Sorry for my questions sir."

"No that's fine lieutenant, you have a right to ask. I guess it's because our government doesn't want to draw unwanted attention. Anyway, there will be six British military personnel travelling with the van. That is the information I've been given, also that they won't be in uniform. You can begin to understand why our government doesn't want the douane asking embarrassing questions."

Lieutenant Beaufort shook his head. He found the whole thing highly unusual, not to mention suspect. But orders were orders. Ten minutes later he was rounding up volunteers for the early morning task force. It didn't take long, it would mean overtime and the lieutenant had presented the assignment as something of an adventure. As he was about to catch up with paperwork in his office, Colette caught him.

"Monsieur Beaufort."

"Lieutenant you mean." Colette punched him on the arm.

"Don't you start. The Capitaine's wife, Monsieur Maubert's wife has been trying to get hold of you. Can you ring her?" The lieutenant had seen he'd received a couple of missed calls. He nodded.

"Will do."

"What's he like? The new capitaine. I'm a little surprised to see you've come out alive!"

The lieutenant grinned at Colette's false show of concern.

"I'm glad you care Colette. Actually, you know, I think he's ok. I think he'll be alright."

Hervelinghen, France

In the tiny hamlet of Hervelinghen not far from Cap Blanc Nez. In the kitchen of a low, long whitewashed house, with a red tile roof. Typical of the region. Facing each other across the kitchen table, sat a young couple, Jean and Camille. The house belonged to Camille's parents, and she still lived with them. Jean lived in a room above the café where he worked. Le Week End in Sangatte. That evening Camille's parents were out for a few hours visiting friends. Normally the couple would have taken full advantage of their freedom and spent the hours naked in her bed. It would have made a nice change from Jean's car.

Instead the couple were deep in conversation, an intense sometimes heated conversation. The conversation revolved around what they might have seen that night on Cap Blanc Nez. Jean was adamant they'd seen Capitaine Maubert pushed to his death. Camille was adamant it was only a maybe. Anyway why risk going to the gendarmerie, Camille argued. Those bastards would probably only try and pin it on us.

Jean admitted Camille may be right. From personal experience the gendarmes had never treated him well. The West African expression, 'give a man a uniform,' had certainly, as far as he was concerned been very apt in his run-ins with them. However Jean had a strong sense of duty and the American's question at the press conference had stirred that sense.

The earlier than expected arrival of Camille's parents cut short the discussion. They agreed to leave it for another day at least.

"A good job we stayed in the kitchen." Camille whispered, imagine if we hadn't. They were both still giggling when her parents entered.

"What do you two find so funny?" Their giggling turned to laughter at her mother's question.

Formby, Lancashire, England

James felt virtually ecstatic on arriving home safely, after work. It always felt good to arrive home after work, but that evening felt extra special.

All day at work he had regularly checked his phone. The only messages or calls he had received were from people he knew, friends. Nothing from anybody who may mean him harm. There'd been no one waiting for him outside work, and he was pretty sure nobody had followed him home. And now that he was home, there was no car parked outside with strangers watching his house.

James rarely drank, but that evening he felt like celebrating. It was obvious to him that whoever had wanted him to falsify dozens of death certificates had come to their senses. What they were asking of him was simply impossible, finally the penny had dropped. He'd managed to do one and that hadn't been easy. They'd just have to be content with one now and again. Going to a fridge in his garage he took out a couple of bottles of Stella. Not bothering with a glass he drank from the bottle. My, it felt good.

"What are you celebrating?" His wife asked, settling their child in his highchair.

Chapter 4

Drury Lane, Covent Garden, England

Roger stood across the street looking up at the darkening windows of John's flat. Was it he being stupid or was there a presence about the building. A sad presence as though the place was in mourning. Where the bloody hell are you John? How many times had he asked that question recently? Too many.

After finishing at the bakery in Putney, he had phoned Jane for an update. She had told him that the suspect taken from face recognition had turned out to be a nonstarter. He had over forty alibis. Shit, that had been his one hope. Hopefully, their forensic examination of the CCTV footage may throw something up. And if it did, whoever had tampered with it may have left some clues. They'd have to wait and see.

Standing outside the front door stood a uniformed officer. Poor bugger, he must be so bored. Under the circumstances Jane had considered it a necessity. He knew the lock had also been changed and that the officer held a key for the new one. Roger wanted to have another look around the flat. On the last occasion the circumstances had been a little stressful to say the least. Under those circumstances he may have missed something. He knew SOCOs had gone over everything but what he may see they wouldn't be looking for. They'd be picking up on what the eye couldn't see, where as he would be looking for the bleeding obvious, such as the bloody missing laptop. He was still kicking himself for not thinking of that at the time.

He'd mentioned to Jane that he wanted to have another look around John's flat and she had ensured, at least he hoped that she had ensured, that the officer outside would be expecting him and let him in. He felt it better that the right people knew, rather than try and attempt a second clandestine visit. If he was caught inside without anyone knowing, some awkward questions may be asked. Drury Lane was busy that night. The time meant that office workers were leaving for home and West End tourists were just arriving, their faces lit with expectation.

Rather than cross the road, Roger walked up to Long Acre, returning a few minutes later with a cappuccino along with sachets of sugar and a wooden stirrer. He smiled as he approached the officer handing him the coffee.

"I thought you could do with this. I'm…" The officer cut in.

"I know who you are sir, Roger Denton, Director with the NCA. Since the explosion we've all been shown your mug shot near on a thousand times. Thanks for the coffee." The officer accepted Roger's offering in a manner that told him a coffee was well overdue.

"I've been where you are now, I know what it's like."

"Yeah hellish." The officer busied himself stirring the sugar.

"You do know I'm coming?" The officer nodded.

"Yes, I got the call around an hour ago. There's a lot of people interested in this flat, you're one of a fair few I'm to expect." This was news to Roger.

"Can you tell me who they are?"

"Sorry sir no. Strict orders. Do you want me to let you in? The SOCOs finished a couple of hours ago." The officer, without waiting for an answer, turned and opened the door.

"Thank you, I shouldn't be long." Roger ducked under the officer's arm and mounted the stairs to his ex-colleague's flat. Going from room to room he switched on every light. The flat was eerily silent, as though ghosts had taken over from the human form. Roger had no wish to stay there longer than was necessary. What was he missing. What was staring him in the face. Not the laptop, he was sure there was something else. Speak to me John, speak to me John, his mind whispered. What were you up to in the days before the Hilton? What weren't you telling me? There was that woman, Maureen, or Bree as John had told him she called herself. Why lie about her name? She must have been a honey trap. But for who? Had she been here? To this flat? He couldn't remember if John had told him. Looking around he could see no evidence of a woman having been there. Maybe the SOCOs had found evidence. It was something they were good at. Roger walked from the bedroom back into the lounge and looked out of the window over Drury Lane. There were so many places where somebody interested in his ex-colleague, or even what was happening now, could watch the place without being seen. His team had checked and in an average month there were over twenty flats available to rent in Drury Lane. It would be easy for someone with mal intent to take one on a rolling contract. If John wasn't discovered soon they'd have to check with all the rental agencies. A laborious and thankless task.

Roger's thoughts were interrupted by the sound of somebody coming up the stairs. Surprised, he spun round. He wasn't carrying a weapon, if it wasn't the officer guarding the place he hoped it was someone friendly. Perhaps it was John, back from wherever! It wasn't but it was a face he recognised.

"Hello Roger of the NCA. What are you doing here?"

"I could ask you the same question J J" Roger couldn't remember his name. He recognised him from the Tea House, the man who had given him a card. He had also been at the meeting in Whitehall but hadn't said a word. Just listened. He flicked his wrist in frustration, why couldn't he remember his name?

"Jason, Jason Mortimer. It's ok, I wouldn't expect you to remember. Anyway I prefer to be Mr Anonymous. Why am I here? Because you're here. So why are you here Roger?" The man smiled. His smile wasn't condescending, it was though somehow, disarming. Roger shrugged.

"It's no secret. I'm sure you're aware of our operation."

"Yes a little unfortunate."

"You're being kind, it's a bloody mess. Well in the past Mr Mitchell and I served together. We know each other from a distance, so to speak."

"Except you came to see him, here. Not long ago."

"Yes it's on record," Roger was nervous, what did this guy know? "I wanted a quiet word with John before everything became too official. I hoped he may tell me something that he wouldn't reveal in a normal interview."

"And did he?" The man, Jason, moved to the window. To where Roger had been standing a minute or so before. Roger shook his head. Needlessly because Jason was watching the street, not him.

"No, only that he'd met a new woman, and he wasn't sure whether to trust her or not."

"Ah yes, Maureen Fowlis." Jason continued looking out the window. Roger said nothing. He'd probably be wasting his breath anyway. So Jason already knew, how did he know?. Jason turned to face him. Look, Roger, shall we have a chat?"

"Why not," Roger shrugged his shoulders. "Shall we sit down?" Roger moved to an armchair.

"No not here. We don't know who we're dealing with. For all we know the place could be bugged. Somebody in a little room somewhere could be watching us on a monitor right this minute." Jason proceeded to move from room to room waving his right arm in exaggerated fashion. "Hello, hello whoever you are." He returned to the window, "or someone, somewhere in a flat out there could be using a shotgun mic to listen in on our conversation. No let's go for a little walk." He stared to hum. "Down by the riverside. I'm showing my age." He laughed. "Shall we?" With that he started to descend the stairs. Roger bemused, and confused, followed. This man was out of his league and the fact that he was really pissed him off.

Chapter 4

Gendarmerie Nationale, Calais, France

After speaking to Capitaine Maubert's wife, Lieutenant Beaufort was more than a little concerned. The late capitaine's wife had wanted to speak to him, one to clear her late husband, his ex-boss's name from his alleged infidelity and secondly to let him know that Marie came across as being really scared. Terrified in fact. When he'd asked why, she had told him a story about a severed head being delivered to a woman in London. And that Marie had been hiding the victim whose head it was, and apparently with her husband's full knowledge, at a friend's house just outside Calais. Her friends had disappeared too, along with the man they'd been hiding, and now the severed head of the man had turned up in London. She was worried that the same thing may happen to her friends, perhaps even, as she was involved, delivered to her. Worse still she's worried that whoever had taken her friends, for she's sure that's what happened, may come and take her. She'd been adamant that her friends wouldn't simply disappear. Her last comment hit him between the eyes. Marie had pointed out that everyone who had been involved with hiding this man had either disappeared or turned up dead. Her friends, the migrant who'd they been hiding and CAPITAINE MAUBERT. Madame Maubert couldn't remember the man's name. Ismail? He'd asked but no, Marie hadn't mentioned the man's name. She was sure. He had promised Madame Maubert after she'd given him Marie's number that he'd call her right away.

Sitting in his office, he picked up the phone. Marie must have been talking about Ismail. The migrant who had been interviewed by Capitaine Maubert. Ismail, who had been kidnapped supposedly, along with a number of others, promised safe passage to Royaume-Uni. In a recording given to the late capitaine, he had described his experience and how he'd been lucky to escape. His testimony had led to them raiding the restaurant on the summit of Mont d'Hubert though nothing had been found.

The gendarmerie since, had known Ismail had disappeared. Scarpered was the general assumption, most likely to the other side of La Manche. Why though had they not been told that the couple apparently, who'd been hiding him, had also disappeared. And more worryingly, why had the gendarmerie not been told, that the severed head delivered to an address somewhere in London, was the head of Ismail? Someone apparently their Capitaine had been protecting. That in itself raised a lot of questions. It was the job of the gendarmerie to protect a witness, not an individual. The whole thing stank. And Marie's last observation rang all sorts of alarm bells. He knew about the severed head in London from the news. The British media though had made the connection with another head found somewhere along the south coast, which had turned out to have belonged to a very vicious gangster. The assumption was that both heads were, therefore, gangster related.

He was just about to ring Marie on the number that Madame Maubert had given him, when he had a thought. He rang through to Colette.

"Oui, Monsieur Beaufort."

"Lieutenant," Lieutenant Beaufort joked. "Colette, have we had any communication from les Rosbifs in the last couple of days." Les Rosbifs, (roast beef), is the nickname the French use to describe us, just as we use the nickname frogs. He could hear Colette tapping her keyboard.

"Oui, a Monsieur Denton, Roger Denton rang from something called the NCA wanting to speak to the capitaine. Capitaine Maubert, not the new capitaine. I've sent a note to the fact along with his number to our new capitaine. Interpol apparently, have also been in touch with the commandant, though I'm sure Capitaine Vendroux will already be aware of this."

"Ok, thank you Colette." The lieutenant replaced the receiver. Was this the reason why Paris had sent a new replacement so quickly? And why he'd been appointed by Paris, not locally which is normally the custom? And now there was the escorting of the bodies from the morgue. Sanctioned by the upper echelons of both his country's and the British governments. Something big was going on, he was sure of it. But why wasn't he being kept in the loop? He had a meeting with their new capitaine tomorrow morning. Following the safe escort of the 'special delivery.' He would make notes and prepare questions for Capitaine Vendroux tomorrow. He thought of something else and once more buzzed through to Colette. He waited thirty seconds but there was no answer. He looked at the clock on the wall. Shit, she would have gone home. He'd ask her in the morning. He looked at the number on his note pad, the number for Marie. He was sure the gendarmerie would have it logged somewhere. He dialled using his personal mobile. After a few rings the phone went to voice mail. He was going to leave a message but decided against it. For the next half hour he busied himself with paperwork. It was time to go. Once more he tried Marie, again he got the answer phone. Once more he decided not to leave a voicemail.

Before leaving he went to the capitaine's office to say he was going home and that he'd organised the escort for tomorrow. When he got there Capitaine Vendroux was on the phone. He signalled through the glass in the door that he was leaving. The capitaine mouthed, escort? Lieutenant Beaufort nodded. The capitaine gave him a thumbs up and put his head down concentrating on his call.

The Lieutenant lived in Coulogne, arguably a Calais suburb, though the residents of Coulogne hated it being described so. He arrived to find his dinner prepared on the kitchen table, all he had to do was heat it up. Of course it was card night, his wife was at her friend's house playing cards. There was a group of them, eight or so and they would take it in turns to hold a game at each other's houses. After heating his dinner, the lieutenant poured himself a Ricard and sat down to watch that evening's sport on tv. At ten pm his wife still wasn't home, this was quite normal with card night. With an early start tomorrow he decided he wouldn't wait up, he needed his sleep. Remembering Marie he tried her one more time. It was late but he was sure she wouldn't mind. The phone rang twice and went to answer phone. He screwed up his face in frustration, he'd try her again in the morning.

Back at the gendarmerie, Capitaine Vendroux was also ready for bed. It had been a very long day and he'd driven from Paris that morning. For tonight, he was booked into a hotel in Calais Nord. He was really looking forward to it. From tomorrow, he'd be sleeping in gendarmerie accommodation until he'd sorted out something more permanent. Not too permanent he hoped, for from what he'd seen of Calais so far, he hated the place. After saying goodnight to the officer manning reception, he walked across the car park to where he could see his car. As he neared it, he searched for his keys, they weren't in his pocket. He remembered, he'd given them to an officer on arrival, instructing him to park his car. Swearing the capitaine walked back to reception.

"Are my keys there, the keys to my car?" The officer manning reception looked puzzled, negative, no keys. The capitaine described the officer who'd parked his car for him.

"You mean Manuel sir, he finished over four hours ago."

"And he hasn't left my keys?"

"No sir, sorry sir."

Merde, bloody merde. Calais, he hated the place and everyone in it!

Chapter 4

Covent Garden, London, England

To Roger Denton, considering the circumstances Jason looked incredibly relaxed. Hands in his pockets, and dressed only in a shirt and trousers, it was also apparent he was impervious to the cold. In contrast Roger had an Eton style scarf pulled tight around his neck and his Magee camel coloured peacoat, buttoned up as far as it would go. After leaving the flat Jason strode briskly up Drury Lane towards Long Acre, with Roger struggling to keep alongside. The only thing that slowed him down were people passing in the opposite direction, on a very narrow pavement. It was obvious to Roger that Jason was on a mission.

"Do you fancy a beer?" Normally, Roger would jump at such an offer, but his lack of sleep was beginning to creep up on him and his head was beginning to hurt. A beer or two might kill him off! A beer or two and Jason, Mr Anonymous definitely would. However, he knew he had no choice. He had no idea what the man wanted but he assumed they were playing for the same side and a chat may be useful. He wondered if Jane knew he was here.

"I never say no to a beer," Roger tried to smile. "Have you anywhere in mind?" Jason didn't slow, turning right along Long Acre.

"Yes, the Lamb and Flag, do you know it?" Roger didn't but he remembered John talking about it and said so. "He's got good taste that Mr Mitchell," Jason quickened his pace. Were they in a race?

The two approached The Lamb and Flag via a narrow alley leading off Floral Street. The long and obviously very old bar was packed with early evening trade, almost entirely people who worked or lived locally. Tourists were always easily identifiable and there weren't any that Roger could see. And yet they were but a stone's throw from both Covent Garden Piazza and Leicester Square. The bar was music free and loud with good old conversation. Roger couldn't see for a minute how Jason intended to have a discreet chat in here.

Lamb and Flag, Covent Garden, London

"I love this place," Jason told Roger looking back over his shoulder. "They've got Olivers Island on, do you fancy a pint of that? It'll freshen you up rather than send you to sleep." Roger nodded. Was his lack of sleep that telling? Obviously, it was.

"Yes whatever." Somehow Jason managed to get served quickly and lifted the beers over the heads of others waiting to be served, followed with two plates, each with a scotch egg.

"Upstairs." Jason nodded to a narrow wooden staircase which halfway up, bent back on itself. At the turn there was a door for the ladies' toilet. The bar upstairs was incredibly quiet, almost empty, and if it wasn't for the décor you would think yourself in a different pub. To the left of the room were two large sash windows and the only other people there were sitting at two tables in front of these. Jason chose a table at the opposite end of the room. They were on their own, incredible considering where they were. Good choice thought Roger, this man knows what he's doing. Jason took a long sip on his pint.

"Cheers," he said afterwards and lifted his glass.

"Good choice," Roger congratulated him.

"Yes no one, will be eavesdropping here, if they tried they'd stick out a mile." Roger had to agree, he was right. They would. "It's a great pub too and the best scotch egg you'll ever find." Jason ignoring his knife and fork, picked it up and took a bite. He closed his eyes as he ate, enjoying, for a few seconds, his own little heaven. Roger preferring a knife and fork cut out a quarter and placed it in his mouth. Jason was right, he'd never tasted a scotch egg like it. Finishing his mouthful, Jason dabbed at his face with his napkin and took another swig of beer. "Do you know, your Mr Mitchell and I have something in common." Roger looked at him in surprise. "Yes, we both worked in Covent Garden in the early eighties and fell in love with the place. Once Covent Garden gets you, not the touristy stuff but the soul, it lives with you forever. Look at this place." Jason arced his free arm towards the empty bar.

This represents Covent Garden, the real Covent Garden. Do you know, when I was in my early twenties I used to come up here every Tuesday night. Do you know why?" Roger didn't of course, he shook his head, at the same time devouring another quarter of scotch egg. "They used to hold poetry readings up here. I used to love them, especially in winter. The only light was from the log fire and candles, and the readers were just incredible. Dickens used to drink here and he wouldn't have felt out of place, if he came here during the eighties to one of those poetry readings." Jason looked animated, more animated than discussing John in his flat.

"I can't believe I've never heard of the place." Roger genuinely found it hard to believe he hadn't.

"That's the great thing about it, it's at the centre of everything and yet it's almost invisible. Back in the day, they used to have whole cheeses from Neal's Yard Dairy behind a bar. If you wanted cheese, they'd chisel a piece off and serve with bread and if you were lucky a pickled onion. Sadly, that's gone and so has Neal's Yard, it's been replaced by a modern development called Seven Dials Market. Such a bloody shame."

"Progress," Roger offered.

"Modern vandalism, I call it. That's why I love this place, it never changes. Do you know out front there's still a working gas light. I'm told fuelled by the methane from the pub's toilets, though that may be romantic thinking." Jason laughed. Hardly romantic Roger thought. He couldn't make Jason out, was this idle, sometimes enthused chat designed to drop his own defences. If it was the man was a bloody good actor. Jason laughed again. "Do you know, it may be an urban myth but either way it's a bloody good one. The story is that this pub was the last one in London not to have a toilet for women. It also used to be a venue where bare knuckle fighting took place. In fact, some people still refer to it as the Blood and Bucket. Anyway it was no place for a woman. The pub in more recent times came under pressure to put in a ladies'. Well, you've seen the place it's so old not to mention small and apparently the owners argued that there simply wasn't room. Anyway things soon came to a head and the owners were forced to comply. Well the story goes, they built it where you saw it, on the stairs. I've seen women come close to breaking their leg trying to get in and out. Especially after a few drinks. It's probably not true but it's a great story." Jason laughed whilst finishing what was left of his scotch egg. "Another?" He'd also finished his beer.

"I'll..." Jason held Roger's shoulder.

"No you don't." Jason pushed Roger back into his chair. "Where I work I get these on expenses." Holding up his empty glass, Jason grinned.

Where, who do you work for? Roger was determined to find out before the evening was over. He rubbed his face, he hoped their little chat would be over soon, he was fading fast and really worried about drinking a second beer. In under five minutes Jason was back. Not only was he carrying two fresh pints he also had in his hand a grey plastic mailing bag.

"Special delivery," he dropped the bag on the table before carefully placing the two glasses and sitting down. Roger noticed his demeanour had changed a little. This time Roger decided to start the conversation.

"Who do you work for Jason? Your card, if you don't mind me saying, speaks volumes." Jason took a sip from his beer. Not the long draughts he took with his first beer, this time it was just a sip. Roger's training taught him to pick up on such things, and he wondered if the last half hour of frivolity had been Jason's way of sizing him up. Jason looked serious for a second and then his smile was back.

"I work for the department nobody speaks about, that most don't know about. I'm Mr Anonymous in a department called anonymity. I work for MI nothing." Although Jason was smiling when he said this, Roger sensed he was being serious.

"But you're not anonymous Jason. You're Jason, or am I meant to feel honoured to know that?"

Jason grinned his biggest grin so far.

"How do you know that's my name Roger? You only know because I gave you a card, a card that I could have printed on a machine in a newsagent. Next week I could be Damien or perhaps even Roger. I can be whoever I want you to think I am."

Roger found himself feeling a little stupid. Jason was right of course, a young kid could have printed that card. Jason rescued him from his embarrassment.

"Of course, the powers that be wouldn't let me attend a meeting with the heads of the intelligence agencies, government ministers and even the prime minister if my calling card said Donald Duck. My presence there, will, I hope demonstrate we're batting for the same side."

The man who may or may not be Jason, for the first time looked directly at him. Roger played with his first beer. The man opposite him, by enthusing about Covent Garden had given a small piece of himself away. A very small piece but it was a genuine piece. Roger had no doubt about that. Was this his way of telling him, look you can trust me?

"I don't feel I can give you anything, if I don't know who you work for." Why did he feel guilty saying this to Jason, if he was Jason. Anyway, that was Jason's problem, not his. Roger looked at the man sitting across the table, he'd expected a negative reaction. But there wasn't one, Jason didn't look offended. Quite the opposite, his facial expression was one of understanding.

"I don't want you to tell me anything Roger, I'm here to give you information. Some signposts if you like. That's what I do in my job, give people signposts. Help people to avoid taking the wrong direction."

"Is that what you think I'm doing? Taking the wrong direction?"

"How did your sting go with Mr Mitchell?"

"You know."

Jason smiled.

"Yes, I do, and the one sign you come up against is Dead End."

"Did you get this from Jane?"

"No." Jason took another sip of his beer.

"Look, I'm here to try and save you time. My department isn't equipped to launch an investigation. We keep an eye on things and if we think we can be of help. Well that's why I'm here." Jason grinned again. "Now I want to make one thing clear. Nobody has the faintest idea who destroyed your building, and they did a pretty good job. You'll get this officially soon but there were five explosive devices. All, it looks like, detonated by someone within the building at the time. So now, almost certainly dead."

"A suicide bomber?"

Jason taking another sip of his beer gave a single nod.

"In a sense yes, except the explosives in this case weren't strapped to their body. Somehow they'd managed to smuggle in a remote control. Even more worrying, every corpse, body if you prefer that has been recovered so far has been identified. We've run another security check on each and every one and guess what?" Jason didn't wait for Roger to answer. "Not one has thrown up a hint of suspicion, they all passed. All the bodies found within the NCA building, if they were still alive, and applied for a job today, they'd be accepted. Which means, we, as yet, haven't found the guilty body or there's something seriously wrong with our vetting system."

Roger wrapped both hands around his beer glass.

"Jane sent me a list of the dead. I knew most of them."

Jason, for the first time since they'd arrived in the pub looked deadly serious.

"Yes, it's an awful thought isn't it, that one of them may have…" His voice tailed off. "Anyway, the explosions aren't your problem, what I mean is, it's not your investigation. Your investigation is finding out the meaning of the three severed heads. How they are related and why. And your one lead is your ex-colleague and some would say friend, Mr John Mitchell."

Roger shrugged his shoulders, he wasn't going to deny it. And the severed heads? IF they were related, not how and why. Did Jason know something he didn't? For now, he'd leave it. He had another question.

"Do you think they're related in any way? I mean the explosions and my investigation? It's just that I have this feeling in my gut."

"And they're normally the best, Roger, my man. To be honest we don't know but they do have one thing in common."

Rogers ears pricked up.

"What's that?"

Jason grinned again.

"Whoever's behind both targets of interest, is running rings around you guys, the NCA. You could say they're making fools out of you and we can't have that, can we? And please don't be offended. I'm not directing that at you personally. If I thought you were a fool Roger, I wouldn't be wasting my time with you now."

"So why ARE you here?"

Jason smiled again. Roger felt he should be finding his smile annoying, but for some peculiar reason he didn't.

"I told you. Signposting. By offering you a few bits of what we know, bits that you'd find eventually anyway. We, I'm hoping you can fine tune your investigation. Speed things up, so to speak. Prevent you from wasting your time running up more dead ends."

"I suppose I should say thanks." Roger drained his first beer and took a sip from his second.

"Wait till you here what I have to say. You may not want to thank me at all after." Another smile.

"Try me." Roger's head was beginning to hurt. He needed his bed. He just wanted this man to tell him what he had and go.

Jason took another sip of his beer.

"As we met in Mr Mitchell's London home, let's start there."

"Fair enough." Three middle aged women who'd been sitting at one of the tables in front of a window, pushed their chairs back, the legs scraping the wooden floor. Standing, each prepared for the cold outside before descending the stairs laughing. Jason watched them go.

"I wonder what it's like to be carefree?"

For a second Roger thought he saw a touch of sadness in Jason's eyes. Then the smile was back.

"SOCOs went over the flat, apartment, whatever you want to call it. Even though, as yet we've no idea if a crime has been committed. How did you push that through? The warrant?"

"I'm just being prudent, the normal channels."

Jason raised an eyebrow at this.

"Really? You're good at convincing people. Let's hope civil liberty campaigners never find out."

"Why would they?"

Jason's smile widened.

"I collect information such as this in case such a nugget needs to be used at a later date. That's also my job collecting information. Oh and of course using it when needs be"

Roger thought this sounded rather like a threat and his expression soured. Jason's smile in contrast broadened even more.

"Don't look like that Roger my boy. I'm here to help remember. And if I'm honest, I think you did the right thing. Anyway, I can tell you the SOCOs found three sets of fingerprints in Mr Mitchell's flat. His, yours and I think we can safely assume the third set belongs to this woman he was dallying with. Mrs Maureen Fowlis. You DO know her name?"

Roger had been listening intently, how the fuck did he know about the fingerprints. He doubted if he'd receive that information for another day yet. Jason's question took him by surprise. He nodded.

"Yes."

"How?"

"Face recognition check."

Jason looked thoughtful.

"Why did you do that?"

Roger wanted to kick himself, he was tired. His guard was down.

"I told you Jason, I don't feel I can offer up information, if I don't know who you work for."

Jason of course smiled at this, but this time it was a knowing smile. He knows. Roger's blood pressure rose, he bloody knows why. But how does he know?

Jason, either oblivious to Roger's rise in blood pressure or simply choosing to ignore it, continued.

"Ok, and I assume you've checked her out, as have we. And she's clean, English widow, living off her husband's money in a seaside town close to Calais. Nothing wrong with that. She travelled to the UK a few days ago, the exact details are in there." Jason tapped the grey mailing bag, "and according to border records she has yet to return which suggests she's still here. But where and is she with your Mr Mitchell? Who has conveniently also disappeared. There's evidence of recent sexual activity at the flat but we don't believe Mrs Fowlis was staying there. Which means she may have been staying in a local hotel. To date we haven't been able to access her bank activity to check, as Mrs Fowlis has a French bank account and the French are a little more protective of that information than we are." Good for the French, Roger cheered silently. "It may, therefore, be worth checking the hotels in and around here to see if you can find if she was staying in one of them."

"Ok," Roger, hadn't until now really considered Maureen Fowlis to be a person of interest. Initially he'd thought she may be some sort of honey trap, but after checking her out he'd considered her to be no more than a middle aged thrill seeker. Perhaps he'd been wrong. "What's your interest in her, Jason?"

"None really except she's associated with the missing Mr Mitchell and she seems to have disappeared as well. A little suspicious, don't you think?"

Roger had to admit it was. But he couldn't understand why this man was so interested. If he was, as he appeared to claim, a member of the upper echelons of the security services, why was he so interested in what was, on the surface anyway, a battle between gangsters. A bloody one yes, but normally this would be the exclusive territory of the police and the NCA. Not the intelligence services. Not unless it somehow threatened national security. They, he must know something that the NCA didn't. Had his gut feeling been right all along? That his investigation was somehow connected with the physical destruction of the NCA? Roger decided to air his curiosity.

"Why are you even interested in John, Mr Mitchell? You're not telling me something Jason."

For a few seconds Jason looked thoughtful, his smile slipped. It took him several seconds before he replied.

"Honest answer? I'm not sure we need to be, that's what I want you to find out." Jason slipped his hand into the mailing bag and pulled out a photo. He placed it face up in the centre of the table, towards Roger. "On the day of your sting operation, when you exited the lift on the top floor you thought you remembered two Arab looking women waiting to take your lift. Was one of them her?" Roger picked up the photo. How the hell did Jason know about the two women? Who was feeding him this information? He tried his best to look non plussed whilst studying the woman in the photo. Her figure looked a little familiar, but the clothes were very different as was the face. Roger shook his head.

"No, I don't think either of them was her. Who is she? Where was the photo taken?"

Jason picked up the photo and studied it, as though it were a mere holiday snap.

"Her name is Fatima, though the French now know this name to be false. The photo is taken from hotel CCTV footage. The Hotel de Plage on Calais seafront to be exact. It's where she seduced the local capitaine of the gendarme in Calais. A Capitaine Maubert."

"I know that name, I've been trying to contact him."

"Yes, I know." Jason placed the photo back on the table, "in relation to the severed head delivered to an address in Tottenham. Well, you'll have a hard job now, the man's dead. It's all over the news. What isn't all over the news is that Fatima here, the French believe, to be a professional femme fatale. Just before his death, the capitaine admitted to telling this woman everything about their latest investigation. The one covered in some detail by the world's media. What happens next is a man hiding, after giving information to the gendarme in Calais, disappears and his severed head is delivered to his wife and child, here in London. Fatima, we believe is now in the UK, probably London. What we don't know is who employed her and why, and why is she now over here? When I heard about your incident during your sting, alarm bells started ringing."

"All the persons of interest at The Hilton have disappeared from the CCTV footage. We're currently working to be seen if it's been doctored." Roger didn't know why but he felt it ok to divulge this snippet of information.

"Where have you sent it? In house?"

"In house," Roger confirmed. "It's amazing what you can achieve with AI, you can't believe what you see or don't see any more."

"To use AI you still have to hack into the system." Jason pointed out.

"If we can't find anything, that's the next step, we'll have to have a team of forensics at the hotel. Looking into it. PR wise though that will be a disaster."

"You didn't inform them you were conducting a sting operation at their hotel? Jason's grin could have belonged to a Cheshire cat. Roger shook his head.

"No."

"Rather you than me." Jason's grin had gone though. Without warning, he picked up the photo of Fatima, and turning it over started scribbling on the back. When he'd finished, he pushed it across to Roger. On the back, he'd written an address in East London, a lady's name and a mobile number. "Listen, if your guys don't find anything, send the footage there, to be precise to her. She runs the best lab in the country for this sort of thing. They even develop their own software." Roger studied the address, he'd never heard of them, and said so. Jason laughed. "That's because they're expensive." Roger joined in the laughter, now he knew why.

Two men came up the stairs each carrying a beer in their hand. After looking around they decided on the table in front of the window recently vacated by the three women. They both saw Jason watching and nodded. Jason returned their nod, smiling. Apparently dismissing them, he returned to their conversation.

"So going back to your sting operation, we have two people missing, plus Maureen Fowlis, who is connected to one of the missing." Again, Roger was left wondering where Jason was getting his information. He'd never mentioned, precisely two were missing. John and their plant, Rory. Jason didn't wait for Roger to confirm. "Now, there are several tenuous links to France, which may or may not be relevant. That's what we, you, I think, need to find out" Jason took another sip of his beer. "The obvious connection are the severed heads. One here in the UK, one in Spain and one either in France or the UK. As yet we don't know where the last killing and decapitation took place. Just that the third victim was last seen in France. If decapitation wasn't enough, each head was defaced by having their genitalia stuffed in their mouth. However, there is a distinct difference between the first two and the last. The first two were brutal hatchet jobs, amateurs, thugs. Your head in London was the work of a professional, a surgeon. Secondly, the London head also had his eyes surgically removed. Not gouged out as the media are reporting. Lastly, there was a neat whole in the top of his head. Someone had drilled into the man's brain. Why? As yet, we have no idea. You'll see when you receive the pathology reports. It's worth noting the severed heads found floating off the French coast, had also been the work of a professional. A surgeon. All but one had had their eyes surgically removed. So, the question I have, we have, are the three connected and those found floating in the English Channel, are they also connected? Or is the third, the one delivered to an address here in London an attempt to make it look like it's connected to the two with their mouth's stuffed with their genitalia? In other words to try and throw us off the track? That's a signpost I'm giving you."

Roger ran his hands through his hair. What was already a challenging investigation, had just gotten a whole lot bigger. And from what he'd just been told even more challenging.

"Does Jane know about this?"

On hearing this question, Jason refrained from smiling.

"If she's worth her salt, she should do. As head of the NCA, she has all the right contacts. We haven't told her though and before you ask, no she doesn't know we're having this conversation. And if you don't mind, I'd prefer to keep it that way."

"May I ask why?"

On being asked this, Jason's smile returned. For a few seconds he gazed across the room at the far windows. For seconds only, then and he was back with Roger.

"Primarily because she controls budgets, and I'd doubt if she'd allow you to extend your investigation this far wide. Much of this is departmental crossover. Not strictly NCA."

Roger suddenly twigged.

"You want me to try and do this on the quiet. Off my own back, is how it would look if questions were asked. I could lose my job, along with half the team. And how the hell am I going to sell it to them?"

For the first time that evening, Jason concentrated his stare directly at the man from the NCA. He opened his mouth to say something but Roger hadn't finished.

"And if you don't mind me pointing this out, I still don't know who the hell you are or who you work for. How do I know I can trust you? I can trust Jane."

Jason's smile remained.

"You should be careful where you lay your trust Roger, our departmental philosophy is to trust no one. Not even each other. If the NCA had applied that rule, perhaps your building wouldn't be in such a mess." Roger couldn't help feeling angry. Jane had told him virtually the same thing not that long ago. They weren't idiots at the NCA. This man, Jason? stranger, whoever he was, had, and he didn't want to admit it, just rammed home a very valid point. As an agency, before the explosion, perhaps they had become too trusting. Especially of each other. "You don't have to trust me Roger and adhering to our departmental philosophy you'd be very wise not to. However, as I've told you, I'm just here to give you signposts. Whether you follow them or not is up to you. Now will you let me finish what I've come to tell you, then you can make up your own mind."

Roger played with his glass, he wished he felt more alert.

"You may as well."

"Thank you." Jason smiled, and on this occasion, Roger read in the smile a touch of relief. He sensed what this man was doing with him in a pub, was by no means the norm. Maybe, he was doing it with great risk to himself. He'd give the guy a chance, listen to what he had to say.

Finishing his beer Jason once more glanced across to the windows. Again, within seconds he was back, and talking.

"These are very uncertain times Roger, not to mention dangerous. There was a time when you or I could have hopped on the 'Magic Bus' to Kabul. Not anymore. Today the world is a very dangerous place. Unstable, some would say unhinged world leaders, fanatical religious groups, organised crime with global networks and terrorist cells which have a level of sophistication not to mention budget greater than over half the countries in the world. With ever decreasing budgets and self-serving politicians, we're more and more expected to confront this lot. To protect the Great British public from the risks they pose, whilst having one arm tied behind our back."

Roger couldn't agree more, for the first time that evening he found himself hoping and not doubting that they were both batting for the same side. Jason was on a roll. He continued with his speech.

"If the bureaucrats in Whitehall have their way, we will soon have to fill out a ten-page risk assessment, before we can tackle a suicide bomber in Oxford Street during rush hour. Providing the risk assessment is filled out correctly, it wouldn't matter to them how many people get killed." He either didn't see or ignored Roger's expression of agreement. Hardly stopping for breath Jason continued, though now in lowered tones. "Never has our philosophy,' trust no one,' been more important than today. What has happened to you, the brutal demolition of your offices demonstrates this. Everyone knows, the whole bloody world knows that to achieve whoever it was did, they would have had to have had several people on the inside. Even worse, no one has a clue who's responsible. This fact is scaring everybody in the intelligence services. Everybody is looking over their shoulder. Which is why I'm here with you now.

This investigation I'm pointing you towards, has to, if it's going to succeed, be done under the radar. We can't use normal channels for we have no idea who may be listening. Even the closest members of your team. You give no one the whole picture. Just snippets, I can't tell you but I can suggest, from here on, you work as a team whilst, keeping everyone at arm's length."

"Now to specifics. Do you want another?"

Roger had finished his beer. He shook his head.

"No, no thanks. I need to concentrate." No longer did Roger feel sleepy. What Jason was putting across to him had revitalised his senses.

Jason spread his hands.

"Now to specifics. I've talked about the heads and the tenuous connection with France. The link becomes a little less tenuous, with the mutilated bodies of those poor children turning up in French waters. Children who were meant to be under the protection of our bloody government." For the first time that evening Jason showed a touch of emotion. Disgust even. "You won't know this yet, but a young girl, or at least her body was found on a beach not far from Calais. Now like the poor Albanian children, her body had also been mutilated. The difference is, after a post mortem, it was discovered her mutilation had been carried out by a professional, surgeon. As had the severed heads found floating in the Channel. The ones making world headlines."

"Just like our head in North London." Roger stared into his empty glass.

"You said it, not me."

"When we get those bodies back, we can check. A post mortem will tell us, perhaps even find if they were all carried out by the same surgeon."

"You mean the twelve Albanian children?"

"Yes."

Jason scoffed.

"You'll have a job, our government has plumbed new depths. To avoid what would be an almighty, scandal they've done the dirty with the French government. The bodies are being brought back to the

UK tomorrow morning. Under a cloak of secrecy. After which, they'll conveniently disappear. You're not meant to know about it, and if you put in a request to the French authorities for their return, they'll simply refuse, citing it's a French investigation. You could make a stink, but you'd never be granted the budget for an investigation into what essentially is this government's dirty deed. Now in France, the gendarmerie in Calais were investigating whether the red market was involved. It maybe something you want to look into. The red market is something we've all heard of but no country, till now, has really taken it seriously." Jason turned over his hands. "I've no idea if the red market is relevant in all of this, but the investigation in France has certainly had, maybe even, provoked some shocking consequences. Not least the death of the leader of that investigation."

"Isn't his death thought to be suicide?"

"Not officially, not yet, but only because the paperwork has still to be completed. So yes suicide but a little too convenient wouldn't you say? Oh and by the way, what I've forgotten to say is a gendarme from the same gendarmerie has also gone missing. Now one of the last known sightings of him was in Wissant, just outside Maureen Fowlis's seaside apartment. So perhaps Mrs Fowlis isn't quite as innocent as we believe her to be. And then there's Fatima, sent it looks like to seduce the capitaine, and very successfully it would seem. The million dollar question, WHO sent her." Jason turned his hands back over, placing them flat on the table. "Our sources, tell us this is all connected to something big, very big. But that's all we're hearing, and it's enough to have put the willies up the people who employ me."

"Thus the reason I'm here with you now. It's highly irregular but what I've just told you cannot be investigated using the normal channels. We've no idea how deep and how wide our security and intelligence services have been infiltrated. Judging by what's just happened to you guys and no one having the slightest clue who's responsible, pretty bloody deep and wide. Don't you think? Now for all I know I may be with you, talking to an infiltrator. I've done my research Roger, and I'm pretty sure I'm not or I wouldn't risk being here. Signposts dear fella, I've given you signposts. Whether you wish to explore where they're pointing is up to you. If you do, a friendly word of warning. Tread carefully." Jason stood up. "You have my number but don't use a regular phone when calling me. As Hollywood likes to call them, use a burner. I believe you have a few!" Jason smiled. "Now I really must be going, before I do, put this number into your phone." Roger did as he was asked. "If anyone one from those tables, leaves immediately after I do, text F to that number. That's my messenger, they're in a high signal location and will receive your text within seconds, if not immediately. Good luck Roger."

Roger watched the man who liked to be called Jason disappear down the narrow staircase. There was no way Jason was his real name, he knew that. He eyed the two tables in front of the windows. Seconds after Jason had left one of the woman from a group of two couples disappeared down the staircase. Roger immediately sent a test saying F. Burner phones. Jason mentioning burner phones and the fact he knew he had a few, was another signpost. He was, via the back door telling him that he knew he'd taken John's pay as you go phones. How did he know? Roger thought hard. Unless he'd been in, searched John's flat before him. Another thought struck Roger. If so was he the one who had left John's regular mobile at the bottom of the stairs? Yet another question and no bloody answers. What the hell had he got himself into?

The Royal Lancaster Hotel, Lancaster Gate, London, England

Fatima had again enjoyed dinner in the hotel's Thai restaurant. Still not tired she'd followed up with a couple of pomegranate martinis in the Park Lounge Bar. Once more she'd dressed mixing both Persian and Western styles. The Western, allowed her to show off her sexuality and Persian an air of mystery. She enjoyed the longing looks from men, sometimes women. All desired her but her Persian touches hinted at the untouchable. How many of those admiring her in the bar that evening would, with their imagination, take her up to bed? Pretty much all, Fatima was confident of that, the thought turned her on. Not sexually but the power her sexuality gave her. In her wake lay a trail of ruined lives, men broken because of her. She bore no guilt. In her eyes the men who had been her paid targets, got what they'd deserved. Men were weak, pathetic. Even powerful men. Her thoughts turned to Pierre, now there was a man worthy of the name. Perhaps in his past life he'd been a woman. She wondered where he was now. In France, yes but where in France? Calais?

Fatima suddenly felt tired. Today had almost felt like a holiday. For a time she'd even been able to forget that she was here for work. She found London an amazing city, a great city but she had a habit of sapping every ounce of your energy.

Time for bed. As she slipped off her seat at the bar, she caught two men admiring her. She smiled at both and both quickly looked away. Pathetic, men are pathetic. As she walked out of the bar. Someone up close, someone she hadn't been aware of whispered in her ear.

"Pitgam." Fatima froze. "Keep walking, imagine I'm not here." Fatima did as she was told. "Order breakfast to your room tomorrow but book it tonight. Don't wait till the morning." Fatima waited for more but there was no more. She looked round, nobody. Shaking she continued to her room. Once safely inside she buzzed through to reception and ordered a Shakshouka, along with a continental selection to her room. Feeling exhausted she slipped out of her clothes and naked, walked to the window. London was an exciting city by day but at night it was even more intriguing, inviting those who dared, to a taste of adventure. Fatima felt her body tingle. That day was coming. She could feel it.

Somewhere in Bushey, North London, England

It was close to eleven when Roger eventually arrived home. He'd been up, almost nineteen hours with only a couple of hours sleep the night before. It was too much and he wasn't getting any younger, his body was telling as much. His head hurt and his whole body was restless. That strange restlessness you get when you're overtired. He recognised the feeling, he knew he wouldn't sleep well tonight. And the reason he knew, he couldn't go to bed, not just yet. Retrieving a bulbous glass from a cupboard, he poured himself a large glass of port from a decanter. Port always helped him to sleep and an expensive decanted port was one of the few luxuries he allowed himself. Not bothering to draw the curtains he spread himself on the sofa, luxuriating in the silence. Light from the pub next door threw long shadows across his garden and in places, through his window. Moving shadows and low voices evidenced people making their way home. Laid out on the sofa, Roger as he watched felt rather like a voyeur. For a moment the voyeur felt lonely, he didn't really have any friends. Those he knew were either colleagues or acquaintances. How many people would really care if he died tomorrow? He didn't wait for his mind to answer. He already knew, virtually no one, if anybody at all. He thought back to his strange meeting with the man who'd call himself Jason. The more he thought about it, the weirder it became, and yet somehow he felt Jason, an obvious alias, had been genuine. The woman who had left her table shortly after Jason, had, in just over a minute, returned. She'd probably just been to the toilet but did he really know? London was home to millions of anonymous faces and that was beginning to scare him, whereas he hadn't given it a thought before.

His mind wandered back to John, the woman who'd introduced herself to him as Bree. Something Jason had told him pointed a signpost as he called them, to her perhaps being a femme fatale and possibly a dangerous one. If John was no longer alive, could she be responsible. Jason had said, according to records, assuming she was travelling under her real name, she was still in the country. She hadn't left. He'd take up one of Jason's signposts and get the hotels around Covent Garden checked. He'd make it a priority tomorrow morning. With Jane's persuasion maybe the Met would help with this. It was a positive step. His mind wandered to John's phone. Had Jason placed it at the bottom of John's stairs? And if so, why? When he'd got back to his car, he'd found a message from forensics wanting to come in tomorrow to present what they'd found on the phone. It couldn't be better timing and had left a message for them to come to his new office under Gladstone Park around ten am. He was due to move in at eight. Two hours should be enough time to prepare for them. Although he was excited to see what they'd come up with, he couldn't help feeling nervous, in case they'd found something that incriminated him. He'd given the matter a lot of thought, and as a result had convinced himself that he'd be able to talk himself out of whatever they'd found. As a result he was more excited than nervous and that was a good thing.

Finishing his port, Roger returned to the kitchen, placing his rouge tinted glass in the sink. He glanced at the pile of post he'd picked up from the hallway. Without examining it he decided they were all bills and the post could wait. Undressing, before taking his trousers off he removed a pocket sized recording device from his trouser pocket. Roger preferred his digital recorder to a notebook. The law required him to take notes but his own thoughts and memories he recorded on his machine. On returning to his car, he'd recorded everything he'd remembered from his meeting with Jason. Sliding the machine under his pillow, he pressed play and settled down to sleep.

Whilst Roger slept rays of light from the passing moon slowly crept through the window into his kitchen below. As though the moon was trying to tell him something, its rays highlighted the pile of post lying on a kitchen counter. From the pile of letters and mailshots, a small corner of a card dared to point to its presence. Sadly, the moon's efforts would almost certainly be in vain. By early morning, when the owner of the house arose, its rays will have moved on. The corner of the card would be in shadow or lost in the glow of artificial light. It was imperative that the man living there found that card. The moon shone bright with exasperation.

The Morgue, Centre Hospitalier, Boulogne Sur Mer, France

It wasn't even dawn and Lieutenant Beaufort, along with three other cars from the gendarmerie in Calais, were waiting outside the parking area for the morgue. Daylight was nowhere near ready to put on a show, but from years of living on the coast, the lieutenant recognised the telltale signs which meant it was going to be a fine day. At the last minute, he'd received an order to take unmarked cars, not marked, and that order had wasted a good hour of their time. Why the change of plan, he had no idea. On arrival, it was obvious they weren't going to get anywhere near the morgue itself. The building was surrounded by carefully placed security. To the average person on the street, it would simply look like casual parking. But to the trained eye of the lieutenant, he recognised the eight unmarked cars, all carefully positioned, belonged to the security services. By the morgue's loading and delivery area, just visible from where the lieutenant was parked, a white van was being loaded. He couldn't see the plates but he could see it had right hand drive. This would be the vehicle he'd been ordered to escort. At five am exactly, a tall sharp faced man, dressed in newish blue jeans and a grey jumper, over which hung a dark blue jacket, approached the lieutenant's car. In anticipation the lieutenant lowered his window.

"Are you ready for us?" The man held a card. The lieutenant had never seen one before, but he recognised it as identity for the GIGN. The man's photo matched but he deliberately had his thumb over his name. What the hell was the GIGN doing in all of this?

"As ready as we'll ever be." The lieutenant attempted to sound as confident as he could.

"Superbe," the man from the GIGN tapped the roof. "When the English van leaves you guys take up close positions, two at the front, two at the rear. We will have two vehicles before you and six at the rear. They will interchange so as not to make it obvious we're part of an escort. If one of our vehicles attempts to pass you. let them. Along the way the forward vehicles will block any entrees allowing you to pass without any hinderance. We will not let any random vehicle pass unless we are sure it is absolutely safe to do so. Our job is to deliver the van to the ferry port, and to see it passes the douane without hinderance. Is that understood?" The lieutenant gave a nod.

"Yes sir."

"Good," the man from the GIGN smiled. "Have you ever done anything like this before?" The lieutenant shook his head.

"Non."

"Well enjoy it, it's good fun." With that the man walked back to the morgue and slid into the passenger seat of a dark metallic grey Peugeot 5008. Lieutenant Beaufort's passenger, a female officer in her thirties whose first name was Chloe, turned to look at her boss. Her face spoke of her shock.

"What the hell is going on Lieutenant? Are we escorting a nuclear device? Or has Putin been killed and we're handing his body over to the British?"

"Neither of those' Chloe, I can assure you." The lieutenant chuckled. "But my orders prevent me from telling you. Sorry"

"Pathetic. You're a coward, boss." The lieutenant faced his officer.

"You're right, I am."

The Royal Lancaster Hotel, Lancaster Gate, London, England

Fatima, showered and dressed, looked at her watch. Ten to eight. She'd ordered breakfast at eight, ten minutes to go. She'd spend the time admiring the view from her window, she never tired of it. Outside that morning, was very different to the last few. The sky was bright blue not grey. Not the blue of home or Marseille, there it was a rich blue. Here the blue was paler but in its own way just as beautiful. The street below, she now knew it to be called Bayswater Road, was busy with traffic and people. The road was always busy, what she'd read about London was correct. The city never slept.

There came a knock at the door.

"Room service, your breakfast Madame." Fatima hurried to her door, her heart thumping. On opening she was confronted by a tiny Asian girl, dressed in the hotel uniform, and pushing a trolley with her breakfast and crisp white linen. She waved the girl in, something must have gone wrong. She couldn't believe this young woman was her contact.

The maid entered with the trolley and started to place the various delights on the table by the window. Not one word did she speak as she did this. Finally she poured a perfect cup of coffee, just as Fatima liked it. Pulling a card from her pocket she presented it to Fatima. Fatima automatically reached for a pen, expecting to have to sign. That's what she'd been told to do with every bill presented in the hotel. She took the card, ready to sign but instead of a charge the card had written on it just one word. 'Axsti.'

"Axsti," Fatima murmured.

The young Asian maid said nothing, instead she waved her arm indicating for Fatima to sit down and eat. Smiling, the maid then sat down herself, watching Fatima eat. Fatima found the experience very uncomfortable, but concentrating on the maid's smile, after a few minutes she found herself beginning to relax. The maid's whole expression she somehow found intoxicating. She was finding it harder and harder to take her eyes off her.

Half an hour later, the maid placed the used breakfast ware back on the trolley, covering everything with a crisp white linen cover. She smiled at her customer. The woman was in a deep sleep still in her chair. Leaning over, she gently kissed Fatima on her forehead.

"Ashi," she whispered and quietly left.

Bayswater, London, England

Arif stretched. At last a blue sky. It was still cold but the sky reminded him of home. He didn't fancy the hotel breakfast that morning. He wanted to try a place he'd been told about called, McDonalds. He'd seen one in Queensway. He couldn't wait. As he walked down the path from his hotel, a man sitting at a small round garden table said something to him.

"Pitgam."

Arif stopped in his tracks.

"Walk with me, Arif." Arif did as he was told. As they walked the man passed Arif an envelope. "Congratulations Arif, you've passed your exam with excellent grades. In two days' time you start work at our hospital in Kings Cross. In the envelope you'll find the address of your new home. I promise you it's very nice and within walking distance of where you will be working. The number for a taxi company is also in there. Book them to pick you up from here at two pm. Enjoy your breakfast, Arif."

The man was gone. Arif shook his head. He needed to clear his head. He opened the envelope. Inside he found a single piece of paper with an address and an NW1 postcode along with the number for a taxi company. In a small brown paper pouch, there were two keys. Arif looked up and down the road. There was no one he recognised. It was very strange, he remembered every word of the message he'd been given but nothing about the messenger. He shook his head again. It felt heavy. A good breakfast was what he needed.

NCA's Temporary Offices, Gladstone Park, Cricklewood, North London, England

Roger had slept well, very well. The deep-set tiredness of yesterday had been brushed away by last night's shut eye. It must have been the port he lied to himself. Again he decided to leave the post, he'd check it when he returned home that evening. Bills only depressed him and his mood was depressed enough as it was. Instead he'd spent his time whilst drinking his three morning coffees, listening again to the recording he'd made the night before. His meeting with Jason now seemed years ago, almost a dream, except it hadn't been. As usual his first call that morning had been to Jane. She was still living in a guarded safehouse, with her own home being watched. Once more she had offered him the same option, which again he'd declined. Fatalities had now risen to twenty one, though the good news was, that figure wasn't expected to rise. Thank God for that. The whole area was still closed off, causing travel chaos, though it was hoped, that the Albert Embankment would re-open tomorrow.

Roger was careful not to let slip his meeting with Jason. He did though bring up Maureen Fowlis and that he thought it was worth checking the local hotels to see if she had stayed or still was staying in any. Jane agreed and to speed things up, said she'd contact the Met herself to ask for their help in doing this. Something for which he was extremely grateful.

From his house it had been a short run down the M1 to their new temporary offices. Roger looked at his watch. Thirty five minutes it had taken him, heaven. He was now approaching the entrance to their new premises, a small industrial park not much more than a stone's throw away from Gladstone Park and Dollis Hill House. He'd been instructed to, on entering the industrial park, turn left. As he did so, he saw their covert entrance. A huge sign read Trevillion Electronics. And underneath in metallic lettering, the caption. 'Bringing the future to your office today.' Who the hell had thought that load of crap up, wondered Roger. He knew the NCA did have a so-called marketing department. They must have thought all their chickens had come home to roost when given that job.

Security was discreet but understandably tight, even so, in under ten minutes he was sitting in his new office, God knows how many metres underground. Apart from having no windows and the garish fluorescent light, he actually thought, considering everything had been set up in little over two days, that whoever had, had done a bloody good job. A so called 'centre manager,' gave him a cursory tour. The tech guys were settled in, excellent, and his closest team had their own operations room and a suite of offices. Any interviews though would have to be carried out off site. After what had happened in Vauxhall, only those with the highest security clearance would be allowed entry. Suspects would just have to be interviewed at the nearest secure police stations. What impressed him the most was a small but well fitted out staff restaurant. Staffed he quickly learnt by chefs on loan from the military. The restaurant he knew would have been Jane's doing. She had always been heavily into looking after anyone who worked at the NCA. The apparent infiltration or betrayal, however you wanted to look at it, must have wounded her greatly.

After ordering himself a cappuccino, yes a cappuccino! Roger returned to his new office. First things first, check the phones were working. They were, all three. One a normal line, one secure and a direct line to Jane. He assumed at her safe house. The secure line also had a language translator device fitted. Able, the centre manager, boasted it could recognise one hundred and forty nine different languages. Roger had used one before. They were very impressive and enabled you to have a conversation with just about anyone in the world. Provided you weren't a Geordie as one of his team had found out.

Feeling rather like a kid in a toy shop, Roger logged onto his computer. It worked! He tried logging into the NCA's secured cloud. The system allowed him to. Happy days. The next hour, he spent typing up his case notes, and filing them. Every now and again there was a knock at his door. Invariably it was always one of his team, saying good morning and asking if there was anything special that needed setting up. Roger left that to them, recreate our workplace at Vauxhall he kept repeating. Forensics were coming at ten and he wanted to be ready for them.

At nine thirty Nick knocked on his door, he'd already said morning so it wasn't that. His face looked flushed. He came in, closing the door behind him.

"Sir, you asked uniform to check hotels in and around Covent Garden, starting with the closest to Mr Mitchell's flat in Drury Lane." Nick looked at his notes. "To check if a Maureen Fowlis had stayed or is staying in any?"

"Yes."

"Well uniform have come up with a hit, she was staying at the Fielding Hotel, Broad Court, Covent Garden. Five minutes' walk from Mr Mitchell's flat in Drury Lane."

"What already? I only asked Jane a couple of hours ago. Is she still there?" Roger was on the edge of his seat. Was this the break they'd been so desperately looking for? Nick leant his back against the door.

"From what I gather a normal foot patrol did it, there's stacks in central London. No she's not there now. Left a couple of days ago. Didn't actually book out though, simply left. All her bills were paid. She left a hairbrush." Nick held up his hand, anticipating his bosses next request. "Uniform have already bagged it up sir, it's on its way to the lab. I know the first thing you'd ask is for DNA."

Roger thought. Nick knew when to keep quiet.

"Have you checked to see if there's any CCTV footage? Let's see what Miss Fowlis has been up to during her stay. Have you got the officers details? I'd like to speak to them directly. Ask them to call me here will you, when they've finished their patrolling. Oh and thank them for me. Bloody excellent job."

"Yes sir, will do. Coffee?" Nick nodded to the empty cup on Roger's desk.

"Go on then." Roger stood up quickly. "Whilst I think of it, where's the bloody toilets? They weren't part of the tour!" He shoved his cup in Nicks hand. Nick grinned.

"Follow me."

Chapter 4

GMC Building, Regent's Place, Euston Road, London, England

Heba stood looking up at the glass and grey building towering above her. She felt like pinching herself. She couldn't believe she was here. After failing her medical exams in her home country of Egypt she thought her dreams of ever becoming a practising doctor were over. Worse, after her husband's disappointment that she wouldn't be the bread winner he'd hoped for, he divorced her. Worse, threw her out onto the street. With no immediate family to turn to she had supported herself, through prostitution, using the name Batul. She lived day to day until out of the blue she was approached by a private medical company. Funny she still didn't know what they were called. They'd promised to retain her and make sure she'd pass her exams. Their one condition, she had to sign a contract committing her to ten years, practising in one of their hospitals, somewhere in Europe. She'd been given a choice of three countries. Turkey, Greece or the United Kingdom. She'd chosen the UK because she knew Mo Salah played football there. Somehow it made the UK feel more like home.

After signing, she'd been taken to a medical facility somewhere below ground, in the desert. It was all very strange but the training facilities were second to none. She'd taken the necessary exams on site and had passed with flying colours. Having chosen her country of choice, the company booked her to sit a UK medical exam, PLAB 1 at a GMC examination centre in Cairo. If she passed, she'd be allowed to sit a second exam, PLAB 2 in London. If she passed that she was free to practice in the UK. And now here she was, ready to take PLAB 2. Even more amazing, she was oozing with confidence. Ever since this new company had help train her, she'd felt entirely confident, whereas before she'd always been a bundle of nerves. Everything she'd been taught at the training facility remained fresh in her mind. She'd even started to specialise in brain surgery. Something she'd been promised she could continue studying, here in the UK. Heba looked at her watch. It was time. With a deep breath she entered through the revolving doors.

Formby, Lancashire, England

James felt a lot more relaxed that morning. The first thing he'd done after getting out of bed, was to peek through the curtains to the road outside. The road had been clear. There was the odd passing car of course but no car parked directly outside his drive. He wanted to jump for joy.

After a breakfast of yoghurt and fresh fruit, he bid goodbye to his wife and young son. Minutes later he was pulling out of his drive on his short drive to work. Just over half an hour later he was at his workplace. The General Record Office, in Southport. As he'd done yesterday, all of the way he'd checked in his rear-view mirror to see if anyone was following him. On his arrival he was confident no one had been.

Such was his relief, he almost felt as though he was walking on air. Perhaps he'd try to organise another death certificate today. Then if the bastards did show up, he'd have something more to give them. Surely they'd understand then, that he was doing his best.

The Car Ferry Port, Calais, France

Lieutenant Beaufort and his partner watched as the plain white van with UK plates was waved through by the French douane. The Brits were so bloody intransigent, so bloody protective of their little island, there was no way they'd let the van through without checks. He was wrong. A couple of border force officers stepped out, waving the van through. Seconds later it was gone, out of sight. The first vehicle to be loaded onto the waiting ferry. From here on the van he'd been told, would be escorted by specialist officers from ERSOU in Dover. The van's passage was no longer their responsibility. Thank fuck for that.

He looked across at all the cars that had travelled with the van from the morgue in Boulogne. They were spread out across the car park, and to the lieutenant they reminded him of regularly repeated scenes from American cop movies. This was not the France he'd grown up in, that he was familiar with. This was Calais, not bloody LA.

The man, quite obviously in charge, who had briefly spoken to him outside the morgue in Boulogne tapped on his window.

"Job well done Lieutenant B…"

"Beaufort, the lieutenant helped him." The man from the GIGN, was gracious enough to smile.

"Yes excellent job, I'll send a report to your new capitaine, Capitaine Vendroux. I'll let him know how professional you and your team have been."

"Merci." The lieutenant felt he should say more but couldn't think of anything. As he struggled, a message came through on an earpiece worn by the man congratulating him.

"Well that's it, the van's on the ferry. It's a British problem now. We can all go home. Let us leave first. Give it five minutes then you guys can make your way back to your gendarmerie." He reached in to shake both his and his partner's hands. As he walked back to his car, he waved to the other gendarmes waiting in their cars in thanks. After that, one by one the cars belonging to the GIGN left the parking area to join the N216 approach road. Presumably, the lieutenant thought, on their return to Paris. What a lot of effort for a few dead bodies.

"What the fuck was that all about Lieutenant?" It was obvious that his partner that day, Chloe, wasn't impressed. "What a fucking waste of time."

"You don't know that, Chloe."

"No, because you won't tell me." In response the lieutenant stuck out his tongue and received a punch on his arm for his effort.

"Shall we go home, I've got a date with our new capitaine."

"Word is he's a complete dick head sir."

"Bloody hell, you're in a good mood this morning Chloe."

"Getting up at half three in the morning for that? Are you surprised?" The lieutenant laughed and putting the car into gear manoeuvred out of the car park. The rest of his team followed him leaving the port to its own devices.

Ten minutes later they were back at the gendarmerie. The officers trooped back inside leaving the lieutenant alone sitting in his car. He had a phone call to make. Using his personal mobile, he rang Marie's number. As it did the night before, his call went straight to answer phone. The lieutenant had been a gendarme long enough to trust his senses, and his senses were telling him something was wrong. He didn't know why but his same senses were telling him that to try and go down the official route would be a complete waste of time. Instead, he did something, in all his career as a gendarme, he'd never done before. Using his personal mobile he phoned a civilian, hoping she would help. For the next step he felt discretion was needed, and one thing the gendarmerie was not, was discreet. On the third ring Madame Maubert answered.

"Lieutenant? I recognise your number."

"Morning Madame Maubert."

"Vivienne please."

"Vivienne," the lieutenant felt uncomfortable calling Madame Maubert by her first name. In all the years he had known her, he'd called her Madame Maubert. He hadn't even known she was called Vivienne. "Vivienne, I hope you're not going to be upset at what I'm about to ask."

"I'm sure I won't be lieutenant. One thing with everything that has happened to me over the last few days has given me, is strength." The lieutenant felt relieved, that was the first hurdle over with.

"I'm pleased Madame M.. Vivienne."

"How can I help lieutenant? Lieutenant Beaufort drew a deep breath.

"The girl that came to see you Vivienne, the one that caused all the trouble."

"Marie."

"Yes Marie, have you heard from her since she visited?"

"Non, you said you were going to call her."

"I have been. She's not answering. I'm just a little worried. It's probably nothing but…" Madame Maubert cut in.

"Your gendarme's sixth sense, is telling you otherwise. My husband never stopped talking about his special sense, which came only after years of experience."

"Something like that Vivienne yes." This was turning out to be so much easier than expected. "It's just I can't really get the gendarmerie involved, not yet. I've got nothing to justify it. Only how I feel."

"So what do you want me to do?"

"Try calling her, she may answer to you. Marie, if she's afraid she may not want to answer a number she doesn't recognise." Madame Maubert's response was immediate.

"I'll text her first so she knows it's me calling, and if she still doesn't answer I'll get my daughter to run me over there. See if we can find her at home." The lieutenant thought. The last couple of weeks or so had been weird. People connected with their investigation had a habit of dying or going missing. He didn't want the responsibility if anything, because of him, happened to his late boss's wife.

"I'm not sure I'm happy with the idea of you two visiting her Vivienne."

"Nonsense, why not." Madame Maubert sounded indignant. This was not the meek, obedient homemaker that he'd met in the past.

"I just don't Mada.., Vivienne."

"Why? Because you're worried I might come to some sort of harm? What more harm can I come to than losing my husband and being mocked as the stupid wife on social media? I'm tired of doing nothing lieutenant. Allow me at least to feel useful. Anyway, who on earth would want to harm me?"

You'd be surprised but the lieutenant didn't say it.

"Just be careful Vivienne, there are some very odd people in Calais." Madame Maubert scoffed.

"You don't think I don't know that lieutenant? I've been married to a bloody gendarme for over thirty years. Now please let me feel useful and try not to worry about me."

The lieutenant sighed. He was beginning to regret going down this route.

"Ok Vivienne but promise me you'll call or message me regularly. Oh and on my personal mobile. If you need me urgently and I don't answer, call Colette. You have her mobile, don't you? I'd prefer it if you didn't ring the gendarmerie, just Colette and my mobiles."

To his relief Madame Maubert didn't ask why, she simply agreed.

Ringing off the lieutenant left his car, slamming the door shut. He had five minutes before his meeting with the new capitaine and he needed to speak to Colette first. He'd better bloody hurry.

In Ardres, Madame Maubert after replacing the receiver stood motionless, deep in thought. She wasn't stupid, there was a reason why the lieutenant didn't want to involve the gendarmerie. What was it? She'd only ever been a wife but from that moment she understood what her husband had meant when he'd described to her his sixth sense. She felt it now. Picking up her mobile she sent a text to Marie.

Calais Plage, Calais, France

Having been for a jog Pierre felt on top of the world. The depressing grey wet cold that had dominated the last few days had gone. Replaced by early winter sun and a clear blue sky. The change in the weather reflected exactly his mood.

After gulping down a glass of freshly squeezed orange juice, he disrobed in preparation for a shower. He had to look sharp at the same time looking relaxed. At twelve he had a lunch date with the mayor along with a couple of his favoured contractors and accompanying him would be a couple of business people working covertly for the organisation.

It was important that the meeting went well. He couldn't see why not. He'd been a generous donor to many of the mayor's pet projects. Now it was time to pull in some favours.

NCA's Temporary Offices, Gladstone Park, London, England

On returning to his office Roger found two men waiting for him. Both held out their hands. The taller of the two spoke their introductions.

"I'm Matt, I head the team specialising in video and this is my colleague Rob from digital forensics. I believe you're expecting us."

Roger felt a shiver go up his spine. These two may hold the key to his very future in the NCA. He shook their hands whilst at the same time showing them into his office.

"Sorry for the neatness, I only moved in a couple of hours ago." Both men laughed at his joke, that was promising. Roger looked them up and down. They were both very casually dressed though the adjective casual was in Roger's eyes a bit of a stretch. Polite though. On the quiet he would describe them both as scruffy. And this coming from someone whose last ex-wife, when they were married, often referred to him as 'jumble-man.' From experience, he'd come to realise that for anyone in tech it was their unofficial uniform. Their badge, shouting I am a techy. It would be easy to laugh at them but in this day and age, without them law enforcement would come to a grinding halt.

Just as everyone sat down Nick appeared with a fresh cappuccino. He looked around the office, smiling at the two visitors.

"Nick, these two gentleman are from video and digital forensics." Nick nodded hello. "You might want to join us." Nick nodded again.

"Great I'll grab a chair. Coffee?"

"We have a bigger selection than Starbucks," Roger joked. "Choose your fetish, gentlemen." Nick went off to collect a third chair and three cappuccinos. It was something of a relief to Roger that people who, to him, worked in an alien world, drank, perhaps Britain's, most popular coffee. They all had something in common at least. Even if it was only coffee. After a minute Nick was back with a chair and in five minutes, coffee. For a few more minutes, as they drank, small talk followed during which the two men expressed their condolences for what had happened at the NCA and how shocked everybody was.

"Not as shocked as us." Roger commented, and we now have the not so small task of finding out who did it and how. On mentioning this the two men from digital looked at each other. This wasn't lost on Roger or Nick.

"Something I said?" Roger looked quizzically at the tech men sat opposite. Matt, who appeared to be senior replied.

"Well it may or may not be associated but we've never come across anything like this." As he spoke his colleague fished about in a sturdy black brief case and brought out a smart phone along with a small speaker. Roger recognised the phone immediately as John's. His heart missed a beat. Setting the speaker on the desk, Rob continued with an explanation.

"This phone has been professionally wiped, cleaned if you like. Whoever did it knew what they were doing for we could retrieve nothing from the phone whatsoever. Absolutely nothing. Never have we come across a smart phone that has hasn't given up some sort of information. Not until now." Roger silently sighed with relief. At the same time what the man was telling him was incredibly frustrating. He'd been hoping the phone would provide some clue to John's disappearance. "I say nothing." Rob hadn't finished. "I say nothing, there were though, quite deliberately we think two dialled numbers left on the phone. One of the number's is yours sir." Rob looked directly at Roger. "Your number is also listed in contacts" Rob looked at his notes. "Ah yes, Roger Denton NCA." Roger knew instantly the entry wasn't John's doing. He would never have stored his full name, along with the initials NCA. Roger relayed his thoughts to everyone in the room..

"I did know Mr Mitchell and knew him well enough to believe he would never have stored my number in such a fashion. Certainly not alongside the initials NCA."

Matt replied to this.

"We agree sir. Whoever wiped the phone, we believe deliberately, afterwards entered your contact details. Why? Well, we hope you guys will have a better idea than us. But they must know who you are, and how to recognise your number amongst the contacts in Mr Mitchell's phone." Roger thought hard. Who did he know who also knew John. Someone ex-military it had to be. Anyway, the question would have to wait.

"What's the second number?" Rob positioned the Bluetooth speaker on the edge of Roger's desk.

"We've no idea but listen to this." Going into John's phone he dialled what Roger assumed was the second number. The one that he had also dialled. The number hadn't been recognised. To his surprise, this time there came a ringing tone. The tone rang twice followed by loud, chilling, mocking peals of laughter. Rob ended the call and Matt followed up.

"If we left the call open, we assume the laughter would simply go on for ever. The longest Rob's team left the call open was two hours. There was no break in the laughter."

Roger looked across at Nick, he could see from his expression his thoughts were along the same lines as his. What the fuck?

"Now you two try dialling the number." Rob handed both the NCA officers a plain white postcard. On which, neatly typed there was the second number stored in John's mobile. " Nick went first. Everyone watched whilst he made three attempts. After which he looked up, puzzled.

"I keep getting number not recognized!"

"Crap, you've got brussel fingers, let me have a go" Roger put his speaker phone on and dialled the number on the card. After a few seconds a message sounded.

"The number dialled is not recognised. Please check the number and try again." Roger looked at the two men sat the other side of his desk, his face a picture of puzzlement. It was the exact same message he had got when he had first tried the number. Then how was it with John's phone, they got a ringing tone?

"The number on the card, you're sure it's the number in the phone. You haven't made a mistake?" Both men looked indignant. Both started to speak at once, then Matt let Rob continue.

"We don't know how they've done it but somehow when you use, this phone, Mr Mitchell's phone it uniquely recognises the number and. Well, you've heard the message. We've checked, and the phone is using a standard network. We have no idea how Mr Mitchell's phone is recognising this number. The number's not in service but then again it must be to get that message."

"Have you tried tracing the number?" The question came from Nick. Matt leant forward.

"Yes, but to no avail."

Rob cut in.

" How do you trace a number that's not in service?"

"What about the laughter? Have you broken it down? I know you guys can do that. Have you been able to detect any sort of accent that might give us a clue who we're dealing with.?"

Both men shook their heads in reply to Roger's question.

"No," they both said at once. Rob finished for both.

"The laughter is computer generated."

"Bloody evil sounding laughter." Nick finished his coffee, putting his empty cup on the floor.

"With respect I think it's meant to be." Matt looked nervous as he said this.

"Yes someone's bloody playing with us. That laughter is mocking us." Roger drummed his desk in frustration.

Rob half held up his hand, as though he were back at school.

"Well whoever it is, has access to some exceptional tech and I would say, access to a hell of a lot of money too.

"You mean a state?" Roger asked directly

"I would say so, but that's for you guys to uncover. Sorry." Again Matt looked nervous.

"Ok, ok. What about the CCTV footage. Have you better news on that? Anything there?" This time the two men looked at each other when confronted with Roger's question.

"Possibly." Matt knew this wasn't the answer the director at the NCA wanted.

"What do you mean possibly? Either you have or you haven't"?

"We're still checking." Matt knew he was risking Roger's wrath but he had to be honest. "We've done every test known to us and we can find no evidence of tampering. That doesn't mean it hasn't been, it's just that we haven't found evidence of it. However, having said that there is one peculiarity, and we're looking into that at the moment."

"Peculiarity?" Roger looked across at Nick. "What's that when it's at home?" Matt refused to rise to the bait. He was used to impatient detectives demanding instant and clear cut answers. Life in the forensic, especially tech world, wasn't like that.

"The man who escorted your target out of the bar."

"You mean the guy who the CCTV shows he was there and yet he has a thousand and one bloody alibis who says he wasn't." Again Roger looked across at Nick who smiled acknowledging his boss's exasperation. The process of checking the guy's alibis had become something of an embarrassment and had resulted in the Northamptonshire constabulary issuing an informal apology.

Matt ploughed on. His colleague once again reached into his briefcase and handed him an A4 brown envelope.

"Now the face recognition system uses the DVLA database." Both Nick and Roger needlessly confirmed that it did. Matt already knew. He handed two photographs to the men from the NCA, placing two more copies face up on Roger's desk. "We broke the CCTV footage into a series of stills. This one," he tapped the one on Roger's left is a close up of the man's face taken from one of the stills from the CCTV footage. And this one," tapping the photo on Roger's right is taken from the photo the DVLA hold, the one used to provide facial recognition." Both Roger and Nick studied the photos closely. It was Nick who confirmed the obvious.

"They're identical."

"Exactly, and we've checked them digitally. Everything matches, and if the system WAS hacked then these," Matt tapped both photos, "are the hackers first mistake. Using AI possibly, it looks as though they've been able to create a false scenario. Putting someone there who wasn't, whilst hiding the identity of the person who was." Roger leaned forward, his expression completely different from a few seconds ago.

"If this Is the case, will you be able to reestablish the original footage?"

Matt shrugged his shoulders.

"Possibly. To be honest I'm not sure, we've still got a lot of work to do on this. And we're going to need to physically check their CCTV system on site. We need to find out how, if their system was hacked, how the hackers got past their security. If we can do that, the dominos might start to tumble. And if that happens, who knows what we can uncover."

"I knew you were going to say that." Roger leant back in his chair running his fingers through his hair. "Ok, I'll put in the request. There's no way those people could have vanished into thin air. The only answer is the CCTV must have been altered. Even if you guys can't find anything. It has to have been, and this." It was Roger's turn to tap the photos. "Proves it." Matt hadn't finished. He had something else to say and he knew it may draw greater concern.

"There's something else."

"Go on." Roger's expression was one of expectation as was Nick's.

"If someone did hack the CCTV system and they did use an image from…," Matt could see from Roger's change of expression that the penny had dropped. "Use an image from the DVLA database…"

"Then they must have also hacked the DVLA's database to have lifted the photo." Roger finished for him. Both Matt and Rob nodded. Rob took over, giving his colleague a break.

"It's not unknown, the DVLA has had some rather embarrassing data breaches, but to hack in and lift an image without anybody realising does suggest there may be a pretty serious hack. A hack that if we're right, the DVLA is still unaware of."

Nick whistled.

"Shit, how bad could it be? I mean what could be the worst that could happen? And are you sure the hackers have used a picture from the DVLA? Couldn't they have simply taken an image from the internet. "

Matt replied to this.

"Despite first appearances it's fairly simple to spot such a scam. No we've digitally checked both images, they're an exact match. The worst that could happen?" Matt raised both his palms upwards. "Well normally hacks are either done to hold the owners of the database to ransom or to sell data on. Alternatively, whoever's responsible for the hack may simply want to create mischief, play about with the data stored. That however is a lot harder."

"Play about?" Roger sensed what was coming. Matt in response dropped his hands on his lap.

"Well in case of the DVLA for example. You, if you knew how could swap data around. The result would be chaos. Addresses could be changed, photos swapped. Convictions swapped over or even deleted. So many government departments rely on the DVLA database, mainly because the proof of identity for a driving licence is greater than that for a passport. If it's found that the DVLA's database has been compromised, then it strips away a major defence against terrorism. Those who wish us harm could assume just about any identity they wanted. The integrity of the DVLA database is paramount for the security of this country."

For the next fifty minutes the discussion revolved around any number of possibles. It wasn't long before every possibility had been exhausted and the possible turned into the fantastical. The trouble was and everyone there knew it, what at the moment looked like pure fantasy could become, worst case scenario, reality.

"Well what do you think?" Roger asked Nick after they left.

"Think?" Nick paused, looking thoughtful. "I think we've under-estimated what we're dealing with. I think this could turn out to be something big. I've no idea what, who or how. But at the moment I simply have a feeling. And you're right, whoever we're dealing with are playing with us, mocking us. And I have a horrible feeling, watching us too" Roger nodded. Big? His mind went back to last night. His meeting with the man who for now, called himself Jason. Big was the word he'd used. 'Big enough to put the willies up the people who employed him.' The thought was scary.

"Do you think our investigation and the bombing of our offices could be linked?"

"At the moment I don't see how, but I'm beginning to get the feeling they might be."

"But it's just a feeling." Roger finished for him. Nick nodded.

"Yes."

Morgue, Centre Hospitalier, Boulogne Sur Mer

Jean-Paul Hubert, chief pathologist at the morgue in Boulogne sat at his desk sipping a strong café noir. He was feeling very uneasy and in something of a quandary. After the visit from the British, gendarmes from Calais and officers from the GIGN, he had tried to return to work but he'd found it impossible. He considered himself an honourable man. And if someone in his morgue was there because they were a victim of malpractice, then he felt it his duty to help the authorities bring their killer to justice. After what had taken place that morning, he felt he'd been robbed of that duty. The mutilated bodies of twelve young children and two adult males taken from his morgue in the most bizarre circumstances.

Worse, he'd been forced to hand over the physical files of the post mortems he'd done so far and delete all the digital files. They no longer existed in his records. Any enquiries, whether they came from the gendarme or law enforcement in Royaume-Uni, he'd been told to refer to an office and number in Paris. He was under no circumstance to reveal any details of his post mortems. If he did he would lose his licence to practise along with his pension. If anyone asked, all the bodies had been transferred to Paris as the morgue here at Boulogne hadn't the space to store them. Well the last bit was true at least. He hadn't the space.

The whole thing stank and he had no desire to be part of it. He didn't really give a damn about losing his job but he needed his pension. Which was going to win? The need for his pension or his conscience? That was his quandary.

Calais, France

Madame Maubert had tried Marie's number at least ten times. On every attempt she got the answerphone. Starting to become worried herself she'd called her daughter. She hadn't sounded very happy about giving her mother a lift to check on Marie but had, reluctantly after much badgering, agreed.

Now here they were in a narrow street in Calais, a street that consisted mainly of Flemish brick terraced houses, one of which was Marie's. And they were standing outside. They'd knocked and tried ringing the bell but got no answer.

"Perhaps she's a heavy sleeper," the daughter questioned. She could empathise with such a trait. "We don't want to wake her up."

"I don't think anyone's home." Madame Maubert was doing her best to peer through the window but with no inside light and heavy Calaisien lace nets she was finding it impossible.

"Are you looking for Marie? The voice came from behind. Mother and daughter looked round to see a young woman, mid-twenties at a guess, holding a baby.

"Oui." Mother and daughter replied in unison.

"She's not at home."

"Do you know where she is? The young woman ignored Madame Maubert's question. Instead she looked directly at her daughter.

"You dropped her off yesterday, non? I saw you." The daughter nodded.

"Oui."

"I was watching, the whole street watches Marie. Well she never went in. Immediately after you left two men picked her up in their car. Probably customers of hers."

"Customers?" This time the young woman replied to Madame Maubert's question.

"Salope. Well, she hasn't been home since the men took her. I live opposite. I'd have seen." With that the young woman turned and went back into her house.

"Well that was a waste of time." The daughter complained.

Madame Maubert didn't respond. She had other things on her mind. She needed to call Lieutenant Beaufort.

Gendarmerie Nationale, Calais, France

"The capitaine's waiting for you Monsieur Beaufort. He's in his office." Colette still felt odd knowing there was someone else in what she still considered to be Capitaine's Maubert's office. Talk about walking in a dead man's shoes.

Lieutenant Beaufort nodded his thanks and started mounting the stairs. Halfway up he hesitated, turned and jogged back down.

"Colette, Colette," he called using hushed tones. Colette turned and the lieutenant touched her arm. "Colette if the capitaine's wife, I mean Capitaine Maubert's wife phones, ask her to leave a message. Whatever the message is, please whatever you do, do not pass it on to our new capitaine. Save it for me." His eyes pleaded with her but there was no need.

"Of course lieutenant, if that's what you want. It'll be my pleasure."

"Promise?"

"I promise Monsieur Beaufort." Colette meant it. First impressions, she did not like their new capitaine at all. It really would be a pleasure to bypass him. To keep him in the dark.

"You're a star Colette." And after kissing her on the cheek he mounted the stairs two by two.

Capitaine Vendroux, Olivier Vendroux, answered, 'entréz,' at the first knock.

Lieutenant Beaufort entered to find their new capitaine, leaning back in his chair, feet up on the desk whilst enjoying a coffee. It was not at all what he'd expected.

"Sit down lieutenant, I've asked Colette to bring you up some coffee. She must know how you like it."

"She does," the lieutenant conceded. He discreetly looked around the office. Usually when a newcomer takes over an office, the first thing they do is to try and make it look like home. In the case of a man, some stupid boys' toys. Family photos, certificates, nearly always a photo of a dog and perhaps some sporting memorabilia. Anything to make settling in easier. But their new capitaine had made no attempt. Judging by his position that morning, he was at home without all that stuff. There came a knock and Colette entered with a steaming cup of café noir. With only a smile, she left. The capitaine when she'd gone slid his feet off the desk and brought his chair up tight.

"I have to say Colette makes an excellent cup of coffee, is she good at anything else?" The lieutenant simply smiled at what he hoped was the capitaine's idea of a joke. "Congratulations by the way, on an excellent job this morning. Very professionally executed I'm told. I need to thank everyone involved personally. Perhaps you can send them up one by one after we've finished, Lieutenant."

"Of course sir, Am I allowed to ask what that was all about?" In response Capitaine Vendroux folded his arms.

"You may not, lieutenant, just as I cannot either. We do what we are told lieutenant. To start to ask questions only encourages disorder. Do I make my point clear?"

"You do, sir." Though quietly he disagreed.

"And I need to repeat, what happened this morning must never be discussed. Especially outside of this gendarmerie. I hope you made that clear to your team?"

"I have sir, quite clear."

The capitaine smiled.

"Good, I just need to make sure. One of the reasons I want to meet the people involved." The lieutenant had already guessed that was the real reason." Anyway, I just want to go over a few things with you before you and I start working together on a day to day basis."

"Certainly sir, good idea." He watched as the capitaine reached down to the floor and on retrieving a file placed it open on his desk.

"I've printed off some of your capitaine's case notes." The capitaine didn't wait to allow the lieutenant time to comment. "Firstly, I want you to know, that my appointment is only temporary. Only till they find someone more suitable. But before you cheer, that will probably take a little over a year. At least, that's what I'm told to expect."

"I wasn't about to cheer, sir."

"Very polite of you to say so." The capitaine grinned a grin that read, we both know you're lying. "Now first things first. Everyday operations can look after themselves. I want to go over with you the main cases you were working on. And, of course, the main one is the one the whole bloody world is talking about, the heads found in La Manche and that poor girl's body found on the beach. I've been reading your capitaine's notes." He held up the file and dropped it down on the desk. "To me, Capitaine Maubert's views are, were, a bit one directional."

"One directional?"

"Yes, he allowed himself to follow only one direction. This stuff about the red market. Do you really believe that lieutenant?"

"Well," the lieutenant paused, allowing himself time to think. "I can't see the idea should be dismissed."

"Where would they dispose of the bodies? The smell? Killing on an industrial scale would be near impossible to hide. Now out at sea. Yes, that's different. That IS a possibility. Now that I can begin to believe. Even the possibility of some sort of red market operation. But here, on French soil? No, quite impossible. I think you've all been wasting your time. Not to mention resources."

"What about Ismail sir? The capitaine played us a recording. It was very convincing." The lieutenant felt the capitaine's dismissal was premature. Even a touch insulting. However, he did have to concede that he'd often felt the same as their new capitaine.

"Ismail? The poor bugger whose head ended up in London sucking his own cock? He certainly pissed somebody off. But red market, no. I've read the transcript, he was high on drugs. Probably his own. Chances are he didn't pay for them. That's why he ended up sucking his own cock. Drugs not blood is at the bottom of all this. It's always drugs. That's what we need to be looking at. Are there any new dealers in town?" Lieutenant Beaufort didn't disagree but felt the dismissal of the red market theory was unwise and said so.

"I'm not dismissing it lieutenant, I just can't accept it's happening here. In or close to Calais. You lot love a good gossip. There's no way anyone'd be able to hide one body, let alone several." The lieutenant assumed by, 'you lot,' the capitaine was referring to his fellow Calaisiens. He had to admit, the capitaine had a point. He didn't like the terminology his new boss was using, but he was right. To hide one body would be hard enough, let alone a number of them. Still, he wasn't going to give up. He still felt the possibility needed investigating.

"What about the girl? Marie's suggestion, that migrants were disappearing, vanishing without any further communication? Don't you think that should be investigated, sir? "

The capitaine waved his arm, demonstrating what he thought of the suggestion.

"They're migrants, many with a lot to hide. How many of them want to do harm to Europe? Most of them I don't doubt. They're transient by nature and clandestine because most have no bloody right to be here. The British government are coming under a lot of pressure to deal with them and as a result thousands are living in camps or on a bloody prison ship. After all the effort to cross La Manche would you want to end up living a worse life than the one you left? Of course you wouldn't. You'd disappear. Find a job that paid cash in hand. You wouldn't run the risk of being caught because you sent a letter back to auntie whoever, living in the jungle. They're disappearing because they want to disappear. Anyway, why waste French money on a bunch of terrorists. Let the Brits sort them out." The lieutenant could see that he was wasting his breath, but the capitaine's tirade had reminded him of Marie. He wondered whether he ought to bring her up and against his better judgement perhaps, did so. He told his new boss his concerns for her safety. That not only had Ismail been a shock but her friends who had been putting him up had also disappeared. That she was worried the same could happen to her. And to be honest he was beginning to worry as well. It may be wise for the gendarmerie to offer her some sort of protection. Especially after the social media led scandal that had exposed her relationship with Capitaine Maubert and as a result his suicide. If somebody else didn't do harm to Marie, he could see her jumping off Cap Blanc Nez. Just like the capitaine."

Lieutenant Beaufort hadn't been certain what sort of response his concerns would draw from his new capitaine. But to hear him laugh was totally unexpected. When he'd had stopped he apologised for his outburst.

"I'm sorry, I shouldn't have laughed. Marie's not the reason your capitaine committed suicide. Have you not been told about Fatima?"

Fatima, the name in Capitaine Maubert's diary. The lieutenant thought he was the only person who knew about her. And what he knew wasn't much. She was simply a name, nothing else. All the diary revealed was the name. He'd been planning to investigate, and now it looked as though his new capitaine was about to reveal all. He was right.

"Your capitaine was seduced by a femme fatale called Fatima. Not her real name by the way, but her working name. We have no idea who she really is. There's a rumour that she's now in the UK, but that's all it is a rumour. Anyway she successfully seduced your capitaine and he admitted to telling her everything about your investigation. Absolutely bloody everything. He even took her to that guy, what's his name, Is…"

"Ismail," the lieutenant helped out.

"Yes Ismail. Well, your old boss is responsible for his death. He handed him on a plate to the femme fatale and whoever she was working for. That's why he was suspended. Apparently before he jumped he went back to the hotel where it had all happened, asking after her. Bloody idiot. Sorry." The capitaine held up his hand. "Sorry, I shouldn't have said that. Anyway, that's what happened. This Fatima was almost certainly employed by a drug cartel to see what she could find out. And what they found out is, we've been wasting our time running about like headless chickens searching for this red market instead of drugs. We now have to turn the tables, change direction. If these bastards had wanted this girl, Marie, they would have taken her out by now. These drug cartels don't piss about. We will though, search for her missing friends. Hopefully, they're hiding rather than come to any harm. You can be in charge of that investigation if you like."

"Thank you, sir." The lieutenant's head was spinning. He felt as though he'd just been punched by the world's greatest ever boxer. Capitaine Maubert, a femme fatale? Never in a million years. Not the capitaine he knew.

"And." Capitaine Vendroux hadn't finished. He tapped the file on his desk. "Out of respect for the work your gendarmerie has been doing, I'll pass this onto Interpol, with the suggestion that they may look at suspicious shipping in the area. They're better placed to organise a search in international waters than we are. I believe all these bodies that have turned up in your waters were meant to have been sunk far out to sea. It's pure bad luck that they ended up on your doorstep. Now if there's nothing else lieutenant, I need to thank the rest of your team for the excellent job they did today. If they're in the building can you send them up one at a time."

Thank them? Tell them to keep their mouths shut more like. The lieutenant realised it was fruitless trying any further to convince the capitaine to further investigate the missing migrants. If they were missing. He had to admit that their new capitaine may well be right. To have gone missing may well have been their own choice. They may well have been investigating something that simply didn't exist. He reflected on the operation that morning. Those poor mutilated children although ending up on French soil, almost certainly didn't originate from France. If they were from Britain perhaps it was understandable that the British government wanted them returned and to keep it under wraps. The whole operation was starting to make sense if you thought of it in those terms.

Capitaine Vendroux watched the lieutenant leave his office. After he'd shut the door the capitaine picked up the file on his desk and slipped it into his briefcase. He had no intention of delivering it to Interpol. It would be a complete waste of their bloody time. Logging onto his computer he continued to the open file on the severed heads found floating in La Manche, and the girl's body found on the beach. Typing quickly, he entered his own observations and that the investigation, for now was closed with the belief that the initial offence did not take place on French soil. Closing the file he stood up and walked to the window. Apart from vehicles belonging to the gendarmerie the car park was clear. The media that had caused such chaos yesterday had largely gone. Already bored they would be on the search for more tragic or salacious headlines. They disgusted him. Today they would announce officially that Capitaine Maubert's tragic death was to be listed as suicide. No foul play suspected. Hopefully that would see the last of them off. There came a knock at the door.

"Entréz."

A middle aged female officer entered.

"Morning sir. I'm Adjudante Lavigne, Chloe Lavigne." The capitaine waved for her to sit down.

"Come in Chloe, come in. Coffee?"

His charm offensive had begun.

The lieutenant had hardly taken a step in reception when Colette signalled for him to stop by her office.

"It's Marie isn't it?" he asked as soon as he had closed the door.

"Vivienne's asked me to get you to ring her as soon as you came out."

"I'll do it whilst I'm here." The lieutenant rang her mobile. Madame Maubert answered immediately. She'd obviously been waiting for his call. In under ten minutes she had relayed all that had happened that morning. Not being able to raise Marie on the phone. Their consequential visit to Marie's house and what a neighbour had told them.

"Everyone hates her lieutenant, the neighbour referred to her as a slut."

The lieutenant could do little more than advise them both, mother and daughter, to go home. To go home and lock their door. In the French countryside people rarely locked their doors. He was worried that it had sounded condescending when he'd told her, no more detective work. But he'd meant it kindly. The last thing he wanted was to put his ex-boss's wife in any sort of danger. And something very strange was going on. Something that made no sense at all. Finishing the call he saw Colette looking at him expectantly. He needed to think.

"Colette, I need you to contact the Procureurs office. I need a search warrant for…" The lieutenant searched through his notes. Finding Marie's address he jotted it down and slid it across Colette's desk. It's Marie's house, we have Marie's details on file."

"What reason shall I give?" The lieutenant took a deep breath, he was finding it hard to get out what he needed to say.

"Owner of the address is missing. Foul play expected. Possible kidnapping. Life of resident at the address believed to be in imminent danger." The lieutenant paused. "Add this too Colette. Owner of property connected to Ismail, have we got a surname for Ismail, Colette?"

"I can look it up." The lieutenant nodded.

"Ok, do that Colette please. Connected to Ismail whatever his surname is, now known to have been murdered. Also with close connections to two residents of Les Attaques, reported missing. And possible connection to recent death of Capitaine Maubert, of the gendarmerie nationale, Calais." Colette looked up shocked.

"Do you really mean that last sentence lieutenant? A lot of questions will be asked. It might not go down well."

"Yes I do Colette, yes I'm certain. And I need that warrant in hours, not days."

Le Channel Restaurant, Calais, France

In arguably Calais's best and most prestigious restaurant, only minutes' walk from the gendarmerie, sat a group of five men. The mayor, the owner of an electrical company who specialised in wiring new builds, the region's largest developer. Pierre, officially a diamond dealer and respected business man, along with two of his associates.

Pierre was looking forward to the next two or three hours. Not only to the food and fine wine, but to calling in a few favours. They might not realise it but the good residents of Calais owed him.

NCA's Temporary Offices, Gladstone Park, Cricklewood, London, England

Around the same time Pierre was sitting down to lunch in Calais, Roger Denton of the NCA was preparing for an update meeting with Nick. For the current investigation, Nick was now his second in command. After the guys from digital and video forensics had left he'd asked Nick to give him half an hour. He needed to phone Jane.

Jane as usual was full of concern for him, his safety. Especially as since their conversation that morning, MI5 had decided to move her to a different, apparently safer safe house. Roger, until now, with all his years of experience in the NCA, hadn't been aware there were different levels of safety in safe houses. On reflection it did make sense.

Jane listened intently to Roger's account of their meeting with digital forensics. She accepted there may be fall out with the hotel when they disclosed, they had conducted a sting operation on their premises without consulting them first. 'Tough,' had been her only comment. Roger then moved on to the real reason he wanted to talk to her. The DVLA. Jane remained silent as Roger explained the theory that the image of the man escorting Mr Mitchell out of the Sky Bar, the poor teacher in Wellingborough who had alibis galore for the time, that the hotel CCTV placed him at the bar. It had been taken from a still, stored at the DVLA. If this was indeed the case, it looks as though the DVLA's database had been compromised, hacked. And that the DVLA, either knew about it but weren't saying anything, (it wouldn't be the first time), or perhaps worse. They simply didn't know, they weren't aware.

Jane promised to speak to the CEO of the DVLA personally. Immediately after they'd finished this call. Especially as the two men from forensics felt strongly that whoever was responsible had access to some very sophisticated tech. Almost certainly developed by a nation state, if not a group, perhaps terrorist, with close ties to a nation state. It was unlikely, but anyone gaining complete access to the DVLA database could cause chaos. Just before their call ended, Jane asked for the contact details of the two men Roger had met with. The DVLA will almost certainly want to speak with them directly.

No sooner had Roger put the phone down, there came a knock at his door and Nick poked his head in.

"All clear? Safe for me to come in?"

"Password."

"Coffee."

"Right answer, though I'm starving as well."

"Special today is crab stuffed ravioli cooked in a cream and white wine sauce with prawns."

"Bloody hell, what happened to burger, tinned veg and chips?"

"Want me to get you some? We can eat in your office." Roger said yes and Nick disappeared.

Several trips later, the two men were sat in Roger's office. Both with coffee. Roger with the special and Nick with burger and chips.

"You're such a bloody heathen Nick. No sophistication."

Nick accepted his boss's remark, with some pride.

"That's why I'm with the NCA."

"Point taken."

On finishing their food, Roger took the plates back, explaining he needed the toilet again. On returning they got down to the serious stuff.

"Report from the search at Mr Mitchell's house in Goring." Nick dropped a file on Roger's desk. The CSO's found nothing of real interest. Twelve thousand pounds in cash in a safe, but that was about it. There was no phone so Mr Mitchell when there, must have used his mobile. Which of course has already been checked and all we've discovered is someone taking the piss out of us."

"Car?" Roger asked. "I know he had a car."

"Yes, found in the garage. It was checked and the SOCOs don't believe it's been driven for weeks. Which makes sense as his last job, from what we know, included reclaiming a car." Roger nodded, all of this was too sanitary. They were missing something, possibly the bloody obvious again.

"Bank accounts?

"We can only find two bank accounts registered to Mr Mitchell sir. Two different banks. We've requested the last three years statements from both. What we have got is the current balance in each. Seven thousand pounds in one and a little over two grand in the other. A lot of money to some, but not I believe to somebody like Mr Mitchell. Somewhere he must have stashed, a hell of a lot of money."

"I agree." Roger ran his hands though his hair. "But where?"

Nick shrugged his shoulders.

"God knows, it's not easy to hide money these days. Both his house in Goring by the way and the flat in Drury Lane, have no mortgage owing. He owns both outright. The one in Goring is worth a cool three million. Not bad from owning a small bakery."

"We both know the bakery was a front."

"Yes sir, but we have checked the accounts, and it was, is making good money. It may be a front but it's also a good business in its own right. Net profit last financial year was over a hundred thousand pounds. And no reason to suspect there's anything dodgy going on. They've even supplied Kensington Palace." Nick paused. "By the way, the accountant and the guy you spoke to there, the one apparently in charge, want to know what's happening with the business." Roger leant back in his chair.

"For all we know Mr Mitchell may suddenly turn up tomorrow. Knowing the man as I do, I can't see him being exactly hands on. So tell them they can carry on as normal."

"Did you get anything from your interview?" It was Nick's turn to ask a question.

Roger pursed his lips.

"Nothing that I didn't already know. The guy told me that Mr Mitchell had received a debt collecting enquiry, he gave me the number of the guy who had rung. But of course the number belongs to us. It belongs to the phone our plant was using, who's now on the bloody missing list. And of course we know Rory's personal phone hasn't been used since the day of the sting. Where the bloody hell are they both? The not knowing is starting to get on my bloody nerves."

Nick ignored his boss's vocal demonstration of his frustration.

"Going back to the bank accounts sir. What the banks have told us, is his cards haven't been used since the day of the sting. That includes his credit cards."

Roger cut in.

"So either he's dead…"

"Or he's clever and doesn't want to be found." Nick finished off.

"And John, sorry Mr Mitchell, has been trained by His Majesty's government on exactly how to do that." Roger stared at the ceiling. "What a bloody mess. Any good news?"

"We're waiting for the phone records from the bakery. They should be with us tomorrow. "We've received the pathologist's report on the severed head delivered to the address in Tottenham." Nick dropped a file on Roger's desk. "Here's a copy. Officers are currently comparing them to the two similar ones from Langstone and Spain. My personal observation is that the first two were both gangsters and the latest a migrant, trying to get to this country to be with his wife. Apart from the way the heads were found I can't see a connection."

"Gangsters move in mysterious ways," Roger commented dryly. "Dig deep enough and we'll probably find a connection somewhere. One thing we do know, we've received a message from Interpol, that the guy, whose head was delivered in Tottenham was helping the gendarmerie in Calais with their enquiries. That reminds me, I need to speak to them." Roger made a note. "We need to investigate those poor children that are in a morgue over there too. We will have to organise a separate team to look at that. And whoever it is, they need to be discreet. If stuff leaked out it could cause an international incident. For now we need to get them back here so that our own pathologist can examine them."

"Good luck with that, sir."

"Thanks Nick. I have a funny feeling I'll need it. Anything else? What about this Maureen Fowlis? Her name keeps coming up."

"Well, her hairbrush the hotel found, in her room has been sent for testing. We've checked and there's no DNA listing for Maureen Fowlis on the NDNAD. So to date as far as the authorities are concerned, she's been a good girl. There is both public and private CCTV situated on Broad Street outside the Fielding Hotel. We will be able to start looking at the public CCTV, here this afternoon. We're going to hook up three screens with three operators so we can cover the time Mrs Fowlis was staying there without taking days to do it."

"Well hopefully that should throw up something. What about the private CCTV?"

"Officers are on their way as we speak sir, hopefully we can start examining that this afternoon as well."

"Great Nick. Anything else?"

Nick sighed.

"I wish there was, at the moment, as you well know. All we seem to have are questions. It would be nice to find just one answer, from somewhere."

This time it was Roger's turn to sigh.

"Agreed, somebody is playing with us. That's how it feels, and we haven't a bloody clue who."

Nick stood up, pushing back his chair.

"We'll get there, sir. The CCTV footage is their first mistake. Hopefully the forensic guys will be able to find out more."

"Thanks for reminding me Nick. I've got to tell the Hilton that we were conducting a sting operation in their hotel without letting them know."

"Good luck with that sir." And Nick left, laughing.

For a good two minutes after Nick had left Roger sat staring at his desk. Never had he been involved in an investigation with so many open ends, so many loose connections. Did anything connect at all? That was the million dollar question. Were they trying to make things connect when simply they didn't?

John. Was he dead or masterminding a very sophisticated what? That was another question, if so, what? What had he got himself involved him? His disappearance at the Hilton, had been extremely well organised. It must have taken a lot of planning and yet their sting operation had only been set up twenty four hours before. Like the explosion at their offices, the NCA building in Vauxhall, this was beginning to stink of an inside job. An informer on the inside. The scary thing was he had no idea who it could be. He trusted one hundred percent all of his team and yet what had taken place at the hotel simply couldn't have been achieved without somebody having detailed information on their modus operandi for the day. Who could he trust? More to the point, who could he not trust? Nick? His number two, he hated the idea, yet Jason's words kept ringing alarm bells in his head. 'Our department's philosophy is to trust no one, not even each other.' The thought left a horrible taste in his mouth.

Needing a distraction Roger picked up the pathologist's report for the head delivered to an address in Tottenham. The poor woman, how will she ever get over the shock of her husbands severed head being delivered, minus his eyes and his mouth stuffed with his genitalia. He couldn't begin to imagine what she and her children were going through. He hoped they were getting support from the government. He wasn't looking forward to having to interview her and interview her soon they will have to. He scanned the pages of the report. Everything Jason had told him in the Lamb and Flag had been accurate. The decapitation had been executed by a professional, a trained surgeon. As had the removal of the eyes. The test estimated that the man had been killed at least forty eight hours before. Roger came to the drilling into the man's brain. Purpose, he read. Apparently to remove the pineal gland which was missing. Pineal gland? What the hell was that? In all his time from being in law enforcement, Roger couldn't ever remember a pathologist's report mentioning a pineal gland. He made a note to call the pathologist and ask him a few questions. There wasn't much more. They already knew the victim's identity.

And he'd already read the police report. The parcel that had contained the head had been delivered by a well known courier company. Several witnesses had confirmed this. Except that when the courier company had been contacted to see who had sent the parcel, they denied the van was theirs. On the day in question, they didn't even have a delivery booked for that street, let alone the address. The van had later been discovered burnt out on a farm track near Wheathampstead in Hertfordshire. Whoever had destroyed it had done a good job for forensics found nothing to help the investigation. Hours of CCTV had been checked to see if a route could be tracked but whoever had been driving had somehow managed to avoid the roads with cameras. When it was picked up, the courier's logo had not only been removed but the number plate changed too. It had taken a while to understand that on the day in question, the van had displayed two very different number plates. Both when checked were valid. Clones of legitimate number plates on an identical model van.

The DVLA. Was this a connection to the hotel sting? Had whoever cloned the plates had access to the DVLA database? It was a possibility which could mean a possible connection between the severed head in Tottenham and the possible hacking of the CCTV at the Hilton. Possible, possible, possible. When would they be able to prove something was certain?

Roger picked up the condensed files to the first two killings. The beheadings that had started this enquiry. Again Jason was right. These were hatchet jobs. An axe or meat cleaver had probably been used to severe the heads and the report read that the victims were almost certainly alive when the butchery took place. Whereas with the head delivered in Tottenham, the victim it was reported by the pathologist had been dead when his genitalia and head had been severed. So same result but operationally very different. The murder in Langstone had been widely reported. The Tottenham murder could therefore quite easily be a copycat killing. Roger rubbed his scalp in frustration. He had limited resources and there may well be two quite different investigations here, not one.

Once again he wondered how John was involved with all of this. How had he got involved? Jason had mentioned the red market. This had been something of a surprise. He hadn't even considered a connection with the red market. And if he was honest he knew sod all about it. He promised himself to do a little research that afternoon. The NCA would have some files on it.

This train of thought reminded him of the bodies of the butchered Albanian children lying in a morgue in Boulogne. They needed to get them back so their own staff could examine them. And perhaps they could get the pathologist over there to examine the severed head, currently stored in Haringey mortuary. Maybe he could tell whether the same surgeon was responsible. It was a long shot but worth a try.

There came a knock at the door. It was Nick, just back from a brief summing up in the operations room.

"Boss. It may be nothing but one of the boys has just told me." Nick closed the door behind him, talking as he walked. "There's a guy out at Staines or Heathrow, same difference. A Detective Constable Havers, asking a lot of questions about the severed head in Tottenham and the other two. It might be pure curiosity, but our guy says the questions are pretty intense. More than if it were simply curiosity."

"Where is he stationed?"

"Staines, so it would have nothing to do with them."

"And the 'other two'? He's specifically asked about the one the Spanish are helping us with as well?

"So I'm told."

"Well how the hell does he know about that one? It's not common knowledge. It means someone's been blabbering."

"I hadn't thought of that." Nick look frustrated.

"This case is so bloody messy, we need to treat everything with suspicion. We need to find out why this officer's showing such an interest. It might be for a legitimate reason but if not. Well, we need to know and know now. I'll speak to Jane. We need to get his phone records. See who he's been talking to. Jane will be able to move that quickly. Can you message me his name and station.

"Will do." Nick made to leave.

"Nick have you heard of the pineal gland?"

Nick looked puzzled.

"No, I don't think so. Why what is it?"

Roger explained what was entered in the pathologist's report.

"Jeeez, why would anybody do that?"

"That's what we've got to find out. Nick can you, or can you get somebody to give the pathologist a call, ask them why anyone would want to do that. Why would they want a pineal gland?"

"Will do." Nick left, closing the door softly behind him.

Roger's hand hovered over his phone. Who to call first? Jane or the Hilton. He decided on the coward's route and called Jane first.

Portsdown Hill, Hampshire, England

Sea mist shrouded the hill overlooking the city of Portsmouth. As a result the night chill remained and only a few people were out walking their dogs, even fewer taking in the views. On the road running along the top of the hill, hardly visible in the mist a white van travelled at a steady thirty miles an hour. There was nothing about it to warrant any special attention except that it was discreetly escorted by four reasonably new cars. Two out front and two taking up the rear. The sea mist suited the little convoy for they had no wish to draw attention to themselves. Traveling from east to west, as they neared the far side of the hill the convoy pulled into an abandoned Victorian fort. One of a series along the top of the hill, built to defend Portsmouth against a possible invasion by Napoleon. The fort greeting the convoy was due for development. For now though it was still under the ownership of the M.O.D. Once inside the fort's courtyard the van made for a wide metal shutter. Personnel in military fatigues, pulled on a heavy chain and slowly the shutter opened. The van was just low enough to pass under the opening and into what was the beginning of a labyrinth of tunnels. Headlights on, the van drove for a further fifty metres and stopped. Quickly and without making a sound, six personnel who had been traveling in the van got out and walked back up the passageway and into the sea mist. Minutes later except for a few armed personnel the fort was empty. Their orders, to guard the van and its sensitive cargo.

The Royal Lancaster Hotel, Lancaster Gate, London, England

It was past midday when Ariana alias Fatima finally awoke. She felt strange. Not uncomfortable just strange, rather as though she'd just come round from an anaesthetic. She remembered having breakfast but not who delivered it.

Feeling a little shaky she stood up and walked to the window. She half remembered it being sunny that morning and if it had been, it was now nothing but a distant memory for blankets of grey were being drawn across any blue by a stiff northerly breeze. Her room was warm but the image the other side of the glass created a feeling of cold. Fatima shivered. She needed to clear her head and walked quickly to the bathroom. Turning on the shower she disrobed and stepped under the deliciously warm spray.

The enveloping perfume of the hotel shower gel, although familiar, Fatima found at that moment extremely sensual. Never before had she found it so, luxuriating yes but never sensual. It was strange but she didn't question why. Her mind wanted her to, her body wanted her to make the most of the way she was feeling. Using her hands Fatima slowly started to spread the aromatic foam across the upper half of her body. Running her hands underneath her breasts she slowly brought them up over her slowly firming flesh until she reached her nipples.

Slowly she squeezed. Her whole body shivered and she let out a long low moan. The small Asian girl who had delivered her breakfast was now in vision. She was smiling and completely naked. The image Fatima found extremely arousing. She squeezed her nipples again and her body twitched violently as she let out an even stronger moan. Her whole body on fire Fatima moved both hands down to her lower body. Her right hand she moved to in-between her strong thighs, stroking then squeezing her clitoris. Rhythmically she went between patting her clit to squeezing and stroking it, always paying strong attention to her body's rhythm. As her tension rose she slid her left hand to the strong rounded cheeks of her bottom and let three fingers slide up inside. The perfumed gel was now intoxicating and she imagined her hands and fingers to be those of the tiny Asian girl. Her fingers front and back quickened as every nerve in her body reached burning point. And then it came, she screamed as her climax erupted throughout her body. Back and forth her pelvis shook as one orgasm after another followed. As they started to die down Fatima slid down the wall until she was sitting with her legs out front. She rested her head on the tiled wall trying to regain some sort of control over her body. The water continued to cascade over her washing the foam and juices from inside her into the drains beneath London.

It was a whole ten minutes later before Fatima found the strength to stand once more and turn off the water. Not bothering with a towel she stepped out of the bathroom and into her room. Standing in front of the window, she stood on tiptoe stretching her arms above her head as if attempting to touch the ceiling. She felt good. Awake as never before. The Asian girl who minutes ago had brought her so much pleasure was gone from her memory. In her place was a new life, a new person. Fatima could see now, as clearly as day the second person inside her. She was still Ariana, alias Fatima who had escaped the abuses of Iran to pursue a career as a femme fatale. But she was now also, Ariana, a French citizen with a Persian heritage. Her family had been close to the

Shah and after the revolution, with help from the British had managed to escape to Jordan. From Jordan, they'd travelled to Egypt eventually ending up in France. Her mother and father had managed somehow to smuggle the family fortune out of Iran and deposited it in France making them one of the richest families in that country. Her father, with his connections in Iran had spent the remaining years of his life working for both the British and French intelligence services. Ariana, a wealthy socialite owned houses in five different cities including London and Paris. She had invested her fortune wisely and gone from being rich to extremely rich. She still had contacts in Iran which made her potentially valuable to the security services, though none to date had come knocking at her door. She'd never lived in her house in Notting Hill and yet she knew it inside out and her three servants that looked after the house and her needs. The house was currently being decorated which was why she was staying at the Royal Lancaster. There was a delay in finishing the decorating so she'd have to spend another two nights in the hotel. Tomorrow she was due to meet some old friends at an address in Mayfair. Private transport would pick her up at ten tomorrow morning. She was looking forward to it.

This new Ariana in no way felt unusual. It was who she was. Who she had always been. Her room suddenly felt hot, claustrophobic. She needed some air and something to eat. Going to the wardrobe Ariana, alias Fatima picked out her outfit for today.

Bodinnick, Cornwall, England

Claire and her dog, Tammy were on the last stretch of their walk. The last stretch meant taking the Bodinnick Ferry from Fowey across the tidal River Fowey. The walk, one of Claire's favourites, she could join from her doorstep. Records of the walk have even been found recorded in Tudor documents. Called The Hall Walk, the route revolves around the tidal inlet known as Pont Pill. Stretches of the walk are intimate, always interesting and regularly spaced with breathtaking views. The route also includes taking two ferries, the Polruan and the Bodinnick. Not many walks can boast that and it's one of the reasons Claire so loved the route for she loved water just as much as she did the land. Docking at Bodinnick, rather than go straight home she decided first to enjoy a pint in The Old Ferry Inn. She loved her local, even though it was popular with tourists it always managed to maintain a tucked away feeling. After ordering a pint she chose a seat near a window in the rear bar. One of the bar's walls was actually a rock face. You couldn't get much sturdier than that. With Tammy at her feet, Claire was in her element. This was the life she craved. She hated her past and her last remaining ties to it. True it had provided her with the living she now had, her stunning house with stunning views but she now wanted rid of it. Slowly she was cutting her ties but it was taking longer than she wanted and then there was the age old problem of people wanting revenge. She could never relax completely. Her walks with Tammy and sitting in her local was the closest she ever came to it.

Feeling her phone vibrate she reached into her pocket and switched on the screen. A message from her informant. Detective Constable Havers.

'Call me, I have some information for you.'

Claire put her phone away. He could wait. For now she felt a million miles away from that world and wanted to maintain that feeling. Leaning down she nuzzled Tammy's cheek. Tammy responded with a single lick. How she loved her life now. How she loved it.

A Street in Calais, France

Lieutenant Beaufort stood with three fellow officers outside the small terraced house that belonged to Marie. It had taken just three hours to obtain a warrant. Almost a record as far as he knew. He'd had to take a call from the procureur who'd wanted an explanation as to his wording, but all credit to him. After a brief discussion he had acted quickly. The procureur had even wished him good luck.

Now they were waiting for a locksmith so they could gain entry to the house without breaking down the door. Their presence outside Marie's house was beginning to attract attention. Not only were they receiving the usual abuse, but a lot of angry shouts were also being directed at the house's resident, Marie. The word salope was being freely banded about. Watching the proceedings stood a young woman with red streaks in her hair. Something of an anarchist she drew contentment from the scene unfolding. Her photo of that traitor Marie with Capitaine Maubert had caused greater publicity than she could have ever dreamed of. She took personal credit for the capitaine's death and felt no remorse and definitely not sympathy for his widow. It was her fault for marrying a gendarme. What did she expect.

And now this. A squad of gendarmes breaking into that traitor Marie's house. She hoped they'd find her dead inside.

Le Week - End Café/Bar, Sangatte, France

Jean had just two hours to go before he'd finish his shift for the day. It was mid afternoon and apart from a couple who had been walking their dog on the beach the café was empty. As a result the owner had told him to take a break. Thus, he was enjoying a café noir watching the local news on tv. Capitaine Maubert's face appeared on the screen. The report that followed confirmed what most people had suspected.

The relevant authorities had just announced that Capitaine Maubert's death was being officially recorded as suicide from throwing himself off the cliff at Cap Blanc Nez. There followed a brief synopsis of the capitaine's life and achievements ending with the channel's condolences for the capitaine's immediate family and friends. Immediately after followed an announcement by the mayor of a new technology park that was to be built in Calais. The park was to be a funded by both public and private money. The mayor would make a formal announcement in the coming days. But Jean wasn't listening. His head was spinning. He was trying to remember that fateful night when, from his car, they'd witnessed someone fall or had they been pushed off the cliff edge on Cap Blanc Nez?

Finishing his coffee he sent a text to Camille, his girlfriend who had been with him that night. 'Camille, have you seen the news? We have to talk. I can't keep silent. It's wrong. Love you always xxxx.' He knew she wouldn't have seen the news but his message may encourage her to look on social media. He just hoped afterwards that she'd feel the same way he was feeling now. He felt racked with guilt and simply couldn't keep their secret any longer.

NCA's Temporary Offices, Gladstone Park, Cricklewood, London, England

Roger Denton of the NCA, felt at last he was beginning to get somewhere. He'd spoken to Jane and she'd promised to speak to the relevant people about having a closer look at Detective Constable Havers. He'd also spoken to the Hilton. They hadn't been happy but had agreed to all of his requests providing the NCA went through the correct legal channels. He had already started that process and couldn't see there being a problem.

The one fly in the ointment was France. Using the language translator on his phone, he'd given the gendarmerie in Calais a call. Eventually a suspicious sounding receptionist had put his call through to a lady called Colette. Colette had been a lot more helpful to be fair to the initial person who took the call, Roger wasn't sure how well the translation device was working. Certainly, it wasn't perfect his end. Colette had put him through to the gendarmerie's new capitaine, a Capitaine Vendroux.

The new capitaine had been polite but short and direct. No, they couldn't have the bodies back. Because of lack of space, all of the bodies in question had been moved to a morgue in Paris where the relevant authorities were at this moment examining them. For the moment this was a French investigation, not a British one. However, he understood the British authorities' concern and as soon as he received an update he'd promised to pass it on. That was it, he'd politely but firmly refused to answer any further questions. Roger had put the phone down bewildered. At a meeting he'd attended, he had personally heard the Home Secretary say, they needed to bring the bodies back to UK soil and as soon as possible. You couldn't get much higher authority than that. What had happened between then and now? Then he remembered Jason's words. To be sure he remembered correctly he took out his pocket recording device and replayed the voice notes he'd recorded in his car after their meeting. He'd remembered correctly. Jason had told him that the French and British governments had done a deal. That the bodies would disappear and any request from the NCA, or for that matter any authority would be met with a refusal. That the investigation was now a French one and the bodies in question had been moved to Paris. This is exactly what had had just happened. So either the new capitaine in Calais had been in on this and had been lying, or he'd been passing on what he'd been told and believed. Either way, the whole thing was deeply unsatisfactory and from here on he was determined to become a pain in the arse for those responsible. Home Secretary or no Home Secretary.

Angry he logged on to the NCA's missing persons files. The agency maintained a central national database. Thankfully it wasn't his department, he wasn't sure if he had the kind of skills to work on missing persons. To some extent, in contrary to the appearance he presented to others, especially his work colleagues, under his thick skin, was quite a sensitive interior. Dealing with missing persons it was a side of him that could well take over. What he read shocked him. It was a national disgrace. Why weren't the news media shouting about this?

A person is reported missing in the UK every ninety seconds.

The last report revealed that in one year, ninety seven thousand adults were reported missing, and most shockingly, 70,000 children. Even more shocking, the latest research revealed that seven out of ten missing children were never reported to the police. By a rough calculation that meant nearly one hundred and sixty five thousand children went missing every year.

Further reading made Roger feel even more uncomfortable. Many found children it had been discovered had been trafficked for the sex trade. And a high percentage of children reported missing were from local authority care. Just like the poor Albanian children. Roger felt his temperature rising. Britain and especially the news media he felt were asleep at the wheel. How many more Rochdales were there waiting to be discovered? He found it disgusting.

Finally of the children reported missing, there were still one thousand five hundred and fourteen children listed as long term missing. In other words, as yet, never found. Reading through the reports there were a good many reasons for children going missing, but nowhere was the red market mentioned. And yet Jason had referred to it and quite specifically. He must have had a reason. Was there an unspoken horror happening here in the UK, right under their noses? The thought sent shivers down his spine. It was something he was determined to look into but where to start? And would he get the budget for it, let alone the resources. He made a note to speak to his equal heading missing persons. He also made a note to speak to Jane. His list for Jane was building. She'd asked for a face to face tomorrow. Normally he hated the idea but with his growing list of requests, it may be easier than a phone conversation. It was easier to say no on the phone than it was physically facing somebody.

Talking of resources. He'd been forced to pull the remainder of his team keeping watch outside the Hilton. It had to be assumed that John and their plant Rory were no longer in the building. How they had got out without being spotted was a mystery equal to that of the Mary Celeste. Ishaan, when Roger had told him had been sympathetic and to his credit promised that his team would continue to keep a special eye out. What had the Met been playing at losing that man?

Nearing the end of the afternoon, Roger received a surprise phone call from Jane. It was to tell him that she'd spoken to the relevant people in the Met and it turned out that they already had their own suspicions about Detective Constable Havers. Her contact had ramped up that investigation and they'd requested a warrant for his phone records. Jane had also, using NCA resources, organised a phone tap on Mr Haver's registered mobile and his home phone. Hopefully he wasn't using a pay as you go. Everyone would have to wait and see if their investigation brought results. His questions may well turn out to be entirely innocent. Natural curiosity of a detective. And as it turned out, he wasn't always based at Staines. When needs arose, he had on occasion been transferred to help with various investigations right across North London. Another explanation perhaps why he'd shown an interest. Maybe he was privately looking for a connection with the one at Langstone. 'We shall see,' Jane had said before she rang off.

At the end of the day Nick reappeared to give his boss an update. There wasn't much except they had streamed, footage from the local authority CCTV which conveniently covered the entrance to the Fielding Hotel in Broad Court. Three officers had started studying the footage and they'd already captured Maureen Fowlis booking into the hotel. Roger wanted to see. So far he'd only seen images John had sent him from his phone. He wanted to see how this woman moved. Get a feel for her. Was she somehow complicit in all of this or just an innocent, inadvertently caught up in John's shady world? By seeing her Roger could rely on his gut to give him some feedback.

Roger followed Nick into an office where three computers had been set up in a triangle, in the centre of the room. Six officers , two sitting at each desk were watching playbacks of the CCTV, each with a coffee on their desk. Nick led Roger over to a desk by the wall. Touching the mouse the screen shot to life and an astonishing good quality image showed up of Broad Court.

"We can watch the CCTV from two angles. I'm going to show you the clearest but you're welcome to watch the second."

"No that's fine, show me." Roger was trying not to let his impatience show.

Nick zoomed in on the entrance of the hotel."

"Now watch."

Roger watched.

A black cab pulled up and a slightly over dressed, Roger thought, woman alighted. She looked her age and was overweight but carried both well. He could see why men would desire her. She had a certain something, would you like a good time boys?' about her. Roger was no expert but she looked expensively dressed. It was obvious she had money. Tipping her driver, she entered the hotel carrying quite a large handbag and pulling a gold flushed aluminium suitcase on wheels.

"We've checked the suitcase, it's a Rimowa. This woman has money." Nick confirmed Roger's suspicion. "What do you think, sir?"

"First impressions?" Roger laughed. "She reminds me of Mrs Fox out of Dad's Army. Hardly a threat, unless she takes a fancy to you."

Nick chuckled too. He hadn't expected that but he understood his boss's drift.

"Is that it?" Roger asked.

"So far sir, but we've only just started. I've got three teams of two working through the night. Hopefully, we'll have a lot more by the morning."

"Let's hope so. When we've got the relevant paperwork together, digital will take a look at the CCTV at the Hilton. I've also requested a guest list on the day in question as well as a list of everyone who works there. Again I'm just waiting for the relevant legal stuff to be completed, so we can formally request it. Whether it will throw anything up I've no idea. Can you print me off a decent still of her face?"

"Done." Within seconds Roger was holding an A4 image of Maureen Fowlis's face. "Anything on our old building sir. Everyone seems to be keeping very quiet about that.?"

Roger shook his head.

"No, Jane wants to see me tomorrow. I guess she wants to tell me something, she doesn't feel comfortable about, talking over the phone. Perhaps it's that."

"Could be."

"Anyway, I'm off Nick." Roger turned to look at the team examining the CCTV. I guess they're all on overtime.?"

"Of course."

"That'll be another wrist slap, oh well."

Nick laughed.

"Pocket money sir."

"Fuck off," and with that Roger left the room.

Ten minutes later he was on the M1, driving home. He switched on his radio, just in time for the news update. The Albert Embankment was now open. The inconvenience to thousands of Londoners was now over. 'Inconvenience!' What about the dead? Had they been an inconvenience too? 'Of course we mustn't forget about the people who lost...' "Too bloody late," Roger shouted at the radio and turned it off.

GMC Building, Regent's Place, Euston Road, London, England

Heba felt very confident. She'd found the practical exams easy. A lot easier than she ever dared to imagine. Leaving the GMC building, she headed for the Black Sheep Coffee Shop fully intending to celebrate.

"Pitgam." A voice whispered in her ear. "Follow me."

Heba found herself following a man to the busy Euston Road where a black cab was waiting. The voice came again though she wasn't sure it was the man speaking. It was bizarre.

"The cab will take you to your hotel. Your luggage is in the boot. As soon as your results arrive you will be contacted. Good luck Heba."

The man walked off, returning to the entrance of the GMC building. There she saw him talking to someone else.

"Please get in Madame, I shouldn't really be stopping here."

It was the taxi driver. Heba quickly slid into the rear seat and shut the door. She looked again for the stranger but there was no sign of him. Funny she couldn't even remember what he looked like. Just his voice.

Formby, Lancashire, England

James turned his car into his drive. Such was his relief, he felt almost as though he'd won the lottery. Time can play tricks with one's mind and it now felt like years ago when a man had ambushed and threatened him in his car.

Just to be sure, he'd taken a huge risk and obtained another false death certificate. He just hoped that it would never show up on the system as the person registered on the certificate was very much still alive.

On entering the house, he gave his wife and young son a very big hug. Only now did he realise just how lucky he was. He had a wife, a beautiful wife who loved and needed him and a son who, possibly, loved and needed him even more. And it had taken a threat to his tiny paradise to make him realise it. How he, now, cursed his stupidity, and all for a few measly quid. Hugging his wife and son again, he quietly prayed that God would look upon his stupidity, led by greed, with sympathy. And that he'd protect what he'd fought so hard to achieve. He wasn't particularly religious but at that moment he made a promise to himself that before he retired for the night he'd pray and pray hard.

Coulogne, Near Calais, France

Lieutenant Beaufort was home. After a frustrating day that frustration, now he was home, was preventing him from relaxing. He was restless and couldn't sit down. Only pacing his lounge, did he find, helped a little, but only a little. He needed to think clearly. Going to the fridge he pulled out a bottle of 3 Monts beer and expertly removing the cap poured the golden liquid into his favourite glass. Returning to the lounge he walked over to the double 'portes-fenetres, staring out at the square one could loosely call a garden.

They'd found nothing really of interest in Marie's two-bedroom house. The morning's post was still on the mat which backed up her neighbour's story that Marie hadn't been home. The one thing they had found was a diary. A casual look revealed it was mainly used to record appointments, but there were a few notes purveying her feelings or thoughts. They may turn out to be useful. Breaking protocol, he'd brought the diary home. He now had in his possession the diaries of those whom most of Calais presumed were lovers. He wasn't proud of the fact, indeed he felt rather guilty, but after his conversation that morning with his new boss, he was worried they might simply disappear.

The interview with the nosey neighbour hadn't really revealed anything new. She couldn't describe the car that had taken Marie away. 'It was just a car.' Colour? She couldn't remember, silver, possibly light blue, perhaps a touch of both. Argghhh the lieutenant almost choked with frustration. There was hardly any CCTV in Calais, certainly not in the area Marie lived and with such a vague description it would be impossible to track. Her description of the two men was equally frustratingly vague. 'They both looked French,' was the best she could come up with. What was the bloody physical definition of a Frenchman? He'd pushed her but she couldn't or perhaps refused to say. Interviews with Marie's other neighbours hadn't fared any better and it quickly came apparent that Marie wasn't liked. No one had seen anything, and 'good riddance' had been uttered by a couple of individuals.

On his way home Colette had called. Capitaine Vendroux wanted to see him first thing tomorrow. Great, he already knew what that was about. And a policeman from London, England, a Roger Denton had phoned. The same policeman who had been trying to reach Capitaine Maubert, his ex-boss. Colette had said she'd put his call through to the new capitaine. He wondered what he'd wanted and more to the point would his new boss, Capitaine Vendroux even tell him.

And there was something odd about his new boss. He'd been very polite in their meeting that morning. Nice even but he'd not come across as sincere. More as though he was putting on an act. Speaking to a few of his team at the end of the day, the overriding opinion was their new capitaine was a bit of a slime ball. Not to be trusted. That he had his own agenda. He was for himself, not for the gendarmerie. A typical Parisian was the second overriding opinion. And the lieutenant didn't disagree.

Finishing his beer, he went to the fridge and pulled out a second. After pouring the beer into his glass he drank half in one gulp before returning to the lounge.

"Alexa, play T Smidje by Lais."

Where his ex-boss had famously liked hard rock, he enjoyed Flemish folk and often, with his wife, went to see live gigs in traditional estaminets. Especially in Belgium. Their contrasts in musical taste had often caused passionate debate between them. As the trio of female voices kicked in and then the fiddle, the lieutenant couldn't help moving to the music. Soon he was prancing around the lounge, twisting and twisting, his hands high in the air, not caring that some of his beer was airborne. The music he found intoxicating. At last, he was beginning to relax. Coming down from another spin, he froze. Standing in the kitchen doorway was a familiar figure, his wife, and she was grinning from ear to ear.

"How long have you been standing there?" he found it hard to get his words out, he was embarrassingly breathless.

"Long enough," his wife's grin grew larger. The lieutenant went to stop Alexa. "No, don't," his wife stopped him. "Play it again Andre, I'll join you." His wife stood close, facing him holding both of his hands in hers and still with the beer.

"Alexa, play T Smidje by Lais." By the time the fiddles had kicked in the couple were swinging around their lounge like demented teenagers.

Chapter 4

Mont d' Hubert, France

Marie was struggling to open her eyes. Her head felt heavy, very heavy, she was finding it hard to keep it up. She felt something. Something or someone was helping her. They laid her head gently back until it was resting against something soft. Now her eyes, her eyes hurt, there was a light above her, a very, very bright light.

"Open your eyes Marie," the words were softly spoken. Marie's fuddled brain recognised the voice as coming from a woman. "Open your eyes Marie, I'll put some drops in your eyes. They'll relieve the soreness." The words again were softly spoken, encouraging. Marie wanted to oblige, she wanted to please whoever was uttering them. Forcing her lids open she immediately felt a cool liquid running over each eye. The voice had been right, the liquid was soothing, the soreness slowly floating away. Best of all, the light was no longer bright, it was just a normal light. Slowly, very slowly she opened her eyes. The room was unfamiliar, she didn't recognise it. She was strapped in a chair, like a dentist's chair, yet she didn't feel panicked. Quite the reverse, she felt relaxed, calm, SAFE.

Moving her eyes slowly Marie looked around the room she was in. In places, stencilled on the walls were words she recognised as being German. They looked old and some of the letters were badly chipped. Hanging from the ceiling was a swastika. In contrast it didn't appear old, in fact it looked almost new.

A figure, a female figure, dressed in white robes and wearing a face mask appeared in front of her. The softly spoken voice must belong to her. She leant over and placed something in her mouth.

"I need to take your temperature, Marie, I need to make sure you're ok." Marie made no attempt to refuse. She wanted to do everything this woman wanted. "Well done, Marie, that's perfect. Now relax, you need to sleep, I'm going to give you something to help you. You may feel a little prick but that's all. You have a big day tomorrow and you need to be ready for it."

Marie tried to nod but found she couldn't, something was holding her head. Her last image, before she once more lost consciousness, was of the woman leaving her room through a wide metal door. Outside stood a man, and Marie could swear even with her blurred vision, that over his shoulder hung a gun. Everything then went dark.

Sweet dreams, Marie.

Ardres, France

As Marie was falling asleep, not a million miles away Madame Maubert and her daughter were starting the evening with a glass of red wine each. Intense discussion about Marie and what may have happened to her meant the bottle was finished quicker than either had intended. "Sod it her daughter said, we need to enjoy ourselves, Maman, Papa would want us to." Her mother for once agreed.

The second bottle encouraged discussions, emotional memories of a father and a husband. Too quickly the second bottle was finished.

"Troisieme Maman, troisieme Maman. Pour Papa."

Against her better judgement perhaps, her mother agreed. It had got to that stage where she was past caring.

However, this time, her mother declared, we need music.

"No more talking, we need music."

Whilst her daughter went to the kitchen to uncork their third bottle, Madame Maubert stumbled to her husband's office. Turning on his hi-fi, she searched for a CD she knew he had somewhere. After a little cursing she found what she was looking for. Manau – La tribu de Dana. The CD was a single and rare purchase by her. She'd bought it at a music stall in the market at Etaples. Closing the tray, she turned the volume up full and pressed play. Leaving the door open, she returned to the lounge. As the music started, mother and daughter wrapped their arms around each other and started to dance. Both loved the song and as they started to sway, tears rolled down both their cheeks. Their dancing grew increasingly passionate and as the song played time and time again, their hold on each other grew more and more intense. The wine forgotten they danced till they could dance no more. And still the music played.

Hervelinghen, Near Mont d'Hubert, France

At around the time Marie was falling asleep under Montd'Hubert, Lieutenant Beaufort and his wife were starting to dance in Coulogne and Madame Maubert and her daughter were opening their first bottle of wine in Ardres. A young couple, in a low, long white washed farmhouse in Hervelinghen, were drinking beer and were deep in conversation about whether to go to the gendarmerie or not.

Camille's parents were in the lounge, unaware of the passion unfolding in their kitchen. To hide their, sometimes, raised voices Camille, had turned on the radio, tuned to a local music station and turned up the volume. After over an hour of sometimes argumentative discussion and several bottled beers, the couple finally agreed. They had to report what they'd witnessed that night on Cap Blanc Nez, even if it meant they got into trouble. Holding each other's hands across the table both started to cry. More in relief than anything else.

Fate as told in this story before, works in mysterious ways and science has never offered an explanation. But that evening fate must again have been watching, and after, played a part. For as they reached their decision, a new song came on the radio. A song they both knew and loved, their song and the song that they had listening to that fateful night. Without doubt it was fate, Tahitialamaison by Keen V started to play on the radio in the kitchen. Their initial shock quickly turned to laughter and sliding back their chairs, without hesitation, started to dance. Not holding each other but freely, individually as though each had not a care in the world.

A Street in Bushey, North London, England

Around the time Marie was falling asleep under Mont d'Hubert, Lieutenant Beaufort and his wife were starting to dance in Coulogne, Madame Maubert and her daughter were opening their first bottle of wine in Ardres and a young couple were embraced in a passionate discussion in Hervelinghen. Roger Denton of the NCA was parking up outside his house. After being underground all day, he didn't feel like leaving his car, going straight to his house. For a few minutes anyway he wanted to feel he belonged to this world, the real world. A world that contained joy and laughter not just pain and misery. That evening, he felt he needed a complete break from people who worked for law enforcement. He wanted to be amongst people who were, that old cliché, 'human.' Luckily, there was a really good pub next to his house and in he went. It was a weekday and yet the pub was packed. The background music, although not loud, was loud enough and when a popular song came on, shouts went up and those inclined, mostly women, swung into an impromptu dance. The atmosphere was intoxicating and just what Roger Denton needed. He'd only intended to stop for one pint but he was enjoying himself and why not. As the evening passed, the atmosphere became more and more and more partylike. The landlord turned the music up and the man from the NCA found himself joining in the dancing. A dance and a pint, a dance and a pint. That's how the evening continued to pass, time forgotten until suddenly the lights dimmed, and the music stopped. It was chucking out time.

Normally frowning at the noise outside from his lounge, that night he was one of a group singing 'Hey Jude' as they spilled out onto the road. A few paces later, he was hugging the friends he'd made in the last few hours. After wishing everyone a very good night, Roger staggered down to his front door on the side of his house. Stumbling inside, he went to the kitchen fully intending to make himself a coffee. After picking up the kettle, he changed his mind. One more drink, just one more drink. He didn't feel like going to bed, not yet. The pressure of the last two weeks was finally finding a way out and he didn't want to close the escape route. NOT YET. Replacing the kettle, he turned to enter the lounge. Perhaps it was fate, but something caught his eye. Light from the moon strangely picked out the post left on the side from yesterday. He grabbed it, bloody bills. He ought to take a look. They presented better under the influence of alcohol.

In the lounge he turned on a single lamp, threw the post on the coffee table, found himself a glass and from a decanter poured himself a large glass of sherry. There were a lot of people still outside and he walked to the window to watch them. A few were still singing, and he didn't mind. But their singing flicked a switch in his head. That's what he was missing now, music. The evening so far had been full of music. And he still needed music. Roger went over to his pride and joy, a Linn Klimax turntable. He was of the school that said vinyl is best. The high the alcohol had given him in the pub was slowly coming down. His mood had changed, he yearned for something more melancholy. Going to his line of wall to ceiling record cabinets, he selected something listed under folk. Ane Brun, a Norwegian singer songwriter. After carefully wiping the vinyl, Roger placed it on the turntable and gently dropped the arm. Within seconds, Ane's crystal clear voice filled the room singing 'All My Tears.' Roger, standing in front of his window, still holding his glass, started to rock back and forth. He suddenly felt very, very lonely. He didn't really have any friends, only colleagues. He thought of John. He realised now, John possibly, had been the closest thing to a friend he'd ever had. Perhaps that was why he was so obsessed in finding him. As Roger listened to the lyrics, his own tears started to form. If only his team could see him now! His rocking grew a little more eccentric and he took a longer than was sensible sip from his glass. Roger knew he was dangerously drunk, but he simply didn't care. Emptying his glass, he went to get a refill from the decanter. Just as he was about to pour, he spotted the post on the coffee table. He'd better open it. He was crap at remembering to pay bills and wanted to avoid having a service or even two cut off. Tearing at the envelopes, after a glance, he threw them back on the table, nothing to worry about. His aim wasn't perfect, one item of post landed on the floor. Something he hadn't spotted. It was a card from a courier. 'Sorry we missed you. Your parcels have been left in a safe place. Under the door of your garage.'

The doors to his garage were more like stable doors. Couriers were always sliding his deliveries under them. He couldn't remember ordering anything, it was probably from his constantly worrying sister. Her latest worry was of him not eating properly and recently had showered him with Rick Stein Meal Kits. Feeling hungry at the thought Roger refilled his glass and staggered out to his garage. Not bothering to unlock the doors he lay down on his front and reached under, pulling out two square boxes. Putting one on top of the other he staggered back into the house, somehow managing not to spill one drop from his glass. Returning to the lounge he placed both boxes on the coffee table and returned to his kitchen to fetch a knife. Seconds later he was sitting on his sofa. The haunting song 'Lose my Way' dominated the atmosphere. Taking another long sip of sherry, and swaying gently, he, a little less gently, cut down the centre of one of the boxes. After sliding the knife around the edge, he lifted the two halves of the cardboard box. Beneath lay a polystyrene box. Yep, another food parcel. Feeling hungry, he lifted the lid and peered inside. Without warning, he was sick. Dropping his head between his legs, he vomited heavily.

At least he had found John. Well part of him anyway.

Kegworth Hotel, Kegworth. Near East Midlands Airport, England

English roads, Heba was discovering quickly, were something of a nightmare. Four hours they had been stuck on something called the M1.

At last, she was now safe in her room. After unpacking her case she made herself a coffee and threw herself on the bed. How long would she be staying here she wondered. A day, a week, a month? She couldn't wait to start work.

Grabbing the remote she switched on the tv. It was time to find out how good her English was.

Somewhere in East London, England

A rather old, dirty white Ford Transit pulled up outside a typical forties suburban house. Two men got out. On seeing them arrive, three men from the house came out to greet them. After a brief exchange of words two of the men went back into the house, returning minutes later dragging two limp young girls. Late teens possible less. Notes exchanged hands and the two girls were unceremoniously, thrown in the back of the van.

In under a minute the van was on its way. Just over half an hour later, the van pulled up outside another innocuous house. A similar scene followed, though this time, a single girl was placed in the back of the van. The driver looked at his watch. Eleven thirty pm. Three more collections. All in North London. With a bit of luck he'd be home by four. Smiling, he put his van back on the road, heading for the North Circular.

A Street in Bushey, North London, England

Roger had no wish to look inside the box again. And he could guess what, who was in the second box. Staggering to his kitchen he threw the remaining sherry in his glass down the kitchen sink and stuck his head under the tap, turning on the cold. He gasped as the almost freezing water cascaded over his neck and cheeks. Pulling back, he placed his mouth under the gushing water and gulped. Turning the tap, off he shook his head, so violently, it almost caused him to fall over.

Opening a drawer, he pulled out two tea towels and returned to the lounge. Carefully covering his vomit, he once more returned to the kitchen. He had no wish to spend another second in his lounge, not even to turn off Ane Brun, whose voice continued to haunt the room.

Leaning over the kitchen sink again, this time, in case, he vomited, Roger tried to clear his fuzzy mind. He tried looking up, but the kitchen wouldn't stay still. Once more he stared down into the sink. The smell of sherry reached him, and he vomited. Spitting the last burning remnants from his mouth he once more placed his mouth under the tap gulping in more cold water. This time the cold fresh water helped him to feel a little better. He had to think, think clearly and the bloody alcohol wasn't helping.

He had to call this in. But not through the normal channels. Jason's words, 'trust no one,' were ringing around his head. He had to call Jane, but not with his phone. Somebody might be listening in. Roger went to the cupboard under the stairs, where he'd stored John's pay as you go mobiles. It wasn't till the fourth, he found one that was charged, and only then not by much. Continuing to lean over the sink, he dialled Jane's number.

A male voice answered. Of course, personal protection. Every safe house came with personal protection. This number, the number he was phoning with, wouldn't have been listed. Roger quickly explained why he was using a pay as you go phone. Not once did he explain what he had in his house. Just that his call was extremely urgent. The voice on the other end asked him to wait, and thirty seconds later, instructed him that he'd have to run through security before he could put him through to the Director General.

Roger agreed of course and patiently answered the specially prepared security questions, many of his answers including a hidden code. Fifteen minutes it took before security were satisfied and Jane's voice registered on the other end of the line. She understandably sounded anxious.

"Roger, what the hell, are you ok? What's going on?"

"I'm afraid I'm not feeling well, Jane, so please bear with me if I suddenly break off. Oh, and this phone is hardly charged, I need to be quick."

"What's wrong with your phone? PP said that you're worried someone may be listening in. Our phones are encrypted, Roger, I'm told they're pretty much impregnable."

"The users of EncroChat thought so too, Jane."

"Touche, Roger, you have a point. Go ahead."

(Operation Venetic is still arguably the NCA's greatest success. Seven hundred and forty-five arrests were made. This was after the NCA alongside their counterparts in France and Holland managed to infiltrate the EncroChat platform).

"I hope no one's listening to your phone, Jane."

"Just tell me what's wrong, Roger."

Roger did as he was instructed. He related how he'd found John's severed head with his genitalia stuffed in his mouth in a box left by a courier in his garage. That it had been delivered the day before, but he hadn't seen the card. I think we can guess what or who is in the second box, but I don't want to look, he told her. Jane agreed, anyway from here on, forensics had to handle everything. Jane asked for details of the courier. Roger told her but they both new that the card was purely a front. Jane would get a CCTV search operational immediately but if the last case was anything to go by, she doubted whether much would come of it.

Jane was brilliant in a crisis. One of the main reasons she was director general. Within seconds, she had decided on the next steps to be taken, and Roger knew those steps would start taking place immediately.

"We can't have the police rocking up to your house, Roger. We need to keep this low key. So, your neighbours won't suspect a thing. First of all, we need to get you out of there. Whoever we're dealing with knows where you live. Heaven knows what they might try next, and I have no wish to see your genitalia Roger. Dead or alive."

"That's reassuring, Jane, thank you." They both managed a nervous laugh.

"I'll send a car to pick you up, we need to get you somewhere safe, somewhere hard to find. Pack a few bags, anything you might need. As soon as you're gone, I'll get a forensics team to 1, take out your delivery and 2, to go over your house. You've nothing that may be embarrassing for you, Roger, if found, is there?

"Only my vomit, sorry."

"They're used to a lot worse, don't touch it, Roger. A car is already on its way. You need to start getting ready. And until I deem otherwise, I'm going to have a live-in agent in your house and a surveillance car outside or possibly in a room somewhere, if we feel we can trust the owners. I want to know if anyone shows the slightest interest in your property"

"You might try the pub next door, Jane. The landlord's ex-military." He heard Jane scoff.

"I said someone we can trust Roger." They both laughed. "Ok, thanks for the tip. I'll get him checked out. Now get your stuff together, your car is now," there was a pause, presumably Jane was checking. "Twenty minutes away." Roger remembered, they had a meeting that afternoon. Is it still on? Jane confirmed it was and she expected him at two. Bring as many physical files as you can she told him. Nothing can be sent here electronically. Roger was just about to reply, when the battery failed.

Quickly he found two largish holdalls and started throwing clothes in each. It was so hard knowing what to pack. Almost forgetting, he gathered toiletries from the bathroom and last but not least, the bag of pay as you go phones, he'd taken from John's flat in Drury Lane. No sooner had he finished, when he saw a car pull up outside. Leaving his door on the catch, he hurried down the path to his waiting lift. On his left, further down the road, another car was waiting. Blocking the route for anyone who wanted to come up the road. The access was one way. Jane was taking no chances. Throwing his holdalls onto the back seat, Roger followed. No sooner had he closed the door, the car moved off. Roger recognised instantly the precision driving of a professional. He was in safe hands. His chauffer didn't speak a word and Roger was thankful, for if he had to open his mouth, he would almost certainly be sick again.

Roger recognised the route. From the A41, they joined the A5, traveling south into London. Without warning, his driver turned off and, after a number of twists and turns pulled up in a residential street.

"That's your transport from here on, sir." His driver pointed to a silver hatchback in front. Roger got out and with his bags climbed into the back seat of the car indicated. As he did, someone, a man, got out of another car and slid into the seat Roger had just vacated. Within seconds, his original transport pulled out, turning left at the end of the road.

"We have to wait here a while, sir, make sure everything is clear." These were the only words his new driver spoke. Roger saw him looking in the rear-view mirror and held his thumb up, indicating ok. For around twenty minutes, the two sat in silence. After which, his driver must have received some sort of signal, for suddenly, without warning, his driver pulled out. Four or five turns later, they were on the A5, traveling south. Within minutes of joining the A5 a marked police car pulled in behind them. It made no attempt to stop them, it just followed, staying around twenty yards back. After traversing Staples Corner they continued to follow the A5. They passed Wing Yip the Chinese supermarket, shortly after which his driver pulled right into Oxgate Gardens. Roger knew where they were going and he thought he knew why. Minutes later, his theory proved to be correct. The driver pulled into a small industrial park and headed for Trevillion Electronics. The cover for the temporary NCA offices. After passing security, the driver swung the car around and unlocked the doors. As soon as Roger had stepped out, the car had gone.

"Early start, sir?" The security guard was doing his best.

"I can't say it was planned." Roger tried to smile, he still felt as though he may vomit at any moment.

"Never mind sir, we'll soon have you comfortable. Your quarters were designed for the Prime Minister. I'm sure you'll be very comfortable. Let me take your bags."

Roger gratefully handed them over. The security guard placed them on a small trolley and led Roger through his daytime offices. He was surprised how many people were working through the night. One of his team studying the CCTV from Broad Court, saw him and gave him a wave. Roger nodded and smiled back. It was as much as he could cope with.

After passing the staff restaurant the security officer stopped at a lift. Taking an electronic key from his belt he touched a sensor on the wall.

Roger felt the lift whirr into action. The doors opened and they both stepped in. The lift descended silently.

"We're traveling three more floors under Gladstone Park."

That's reassuring Roger thought. Personally, he wasn't sure whether he liked the idea. After coming to a halt, he was led along a passage, passing through a number of sliding doors before stopping in front of a simple iron door, above which were stencilled the letters P M. The security guard pushed and the door swung open.

"I'm afraid somebody's lost the keys, but you needn't worry. You're the only one living down here and the lift is key operated. Apart from security, you will have the only key. The key is programmed so the lift can only travel from this floor to the floor your offices are on. The other floors are out of bounds. Sorry sir." The security guard gave Roger the same style of key he'd used just minutes earlier.

Roger waved it's fine. And lifted his bags from the man's trolley. The security guard recognised the signs of both fatigue and shock. This man needed to be left alone.

"Ok, sir, I'll be off. I hope you get some sleep. There's coffee and tea not to mention water in your quarters. There's also a direct line to the restaurant which is open twenty-four hours and if you order anything. Myself, or one of my colleagues will bring anything you've asked for, down for you."

"Thank you." It was as much as he could say. Roger watched the man disappear down the corridor and turned to examine his room for the night. On inspection one could hardly call it a room. The floor space was around the same as the ground floor of his house. There was a well fitted bathroom, an office, a small dining area, and a quite spacious lounge complete with telly and even Alexa. The latter must have only just been fitted. And finally, a bedroom, also with a tv. There were two phones, one beside the bed and one on a wall in the lounge. Roger tested them both. There was no outside line, just two internal connections, security and the restaurant. In a drawer, Roger found a folder titled 'Nuclear Safety.' Actually, managing a smile, he put it back. Taking his bags to the bedroom, he undressed. He needed a shower. Naked, except for his socks Roger sat on the bed to remove them. It was the last move he made before he fell asleep. Thankfully, the bedroom was the one room which had no CCTV.

Chapter 5

Gendarmerie Nationale, Calais, France

At eight in the morning, a young couple arrived at the gendarmerie nationale in Calais. They were surprised to find a queue at reception. Patiently they waited in line. The gendarme at the desk noticed them immediately. They both looked scared, as though they had both seen a ghost. Using his experience, the gendarme signalled to them.

"Is it urgent, mademoiselle, monsieur?" The couple looked at each other, each searching the other for a response. In the end, in unison, they both nodded.

"Oui, we think so," answered Jean. "It's about your capitaine, the one who is dead."

There was a muttering from those standing in the queue, waiting to be seen.

"Just a minute." The gendarme apologised to the woman first in the queue who wanted to report a missing cat. Almost jogging across reception he tapped on Colette's door and entered.

"Colette, there's a young couple in reception who both look as though they've seen a ghost. They want to see someone about the death of Maubert. God knows what it's about. I'm dealing with a load of crap out there. Can you keep them safe in here for a few minutes. That is until I'm free?"

"Of course," Colette never refused anybody. "I'll come out with you."

Minutes later, the couple Jean and Camille were sitting in Colette's office drinking coffee. Jean had actually asked for a beer! At eight in the morning! I always start with one at the café where I work he explained, on seeing Colette's shocked look.

"Sorry we don't provide beer, oh but our new Capitaine might have some. Our old capitaine used to have quite a bar in his office." Colette laughed in an attempt to lighten the atmosphere. It was obvious that the couple were very nervous and didn't want to be there. They must have good reason to put themselves through such self-torture.

"It's him we want to talk to somebody about." The young man was rubbing his hands as he said this. His partner looked as though she was going to be sick. Colette stayed silent, allowing the young man to continue at his own pace. "You see we were there." Jean stared at the floor.

"You were there?"

"Oui," the young man, Jean wiped away tears with his forearm. "Oui, on Cap Blanc Nez, when your capitaine died."

Colette felt her stomach scrunch into a ball, she was finding it hard to keep her composure.

"Yes, we were in my car," he looked across at Camille for support, but she was staring at the floor, her body shaking as she struggled to hold back the tears forming inside. Jean inhaled deeply, he needed to feel the air in his lungs. ""Yes, we were there," he paused again, struggling to get his words out. Then all of a sudden, the floodgates opened. The words came tumbling one after another. "We were there, we saw what happened. Your capitaine didn't commit suicide. He was pushed!" The couple started to cry. Jean spoke again. "I'm sorry we didn't come forward earlier, we were scared." Jean almost collapsed as he said this.

Colette was frozen. She was in shock and struggling to know what to do. Gathering herself she touched both on their shoulders

"Don't worry you two. You're not in trouble. You've done the right thing. I think you need to speak to our new Capitaine. Wait here a minute. I'll go and tell him you're here." With that Colette closed the door and bounded up the stairs three by three. The gendarme at the reception desk watched her go. Colette never bounded up the stairs three by three. Whatever the young couple had told her, it must be dynamite.

A few minutes later he saw Colette return and escort the young couple up the stairs to the Capitaine's office. As she descended a second time she met with Lieutenant Beaufort just about to mount the stairs himself. Colette put her hand to his chest.

"You can't see the capitaine, not just yet."

"But he wants to see me, first......" Colette stopped him.

"First thing, I know. But you'll have to wait. Come into my office. I'll explain." The lieutenant did as he was asked. More coffee was poured, and Colette revealed what the couple had told her.

"Bloody hell, this changes everything." Lieutenant Beaufort was struggling to take in what he had just been told.

As he struggled to understand, the young couple came bounding down the stairs and ran through reception to the car park. Colette rushed after them, but she was too late. The couple were already driving away. She was just in time though to catch the expression on the young woman's face. She no longer, looked shocked, her expression had changed to one of anger.

When Colette returned, she found Lieutenant Beaufort in reception. Behind the reception desk, the gendarme operating was taking everything in.

"What the hell was all that about?" The lieutenant searched for an answer from Colette.

"I've no idea but you'll soon find out. You've got a meeting with the capitaine. Remember?"

The lieutenant didn't need reminding, he started to climb the stairs one by one.

Ardres, France

Madame Maubert stood in her shower. Cold water doing its best to wash away yesterday's over indulgence. She hadn't drunk like that since she'd been a teenager. In fact, the night she'd met her future husband. Now deceased. Her thoughts turned to Marie and whether the gendarmes had had any luck in their search for her. She made a mental note to ring Lieutenant Beaufort.

For now, though, she had to concentrate on her own affairs. Her husband's funeral was scheduled for the next day. It was quick, she knew, but she wanted everything over and done with. Over and done with, so she could grieve properly without all the back chat and pitying looks.

Normally it was the custom to lay out the deceased at home, in an open coffin so everyone could come and say their last farewell. Her daughter and she had decided that this would be a bad idea. There was the danger the whole thing could turn into a circus. The new capitaine, Capitaine Vendroux had kindly offered to transport her husband's body in one of their vans. It seemed appropriate. They would travel to the cemetery, Cimietiere Sud, to pay their respects and witness what she had requested to be a short and simple ceremony. Her one step away from this was to accept Capitaine Vendroux's offer that six of his gendarmes would bear her husband's coffin. He would also ensure the media would not be too invasive. He was a lovely man, Capitaine Vendroux.

Chapter 5

Mont d'Hubert, near Calais, France

Deep under Mont d'Hubert, a doctor was doing tests on a young woman called Marie. She's not ready yet he concluded. We need her brain to be totally relaxed. And it's not, there's too much activity. We will take a look at her again tomorrow. Hopefully by then her brain will be one hundred percent relaxed.

"Did you hear that Marie?" It was the soft voice Marie loved, she smiled. "You need to stop thinking, just let go, enjoy yourself."

Marie giggled, this was fun. The nurse smiled at the doctor.

"I'll take her back to her room, here we go Marie. Wheeeeeee."

Marie didn't stop smiling.

A House in Mayfair, London

Ariana's, alias Fatima's car had been waiting for her, outside the Royal Lancaster Hotel dead on 10 am. The car smelt and looked new. There wasn't a mark anywhere. Her journey turned out to be quick. Within no time at all, her driver had deposited her at a house she'd been in before. The house belonging to Orme, though she still doubted that.

As last time, the door opened without anyone knocking. There were a couple of security cameras outside, and Fatima assumed somebody must be watching the entrance, twenty-four seven. Inside, a young woman wearing elaborate Saudi style robes ushered Fatima to follow her. This time rather than mounting the curvaceous staircase ahead, she was led down a simpler affair into a basement. From the stairs, Fatima followed the woman along a dark, softly lit corridor with a carpet so soft and so deep that it was almost like walking on water. In between the dimmed lamps were hung paintings, all classic Arabian scenes from a century or two before. On reaching the end of the corridor, the young woman pushed on, what looked like, a leathered padded door.

"Please," the young woman said in English. "Please, come in." She held the door open, allowing Fatima space to pass. Fatima swept into the room, her long robes,(for she'd thought it wise to dress in traditional Muslim attire), kissing the carpet, creating the sound of a soft breeze. The room she found herself in was not at all what you could call a standard room. For a start, it was perfectly round. The ceiling was decorated with gold rays extending from a central black circle. The walls were painted, classic British racing green on which hung paintings depicting scenes from just about every world religion. In-between were variations of the Croix d'Agadez. Dominating the room and central to it, was a huge highly polished round table. At its centre stood an elaborate four-armed candlestick with a pair of serpents curled around the central stem. The only light shone from the circumference of the black circle giving the impression that the room was lit by a black sun. At the far side of the room stood two women, one standing around five foot two tall was almost certainly Chinese, the other at around six foot had classic Eastern European features. Both smiled as Fatima entered but said nothing.

Softly the door closed behind her. The young woman who had shown her in was gone. Fatima found herself feeling a little uncomfortable, she was uncertain what to say or do. Her quandary ended when a lady stepped out of the shadows to her left. Until she moved she'd been cleverly concealed in what Fatima now realised was a deliberate darkness, a shadow formed by the light streaming from the black circle above. The woman wore a traditional black abaya and black hijab, as she turned to look at Fatima, she recognised instantly who the woman was. It was Orme. As her eyes caught hers, Fatima felt her legs begin to tremble. What power did this woman hold over her?

"Good morning, Ariana, it's lovely to see you. May I introduce you to two ladies you will be working with in the near future." Orme waved to the woman or rather girl, for she looked really young, who Fatima had assumed to be Chinese.

"This is Cuiping, she's originally from China." So, she'd been right. The girl from China, Cuiping walked around the table and took Fatima's hand in hers. Close up Fatima could see the girl was indeed a woman.

"Welcome Ariana, it's lovely to meet you."

"You too."

"And this is Yuliia," Orme waved to the second woman. "She is originally from Ukraine." Yuliia walked around the other side of the table and took Fatima's remaining hand.

"It's a pleasure to meet you, Ariana."

"You too." Fatima was uncertain how else to answer.

"Please all of you sit down." Orme gestured to chairs that were placed neatly around the round table. Each took a seat, Orme remained standing. "Over the next few weeks you will in a sense be working as a team. You all have that certain skill, to hold power over men. This skill in the near future will be needed as its never been needed before. I hope you will all enjoy the challenge. I want you to spend this morning getting to know each other. But please no talking about the work you've already done for us. That is my only rule. It's not a request, it's my rule." Orme looked at each of them in turn, making sure they understood. "In a couple of hours, we will break for lunch. Where you go is up to you. Please be back here for two, when you will each meet your new contact and guardian. After that you're free to go and enjoy yourselves, but please not together. You cannot be seen outside this house with each other unless we specifically ask you. Understood?" The three women nodded. "Good, Nefret will bring you some refreshment, please enjoy getting to know one another." With that, Orme left the room. So silent so gracefully did she move, Fatima, if she didn't know better, could have sworn she was floating on air.

For a few seconds after Orme had left, there was an uncomfortable silence between the three women. It was Cuiping who attempted to break the ice.

"Do you speak English, Ariana? Orme didn't say where you're from."

"A little," Fatima started. Both women laughed.

"We all say a little," Yuliia explained their mirth.

"The men like it though, when we tell them a little. The English men I think find it exciting." Laughed Cuiping. Yuliia put a finger to her lips.

"Shhhh, we're not meant to talk about that."

"Oh no," Cuiping laughed again. Her laugh was physical as well as vocal. Each time she laughed she raised both hands and rocked. It was an endearing quality.

"So where are you from Ariana?" Yuliia returned to Cuiping's original question. "And how did you get here?"

"Am I allowed to tell you?" Fatima wasn't sure. Both women nodded.

"Oh yes," Cuiping clapped her hands. "It's encouraged, if it wasn't for the, well Orme I'd probably be dead on the streets by now." For the first time since Fatima entered the room, Cuiping looked serious. Just as Fatima was about to reveal where she was from. Nefret arrived with a young man dressed in the classic black and white of a waiter, pushing a trolley.

"I've brought a bit of everything, soft drinks, water, Persian tea, bubble tea and of course coffee. There's also a selection of biscuits and some baklava which have been made fresh, in this house. Nefret lay a crisp white drape on one side of the table and the young man in black and white gently placed the refreshments on top. "Have fun," Nefret smiled and left, the young man following though he left the trolley. Each woman's choice of beverage spoke volumes of where they were from. Fatima chose the mint, (Persian), tea. Yuliia coffee and Cuiping bubble tea.

"So you're Persian Ariana?" Both women asked the question at the same time and laughed. The ice was broken.

Ariana, alias Fatima shed her initial nervousness. Removing her hijab, she related her early upbringing. The abuse she'd suffered as a teenager and as a young woman. Her eventual escape to France where she was now employed by, well you know who. Her two new companions had very similar stories. Cuiping had been a nurse in China. She had been married to a successful businessman who dared to question the communist system. Her husband as a result had been thrown into jail and Cuiping, to avoid a similar fate, had escaped to Hong Kong. Her life there hadn't been easy as she, at the time spoke only Mandarin, whereas natives from Hong Kong spoke Cantonese. Mandarin speakers were, in the main, treated with suspicion. As a result, work had been hard to come by and she had had to turn to prostitution to make ends meet. One of her customers had offered her work in Dubai. She had jumped at it, only to find when she got there, that she was expected to work as a full-time prostitute. Entertaining up to twenty men a day. She had been rescued from her hell by another client who smuggled her across the desert to Egypt. From there she'd been smuggled across Europe into England. Once in England somehow, she'd lost contact with the man who had been helping her. Not speaking any English, she'd plied her trade in Chinatown, London. It was there she was rescued by, the organisation. No one seemed to know its name. They had helped her to learn English and put her through medical exams so she could find genuine work. She had already met her target and had succeeded in seducing them. She couldn't say any more except her target wasn't a man but a woman, and she enjoyed her work with her.

Yuliia's story was very similar, just a different place. She was born and brought up in Odessa Ukraine. She'd loved her city, but work was scarce and poverty rife. She was offered work in Istanbul by an agency run by a woman. The work would be working in an international hotel and the money much more than she could earn locally. Yuliia had been well aware of trafficking horror stories, but as the agency was being run by a woman, she'd felt she was safe. The work genuine. The woman was even traveling out with her along with four other women lured by the salary. When they arrived, they were picked up outside the airport in a minibus. The Ukrainian woman from the agency never left the airport. The minibus took them to a sordid flat above a night club and there she had been forced to work as a dancer and escort. Long legged blonde women were at a premium. One night after being brutally beaten by a customer she'd decided to take her chances and escaped, taking the man's wallet with her. Having had her passport taken from her, she'd used her sexuality to travel across Europe. Initially, she'd intended returning to her family in Ukraine, but after a chance meeting in a bar in Budapest, she was persuaded to look for work in England. This time she was prepared for the falsehoods, but her contact had turned out to be genuine. He had driven her to Calais where she'd been introduced to a wealthy man she only knew as Pierre. Fatima sat up on hearing this. He could only be her Pierre. Pierre had organised a passport for her. A UK one and had been flown right into the heart of London. The city airport or something like that. Once in London, she had slowly been introduced to influential men, mainly in what was called, The City. The role the organisation had wanted her to play was as a femme fatale, gathering information and influencing decisions. She loved her work, the men she was asked to seduce always treated her well and the money she'd earned was beyond her wildest dreams. Yuliia stopped, worried that she'd said too much. Fatima asked where they both lived, and both replied that the organisation had provided them with modern apartments.

"Why are we meeting here, in this room?" Fatima asked. Cuiping shrugged her shoulders.

"Whenever there's a meeting, it's always held in here. Nefret told me once it's because this room is safe. No one can listen in. I asked her what she meant by that, but she clammed up after. I think that's the expression the English use, clammed up." Cuiping laughed her infectious laugh. Fatima was puzzled, she hardly spoke English and yet she was understanding every word.

The time flew. The three women all had something in common and they felt comfortable in one another's company. Stories and laughter walked side by side. When Nefret reappeared the three were almost partying.

"Lunchtime ladies. Orme needs this room. Please follow me."

Nefret led them back up to the grandiose hall where she let Cuiping and Yuliia leave five minutes apart. Not together, she reminded them. And don't be late, 2 pm sharp. Back here. Fatima expected the same, but Nefret held her hand.

"We have something in common. I'm from Persia too," she whispered to Fatima. Will you join me for lunch? I know a great little place only minutes from here. Orme won't mind she trusts me."

Fatima was secretly delighted. Her trade was a lonely one. She knew nobody she could trust and although London was exciting, she hadn't as yet found it a particularly friendly place. It was certainly a city you could easily disappear in, and nobody would notice.

Nefret led her, always holding her by the hand, to a secluded square called Shepherd Market. The square had a multitude of restaurants and outside one, called Ferdii, there was a small queue. Nefret joined it. Nearly everybody else in the queue looked to be either Arab or Persian.

"I love this place," Nefret's eyes reflected her enthusiasm. It's French run but they have a restaurant in Saudi, the reason why everyone queuing is like us." Nefret laughed. It was the first time Fatima had heard her laugh. And it revealed a completely different side to a person, who up until now, had hardly spoken a word. And when she had it had been mostly formal. "Kim Kardashian famously likes their cheese-burger. Perhaps another reason." Nefret laughed again. "Personally,

I like their vegetarian food. We can choose a mix." Nefret squeezed Fatima's hand tightly.

She's like a little girl let out to play was Fatima's impression. And it struck her that Nefret's existence was probably very similar to hers. A lonely one.

Nefret was right. The food was really good, and Fatima was surprised just how many Arabian women were eating there. Whilst they ate, Fatima attempted to explore Nefret's history but, in that, she was extremely guarded. In reverse, Nefret quizzed Fatima continuously about how life in Persia. Iran was like now. Fatima couldn't really tell her much as she'd been out of the country too long. Once or twice, Fatima attempted to ask questions about Orme, but each time Nefret batted them away. All she would say was that Orme had been really kind to her and that for the first time in her life, she felt safe. There was a story there somewhere, but Fatima wasn't going to find out what it was. Not today, at any rate. Time, predictably passed too quickly, and in what seemed like no time at all, Fatima was being led back to Orme's house.

On entering there was no sign of the other two woman. Once more Fatima was led down the stairs to the basement but this time rather than follow the corridor to the round room, she was led into a room through one of the side doors. This room was small in comparison, just three leather armchairs, a small table and a drinks cabinet. In one of the chairs, sat a man, in his late sixties perhaps, Fatima judged, and going by his appearance, almost certainly English. As Fatima entered the room, the man stood up. He was tall, a little lanky and wearing the classic attire that foreigners tend to imagine all English gentry wear. He held out a hand.

"Lovely to meet you, am I to call you Ariana or Fatima?" The man grinned.

"Ariana," Fatima heard Nefret whisper behind her.

"Yes of course, just my little joke." Nefret left, closing the door behind her. "How are you Ariana, my name's Charles, couldn't be more English could it." He laughed loudly. "Please sit, take a seat, Ariana." Fatima chose a chair nearest the door. She wasn't sure how comfortable she felt with this man. He was affable, friendly yes, but she felt that it wouldn't be wise to cross him.

Charles sat back in his chair as though he were relaxing at home. His long legs crossed and his arms resting on the arms of his chair. Fatima felt his eyes examining her and wasn't sure if she liked the attention.

"Funny old world, isn't it?" Charles smiled a smile that was completely artificial. "You, me, from completely different backgrounds and yet here we both are, thrown together working for the same cause." He laughed. Fatima had no idea what he was talking about, what cause? Charles hadn't finished talking. "I can see why everybody raves about you Ariana, you're a stunner. You're perfect. Your target, I know him well. You'll have him eating out of the palm of your hand, in no time."

The more he spoke the more Fatima disliked Charles. In his case old fashioned values seemed to mean being chauvinistic. Charles wasn't stupid, and he could see his manner wasn't going down well.

"Ignore me, Ariana, I can be a bit too full on sometimes. My wife is continually telling me off." So, he's got a wife. Fatima tucked this snippet away. "Now, why we're both here. Do you mind?" He didn't wait for Fatima to answer. Charles stood up and poured himself a large whisky from the drink's cabinet. He didn't offer Fatima a glass. Instead, he sat back down, rolling the glass between his two hands. "Now Ariana, down to business. First you need to know a little bit about me. I'm ex-military. I once did devilish work for Her Majesty's government. Later on, I joined MI6, where I did even dirtier work. Oh you know what MI6 is?" Fatima nodded, she did. Mainly from watching English spy films but she wasn't about to admit that. "Good, good." Charles looked pleased. "Well, I still keep my hand in, young Fatima, except

I no longer get paid. Since I've retired, I've less and less liked the way our country, the western world is going. We're a bunch of hypocrites who think we can tell the rest of the world how to behave." Fatima didn't disagree with that. "Hence in my own little way I'm trying to do something about it. The reason I joined the er, the er organisation. Well, you know how it is." Fatima didn't at all. She hadn't a clue.

"Anyway," Charles brushed it off. "Tomorrow, you and I are going out to dinner. In a little wine bar come restaurant just behind Harrods. It's very popular with serving MPs. Eating there is something of a status symbol for them, a bit like owning a house in WC1." Charles laughed again, he apparently liked his own jokes. Fatima smiled politely, in truth she hadn't a clue what he was talking about. "Anyway." He liked that word, Fatima observed. "Anyway, tomorrow we will be dining there with your target. Before we do, I need to tell you about our relationship. This is him, by the way." Charles took a coloured photograph from his inside jacket pocket and handed it to Fatima. Fatima looked at the photo, his face looked familiar. "I need to take that back, Ariana. Sorry." Fatima handed the photo back. Charles without looking what he was doing returned the photo to his pocket. He took a long sip from his glass and wiped his mouth with the back of his hand. "It's important he feels comfortable in your company Ariana, that he quickly dismisses you from being a potential threat. He knows I'm bringing you tomorrow and MI5 will have already checked you out. I had to give them your details you see. The organisation I'm told have drilled your new identity into you?"

"Yes they have." Fatima wouldn't have used the word drilled, but yes she knew every square millimetre of her new identity.

"Good, good. One thing I will say for the organisation, they're always very thorough."

For the next three hours, Charles in between telling poor jokes briefed Fatima on their supposed relationship and their dinner date with her target. He refused to tell her his name as it was important she appeared genuinely surprised when she was introduced. Showing her the photo was a risk he felt he had to take. He hadn't wanted her targeting the wrong man. It had happened in the past. As the afternoon progressed, Fatima slowly began to relax and at one point even accepted a pale sherry. Her first impressions she now felt had been wrong. Yes Charles had traits left over from a certain era but ignoring that, he was charming and sometimes even funny. By the end of their meeting, Fatima found she'd actually started to enjoy his company.

By the time she left the house, dusk was beginning to fall. Nefret had offered her a car, but Fatima had said she'd prefer to walk. After being shut up in that small windowless room all afternoon, she felt she needed some air. Nefret had squeezed her hands goodbye. There'd been no sign of Cuiping or Yuliia. She wondered where they both were. No matter, she was sure they'd all meet again, and soon. She was looking forward to it.

NCA's Temporary Offices, Gladstone Park. Cricklewood, London, England

Blinded by the light. That's exactly what Roger experienced when he gently opened his eyes. His head was thumping and his mouth sore, and still with the taste of his own vomit. Gingerly he sat up trying to remember where the hell he was. Slowly everything started coming back. Shit, what a night. He looked at his watch. Nine fifty. Shit. Why hadn't anyone woken him. Treading carefully to the bathroom he turned on the shower. He filled a glass with cold water from the tap. On the bedside table, there was a packet of Ibuprofen, liquid capsules. Sod what the label said, he took four. Feeling better, simply with the thought that they would soon start to kick in, Roger returned to have a shower.

The water was deliciously hot and for several minutes he simply stood there with both his hands on his head, enjoying nature's greatest gift. By half past ten, he was shaved and dressed. His stomach was still telling him not to mess with it but otherwise he felt ok. His headache had gone.

Taking the key security had given him he returned to the lift. Exiting he began to understand the expression, 'walk of shame.' Before today he thought the expression applied only to women. How wrong he had been. As he made his way to his office, he felt as though every single pair of eyes were upon him. For the first time in his career he felt as though he'd lost control, ashamed.

No sooner had he sat in his office when Nick appeared, carrying a cup of freshly made cappuccino.

"I thought you might need this boss." Nick placed the coffee and without being asked sat himself down. "Are you ok?"

Roger smiled weakly.

"I think so. I've had a bit of a night."

"I think that's a bit of an understatement sir." Nick studied his boss carefully. "Are you ready for an update? There's quite a lot. By the way, Jane called. She wants you to ring her as soon as you feel well enough." Roger groaned. "Sorry boss, just giving you the message. She did tell me to tell you, that we're monitoring Detective Constable Havers' mobile. There's also a tap on his landline and covert mics in his house. When Jane shouts, everyone listens."

Roger managed a laugh. He was right, nobody messed with the head of the NCA. Nick leant forward.

"We've already got a brief summary back from the pathologist. Do you feel well enough to hear it?"

"Just the important bits, no bloody gore." It was Nicks turn to laugh.

"Ok, sir. Well first things first. The second box, as we probably all assumed, it contained the head of our man, Rory."

"Bastards."

"Yes and he was presented in the same fashion as all the other heads. His genita...."

"Yes, yes Nick, I get the picture. Anything else?"

"Sorry sir. Yes. Mr Mitchell. The pathologist said that he had received a severe beating before he was killed. That the beating probably killed him, and chances are, that the beating took place at the hotel. Though we can't be sure of this until we've found evidence."

"Shit, how many rooms has that hotel got?

"I've already checked, four hundred and fifty-three, and that's assuming he was killed in one of the rooms. It could have happened in a service area."

"I thought I'd got rid of my headache, it's already coming back." Roger massaged his scalp. "Go on."

"Like the head in North London, both decapitations were professional. Performed by a surgeon, as were both castrations. The pathologist is in no doubt about that. And his initial findings suggest both operations were carried out at least twenty-four hours after the two men had been killed."

"So?"

"So, my thoughts sir, and that of nearly all of the team. The two were almost certainly killed in the hotel and somehow moved to a location where the bodies were operated on."

"But how the hell could they have got two dead men past our surveillance? Roger finished his coffee.

"Your guess is as good as mine. Nobody has an idea." Roger sighed. What a bloody mess. Never had he felt so helpless in an investigation. Everything was moving so fast and whoever they were looking for appeared to be miles ahead. Not just a step.

"Anything else?"

Nick smiled.

"Yes, we've finished studying the CCTV in Broad Court. Do you feel well enough to take a look.?"

"I'll have to." Roger went to stand up and stopped. He'd remembered something. "Nick you know those bodies in France. The twelve kids."

"Yes of course."

"Well yesterday I phoned the gendarmerie in Calais. I spoke to the new guy in charge. He cut me off point blank. He told me the bodies had been moved to Paris. That it was now a French investigation. Not British."

"That's crap, you should speak to Jane."

"I will." Roger stood up. "Right show me what you've got."

Gendarmerie Nationale, Calais, France

Lieutenant Beaufort knocked once and entered. Just as the first time he'd met their new capitaine. Capitaine Vendroux was leaning back in his chair with his feet resting on the desk. He didn't remove them and failed to offer the lieutenant a chair.

"Lieutenant Beaufort. Yesterday you requested a warrant from the procureur, to search an address in Calais?"

"Yes sir?"

"Why, and why wasn't I, haven't I, been informed"?

Lieutenant Beaufort listed his reasons. The main one being that Marie had gone missing, possibly kidnapped, and he'd feared her life may be in danger. Indeed, that morning, his fear hadn't changed. He'd not informed the capitaine because he was busy interviewing. This was a lie of course. And he was going to inform him now, this morning. From the expression on the capitaine's face, Lieutenant Beaufort felt his reasons had been accepted.

"And what about the wording? The death of Capitaine Maubert?"

"Everyone connected to this investigation, sir, has either turned up dead or are missing. I thought it appropriate to include his death in the warrant. And I understand from Colette that a couple may have been witness to his death and thrown doubt on our assumption that it was suicide."

Capitaine Vendroux removed his feet from his desk and leant even further back, his previous expression of nonchalance replaced with a look of displeasure.

"Colette has no business telling you what witnesses have to say when they enter our gendarmerie. She's a bloody civil secretary, not a gendarme. I shall have words with her. And, you mean, that young couple? What a bloody joke. They're not sure what they saw. Possibly it could have been a trick of the light. They only thought, THOUGHT they saw something. Overactive imaginations that's what it is. It's bloody obvious your ex-capitaine took the coward's way out. He just couldn't face the music. And after everything his poor wife has been through, I'm not going to make her grief worse by conducting a murder investigation based on the testimony of a couple of immature young adults? Is that clear?

"Yes sir." Lieutenant Beaufort was stunned.

"Now you know it's your ex-capitaine's funeral tomorrow"?

"Yes sir."

"His wife, Vivienne, lovely woman wants to keep it low key. I've persuaded her though to accept six uniformed officers to carry the coffin, and I think it would be a nice touch if you could pick her and her daughter up and take them back. What do you think, lieutenant?"

"Yes, it would be an honour sir. Good idea."

"I think so." The expression of annoyance on the capitaine's face had gone. "The funeral's at two in the afternoon so best pick them up around twelve thirty. Just to be sure."

"Yes sir, will do."

"Right, you'd better get on lieutenant. Marie's house, have the PTS(SOCOs), found anything yet?"

"They've only just gone in, I'll probably know more this afternoon." Capitaine Vendroux spread his hands.

"Good, well keep me informed."

"Yes sir." Lieutenant Beaufort made to leave.

"Oh, and lieutenant, you did the right thing with the warrant. But you need to keep me informed. I can't run a good ship without knowing what's going on."

"Yes sir, will do," and the lieutenant left closing the door gently behind him. Through the final crack he saw the capitaine once more rest his feet on the desk. Returning to reception he knocked on Colette's door. He had to warn her that their new capitaine wasn't happy. He relayed what the capitaine had told him. Colette looked shocked. That young couple she told him were scared witless. They hadn't come in before as they thought they may get into trouble. They didn't give me the impression, that they were suffering from a fervent imagination. Not at all, she wanted to drive her view home.

Lieutenant Beaufort left her with a feeling of great unease. Something wasn't right. Nothing had been right since the storm. Stuff was going on he simply didn't understand. Whoever they were looking for, he felt they were kilometres ahead of them. Not just a step, kilometres.

Bodinnick, Cornwall

The time was just gone two in the afternoon. Claire had enjoyed lunch in Fowey and was now relaxing in a lounge chair enjoying the view along the Fowey estuary and out to sea. Her dog Tammy lay at her feet and she was trying to find the energy to take her for a walk. At that moment though, the wine she'd enjoyed with her meal was winning. She felt relaxed, snug, not wanting to move.

Just as her eyes were closing Claire's mobile rang. She looked at the screen. Havers, about bloody time.

"Afternoon detective, about bloody time."

"I have to be careful, Claire. With everything that's going on, everybody's under suspicion."

"Do the Met pay you as well as I do?"

"No Claire, you know they don't and I'm truly grateful, but I still can't afford to lose my job."

"Just tell me what've got, detective."

"What I've got, Claire, is two new severed heads delivered to a director of the NCA. One head, is actually an officer with the NCA."

Claire listened carefully. What the hell was going on? Who was doing this?

"How are you getting this information Havers? You're sure you're not bullshitting me?"

"That's my business, Claire, let's just say I know someone in the agency, someone who needs the money. Are you listening Claire?" Claire ignored him. Snivelling little creep.

"Have they any idea, who's responsible?

"No. Are you sure it's not your doing Claire?"

"No, it's bloody not."

"Then what's your interest?"

"I don't pay you to ask questions, Havers." Insolent fucker, how dare he. Tammy stirred. In her anger, Claire had moved her feet. She reached down and stroked her head, at the same time making soothing noises.

"Fair enough, you don't. The two delivered to the NCA are similar in that they are the work of a surgeon. So, I assume that whoever's investigating will assume they're all the work of the same person. The other two, the one on the south coast and the one in Spain, are different, in that, they weren't done by a surgeon. The heads had been hacked off not cut. Would you know anything about that, Claire?"

"I told you Havers, I don't pay you to ask questions."

You haven't denied it. Detective Constable Havers made a mental note.

"Anything else detective?"

"No, Claire, that's it. And that's more than enough, way above what you pay me for."

"You'll receive payment tomorrow, the usual method."

"Thank you, Claire."

Claire rang off, 'dick head' she said to Tammy. Tammy sighed, she had heard it all before. Claire fingered her mobile. She was pretty certain Ryan, her muscle, wouldn't, not without her say so, but she had to be sure. She dialled a number she had under her contacts as a favourite. Favourite. Bloody ridiculous. Why couldn't the phone company come up with something more appropriate, like work. No way was Ryan a favourite.

Ryan answered after the third ring. He always did. Sometimes Claire thought Ryan was forever holding his phone in his hand waiting for her call.

"Ma'am."

"Ryan. Ryan, I want you to promise me something."

"Of course."

"Promise me you had nothing to do with that beheading in Tottenham."

"I've already told you that Ma'am. I promise."

"Now there's two more, Ryan. Are you sure you had nothing to do with these? You're not working for somebody else?"

"I promise you Ma'am. Only the two you ordered. Hang on Ma'am, there's someone at the door. I'll be right back."

Claire heard him walk off and in conversation with whoever it was at the door. She waited and waited and waited. After holding for ten minutes, she put the phone down. What the fuck was Ryan playing at? Frustrated, Claire waved Tammy's lead. She was surrounded by dick heads. Give her, her dog any day.

"Come on Tammy, walkies."

In an office in London, the phone conversation between Detective Constable Havers and the woman in Cornwall had been listened to and recorded. Trace the call, the officer in charge had instructed. We need to know to whom he was speaking. And get a feed on her mobile, quickly. We need to know everyone SHE speaks to, too.

Le Weekend Café/Bar. Sangatte, France

Jean and Camille sat in the café where he worked, each drinking a beer. In fact it was the third beer for both. They had also ordered something to eat. The owner watched them from behind the bar. He sensed something was wrong.

After all the build-up, the stress of going to the gendarmerie, the arguments whether it was the right thing to do. They'd been sent away by the officer in charge, as though they were nothing more than silly little children. Whereas before, they'd both been nervous, undecided. Now both were furious. Over their meal they discussed what to do, how to put things right. By the time dessert was delivered, they'd made up their mind. They had to tell the Capitaine's wife. No matter how much it would hurt her, she had to know the truth. If the gendarmerie wouldn't listen to them, they'd have to go to the widow directly. Perhaps her anger would force a new investigation.

Exhausted by their morning's experience, the two decided to go tomorrow morning. They would find her address on social media.

Mind made up Jean asked his boss if he could take the next day as holiday. Sensing whatever it was meant a lot to his employee he readily agreed. Just don't be late the day after.

The two drove off with grim determination set in stone between them. Never, never had each other felt as close to the other as they did at that moment. With luck, Camille's parents weren't home yet, and they could turn that closeness into passion.

NCA's Temporary Offices, Gladstone Park. Cricklewood, London

Roger stood staring at the screen in front of him. Playing out on screen was the lady known to them as Maureen Fowlis along with his ex-colleague and friend John Mitchell. They both looked happy, very drunk and into each other. Much later, John appeared, on his own leaving the hotel.

"He, Mr Mitchell. Never returns to the hotel. Not whilst Ms Fowlis is there. We see her come and go but the next real item of interest is this."

The operator switched to another screen. This time it showed Maureen Fowlis, again apparently drunk, though this time with a much younger man, possibly even an adolescent. The man was caught on CCTV leaving the hotel at three in the morning.

"Do we know who that is?" Roger asked.

Nick replied without hesitation.

"Yes, we did a facial recognition check. He's one Nicholas Burrows of Eggleton Drive, Tring. Nineteen years of age. Reported missing by his parents the next day."

"Any other sightings of him?"

"Yes boss, CCTV captured him walking along Long Acre. He disappeared in a black spot between two cameras. If someone meant him harm, they knew what they were doing. They knew they weren't on camera."

"Any more on Maureen Fowlis?"

The operator turned.

"Yes boss. This is the last sighting of Maureen Fowlis. She left the hotel later that day but never returned. You will notice, she isn't wheeling the suitcase she arrived with. Now watch this." The operator switched to another screen. Everyone watched as a man was captured on camera, wheeling out, what was unmistakably, Ms Fowlis's suitcase.

"Have we got a face recognition check on this guy?" Roger asked.

Nick lent his arm over the screen.

"Yes boss. I'm afraid you're not going to like this. He turned to the operator. "Can you zoom in." The operator zoomed in till just the man's face was visible. "Recognise him?"

Roger strained to recognise him. His face looked familiar, but he just couldn't place him. Nick helped him out.

"Mr Peter Fitch of Burns Road, Wellingborough."

"What the Peter Fitch interviewed over the Sky Bar?" Roger now recognised him instantly

"The very same, and, yes, we checked him out immediately. On that day, he was teaching. Just as last time. And in the evening, he was taking extra studies. Again, just as last time. There is no way he could have been wheeling out Ms Fowlis's suitcase. And yes, we've tried tracing his movements on CCTV and like the young man, he disappears between cameras. Digital forensics are already checking the local authorities' CCTV. I think it's obvious now that both the hotel's and the local authorities' CCTV has been hacked."

"Not to mention the DVLA," Roger reminded him.

"Exactly, and the phone company. Whoever we're dealing with sir they have some serious capabilities. Way beyond what we have."

"It's got to be a state sir." A voice from one of his team. "Who else could finance an operation like this?"

Nick joined in.

"Do you think Mr Mitchell could have still been working for the intelligent services? Unofficially. It has been known."

"Well, if he was, I knew nothing about it. And if he was, what was so important? Why this mass murder? Why tease us? Because that's what they're bloody doing. Messing with us."

The room fell silent, all allowing their boss time and space to calm down. Nick spoke next.

"Jane's coming over boss. She doesn't want you leaving here. Not for now. She says she has something for you. Something she doesn't want to talk about over the phone."

Roger wasn't listening. His mind was in overdrive.

"Maureen Fowlis. She's connected to two murders and two missing people. One a gendarme in France. If not her directly, whoever is connected to her is extremely dangerous. I want her details and photos distributed to every force in the UK. We also need to find out what the authorities know about her in France. We won't go public, not yet. But if we can't find her we're going have to use the media. We need to find her and find out who she really is. I've no doubt she targeted John Mitchell and now he's dead. And this Peter Fitch of Wellingborough. Is he really squeaky clean or is he really clever. If he is clean, why did whoever it was, put his mug on CCTV? Why choose this man, Peter Fitch. There has to be a reason, a connection somewhere. We need to find it." There were several 'yes, sirs' sounding from his team. "What were you saying Nick?"

Chapter 5

A Newspaper Office, Portsmouth, England

Steven Hunter had been with the newspaper for as long as he could remember. Educated at the then comprehensive on Hayling Island, he'd studied English Lit at South Downs College before joining the local rag in Portsmouth as an apprentice. At first, he'd specialised in sport, mainly because he supported Pompey, (the local football team), and had wanted to cover their matches. As he matured so did his ambition as a journalist. At first, he covered local fetes, missing pets, that sort of thing, but as time went on he started to prove his worth as an investigative journalist, and now he was the rags only journalist of that genre. He wasn't sensationalist and thus had gained respect from all quarters. Both the police and the criminal underworld. He'd quickly come to learn that the criminal world had standards too and they would pass on information if someone wasn't, in their eyes, behaving correctly. Over the years he'd assembled a myriad of quality contacts. Contacts that trusted him to do the 'right thing.'

One of those contacts had just got off the phone. He worked on the peripherals of the military, mainly the Royal Navy. Something had occurred earlier in the day that had caused a great deal of concern between those involved. A delivery had been made to a disused fort on Portsdown Hill, a fort still in the ownership of His Majesty's Government. The fort was now guarded. He hadn't seen the delivery himself, but word was going around that the cargo had been the bodies of twelve mutilated children along with two adults. The delivery to an abandoned fort was unusual enough but if the rumours were true, well his contact had thought he should know.

Steven thought hard about the call. He could hardly go up to the fort asking to see for himself. The navy would give him short shrift. But he knew someone, someone he respected, who may be able to ask some difficult questions. He picked up the phone on his desk. A woman answered.

"Havant police, how can I help you."

"Can you put me through to D.I. Johnson please."

"One minute, may I ask who's calling please?" Steven gave the policewoman manning the phones his name. "Oh, hello Steven, I thought it was you. One minute I'll see if he's available." Seconds later, a man's voice came on the phone.

"Hello Stevie, how are you?"

"You know how it is Phil, not bad but I wish it was better."

"Don't tell me that, don't I know it. Anyway what can I do for you. Or rather you do for me?"

Steven took a deep breath before relaying the conversation he'd just had with his contact.

"Is he reliable?" was the D.I.'s first question.

"Always has been, one of my best. Never lied to me in the past."

"And you won't give me his name?"

"Don't be silly."

"Ok Steven, I'll look into it. And thank you."

"You'll keep me informed Phil."

"That goes without saying, thanks again."

"Thanks, and good luck." The phone went dead.

D.I. Phillip Johnson stood up and walked to the window. He looked across to the town hall. What secrets were there in that building? What was the mystery, the secrecy around the delivery on Portsdown Hill? Over the years, he'd quickly come to learn that the biggest, dirtiest secrets were almost always within the civil service, all avenues of government. The NHS, the military, the intelligence services, and yes even the police force.

His investigation into the brutal murder in Langstone had somehow rightly or wrongly become entwined loosely with the goings on around

Calais France. Roger Denton had mentioned something about twelve Albanian children that had been discovered dead on a boat floating in the English Channel. He hadn't told him a lot more, only that the children may have been under the care of social services in various towns along the south coast. Mr Denton had asked him to discreetly make some enquiries. He'd emphasised the word discreetly. This was unusual. Normally it was, 'rock a few boats.'

What was going on? What hadn't he been told? After the explosion at the NCA building in Vauxhall, Lambeth he'd left Mr Denton alone. Assuming he had enough on his plate. Anyway, his investigation wasn't really going anywhere. He'd had nothing new to report. That is until now. He picked up the phone.

A House in Coulogne, near Calais, France

Lieutenant Beaufort sat in his lounge with a small black book resting open on his lap. He was reading Marie's diary. The ASPTS team had found nothing of consequence in Marie's house. In fact it was apparent that she lived a very simple existence. One would never had imagined that for years she had been a real pain in the gendarmerie's side. Now reading her diary the lieutenant felt as though he was reading the diary of a ghost.

Like Capitaine Maubert's diary, Marie's diary didn't contain much. There was an entry where she registered being roughed up by a number of migrants, spurred on she suspected by a so-called colleague, female at that. The lieutenant, reading her name, knew instantly who she was. She was a well-known anarchist and a real pain in the arse. There were some very favourable remarks about the late Capitaine Maubert and the gendarmerie wanting to help. And some very distressing entries about the photographs posted on social media of she and the capitaine.

Her entries confirmed what she had told Madame Maubert. That the apparent kiss was not at all how it was portrayed on social media. It had really upset her. There was almost a page questioning whether to meet the capitaine's wife. Whether she would be believed. Whether her visit would simply cause the poor woman more pain.

He closed the diary with a heavy heart. And now the possibility that his ex-capitaine's death may not have been suicide at all, but murder. With the official door firmly closed by his new boss, if he was going to make enquiries, he'd have to ensure they were made under the radar. It wouldn't be easy, and he risked losing his job but there were principles at stake. His conscience simply wouldn't let him ignore the alternative. He needed a beer. There was one 3 Monts left in the fridge, he stood up to get it. In the kitchen his wife was busy pressing his spare uniform. The uniform he would wear at his ex-boss's funeral tomorrow. The funeral would mark the ending of a chapter. A new chapter was about to begin, and the lieutenant had a feeling in his gut that he wasn't going to enjoy it. Kissing his wife on her forehead, he poured himself a beer. His gut was also telling him he may be drinking a lot of these in the near future. That he didn't mind.

An Office in South London, England

They'd traced the call by Havers to a woman living in Bodinnick, Cornwall. They had also managed to get a feed on her phone and her very next call had been to a man living at an address in Enfield, North London. It had been to a landline, and they had an address. A team was already on its way. There would be no attempted contact, just covert surveillance.

A background check was currently underway into the woman in Bodinnick. Initial findings had been quite startling. She was very well known to the police, especially in Liverpool but despite numerous attempts by the constabulary there, had always avoided being convicted by a court. A covert operation on her house was currently being put together by the covert operations unit belonging to the Devon and Cornwall police. An armed response unit was also being placed on standby. And a raid on the woman's property was being planned for midday the next day. Two officers from the NCA would be attending. Detective Constable Havers was due to start his next shift at midday tomorrow. To avoid unwanted attention it had been decided that he would be arrested as he joined his shift. His house and his phones were continuing to be monitored and would be, throughout the night.

Everything that was taking place was being relayed to Jane of the NCA as it happened. Shortly she would be leaving her safe house for a meeting with Roger Denton. She was looking forward to giving him some positive news.

The Old Ferry Inn. Bodinnick, Cornwall, England

Claire sat at her favourite table in the back bar of the pub. Tammy at her feet was enjoying the attention of fellow drinkers. There were a few in the pub that night she didn't recognise. Unusual for the time of year.

Havers call had annoyed her. In truth it had reminded her just how much she wanted to retire. To be rid of the world that had given her her living. She no longer wanted to be part of it. She detested it. All she desired now was the quiet life with her best friend, Tammy. To go on long country walks and discover many of the county's hostelries. That evening she made a promise to herself. She was retiring. There would be those cheering from the roof tops, and she hoped beyond hope that that's all they would do, cheer. Not look for revenge. It was a risk she'd have to take. In any case her house had a good alarm system, CCTV and if all else failed she had hidden in her lounge a Beretta 9000 pistol. Fully loaded in readiness.

Enjoying the effect of the beer, Claire reached down and stroked her beloved Tammy.

"It's just you and me girl from now on. No more shit I promise," Claire murmured. Tammy in response rolled over on her back with all four legs in the air. Claire sighed. "You have no pride girl" and leant back in her chair a smile fixed on her face. Never had she felt so contented.

NCA's Temporary Offices, Gladstone Park. Cricklewood, London, England

Roger Denton of the NCA sat in his office, head in his hands. Last night was catching up on him fast. His headache had returned.

"You ought to try and eat something boss, you'll feel better for it. And you'll need to feel on form when Jane arrives." Nick was all concern.

"Get me a yoghurt and some fresh oranges can you Nick. No on second thoughts, make it a banana."

Whilst he was gone Roger once more started going over some of the reports. Nothing made sense. Everything was just a big bloody mess. They were no nearer finding out who was responsible for the deaths in Spain and Langstone on the south coast. Nick returned and along with the yoghurt and banana he had an expression that read, 'how do I tell the boss.'

"Thanks, and what is it, Nick?"

"Have you still got your sense of humour, sir?"

"Try me." Roger sucked his first spoonful of yoghurt.

"We've been looking at the CCTV at the time Ms Fowlis and the young lad, Nicholas Burrows disappeared. We've come up with something, but you're not going to like it."

Roger finished his yoghurt and started on his banana. The yoghurt had finally ridden his mouth of the taste stubbornly lingering from being ill.

"It can't be shittier than the shit of the last few weeks. Let's have some more shit."

Nick drew in his breath and pursed his lips in readiness.

"Ok sir. Well, we found a car, the same car. Seconds before and after Ms Fowlis and Mr Burrows disappeared. It's a Citroen C3 hatchback. MS Fowlis we now assume got into a black cab outside the El Pacifico restaurant in Langley Street, only minutes from where she was staying. We know she never returned to her hotel. I say assume because the CCTV doesn't actually show her getting in. Just that the taxi slows as she exits the restaurant. A man is seen waving her off, but his face isn't visible and there's no trace of him on CCTV elsewhere in the area. Only with him entering the restaurant with Ms Fowlis and even then, you can only see the back of his head. This man knows what he's doing."

Roger finished his banana and threw the skin in his bin.

"But that's good news, isn't it? Surely, you've done an ANPR check on both vehicles?"

"Yes of course, and that's where it all goes wrong. Where it starts to unravel. Where shit happens."

Roger pulled a face.

"The Citroen, it's registered to one Peter Fitch, Burns Road, Wellingborough."

"That little shit again, he must be lying."

"Wait sir. We contacted Peter Fitch. In fact he's so pissed off with us now he's employed a solicitor."

"Good for bloody him."

"Yes well, guess what? He does own the exact same make, model and colour car captured on CCTV. Only he can prove that his car was in Wellingborough at the times in question."

"How can he prove it? I don't believe him."

"CCTV. At the time Ms Fowlis disappeared, his car was in the school car park. The school where he teaches, they have CCTV and it was parked there all day. Mr Fitch didn't even leave during lunch. And during the hours, the early hours when Mr Burrows disappeared, his car was parked outside his house, where guess what. He has CCTV. So does his neighbour. His car was parked there all night."

Roger leant his elbows on his desk and placed his head in his hands.

"Fuck, what about the taxi? Does Mr Fitch own that too?"

Nick managed to laugh.

"No but this takes the biscuit. From the CCTV footage it's one of ours. A specially constructed TX4, bullet proof and with armoured glass. Used in special ops or to carry members of the intelligence services considered, 'at risk.' Jane will be travelling in one today."

"And I guess it wasn't stolen."

"No, at the time this car was recorded, our car was being used by MI6, transporting a Russian squealer between safe houses."

"Fuck, fuck, fuck." Do MI5 or MI6 know?"

"Not yet, but somebody's going to have to tell them."

"Let me speak to Jane first."

"Yes sir. You do know that SOCO's are going over your house?"

Roger smiled a smile of reluctant acceptance.

"Yes, have they found anything? Cameras? Listening devices?

"No, nothing. I'm told they're going to give it up soon, early evening. I'm sure Jane will have more details. They're going to keep a car just down the street. Keep your house under surveillance. Make sure nobody tries anything.

"That's reassuring." Nick caught his boss's sarcasm right in the face. "What time is she due to arrive?"

Nick looked at his watch.

"She's on her way. Any minute now I should think."

As he spoke, people were moving outside. Three men were escorting a woman through the offices. Jane, but the woman didn't look like Jane. Jane was blonde and wore her hair in a bob. This woman was brunette, and her hair tumbled below her shoulders.

Just as the woman was escorted into his office, Roger's phone rang. It was D.I. Johnson from Havant. He pressed a button that sent a message. 'I'll call you back.' The woman sat down instructing the men guarding her to wait outside. No one was allowed to come in. They weren't to be disturbed. Once the door closed, the woman pulled at her hair. Off came a very convincing wig revealing bright blonde hair styled in a bob. Jane.

"Sorry I'm late Roger. Lots going on, and we have lots to get through." Jane was always direct, 'Business business,' as the French say. As she spoke, she pulled up a colourful silk scarf hiding beneath her blouse. The silk scarf was Jane's signature. It was her identity. Roger had never seen her not wearing one.

A Street in Enfield, North London, England

Three cars pulled up outside, or as close as they could get outside, a house in a residential street in Enfield. The house was typical of one from the late forties, with a bow window and quite a large front garden. The garden looked well cared for and all the roses had been pruned ready for winter. Everything looked normal except the front door was wide open. Looking in from the outside it gave the appearance of someone who'd left in a hurry. So much of a hurry they hadn't bothered to close the door.

The lead officer opened her mic so everyone could hear.

"What do you think, guys and gals? Do we sit and wait, or do we go in? Any suggestions?" Leaving everyone to think she radioed their situation to control. The instruction she received was to go in but proceed with great caution. Take firearms with you. What control meant by this was to be escorted by armed officers, of which there were three with the team. Opening up her mic again, the lead officer relayed what control had instructed.

"We're going in, I need two armed officers with me, sort it out between the three of you, and please no fisticuffs. The remaining shooter I need to cover the front door and alleyway down the side of the house. Just in case. Everyone, keep your radios open."

There was no arguing. In seconds everyone was in position. An armed officer entered the house first, followed by the lead officer followed by the second officer with a firearm. The hallway led to a kitchen at the back. The door was ajar, with a door on the left leading to, presumably the lounge. To the right, stairs led up to the next floor. There was not a sound coming from anywhere, and one thing you learnt very quickly in the services, was to treat silence as a greater danger than sound. The atmosphere was tense. Everybody felt tense. In an alcove to the left, just after the door to the lounge there was a small table with a telephone. The receiver was off and hanging by its cord, almost touching the carpet. But it wasn't this that caught the eye of the lead firearms officer or the lead officer following him in. It was the briefcase in front.

"OUT," screamed the lead officer but it was too late. There came a blinding flash, followed by a split second's silence followed by a roar. Flesh splattered the woodchipped wallpaper and ceiling before the house rose and caved in on itself. A second smaller explosion sent splinters of masonry skywards before dust settled followed by an eerie silence. One officer radioed into control, screaming what had just taken place, requesting immediate assistance, while the second ran to the third armed officer who was lying bloodied on the grass.

Within minutes, fire engines and ambulances were on the scene with police cordoning off the area. Immediate residents were escorted away. The explosion was almost certainly the result of escaping gas. To stay could be extremely dangerous.

A Street in Bushey, North London, England

He hated wearing coveralls. They made him sweat, feel claustrophobic. Thank heavens he would still be free of them. After watching his colleague mount the stairs he returned to the lounge. They had already checked it over but there was something else he had to do.

Staring out of the window he searched in his pocket. Fingering a piece of plastic he said a prayer and pressed. For a second he felt a rush of air and lived long enough to see the car parked out front flip on its side.

He died with a smile on his face. The people who had trained him had been right, death was painless.

NCA's Temporary Offices, Gladstone Park. Cricklewood, London, England

For the next three hours, the two went over every avenue of their operations. Jane took the revelation of the black cab very badly. It meant that the NCA had definitely been infiltrated. In truth, they both knew it anyway, but this was further evidence. In return, Jane had shocking news for Roger. She told him of their surveillance of Detective Constable Havers, of their recording of his telephone conversation with a 'gangster woman,' now living in Cornwall. That their conversation had revealed there was a mole, not just in the NCA but in Roger's department. Jason's words came flooding back. 'Trust no one. Not even each other.' The thought that one of his team was passing information, confidential information to someone on the outside, made him feel sick to the stomach.

Roger detailed what they had found out about Maureen Fowlis, about the CCTV footage and the constant connection to Peter Fitch of Burns Road, Wellingborough. Jane in return detailed their operation in bringing down Detective Constable Havers and the people he was feeding information to. She was confident that they had found the person responsible for ordering the brutal murders in Spain and on the south coast.

Roger finished by going over his dealings with the gendarmerie in France. About their refusal to return the bodies of the twelve mutilated children. That according to the capitaine the bodies had been moved to Paris, that they were no longer the concern of the British authorities, that they were now France's concern.

"After our meeting with the home secretary, I thought it would have been a simple formality." Roger told her.

"Ok, leave it with me, Roger, I'll ask the right people."

Roger wanted to believe her, but he felt her promise somehow lacked conviction. Again his mind remembered Jason's words. Just how close are you to the government Jane? He pushed his thought, his doubt aside. He'd known Jane forever, or so it seemed, and in the past, she'd often expressed her dissatisfaction of the government. Their dirty tricks.

Their final subject was all about him. His safety. What had happened at his house had been a shock, but if someone had wanted him dead, Roger pointed out. They would have done it by now. For him, he told Jane, it was more of a worry why, whoever it was. Wanted to keep him alive.

Anyhow they both agreed, that for now it was better if Roger stayed within the confines of the new offices. He was safe here. And let's not forget Jane reminded him. You're living in accommodation designed to house the Prime Minister. Not bad, not bad at all, for a mere director with the NCA. Yes, in a nuclear war Roger wanted to point out but didn't.

As Jane was tucking away her scarf and adjusting her wig one of her security knocked and entered, by his side stood Nick. Both men looked as though they had something to say.

"Nick?"

"Sir, sorry Jane."

Jane smiled.

"I thought you'd both want to know. We've had the call lists back from the phone company. The one for Mr Mitchell's phone."

"And?" This came from Jane.

"There aren't any. I mean there aren't any calls. What I mean is, the bills have gone out. Mr Mitchell has paid them but the calls, or the data that made up those bills has been wiped from the system. I've been on to the phone company but to be honest they haven't a clue. All they keep telling me is that it's never happened before, and they don't know how it could have happened. That they're looking into it."

"Better get our guys to look into it to with them," Jane instructed

Resources, resources, resources thought Roger, give me the resources but kept quiet.

"Ma'am, there's been an incident," As the man from Jane's team spoke, one of Rogers team appeared and whispered something in Nicks ear. Both Jane and Roger heard Nick whisper, 'are you sure?'

"What incident?" Jane demanded

"The house in Enfield, the one we're placing under surveillance. There's been an explosion. Three dead and an officer badly injured. Critical."

As both Roger and Jane stood shocked, Nick stepped forward.

"Sorry. I'm afraid I have to report another explosion." Nick looked directly at his boss. "I'm sorry sir but there's been another explosion. It's your house in Bushey, sir. There's been an explosion there. I'm afraid your house has been razed to the ground. There were two SOCOs inside at the time. Both dead, I'm afraid. I'm sorry, sir." Nick looked at Jane. "I'm sorry, Ma'am."

Chapter 6

Roger sat down, stunned. The alcohol and stresses combined from the night before had been steadily catching up with him and now this. This, the latest news was like a bullet through the heart. He was normally unshakable in any crisis but at that moment, he felt crushed. Their foe, if you could call them that, were running rings not only around the NCA but him personally. He honestly hadn't a clue which way to turn. Strangely at that very moment he wished Jason were there beside him. He was a complete stranger, and Jason almost certainly wasn't his name but for some peculiar reason he felt he was the one person he could trust.

Jane, in contrast, didn't hesitate. Within seconds she was on the phone to both her teams in Bodinnick Cornwall and more urgently to the team keeping Detective Constable Havers' house under covert surveillance. Under no circumstances were the team to enter the house. Circumstances may well tempt them, but circumstance may be a front, a trick to lure them in. Only I can give the order for you to move in Jane reiterated. The team in return told her that there was no sign of Mr Havers. Lights had come on in the house, but from experience the detective suspected they'd been switched on either by a timer or a mobile phone. The house felt empty to him.

Happy her warnings had been heeded, Jane spoke directly to Roger.

"We need background checks on Havers. Yes, I know he's a policeman and checks will have already been carried out but recent events have told us that the Met's checks are perhaps not as tight as they should be. I want a deep deep check on Havers. What pets he's kept, hobbies, what toilet paper he wipes his bum with everything. Once we have him in custody, we can start knocking on doors. But not until then. And this guy in Enfield Ryan, Rya?

"A Mister Ryan Hedges." The agent who had broken the news about the explosion, helped her out.

"Thank you. This Mr Ryan Hedges, we need a background check on him. A thorough one, not just a surface check. We need to know the connection between him and this Claire woman down in Cornwall. And is there a direct connection between him and Havers? We need to find out. WE need to obtain their phone records. I have a magistrate on standby who is aware of the seriousness of our investigation. She will issue any warrants needed." Jane leant forward and scribbled her details on some note paper. Roger passed them directly to Nick. Jane stood up. "I need to go. Is your house insured, Roger?"

"Yes I think so."

Jane could see her top man was on the edge. She'd witnessed the signs many, many times before.

"If you have any problems on that front Roger let me know. I'll see to it that the NCA will cover any loss. I don't want you to worry. More importantly I think right at this moment I need you to rest. I forbid you to leave this building. Tomorrow I need you back on the case. Chin up Roger. We'll get these bastards."

Roger smiled ruefully.

"We will, Roger, trust me." With that, Jane left.

Nick remained in Roger's office.

"I feel stupid, asking sir, because of course you're not. But are you alright?

"No of course I'm bloody not." Roger managed to laugh as he said it. "Can you start actioning that lot, Nick? And remember we have a mole amongst us. Be careful what you say and to whom."

Nick pretended to punch the wall.

"I can't bloody believe it. I count every man and woman out there as both a colleague and a friend. I just can't believe anyone of them would betray us in this way."

"I know but one of them has, and it leaves a worst taste in one's mouth than last night's vomit."

Nick managed a smile.

"I'm glad you haven't lost your sense of humour. You need to rest boss. Can I get you anything?"

"Does that restaurant have any alcohol?"

"No but there's a fully stocked bar. You don't imagine a bunch of MPs could shelter here without a bar, do you? Probably all tax free as well. What do you want?"

"If they've got it a brandy. Brandy helps settle the stomach. You'd better make it a large one Nick." When Nick had gone in search of his boss's saviour, Roger pulled his recording machine out of an open drawer. Knowing how he'd felt, he'd recorded every word since Jane had entered his office. He'd listen to the recording in bed. Nick returned with both a bottle and a glass.

"Bloody hell sir, Parliament don't do things by halves. Look what I've found." Nick held up the bottle. "Ferrand Legendaire."

"That means nothing to me Nick."

"And you have the cheek to call me a heathen, boss. Just drink it but savour it. This stuff's around one hundred pound a glass."

"Wasted on me then, but thanks Nick."

"Don't say thanks to me, say thanks to His Majesty's government."

Roger raised his empty glass.

"CHEERS."

Chapter 7

A Street in Ealing. West London, England

Jane told her driver to stop by her house in leafy Ealing. She needed a few things. There was only so long you could stay in a safehouse living out of a suitcase without topping up. She also wanted to get some personal effects to make her safe house feel more like home.

Her driver watched her enter. He was very unhappy about her request, especially after what had taken place only hours earlier. But saying no to Jane, Director General of the NCA, was almost an impossibility. He watched as she searched for her key and entered. Behind in a highly polished Santorini black F-Pace Jaguar, two men got out and paced up and down outside. The intelligence services were taking no chances. In under five minutes Jane returned carrying a small leather bag in one hand and a supermarket carrier in her other. Photos she told her driver raising the supermarket carrier. And women's stuff she told him raising the other.

"I wouldn't understand that Ma'am."

"No you wouldn't."

Ardres, France
The Following Day

Lieutenant Beaufort had spent almost the entire morning polishing and cleaning his car. Now sitting outside Madame Maubert's, he found himself still checking for marks. Seeing the front door open, he jumped out to greet mother and daughter. After kissing both on the cheeks, he opened the rear door of his car, allowing them to glide in. Neither, he noticed, were wearing black, indeed if anything they looked as if they were both dressed for a wedding.

Hardly a word was spoken on their way to the cemetery. Lieutenant Beaufort told friends and colleagues afterwards, that the drive to the cemetery was possibly the hardest hour of his life. When they arrived, the van carrying the body and coffin of Capitaine Maubert was already parked outside. Six uniformed officers stood to attention waiting to carry out their duty as pallbearers. Thankfully, there were only a handful of photographers and they were being kept well back by local police.

Madame Maubert had insisted on a simple ceremony only, and for it to be held beside the grave. Only a handful of close friends and relatives including her mother were in attendance. Instead of flowers, her mother had brought with her a simple white china plate, on which, and beautifully presented, a baba au rhum. The gesture could have been interpreted as comical by those attending, but it wasn't. Everyone there recognised it to be a very personal tribute. The transportation of the coffin by the gendarmes was appropriate. Her husband had lived and died for his gendarmerie. Both Madame Maubert and her daughter were determined not to cry. Indeed, it was telling that the only tears shed were by the gendarmes themselves. After earth had been thrown, all retired to their transport.

The new capitaine had organised a wake to be held at Le Bistrot de la Place, Place de l'Europe in nearby Marck. He'd told everyone that the gendarmerie was paying for it, but the rumour was that he'd paid for it out of his own pocket. He'd declined to attend as hadn't known the man personally and felt it would have made things difficult for his widow. He had though, allowed Colette to attend and at the bistrot, she sat at the same table as mother and daughter.

Absent was the Mayor. He'd sent flowers along with his condolences. He'd wanted to attend but he had to head a media conference organised before the date of the funeral. At around the same time the funeral party were tucking into a fine lunch at the Bistrot de la Place, journalists were tucking into a buffet laid on by the mayor at Calais's Hotel de Ville.

After everyone had eaten, the mayor was joined on stage by owners of several local businesses, they would, the mayor declared, all benefit from his announcement as would the good people of Calais. He went on to announce that Calais would benefit from a cutting-edge technology park. As part of the deal a new chip making company to compete with the likes of Silicon Valley and Taiwan would be building not just a chip making factory, but a state-of-the-art research and development facility. Alongside this company, a deal had been struck with an up-and-coming international company specialising in developing and manufacturing the very latest audio and video communication systems. The company already had factories in Turkey and the UK and the fact that they also want to lay roots, not just in France but Calais was testament to the forward thinking of the town. And that wasn't all. Calais had, only recently, built one new hospital and as part of the deal they would gain yet another. New Dawn, a rapidly expanding private health care service, wanted to build not only a hospital but a research centre. One of the main reasons Calais had been chosen was the town's strong relation with the UK, in particular, that country's health service.

The park was to be jointly funded by private and public money and the land would be provided freely by the good people of Calais. The money and employment the project would bring to the area was unparalleled, and the project was expected to attract some of the best minds from around the world. Thus luxury housing would be needed, and licenses would be granted to a number of local firms. It was win, win, win for Calais.

Pierre listened to the announcement whist driving to his hometown, Bree in Belgium. The longer the mayor spoke, the wider his grin. The whole thing had been easier than he'd ever expected. It was such a shame people had to die along the way. For a few seconds, his conscience was bloodied. But only for a few seconds. He was looking forward to the future. As he drove, he, switched channels. Moby – Extreme Ways came on the radio. As he listened, he pressed his foot harder on the accelerator. The music reminded him of the Bourne films. He loved them. They were great but they were fiction. This was reality. His grin widened, so wide it threatened to split his face.

Mont d'Hubert, France

Marie felt sleepy, why was she always sleepy. The soft voice spoke to her, that deliciously soft voice. She loved hearing that voice.

"Relax, Marie, don't try and move."

Marie wasn't, she didn't want to move. She wanted to stay just where she was. In the most comfortable chair in the world.

A man dressed in white coveralls studied his instruments. Satisfied, he stood up wiping his disposable glove covered hands down his front. There really wasn't any need, for his gloves were spotless.

"She's ready," he spoke to the lady with the soft voice.

"Did you hear that, Marie. You're going to be the first. You my lovely will go down in history."

Marie smiled, she was so happy.

The man in white took off his gloves.

"I need to let Orme know. If this succeeds, we need to be ready for the next stage."

Marie continued to smile.

Bodinnick , Cornwall

A well-known courier pulled up outside the Old Ferry Inn in Bodinnick, Cornwall. The uniformed driver got out, and opening up the back, took out a parcel. Reading the address, he looked up and down the steeply sloping road. There was a car parked just in front of his van and there was someone in it. He tapped on the window and the driver lowered the glass.

"Excuse me mate, you've no idea where this address is?" He showed the driver the label.

The driver was careful not to show his exasperation, it was the house they had under surveillance. They were ready to go in. They needed this idiot out of the way and out of the way fast.

"It's just there, mate." The driver pointed. "The second house along the path."

"Ah, the very des res," the driver joked. "Thanks, mate." The driver walked off whistling. The team watched him knock the door, hand a parcel to a woman, retrieve a signature and leave. As he drove off, he waved his thanks, but the driver of the car and his team weren't taking notice. The woman had closed the door quickly, too quickly. They didn't watch the van as it turned right just before the ferry onto the main road out of the village.

Claire accepted the parcel, funny, she couldn't remember ordering anything. As she signed something caught her eye. On the road she spotted a parked car, a parked car with two men. They were watching her. She knew instantly what was coming.

"Tammy get back," she screamed at her dog. Tammy looked confused, she couldn't understand what was happening.

There followed a serious of loud knocks on her door. Her dog started barking, tail wagging.

"Tammy, get fucking back, will you."

"Police, open up. Open up, madam, or we'll have to break down the door. We have a warrant to search this house."

"Fuck off and fuck you," shouted Claire bearing her Beretta 9000.

"Stand back madam, we're coming in and armed officers will be attending." There came a loud crashing sound as a ram was swung against the door. The dog started to leap at the door.

"Tammy, get the fuck back." The dog did as she was told. Claire levelled her pistol. There was a loud crack as she fired and a scream from the other side of the door.

"I fucking told you," Claire screamed. "I fucking told you to fuck off." She aimed her gun again. There came a second crack. This crack sounded different. A split second after the sound of splintering glass followed by a thud, as Claire fell to the floor blood oozing from her side.

She knew instantly that she was going to die, that she had only seconds left on this earth. She felt a wetness on her cheek, through the blur in front of her she realised it was her beloved Tammy. Not understanding what was going on, only that her mistress and the love of her life was hurt.

'You stupid cow Claire why didn't you retire earlier, you had it all.' Claire scolded herself. As a beautiful garden appeared around her, she felt Tammy's tongue on her cheek once more. Her dog was her biggest regret. She prayed hard that somebody would give her a good home. Tears started to roll down her cheeks and then the world she was in, was gone. Instead, she found herself walking through a garden. A beautiful garden with lovely scents and bird song. Normally she'd have welcomed such as her garden, but she was already missing her best friend.

One of the officers knelt, feeling the slumped woman's neck, at the same time stroking her dog.

"Shit, she's dead. Jane's going to go nuts."

"I had to shoot, she was going to shoot again." The armed officer who had been stationed outside her window defended his action.

Outside a colleague was receiving first aid. He had been shot in the cheek. He wasn't going to die but he was a bloody mess.

Standing, the officer who had declared Claire to be dead, barked orders.

"Right, let's get this place secured. We need to have uniforms knocking on doors and asking questions. Officers with experience only. We need SOCOs here like yesterday."

"Don't we take a look around first?"

"No we've fucked up already, I don't want us messing anything else up."

"What about the parcel?"

"Let forensics deal with it. Will someone put a lead on the dog, she's beginning to get upset."

The Police Station, Staines, London, England

It was gone one in the afternoon and Detective Constable Havers hadn't appeared for his shift. He'd been due to start at midday. The team detailed to arrest him weren't stupid. The officer had obviously got wind that something was up. He'd done a disappearing act.

They checked with the team carrying out surveillance outside his house. Nothing, not a sign. Not a sign since they'd arrived.

The officer in charge radioed in his report.

"Someone's tipped him off, someone in the know. One of us probably. He's almost certainly done a runner."

Those in charge moved fast. DC Havers' image and details were wired to every police force in the UK. Just to be sure, the same details were also sent to Interpol.

NCA's Temporary Offices. Gladstone Park, North London, England

Considering everything that had happened, Roger felt surprisingly well that morning. Refreshed definitely, positive, yes. God knows why. Cheerful? Well, he didn't feel sad. He was still finding it hard to come to terms that all he had to do, to come to work was take a lift. As soon as he stepped out, Nick grabbed his arm.

"There's someone waiting for you, boss. They're in your office. He wouldn't give his name but he's high clearance. Not the sort of person we normally come in contact with."

"Ok," he looked at his watch. One pm. ONE PM!!!! "Fuck, Nick, it's bloody one in the afternoon. Have I been asleep all this time?"

Nick nodded.

"It was probably the Ferrand Legendaire, oh, and Jane rang."

"Shit."

"No she told me to let you sleep."

"Yes that's what she told YOU. What does she want? Any idea?"

"There's been some more developments boss."

"Good or bad?"

Nick pulled a quizzical expression.

"Not good but not entirely bad. You'd better see this bloke. He's been waiting for at least half an hour. I'm just about to bring him fresh coffee, do you want some?"

"Of course." One bloody o'clock, Roger still couldn't believe it. And he couldn't believe who was sitting in his office, waiting to see him. Jason, bloody JASON. Jason didn't bother standing up but simply smiled as Roger walked through the door.

"I prefer the Lamb and Flag," he smiled that disarming smile of his.

"The bar here's not bad," Roger countered.

"I don't doubt, the first thing parliament would have planned for, for a place like this, is a good bar."

They both laughed.

"I must say I'm surprised to see you turning up here. I thought you wanted to remain anonymous."

"And so I am. My security clearance allows me to order you and your colleague to keep my visit secret. Your security didn't even check my name. Just my photo and my security clearance. Their computer would have told them not to mess with me."

He smiled that smile.

"So why are you here?"

"Signposts and to say how sorry I am about your house."

"And the poor buggers inside." Roger remarked.

The atmosphere turned solemn. Nick entered.

"Bloody hell has somebody died?"

"YES," Jason answered at the same time. Red faced Nick placed the two coffees on the desk and backed out.

"You remember what we talked about? About conducting your investigation under the radar? Well, I think recent events proves my point. Trust no one Roger, trust no one. There are obviously people who are working for us who also have another bat. You don't know who they are, and I certainly don't, which is why I came to you." Jason took a long sip of his coffee. "I tell you what the coffee is bloody good here." He looked up from his cup. "You know, you won't have been told yet, but I CAN tell you, that the method to blow your house was the same used for the NCA offices."

"What the..."

"Yes, the explosives were within your walls and set off by close quarters remote control. One of the dead SOCOs Roger. One of the two set off the explosion and was prepared to die to do it. Have you had any work done on your house recently?"

Roger thought.

"I had a chimney taken out, but that was four maybe five years ago."

Jason smiled.

"I'm not a betting man but I bet that's when and where the explosives were planted. If I were you, I'd take a look at who did the work."

Jason looked at his watch.

"I'm going to have to go. I came to give you my new card. He handed another plainly printed card to Roger. It had printed a new name, 'Donald Anas,' and a new number. Only contact me on that number using a pay as you go. I hate the word burner. So American. I refuse to adopt it. And never leave a message. If you ring and I don't answer I'll call you back. Now signposts. There is I believe a French connection. But under the radar Roger, under the radar. Thank your man for the coffee won't you. Keep in touch."

Roger placed the card safely in his wallet. He looked at his phone. There'd been another missed call from D.I. Johnson down in Havant. To have rung twice it must be important. Frustratingly his call had passed direct to answer phone. He needed the toilet. On his way he met Nick.

"Nick, any chance of another coffee?"

"I must be the bloody highest paid waiter in the land."

"Yes, sorry Nick, the next one I'll get myself."

When Roger returned to his office Nick was already there with his fresh coffee.

"Thanks Nick."

"Who was that guy?"

Roger attempted to present an air of nonchalance and failed miserably.

"Someone from one of the intelligence agencies. He wanted to know our progress. With all the shit, everyone's scrabbling around looking for answers. Why do you ask?"

Nick shrugged his shoulders.

"Security were treating him as though he were bloody royalty."

"In intelligence terms he may well be. Oh, and Nick not a word that he was here. Ok?"

"Don't worry, I've already promised the man himself and security have already told me that I can say goodbye to my balls if I do." Nick paused. "Don't forget to call Jane."

"Ok, shut the door will you."

Nick did as he was told. Next Roger called Jane. She filled him in on events in Cornwall and Staines. That Detective Constable Havers has gone awol. There's no trace of him. Police services around the country are looking for him. No more bodies had been found, in the rubble at the NCA offices, which was good news. After prompting she promised that she'd ring her equivalent in France, to see what the hell was going on with the bodies of the twelve mutilated children, they'd been expecting them to be returned. One problem she could see was that, technically, the unfortunate children weren't British citizens. And that might have thrown a spanner in the works. After asking how he was, Jane had rung off.

During the afternoon, Roger had tried ringing D.I. Johnson twice more but to no avail. On each occasion, his phone went direct to answer phone. He'd tried ringing Havant police station too but all they could tell him was that D.I. Johnson was out meeting someone. They were very sorry but that's all they knew. That's all he'd told them.

He'd been informed that tomorrow they'd receive the relevant paperwork to satisfy the Hilton. So that was at last some sort of progress.

Otherwise every other search was in progress and the telephone company responsible for John's mobile were attending tomorrow with digital forensics. Progress of a sort. By seven in the evening Roger was ready to retire. Not seeing the outside world all day was beginning to play with his mind. Something, temporarily anyway, only a good night's sleep could help with. He had another look at the card the man previously known as Jason had given him. Donald Anas. He wondered if he'd ever discover his real name and which agency he worked for. Why should he trust this bloody man? He was just about to leave his office when there came a knock on the door. It was security. Now what?

"Sorry, sir, this has been waiting for you in our offices. It was delivered this morning, addressed for your personal attention. It's been checked for traces of explosive and given the all clear. In his hands, the guard held a parcel. Square and just large enough to hold a football. The guard made to give it to him, but Roger recoiled. He had seen a parcel exactly like that before. In fact, two parcels. He knew exactly what was inside.

Formby, Lancashire, England

Holding her baby, Mrs Wade kept leaving her house, walking down their drive and peering up the road. It was almost half past seven and her husband, James should have been home. At least by five. Where was he?

She'd rung his workplace, the General Register Office in Southport, and they'd told her he'd left there at four pm. He should have been home ages ago. If ever he was late, he always rang. She'd tried ringing him, but his phone was off. It was never off. By eight pm, she'd had enough. She was at her wits end.

She called the police. Give it twenty-four hours and if your husband's still not home we'll list him officially as missing they told her. Why wouldn't they listen to her. She knew her husband. He was missing, something terrible had happened. She could feel it. What else could she do. If the police weren't interested who could she turn to? There was no one. Clutching their baby to her chest she began to sob uncontrollably.

Ardres, France

The funeral had passed better than expected. In fact, at the wake Madame Maubert and her daughter had often been caught laughing. Colette had drunk too much, and she was now also hitching a lift with the lieutenant. After dropping off Madame Maubert and her daughter, he would drive her back to Calais.

He was now parked up outside his ex-capitaine's house on the perimeter of Ardres. The warmth of his car had sent all three of his passengers to sleep. Gently, he woke Madame Maubert and her daughter. At the same time, Colette started to snore. This brought giggles from the two ladies in the back seat. Opening the rear door, the lieutenant smiled. Giggling was good, life must go on.

After kissing the two women twice on each cheek, he got back into his car to watch them safely enter their house. As they approached their front door, he saw movement. There were two other persons there. From their outline they appeared to be a man and a woman. A young man and woman. The lieutenant thought the two looked familiar. He put his hand on the door, ready to open it in case he was needed. He watched the four engage in conversation. The conversation appeared to be cordial. Next, all four entered the house. All good. The lieutenant started the engine, Colette was next. He gently closed her mouth. It was at that moment he heard the scream.

Gendarmerie Nationale, Calais, France

Capitaine Olivier Vendroux stood with his hands in his pockets staring at the view out of his window. It was already dark and the scene and weather outside sent shivers down his spine. He hated this time of year. The weather was already demonstrating the months of misery to come. And being by the grey miserable La Manche, the demonstration was even more pronounced. From what he'd seen so far, he hated Calais, he hated his gendarmerie, and he found the people who worked there, simple and lacking in culture. And their accent, it disfigured the most beautiful language in the world.

Give him Paris any day. There, culture oozed from every corner. The weather was warm even when it was cold. And people spoke eloquently, even the clochard begging for money. And why whenever he asked a question in Calais, the initial response was the sound of a sheep! He really hoped his term here was to be short.

He looked at his watch. Despite outside appearances it was still early. His accommodation was depressing. He had no wish to retire there yet. He needed a thrill, something that would excite him. Stimulate his bruised nerves. Cap Blanc Nez. Everyone was talking about the place as though it was some sort of Devil's palace. It was where his predecessor had met his death and a photographer not long before. Both had met their deaths by falling over the edge.

The wind outside was strengthening but that would add to the thrill. He made his mind up to drive up to the summit of Cap Blanc Nez. He wanted to see for himself what all the fuss was about. The thrill seeker within needed to be satisfied. Calais, he found boring, at last, here was a chance to satisfy the growing yearning within. He would stand on the summit, at the very edge of the precipice. Challenge the wind to do its worst. Where both Rommel and Hitler had once stood, their eyes looking enviously on the island across the water. And more recently where two men had plunged to their deaths. And the biggest thrill of all, feeling his predecessor, falling. Bouncing off the cliff before hitting the water below. Olivier Vendroux felt sick with excitement. Grabbing his car keys he made for the exit. He couldn't wait.

A Wine Bar and Restaurant Near Harrods. London, England.

Charles had picked her up in a Rolls Royce. He was very smartly dressed wearing a light- coloured suit with an open neck shirt and a neatly crafted sage green silk cravat. Their conversation on the way was light and made easier by a pale golden sherry served from a mini bar.

By the time they were dropped off outside the wine bar, Ariana, alias Fatima felt very much at ease. For the evening she'd chosen a tight wearing bottle green dress, which was neither low cut or above the knees. But what it did do was accentuate her burlesque figure. Around her neck she wore a simple black choker with a single pearl clasp. As a final touch, she had added a little glitter to her luxuriant Persian hair. She knew she looked good and was confident in her own skin. She knew also that she would have the attention of the room. Desire from the men, envy from the women.

Charles' card was taken at the door.

"Not everybody gets in here, you know," he smiled. "You have to have," he coughed with his hand on his mouth. There was a glint in his eye. "You have to have certain credentials. This way. Charles motioned with his arm. "We're downstairs. Opposite to the old Ivy. Here all the important people are below ground." He laughed. Fatima hadn't a clue what he was talking about.

Fatima followed him down the stairs into a large and busy space decorated in traditional Italian style. She counted at least eighteen round tables, some of them small, designed for couples with most being large for groups of eight. Even more, every table was taken, and most were full. Charles led her to a table to their left. Gazing around the room Fatima found so many of the faces familiar. She was sure she'd never met anyone there so there must be another reason. Public figures or celebrities, perhaps. Fatima had never really been interested in either. She preferred to judge a person by their character, and she was nearly always disappointed. Just as they were nearing their table, a table with two free chairs, Fatima saw somebody she recognised. Cuiping was sitting at a table with three other women. She was laughing and involved in deep conversation with her fellow diners. Fatima allowed her gaze to rest only for a few seconds. They had reached their table. A man stood up. Fatima recognised him instantly from the photo Charles had shown her.

"Ariana, let me introduce you."

The man who was standing took her hand. Fatima could see by the look in his eyes that he approved. He was very discreet, but eyes were almost impossible to disguise.

"Ariana, this is Stephan, and this is his wife, Henrietta." Henrietta didn't stand up but blew a kiss. She was a remarkably plain woman with pale skin, thin lips and straight, easy to manage dark shoulder length hair. Her beauty lay beneath her skin. Fatima could tell simply by examining her eyes that the apparent subservient wife had an intelligence beyond her husband's and a kindness that prevented her from being judgemental in any way. Fatima instantly liked the woman. The man she now knew as Stephan, and her next target kissed her hand. Again, his desire was very discreet but his lips remained on her skin, seconds longer than was necessary. Fatima took an instant dislike to him. If this man was her target, then her professionalism would be tested to her limits. The man sat down, his bulging midriff hiding the rather expensive looking belt securing his trousers. As Fatima sat, smoothing her dress with her hands, Charles finished his introduction.

"Ariana, Stephan is our Home Secretary."

A Safehouse Somewhere in South London, England

At the time Fatima was being introduced to the Home Secretary, Jane was busy trying to make the safehouse she was in, more like a home. After taking off her wig and unpacking her bag, she busied herself placing family photographs around the place. No matter how hard she tried every photo somehow looked out of place. The safehouse still felt like temporary lodgings, nothing like home.

Satisfied that she'd done her best but still frustratingly unsatisfied with her surroundings, she poured herself a glass of red and looked at herself in the mirror. With both her hands she cushioned her bob and loosened her scarf. You don't look bad for your age, she told herself, especially considering the day to day stresses you have to endure. Jane puffed out her lips, just as adolescent girls do when taking a selfie. She laughed. She looked ridiculous. Going to the rather stoic lounge, even with her recently added photos, she sat down wanting to watch some mediocre TV. She'd had a hard time recently, that was an understatement. And watching a bit of good rubbish on the telly would do her the world of good.

A House Somewhere in Mayfair, London

At the time Fatima was being introduced to the Home Secretary, Orme still dressed in a traditional black burqa and hijab, was standing at a large sash window with views over Mount Street Gardens. Mayfair's one public park, and arguably, London's most intimate. She loved the view of the park at night. The light, thrown from the houses surrounding it, gave the park, she thought, something of a Peter Pan appeal.

In one hand, she held a clear heavy plastic cube. Inside floating in a thick clear liquid, there was what appeared to be a pale miniature pinecone. Orme examined it using only the light from the moon and the lights outside. She found it mesmerising, quite beautiful.

There was a knock at the door and a woman entered. Throwing her coat on a nearby chair the woman tussled with her hair. Within a couple of minutes, her hair had joined her coat on the chair. Breathing a sigh of relief, she shook her head letting her blonde hair find its natural place in her bob. Reaching into her blouse, she pulled out a colourful silk scarf and proceeded to adjust its position around her neck.

"Hello, Jane," Orme turned to look at her. "Axsti."

"Axsti."

"Come look at this." Orme raised the cube high above her head. Jane joined her. To her, the object floating inside looked rather like a miniature Jerusalem artichoke.

"Just think, Jane, if our theories are proved to be correct, with this little beauty we may be able to control all humanity. If not some, enough for our plans at least."

Jane tried to meet Orme's enthusiasm. She was beginning to worry about what she'd got herself into. Her conscience was bloodied enough, she didn't want it to be bloodied any further.

Chapter
8

In Bristol, a man was almost apoplectic with, whom he considered, an idiot on the other end of the phone. All he wanted to do was renew his car insurance and this idiot was telling him he couldn't. That according to DVLA's records, he was banned for six months. What rubbish, he'd never ever had points on his licence.

In Southampton the police stopped a middle-aged woman. Her driving was fine but after passing an ANPR camera she'd flagged as having no insurance. Rubbish she told the two, she considered rude, police officers. And reached into her glove compartment.

In Leeds, an excited twenty one year old opened her letter from the DVLA. She knew what the envelope contained. It was her first ever driving licence. Trembling with excitement, she held the piece of plastic in both hands. What she saw caused her expression to drop.

"Is this some kind of sick joke."

She showed her licence to her mother. Instead of a photo of her face, she found the face of a sheep staring back at her!

Call after call started to come into the DVLA's contact centre. By 8 pm their website had crashed.

To Be Continued – Available Soon

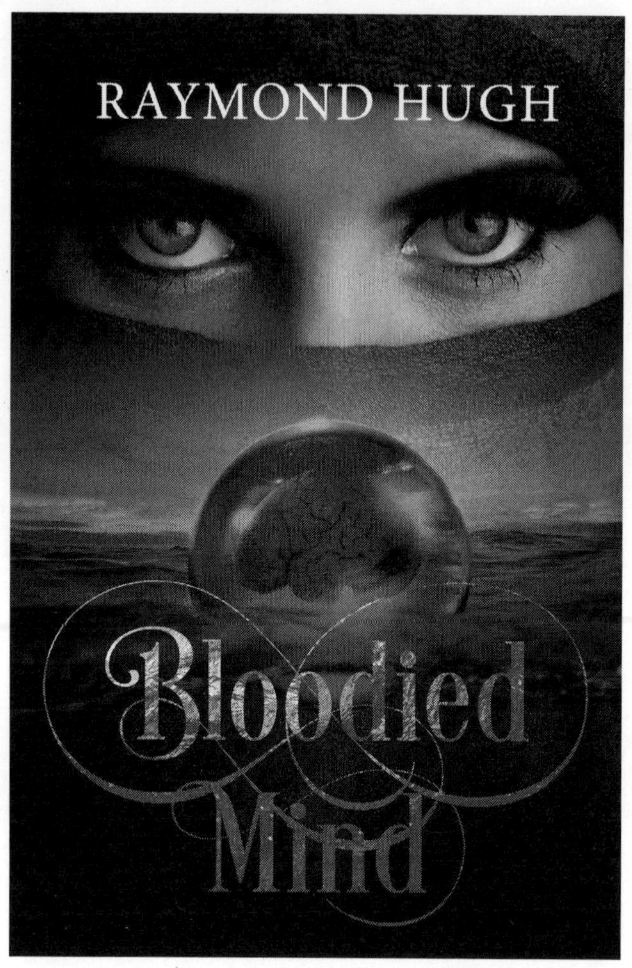